LOUISIANA HOTSHOT

"[A] stroke of genius. *Louisiana Hotshot* is fresh, fast and touching. Just like New Orleans [it] has a lot of 'tude, and a big heart."

D0054394

JULIE SMITH

A TALBA WALLIS NOVEL

Also by Julie Smith

Louisiana Hotshot

JULIE SMITH

TOR®

A TOM DOHERTY ASSOCIATES BOOK
NEW YORK

This is a work of fiction. All the characters and events portrayed in this book are either products of the author's imagination or are used fictitiously.

LOUISIANA HOTSHOT

A Tor Book
Published by Tom Doherty Associates, LLC
175 Fifth Avenue
New York, NY 10010

www.tor.com

Tor® is a registered trademark of Tom Doherty Associates, LLC.

ISBN: 0-765-34292-8
Library of Congress Catalog Card Number: 2001018958

First edition: May 2001
First mass market edition: August 2002

Printed in the United States of America

0 9 8 7 6 5 4 3 2 1

To Steve and Dianne

Acknowledgments

So much goes into a book and so many people contribute! Some are sources of information, some sources of inspiration, and some are sources for the sources. In the course of writing this one, Chris Wiltz, Betsy Petersen, Marigny Pecot, Prieur and Mathilde Leary, A.J. Valenti, Linda Buczek, Chuck Hustmyre, Andy J. Forest, Ken White, Sonya Hardy, Roger at Spytek 2000, and Pat Brady generously provided counsel and shared their expertise. I'm hugely grateful to them all, as well as to my agents, Charlotte Sheedy and Vicky Bijur; and to Win Blevins, the kind of editor they don't make any more. Finally, my most special thanks of all go to Lee Pryor, untier of plot knots, tireless location-finder, and the kind of husband they don't make anymore.

Chapter One

Nerd wanted. Nerdette wouldn't be *too* bad. Young hotshot, under thirty, 5 yrs. computer, 10 yrs. investigative exp. Harvard ed., no visible piercings. Must play the computer like Horowitz played piano. Slave wages.

Huh. This one see you comin'—he as picky as you."

"Let me see that." Unbelieving, Talba Wallis grabbed for the classifieds. She was having breakfast with her mother at the old black-painted table, trying to ignore Miz Clara's morning meddling.

Talba had nothing against getting a job, indeed fully intended to. She merely preferred to peruse the *Times-Picayune* ads at her own pace, if at all. The best jobs in her field would be on the Internet, so why bother?

However, she had to admit her mother had happened on a rare gem—an honest ad. The kind you usually saw only in the personals: "Fat toad, sixty-five, stinks, seeks hard-bodied blue-eyed blonde for hideous perversions. Must be 18 and star of own TV series."

"Must be some kind of joke," Miz Clara said. "Nobody under thirty with all that experience."

Hardly hearing, Talba took the paper and wandered toward her room. Who the hell would place an ad like that? It was easy enough to find out, and she couldn't resist—it was a slow Sunday morning. Darryl had his kid for the weekend.

Actually, she met quite a few of the criteria. She was under thirty, had no visible piercings, did have investigative experience, and was, in fact, the Horowitz of the computer. She'd probably be employed if she weren't so damn good. In fact, she certainly would be—she'd just quit a cushy gig at United Oil out of pure boredom. Elsewhere, there were plenty of jobs for an African-American nerd of her distinction, but Talba was a New Orleanian through and through. Her mama was here, and her boyfriend was here but that was only part of it.

Her heart was here.

The last line of the ad said "Fax résumé," and gave a number. That was all she needed. A few strokes of the keyboard and she had a name: Edward Valentino.

A few more and she had another: E. V. Anthony Investigations. A detective agency on Carondelet. No web site.

"Well, well, well, well, well. What can we deduce from this?" she mumbled to herself, thoroughly delighted. Her mentor, Gene Allred, had told her he got a good percentage of his work from being first in the phonebook—therefore, given the "E. V.," there probably was no Anthony. Carondelet Street was in the CBD, or Central Business District—therefore maybe Valentino was a pretty respectable guy (which was more than she could say for Allred.)

She grabbed for the Yellow Pages. Aha, an ad. Twenty-five years' experience. Specializing in criminal defense, undercover, divorce, child custody, missing persons, insurance, prenuptial. In other words, not specializing.

Interesting, though—the ad didn't mention too much about background checks. Corporate and prenuptial might cover that, but something told Talba Mr. Valentino didn't care much for doing heavy computer searches.

Well, hell. That was a nerd's job. She got back on the net and sometime after lunch had a stack of papers half an inch thick. An excellent day's work. She decided to give her mother a treat.

"Come on, Mama. Let's take a ride." Miz Clara was dozing in front of the television set.

"Where ya want to go?"

"Let's go see Aunt Carrie. I've got this nice car—we might as well use it." She had bought a five-year-old Camry out of her United Oil earnings.

Miz Clara said, "Hmmph. Not nice *enough*."

"Oh, yeah, I think so. In this neighborhood, I think it's quite nice enough." Her mama lived in a run-down cottage in the Ninth Ward, on a block poetically situated between Desire and Piety. A better car would just be a better target.

Miz Clara went off to trade her floppy old blue slippers for a pair of Nikes, and find herself a wig to wear. When she came back, she said, "What you been doin' in there by ya self?"

"Writing poetry," said Talba, and Miz Clara shut up.

It was eight-forty-five the next morning when Talba tried the door marked E. V. Anthony. It was locked. Good. That probably meant they came in at nine.

She found a ladies' room in which to replenish her lipstick, and returned to stand guard. At approximately nine-oh-five, a young white woman unlocked the door. "Are you waiting for someone?"

"Edward Valentino."

"Come on in. Do you have an appointment?"

"No. Just taking a chance."

"Can I help you with anything?"

"Oh, no thanks. I'll just read a magazine." It was obvious the woman was dying of curiosity, but Talba figured once was enough to tell her story.

It was another few minutes—twenty maybe—before a stocky man came in, a man who'd be sixty-five in a matter of days, stood five-feet-ten, and limped a little. Not even giving him a chance to greet the help, she rose and extended her hand. "Mr. Valentino, I presume."

"Good morning. Good morning," he said, clearly a little flustered.

"I didn't know about the limp."

"Say that again?" Now he was irritated.

Talba noticed that he said "dat" for "that." He had the kind of New Orleans accent that sounded, for all the world, as if he'd grown up in Brooklyn. She held up her file. "Everything else was on the Internet. But I missed the limp." She nodded at the secretary. "You're Eileen Fisher, aren't you?" She turned back to Valentino. "And you're about to have a birthday. Congratulations."

Smoke was starting to come out of Valentino's ears. "What the hell is this?" *What da hell is dis?*

"This," she said, "is a young hotshot, able to play the computer like Horowitz tickled the ivories. No visible piercings and well under thirty. Talba Wallis at your service."

Valentino looked exhausted, but he stuck out his hand manfully. "Eddie Valentino. You gotta be a friend of Angela's."

"Angela? I must be missing something."

"Come on, come on. Angela put ya up to this."

"Angela. Your wife's name is Audrey, it can't be . . . oh! Daughter. She must be your daughter."

He was laughing now. "Angie, Angie—don't you ever give up?"

"Mr. Valentino, I'm as much of a hotshot as you're gonna get, but your daughter's name wasn't in any of the databases. Now if I'd known I was going to need it, I could have had it in two seconds."

A look of astonishment spread over his features. Talba figured he was starting to catch on. "How'd you know who placed the ad?"

Talba shrugged. "You advertised for an investigator. I investigated."

Valentino closed his eyes and shook his head slowly, a man clearly at the end of his rope. "Eileen, you got any coffee?"

"Yes sir. Of course." The girl looked terrified.

"Bring us some, will ya? Ms. Wallis, come on in." He led the way to one of three other rooms she could see, another of which seemed to be a combination coffee and copy room. Valentino's office wasn't a whole lot grander. He turned on a light and slipped behind a desk, gesturing at two facing chairs. Talba took one, and for the first time really looked at him.

His hair was salt-and-pepper, not yet white, and not soon to be, but his face was deeply lined. Almost as if it had been carved out of a once-handsome, very Mediterranean demeanor that had become, for some reason, very tired. Deeply, deeply tired. The bags under his eyes were duffels. She almost asked if he were getting enough sleep.

"Start at the beginning, Ms. Wallis."

She passed him most of the file, holding back her ace in the hole. "Here's the background check I did on you, complete with driving record and newspaper clips. I see you worked on the Houlihan case."

He nodded impatiently. "Yeah, yeah. Okay, you're a hotshot. Ya went to Harvard?" Eileen brought in a couple of mugs of coffee, and he had his to his face almost before he'd finished speaking.

"Xavier. Computer skills mostly self-taught, except for five years at TeleSyst. Five years off and on, I mean—some of it was summer stuff while I was in school. But I bow to the applicant who did go to Harvard *and* brings you a package like this."

"Pretty pushy broad, aren't ya?" His eyes crinkled a little. He was starting to loosen up. Talba knew guys like this—the way they showed they liked you was to get insulting.

Best to let it go, she thought. Stow the righteous indignation. She gave him a grin instead. "I try to be." He had drunk about half his coffee by now, and it was doing him a world of good. His skin was looking less gray, his eyes starting to show some spirit, the purple of the duffels smoothing to puce.

What's in that stuff? she thought, and took a sip herself. If she hadn't already been sitting, it would have knocked her on her butt.

"How much investigative experience ya had?"

"About two months." She paused. "Not counting the ten minutes I spent on this." Gesturing grandly at the pile she'd given him.

He didn't crack a smile, and she made a mental note to lay off the bragging. It wasn't going over. "I'm just kidding. It really took me about an hour and a half."

"You tellin' me the truth?" *Da trut'.*

She made an attempt to look modest, but it was something she hadn't tried before; she wasn't sure she succeeded. "Yes sir. Give or take."

"Tell me about your experience."

"Well, it was a funny thing. I had a problem I needed a private eye for. So I picked one out of the phonebook, and the guy hired me."

"Oh, yeah? Who was that?"

"Gene Allred."

He leaned forward a little, and his eyes threw off

sparks like a couple of mini-fires. The guy had some-thing she hadn't seen at first. "Gene Allred? I knew Gene Allred. Crooked son of a bitch."

Talba laughed. "Guess you right." She hardly ever lapsed into dialect, but this guy was such an old-time New Orleanian, it was catching. "A little sleazy, but he sure could detect."

"What was so special about ya he just had to hire ya?"

"He said I had the right demographics."

Valentino raised an eyebrow.

"Meaning I could go undercover in places he couldn't. That and my computer skills. Gene was kind of a Luddite."

"A what?"

"Luddite. You're one too, aren't you?"

"I'll let ya know when ya clue me in what ya talkin' about."

"A Luddite is somebody who'd rather give the government thirty-four cents than send e-mail."

"I got no time for that crap."

"I rest my case. But an awful lot of detective work is done on computers these days. Which must be why you advertised."

"It ain't the business it was." Valentino's shoulders sagged forward as if he'd just suffered a defeat. Talba hated seeing him that way; found it made her truly sad, and noticed for the first time the sadness in the detective's eyes. The sadness, and the intel-ligence; and the kindness.

Oh shit, she thought, realizing she had started to care about him. She recognized instantly that it wasn't a sexual thing—never could be, never would be. She had a great boyfriend, a dynamite boyfriend, and this dude was white, married, old enough to be her father, and so depressed he probably couldn't get it up. Definitely not sexual, but definitely something, and something she thought she recognized. Something not too healthy.

Valentino's eyes—the sad, intelligent, oh-so-kind eyes, the terribly caring, deeply understanding, tender-as-the-night eyes, were the sort of eyes sometimes referred to as soulful; the sort that, in a young, attractive man were almost guaranteed to get a young woman in trouble.

She had seen those eyes before, seen them on many an attractive, hurt, tough, scary young face; and she had followed them where they had led and had gotten in the kind of trouble they invariably got you in. She was such a sucker for that kind of thing her mother and brother had sunk to trying an intervention to get her to dump her last boyfriend, the one before Darryl, the one she now recognized was the second biggest asshole in the city of New Orleans (she being the biggest for not seeing it sooner).

She knew perfectly well why these eyes were so attractive. They were irresistible because they were the only soft thing in a hard face; a worldly, leather-tough face that had seen it all and dealt with it, a face you wouldn't want to mess with. They were a cry for help from a soul that desired no help, wanted no help, chose no help, couldn't in any way *be* helped.

They were not eyes that cried, they were themselves the tears; they were the fatal tip-off that that mutilated and now aggressively armored soul needed to be kissed and made well. That the imaginary tears must be wiped away: crying, desperate eyes replaced by the carefree, corner-crinkled eyes of a man who has just been made to laugh by his beloved; or the devoted, follow-you-to-the-grave eyes of a man who has just made love to her. Or to anyone. Or to a plank with a mink-lined hole in it.

Oh, yes. Talba was not only under thirty, but well

under twenty-five, and already she knew everything about eyes like that—everything except what they meant when they were underscored by velvet-soft pouches so big they needed a bra; so bloodstained, so seemingly bruised you wanted to order emergency ice. What they meant when they sometimes sparked like small fires and peered from the head of an old white man who said "dese" and "dose."

When Eddie Valentino spoke again, interrupting her silent ocular love song, she nearly did a double take. "I'll think about it, Ms. Wallis."

"You'll think about it? Here I stay up half the night to show you what I can do, and then I get here before sunrise, and you'll *think* about it?"

And for the first time in the interview, sad, soulful Eddie Valentino really did smile—a broad, amused, gotcha smile. "I thought it only took you ten minutes. Hour and a half at the most."

"I'm making a point, Mr. Valentino. I tend to ex-agggerate when I'm making a point. And the point is, I'm your hotshot. Who else was here before your door opened with a complete dossier on you? I mean, what's the definition of a hotshot?"

He smiled again, "You're a ball of fire, all right. I just gotta sleep on it, that's all."

"Oh. Well." Twice Talba had made him smile. Maybe that's what her mission was; maybe that was all she was meant to do. Of course he had to sleep on it. What was she thinking?

I'm believing my own P.R., she thought, and felt embarrassed. *What did I think he was going to do? Welcome me like a long-lost daughter?*

Chapter Two

Eddie rubbed his eyes. *Whoa,* he thought. *Pushy. I better get some more coffee.* He watched her indignant tail switch out of the office, and thought how tired he was; how much he wished he had Talba Wallis's energy. How much, in fact, he wished he were her age again.

He forebore to ask Eileen to bring him a cuppa joe—lately everything he did was construed as being old, infirm, or otherwise messed up—and limped in to get one for himself.

Hell, he thought. *Just hell.* And tried calling his daughter. Of course he didn't get her. He never got her. He tried her on her cell phone.

"Yeah?" she said. Just like that.

"Ya gotta talk like a truck driver?"

"Dad, I'm in court. Judge Hart's gonna ream me out—I forgot to turn my phone off." She hung up.

What the hell was *with* girls anymore? Or maybe it was just Angie. Maybe she was a dyke. There were people who said so.

Hell, he thought again, not sure why he was in such a crummy mood.

He figured he'd wasted enough time. Sighing, he turned on the damn computer. He'd lost his zest for the job, really lost it. These days, fifty percent of it—thirty, anyhow—had to be done on a computer—and the damn thing made his eyes hurt. Made his wrists hurt. Oh, yeah. Carpal tunnel, the whole thing. It gave him the worst headaches he'd ever had in his life. So bad Audrey and Angie kept hounding him to go to the doctor.

Yeah, right. He was sure gonna go to some pansy-assed doctor. When hell froze over. He didn't even want to go when he got hurt; figured the leg would heal on its own, and it might have. He just would have bled to death first.

Well, Angie was right about one thing—something had to give. He just didn't know what.

On the whole it turned out to be an okay morning. He'd done two employment checks and one premarital when his daughter breezed in. He was glad to see her. It meant he could turn the damn machine off, rest his eyes a little.

"Angie! Help yaself to coffee."

"No thanks. My damn client didn't show. Hearing got postponed." She was wearing a black tailored suit. That was all she ever wore these days—all any women ever wore, seemed like.

He passed her yesterday's *Times-Picayune,* the section with his ad circled. He knew she wouldn't have seen it—nobody reads classifieds unless they're looking for a job.

"Daddy! Don't tell me you ran this."

"Ya didn't want me to? Ya wrote it, didn't ya?"

"I was just trying to illustrate that the person you claim to want doesn't exist."

"I happened to interview a very qualified applicant already."

"Oh, yeah?" She brightened up, smiling like the old Angie, the little kid he never wanted to lose. It really pissed him off that she grew up. "What's he like?"

"Kind of like God," he said. He'd been waiting to deliver that line.

"What?" She spoke in the tone of a mother whose kid has just told another tall one.

"You heard me." He was enjoying this.

"What in the name of all that's holy does Eddie Valentino find godlike about a computer nerd?"

"She's black." Eddie couldn't help it, he had a weakness for dumb jokes. The older the better.

Angie didn't even laugh, way too snotty to even be bothered. She was so staggered by the information she just repeated what Eddie had said: "She's black?"

"What's wrong? Ya prejudiced?"

"No, but you—uh—"

"Ya got me wrong, Angie—I'm not prejudiced. I don't like pushy broads, that's all."

"What about Mama?"

"I'm stuck with her."

"What about me?"

"Can't stand ya." He swatted her face ever so gently, and gave her a half smile.

"Oh, *Daddy*." Like a fourteen-year-old. He liked it. "Tell me about the applicant. What's her name?"

"Hell if I know." He shuffled some papers. "Talba Wallis."

"How old is she?"

" 'Bout twenty-two. Twenty-three, maybe."

"That's way too young to have the experience you wanted. She must have gone to Harvard."

"Xavier."

Angie was looking exasperated. Eddie hadn't had so much fun in a month. Teasing his daughter was one of his greatest pleasures, especially since she hated it so much. It kind of got her back for having the gall to grow up. "Well, what the hell was so qualified?"

"She passed on faxing a résumé. Showed up at my door before I did this morning. With this." Eddie handed over the dossier Talba had compiled on him.

"Holy shit."

"Angela. There's no need for foul language."

"Is this what I think it is?" She ignored him. Went right about her business as if he'd never spoken. He didn't know what to do about it when kids got out of control. Nothing he'd ever tried had worked worth a damn.

"Yeah, it's what you think it is. Said it took her an hour and a half."

"Holy shit," she said again. "Did you hire her?"

"No, I didn't hire her. She's pushy."

"In a good way, it sounds like." She was treating him like he was the child.

"I been workin'. I haven't even had time to do a background check."

"Well, what are we waiting for? Let's do it now."

He liked that idea. Angie could do a background check as well as he could—better, probably. She was about ten times as good as he was on the computer, which would have intimidated him if he had any respect for the damn machine. A video camera—now that was a piece of hardware he could love. Computers were just something outside his purview, like sewing. He could work fine with Angie without feeling like a sack of shit. But what appealed to him about the idea, if she was going to help him, she was going to stay with him a while. Maybe she'd even have lunch with him.

He got up and gave her his chair. "I'll just be in the video room."

Angie was leaning forward, her fingers racing.

"Hey, Dad, wait. I've got something. She's got a web site. Your little applicant's got a web site, and you don't even have one yourself! You gotta get this girl. She's hot stuff."

"Yeah, yeah, she mentioned it."

"Her web site? I should think."

"No, the hot stuff part."

"Holy shit." She was leaning intently, as if she didn't care if she fell into the screen.

"Angela. Language."

"She's a poet. Omigod, I've *heard* of her. Is this woman for real? Why would she want to work for you?"

"Whaddaya mean, poet?"

"Take a look at this." She turned the computer screen toward him.

Slowly, his bullshit detector turned on "high," he walked back around his desk. "What the fuck? (Excuse my French.) AKA The Baroness de Pontalba, for Christ's sake? She's been dead for a century. *And* she was white."

Angela was looking way too amused to suit him. "Did you say something about foul language, Daddy dear?"

"I got a double standard; you know that."

"Yes, Daddy." He hated it when she gave him that suppressed-grin thing. "Listen, I know about this woman. They call her the Baroness—it's her nom de plume."

"I'm gonna nom her plume," he said automatically, and finally looked at the screen. There, sure enough, was the applicant in some kind of purple flowing thing with a turban on her head. A goddam turban. "I guess she's an African baroness," he muttered. "Why in the hell does a poet want to be a detective?"

"No money in poetry," Angie said. "They have to have day jobs. Hey, look, here's a schedule of readings. There's one tonight. Shall we go?" Evidently, it was a rhetorical question. Her fingers were working again. "Ah. Here it is. I thought I remembered this." She'd somehow, in the flash of a fingernail (Angie wore Mandarin Red) pulled up a *Times-Picayune* story. "Great big piece by Jane Storey."

"Let me see that." Eddie pulled the screen toward him and read the piece aloud, as naturally as he'd once read his daughter *The Cat in the Hat*. "Yeah, she said she worked for Allred."

Angie nodded. "I guess it was around the time he had that unfortunate collision with a hunk of hot lead."

He stared at her. "What you been readin'? You're talkin' funny." Without waiting for an answer, he kept putting things together. His head started bobbing, as if a puppeteer were running it. "Yeah. Yeah. She checks out. Looks like she's who she says she is. Damn. She helped break the Russell Fortier case."

Angie leaned back in her dad's chair, looking smug—as if the entire female sex had been challenged and had passed the test. "Dad, you've got a problem."

"What's that, baby?" He was still staring at the screen, distracted.

"She's not going to go for those slave wages you're offering."

"Who's offerin'? I don't know if I could work with a woman like that."

"A woman like what? Black or female?" His daughter's voice was cool, but her eyes were hot and dangerous. She could turn on him like a snake—she had a history of this.

"I'm not prejudiced, Angie."

She said, "I ought to know whether you are or not," and walked out, scooping up her purse on her way.

I could call her back, he thought. *Maybe she'll go to*

lunch, anyway. But physically, he couldn't. His throat had closed. When that chasm opened between them, that Grand Canyon of a thing that cracked open as suddenly as a fissure in an earthquake, he felt as if someone were sitting on his chest, squeezing the air out of him. The world turned gray, and he floated above himself, watching his body, shriveled and ancient, lying in a hospital bed and facing a wall, a gray wall in a gray world, perhaps for all eternity.

It hadn't always been this way. He didn't know what was happening to him, exactly, except that it was a form of hopelessness and it wasn't about Angie. Or wasn't all about Angie. He sensed that it was partly about his impending birthday, and wondered if it happened to everyone, and if so, if it ever went away.

He decided against lunch; it would only prolong life.

It was three when Audrey called, and his stomach was sour from too many cups of coffee. "EdDEE," she said, the way people in their old neighborhood called each other. He'd say "AuDREE" if he wanted her. "Ya want meat loaf and red gravy tonight?"

His stomach growled. He wanted some now, he realized. He wanted some bad.

"Come home early," she said. "The poetry readin's at seven."

"What? The what's at seven?"

"The thing Angie's taking us to. I thought y'all talked about it."

Damn, he thought. *Why bother thinking up a good name for your kid? We might as well have called her Devila.* He said, "Okay, Audrey. I'm leavin' early, anyway."

"Why? You don't feel well?"

He almost said, *The goddam screen. It's giving me a headache*. But he caught himself. By now, Angela would have rounded her up; the two women would be irrevocably locked into a conspiracy against him, a mission to get him to hire a nerd to save him from himself. This nerd, apparently. The one who thought she was royalty. *Why the hell Baroness Pontalba?* he wondered, and thought with resignation, *I bet I'm about to find out*.

Some four hours later, full of the promised protein and tomato concoction as well as a mountain of mashed potatoes, he and his wife and daughter (who'd not-so-coincidentally been invited to dinner) found themselves at a restaurant on North Carrollton it would never have occurred to them to patronize in other circumstances. Or Audrey and Eddie, at any rate. For all Eddie knew, it was Angie's favorite hangout.

Reggie and Chaz was a black-owned restaurant for starters, a gay-owned joint for a follow-up. It was fairly new as well. All those facts added up to a hip restaurant, a multicultural, happening kind of restaurant, of a sort that would normally have merely bewildered the elder Valentinos, who leaned more toward the likes of Mandina's. Tonight, they got the hang of it, though; it was a venue for Art.

If that was what poetry was: Eddie really wouldn't know.

He looked around him. The place had a little bar, which was fortunate, since the three of them had already eaten dinner and would certainly be expected to spend money for the privilege of this great artistic experience. Aside from that, though, to say it was simple would be bragging on it. *Ah, no*, Eddie thought. *That's not fair*. It was simple, but it had flair. The walls were tastefully dotted with masks, most of them grotesque, some of them African, presumably; some Indonesian; some Mexican, certainly. Not ex-

pensive, but, boy, did they make a statement. Woven
Guatemalan belts hung from the ceiling like so
many colorful snakes—or like confetti, Eddie
thought.

Grudgingly, he had to admit there was something
festive about it.

The crowd was mixed—salt and pepper, young
and old, hip and conventional. *Sure*, Eddie thought.
*Poets and their parents. You don't have to be a detective
to get the hang of that one.*

He was surprised when the first poet to read was
older than he was, a distinguished black man, professor type, in a handsome dark suit.

Several poets were evidently about to perform,
singing for their supper, which was being served at
a large raucous table more or less in the middle of
the restaurant. The applicant was there, looking totally different from the businesslike young woman
who'd called on him that morning. She wore a cobalt blue, silky flowing thing, like the one in the
picture on her web site, and she had something on
her head that looked like two silk scarves somehow
woven and twisted together and tied across her forehead, Indian-fashion. He hadn't thought about her
appearance that morning, other than to register
that she had a lot of hair, but now he noted that he
was looking at a very striking woman. How did
women do that? he thought. Turn from mice to
birds of paradise, depending on the time of day?

He looked at his wife and daughter. Angie had
changed into black jeans and a black T-shirt, and
Audrey was wearing a soft green pantsuit. Celadon,
she called it. Any man in the room would look at
either of them; probably had by now. Italian women
didn't do the metamorphosis thing, he thought—
didn't need to.

The black man was going on and on about something historical. He was boring the pants off Eddie.

Poetry! Jesus Christ, what he did to please his women. He was going to bust a gut if the guy didn't shut up soon.

He had by now managed to secure a scotch and water, and he clutched it like a baby clutches a bottle, figuring there was one tried-and-true way to stave off the worst boredom in the world. He ought to know—he'd done it often enough before. The poem was about slavery, and it quickly went from boring to angry—or at least the poet was angry. Eddie wasn't; he was merely uncomfortable at the man's rising voice. He sipped away at the scotch, vaguely noticing that Audrey was giving him a disapproving look. (She herself was slurping on a white wine, but in her book that wasn't the point—she liked being boss of herself *and* Eddie.)

The poet finished, to a faint flutter of applause—evidently the rest of the audience was as difficult as Eddie. And after him came a white woman, housewife type, who read obscene limericks. That he hadn't expected, and he was oddly disappointed. If he was going to have an intellectual experience, then let it be shaggy-haired, dammit, even if it bored him to the toenails.

After the white woman came a black woman who'd had a job where people treated her badly. White people, of course. Too bad, but was it poetry? He was in critic mode by now, and also on his second drink. He was kind of enjoying hating it all so much.

Three more poets came after the black woman, but when Eddie tried later to remember them, he found they all ran together, but it couldn't have been the scotch, because what he heard after that he remembered vividly.

He was just ordering a third drink when the emcee said, "And now for our star attraction—someone who got her start at Reggie and Chaz, one of our very first readers, a young lady who's starting to make her mark in the poetry world—the Baroness de Pontalba." The guy sounded like some asshole on TV.

Eddie settled down in his chair, getting comfortable and feeling grumpy, as the applicant flowed forward. *The deep blue sea herself,* he thought, and decided he had an aptitude for this crap himself—probably a lot more than the rest of these bozos.

He was paying for his drink while she introduced her first poem, but the gist of it seemed to be that some other poet that she didn't even seem to mind stealing from had written some idiot thing about a cat having three names and she, Miss Talba de Baroness (he was proud of himself for that one) was like a little pussycat herself. He figured he was about to get a month's worth of ribbing material for Audrey and Angie out of this one.

One thing, though. The woman's voice was like cream. Or maple syrup, maybe.

No, it was butterscotch. Yeah. Unbearably sugary and sweet and exotic. Less familiar than chocolate, yet with more personality. Gentler. More tantalizing. Maybe the best stuff in the world, if you didn't count oyster po' boys. When he was a kid, he didn't give a damn for chocolate. Give him butterscotch every time.

"I am like a cat," the poet said.

For Christ's sake, give me a break, he thought. And then she really got going.

When I was born, I was a little piece of toffee.
Brown toffee.
Soft and sweet and just as innocent as the baby
*   Jesus.*
Just as innocent as my mama.
Or maybe I should say my sweet mama was just as
*   innocent as*

her own sweet baby.
My sweet mama was so proud.

My sweet mama was so proud.
Even though her own sweet baby was born at
      Charity Hospital—
(Couldn't have been worse—there ain't really no St.
      James
Infirmary)
She was lyin' there at Charity like Cleopatra in
      exile, and
she says to the Pill Man, the one who pulled her
      baby out of
her womb and stopped that relentless screaming
      pain—
She says to that nice young man,
"What you think I ought to name my baby?"
My mama so proud of her little piece of toffee,
She wants to name her somethin' fine.
Somethin' fancy.
Somethin' so special ain' no other little girl got the
same name.
And the doctor say, "Name that girl Urethra."
And my mama, she just as pleased, and she so
      proud,
And she say, "That's a beautiful name. Ain'
      nobody in my neighborhood name Urethra.
We got Sallies amd we got Janes and we got
      Melissas and
Saras—we got LaTonyas, just startin' to have
      Keishas—but
ain' nobody else name Urethra.
I'm gon' name my baby Urethra for sure."
And that's my first name—the one they put on my
      birth certificate.
I am named Urethra. Now ain't that a beautiful
      name?
But somebody knew. Somebody in our neighborhood.

*Somebody told my sweet mama she name her little
    candy girl
after some ol' tube you piss through.*

*My name is Piss Tube.
My name is Pee Place.
My name is Exit for Excreta.
And my sweet mama so proud.*

*Now she call me Sandra.
I never did find out why.
Must be for the sand got in her eyes when she listen
    to
that white man.
Do I look like a Sandra to you?
My name is Urethra.
My name is Exit for Excreta.*

*And I am a baroness.
Because a cat has three names and I am like a cat.
My sweet mama's broken and weak now,
After what that white man did to her—
She never did trust no one again, black or white.
And I can never say again, "My mama's proud."
I didn't want no African name,
'Cause I am African-American, love it or hate it,
And I didn't want no LaTonya, I didn't want no
    La Keisha,
Latifah, Tanisha, Marquita, Shamika—
White asshole steal somethin' from me.
I'm gon' steal somethin' right back.*

*I
AM THE BARONESS DE PONTALBA,
AND YOU
can kiss my aristocratic black ass.*

Shock value, he thought. *She's just going for shock
value. Everybody's heard that stuff about the interns at*

Charity Hospital, but nobody believes it. It's just a story, for Christ's sake. This is the kind of thing keeps the races apart. This girl isn't doing anybody any good with this kind of crap.

Still. The poem made him feel a little shaky. Awkward, kind of. He stole a glance at his wife and saw she was staring at Angie, who was in tears. Good. A way out. "Angie, ya so softhearted," he said.

"I don't see what's wrong with her," Audrey said. "I thought it was supposed to be funny."

"Supposed to be. Sure—*supposed* to be," he said, "Well, I thought it was supposed to be sad and funny at the same time, but I don't think it was either one, 'cause I don't believe a word of it. I think the Baroness is a hype artist."

Angie gave him an, "oh, Daddy" look, and the poet started up again.

"That's from a series of poems I've written—still writing, matter of fact—about my favorite subject: The Baroness Myself. 'Course, I wouldn't want you to think I'm self-involved or anything, but after a hard day of makin' up verses, I find I still don't have enough to cover the rent and shrink bills both. So I just get up and dive a little deeper the next day and put off that shrink appointment until the Hollywood money starts to roll in, and whatever I write keeps me sane. So y'all are going to have to forgive me if these things sound a little crazy." She paused a second, and Eddie nodded to himself, thinking she really was an excellent performer. "Got another one for you. It's called 'Queen of the May.'"

Other girls' daddies are po-licemen,
bankers, lawyers, tubewinders, tolltakers,
worthless layabouts, drug dealers,
And cable TV installers.
Mmm-mmm.

Not my daddy.
My daddy ain' nothin' like nobody else's daddy.

My daddy say, you ain't no Baroness,
You Queen of the May
And I . . .
Am your faithful servant, at your service today.
Your Majesty, honey,
Come fly a kite with me.

And he take me out to the park to fly a kite,
And I cry 'cause only the kite can fly and not me.
And he say, lucky for you we in the Enchanted
   Park.

Enchanted Park? I say.
He got my attention now.
"Only park in the history of the world
   Got flyin' horses.
    You ever fly on a horse?"
And I say, "Daddy I never even rode on a horse."
And we fly on the flyin' horses
And I cry 'cause they ain't even real,
And already
I seen too many things match that *description.*

But he say, you want a horse? I'll get you a horse.
Great big chestnut horse
With a long silky mane and
A hand-tooled leather saddle,
And he be real big and warm
And make you feel safe like nothin' ever did in this
   world.

Mmmm hmmmm.
Other girls' daddies be plumbers,
accountants, shoe salesmen,
bus drivers, bail bondsmen,

Preachers, and the random city councilman.
Not my daddy.
My daddy my faithful servant,
Do anything I want
Anytime I want
Because I . . .
Am Queen of the May.

So he get me that great big chestnut horse
And he put me up on top,
And I never in my life felt anything so big and
    warm and safe
Except my own sweet daddy's lap when I climb up
    and give him a hug.

Every mornin' now my mama come in,
Come floppin' in in her funny ol' fuzzy slippers
And she say, Girl, why you sleep so late?
Who you think you is?
You think you Queen of the May?
And I say, five minutes, Mama, jus' five minutes
    more.
And I close my eyes
And I saddle up my horse
And we go flyin' off again.
And I never in my life felt anything so big and
    warm and safe.

It's her voice, Eddie thought. *It's her goddam voice.*
That and the scotch. He felt like crying, and he had
to blame it on something. Audrey was cocking an
eyebrow at him. He wasn't actually tearing up, but
he turned away just in case.

He hated this woman. Actually hated her. He
could probably hire her for pennies, but he was willing to pay a living wage just to get her out of his
life. Tomorrow he'd bite the bullet and run a real

ad and get some young male hotshot. Angie had made her point.

The poet read some other stuff and it was quite a bit lighter, kind of funny, some of it. He even half-way enjoyed it, now that his decision was made.

And then it was over, and everyone was standing and chattering, and she was coming. She was headed right for him, cobalt folds flying about her, holding out her hand as graciously as a queen. The woman was scary.

"Why, Eddie Valentino, I never figured you for a poetry lover."

"My wife made me come."

He could hear Audrey gasp at his side, but the Baroness was utterly unfazed. "Audrey? Delighted to meet you. And you must be Angie. It's so lovely of you to come. Will you come meet my mama?"

Then, somehow, they got sucked up into the maelstrom of people around her and Audrey was falling in love with the woman the Baroness said was her mama: "She calls herself Miz Clara, but you can probably call her 'Miz' for short."

Angie was trading wisecracks with some black guy—good-looking dude, way too handsome for Eddie's taste—who was probably the poet's boy-friend or husband or something, and he was forced to talk to the damn woman herself.

"Tell me something, Miss, um . . . Miss . . ." He'd forgotten her name.

"Why don't you call me 'Your Grace'?"

"Uh, tell me something. Where'd you go to school?"

"Harvard. I told you that." She was laughing at him.

"Oh, yeah, Xavier. Ya graduate?"

She nodded. "With honors."

"Well, you talk like an educated lady. Why ya write ya poetry in ebonics—idn't that what they call it?"

He was proud of himself for remembering.

"You really want to know?"

Not really, he thought, but he had to talk about something. "It just seems like kind of a waste of education."

"I do it because that's how I hear it."

He thought she'd say more, but she didn't. Superior bitch. He truly hated her.

Chapter Three

Before it was over, Talba had managed to get him together with Miz Clara. The Baroness might be too much for him—she was pretty sure she was—but no one, at least no one like Eddie, could resist Miz Clara when she was in church-lady mode. She came to Talba's readings dressed to uphold the family honor in the face of her daughter's outlandish persona, and that meant panty hose, heels, tight little dress with peplum, and Sunday-best, not-a-hair-out-of-place wig-hat-on-her-head. She worked as a housecleaner, which she would probably work into the conversation, just because she liked to get it out there in case it was an issue, and Talba figured that could work to her advantage. It would show that she came from modest beginnings and therefore couldn't be too threatening.

Talba had kept an ear cocked while she talked to Eddie's very hip daughter—whom she liked a lot—and heard Miz Clara going on about how honored she was that Eddie had come to hear her humble daughter and even brought his exalted family. She might not actually have used those precise adjectives, but Talba thought there was something downright Japanese about the way she carried on about the honor he and his were heaping on her and hers by their luminescent presence. Her mother must really want her to get a job.

Her brother Corey already held one of the three positions Miz Clara deemed acceptable for her offspring, the other two being president and Speaker of the House. Corey was a doctor. Miz Clara hadn't signed up for a poet.

Worse, she hated most of Talba's poetry, because it revealed too much about the family. What she did like was the adulation it got her daughter, which Miz Clara felt reflected so well on her it actually *was* hers. And so, gradually, ever so gradually, she'd become willing for Talba not to go off to Palo Alto and become an Internet millionaire, so long as she did some kind of honest work. Evidently, she'd liked Audrey enough to make Eddie okay with her. And okay in Miz Clara's book meant she was going to stay on Talba's back—and maybe Eddie's—till Eddie hired her.

That morning she had knocked on Talba's door, and shouted, "Girl, who you think you are? Queen of the May?"

Talba smiled. "Come on in, Mama. I'm sorry you hate that poem so much."

"Hmmmf. Describe *you*, all right. Got coffee made."

Talba had stayed out late with Darryl after the reading—she found it took her hours to wind down from these things—and had slept much longer than usual, too long to join her mother for coffee, as usual.

When Miz Clara had left, and she had drunk her

coffee and worked up her nerve, she took a breath and called Eddie. "Mr. Valentino? I just wanted to thank you again for coming to my reading. I was really very touched and just wanted to say . . ."

But he interrupted her. "Ya busy this morning? Why don't ya come on in?"

For what? she thought. *Am I hired?* But she didn't ask. What the hell, she wasn't busy. She put on her one good suit.

Eileen Fisher looked up only briefly. "He said to send you right in."

Talba thought he looked a little better this morning—maybe a little less tired. Probably a load off his shoulders, knowing he was about to get such a competent assistant.

"Ms. Wallis, ya got an investigator's license?"

"License? Well, no, I thought if I worked for you . . . why? Do I need one?"

"To be an investigator ya do."

Fool. She hadn't checked *that* out. "What do I have to do to get one?"

"Ya gotta go to Delgado or UNO and take a course. Take ya coupla weekends. But you gotta wait till they give the class."

"Oh." She sat still for a moment, taking it in. Finally, she said, "Well. I'm in your office. There must be some reason for it."

"I'm willing to take you on as an apprentice while ya get ya license."

"I see."

"And I was wonderin'. You're so good with the computer—ya got a program for keeping books?"

"You want me to keep the books as well?

He shrugged. "Not that much to do. It's just a pain in the ass if ya don't have the software."

"You want me to do two jobs? Is that it?"

"Well, ya won't be doing that much investigating— mostly just tagging around with me and learning.

With your skills, the bookkeeping won't take ya more than a few hours a month. I'd say it's about three-quarters of a job, really."

"Wait a minute. None of that's my real job—what you really want's a computer jockey, right?"

He leaned forward, getting aggressive on her. "That's nothin'. That's like a hobby for ya."

She was considering flouncing out of the office when suddenly she noticed something she'd never seen in this man before. Somewhere between the lizardly hoods of his eyes and the purple luggage below was a glint of amusement. He was playing with her.

She reached for the file she'd withheld from him the day before, the one that held his financial report, setting it provocatively on his desk. "You're right. Piece of cake for a hotshot like me. But you don't know me—how come you'd trust me with the books?"

"I wouldn't. I'm gonna micromanage ya until I'm sure ya've got the hang of it."

"I mean, how do you know I'm honest?"

"Are you serious, young lady? You should never have introduced me to ya mama—you don't do right, Miz Clara'll be the first to know."

If he was the laughing type, he'd be roaring at this point.

She concealed her irritation. "What kind of salary did you have in mind?"

"Tell me what ya lookin' for." He looked like a buzzard circling prey so helpless it already stank.

She said, "Oh, about eighty grand."

He did a histrionic double take. "Grand is right, Your Majesty. We're talkin' grandiose."

"Your Grace will do." She gave him a full-wattage smile.

"I was thinking more like twenty-five."

Good, she thought. *Excellent. He was probably really thinking about seventeen.*

She opened the folder. "Well, now, I've already given a little attention to your books."

He snatched the folder out of her hands. "Where'd you get this?"

"Same place that high-priced service of yours gets it. You've got one, don't you? You probably pay them twenty-five a year. I can save you that much just by doing your financial checks for you. So look—take that twenty-five and the twenty-five you just offered—I'll do it for fifty."

The amusement was gone now. He was starting to look dangerous. "You got some nerve, ya know that?"

Talba was wondering if she'd gone too far when a timid voice spoke behind her. "Mr. Valentino?"

"What is it, Eileen?" His voice was furious. Talba could see the woman wince, bracing for a temper that he probably didn't bother controlling if he didn't feel like it.

"I've got a call for Ms. Wallis."

"Ms . . . Ms . . ." He seemed to be struggling to remember who the hell Ms. Wallis might be.

"May I take it here?" Talba asked coolly, and picked up the phone.

"Did I get you at a bad time?" It was Darryl.

"Couldn't be worse. How'd you find me?"

"Took a chance. Listen, there's no time to talk. I'm sending you a client. You got the job, I presume."

For the benefit of Valentino, who was hanging on her every word, Talba said, "I see. You're sending us a client."

"Look, it's a lady whose kid goes to another school. She just made a scene in the counselor's office, and I thought of a brilliant way to get her out of here."

"Uh-huh. What was that?"

"Suggested a hotshot P.I. Oh, shit, she's yelling again. Listen, I've got to go."

Talba set the receiver down, wondering what this was going to do to her negotiation. She decided not to go the apologetic route. Instead, she smiled and held out her hands. "Well. Looks like I'm a rain-maker."

"You're mighty damn big for ya britches, you know that?"

"Actually, I'm a little embarrassed about that—I didn't solicit it; it just happened."

"And how exactly would you define 'it'?" he asked.

"A friend said he had a client for us. No details; no nothing."

Valentino shook his head. "Well, I can't pay you fifty thousand dollars."

He damn sure could, she thought. She knew exactly what he was taking in. But she said, "Okay. Forty-five."

Eileen Fisher appeared again. "Another call for Ms. Wallis."

Again, Talba picked up. "This is Aziza Scott. Darryl Boucree called about me."

"Yes, Mrs. Scott. But he didn't tell me what it was about."

"I'm calling from the car. See you in ten."

Valentino seemed hardly to notice the interruption. "Twenty-seven tops," he said.

Tops, my ass, Talba thought, and tried not to think about what Darryl was sending them. She was starting to perspire, partly from fear, and partly from the realization that she was doing it, she was going to get what she wanted. "Forty plus benefits."

"Of course benefits," Eddie said. "Think I'm a piker? Twenty-seven and benefits."

Several thousand dollars later, when they had finally shaken hands, a well-dressed woman arrived, nervously twisting the nice-sized diamond she wore. Talba breathed a sigh of relief—apparently, she was able to afford an apprentice hotshot.

Valentino was suddenly the perfect host. "Come in, come in, Mrs. Scott. Would you like a cup of coffee?"

The woman was tall, African-American, straight-haired, straight-nosed, and probably, if her clothes were any indication, straitlaced. She was dressed for the business world, and from the looks of her gray suit and gold jewelry, high up in it. Talba thought she looked like a bank officer.

The woman addressed herself to Talba. "Mr. Boucree seemed to think you'd be able to relate to my daughter."

"Mr. Valentino and I work as a team. Excuse me a moment, will you? I'll get another chair." She was making it up as she went along, but it seemed to be working. The woman relaxed and sat.

When Talba came back with the chair, Eddie was already talking. "What can we do for you?"

"My daughter's been molested."

Talba gasped, but she kept quiet, taking a cue from Eddie, who shook his head slowly, murmuring, "Mmm. Mmm. Mmm."

"The thing is, no one will *do* anything!" Scott sounded whiny and at the end of her rope.

"I'm so sorry." Talba said, no longer able to contain herself.

"She still has braces on her teeth." The woman was twisting a tissue, but maybe, just maybe, she didn't seem quite as anguished as Miz Clara might have been in her situation.

"Why don't you start at the beginning," Eddie said quietly.

Aziza Scott took a breath. "I read her diary. I don't like to admit it, but I didn't know what else to do. She wasn't acting right. Nothing made her happy all of a sudden—she was sullen and pouty all the time instead of only three-quarters of it." She tried out a smile on this one, but none of the three of them had the stomach for it. "I thought maybe I could find out what was bothering her."

Talba didn't think this was a first, the thing with the diary.

"It was in there."

"That she'd been molested?"

"That she'd had sex. Here. You read it."

She handed it to Talba, opened to a page with a section marked in yellow highlighter, and Eddie had no choice but to wait until she'd read it.

He picked me over Shaneel! Bet that's never happened to her in her whole life. "You," he said. "Come with me." Just like that. As soon as we were in the bedroom, he said, "Baby, you beautiful. Anybody ever tell you that? You got a bottom like somethin' out of the movies. You want me to rub your back? Come on. Let's go over to the bed."

Well! I'm embarrassed to write what happened next—stuff I never even heard of. Wow. I can honestly say he taught me things about my body I never suspected. Oh, yeah—all right! That part was real good. But it still hurt when we did it.

Why doesn't anyone ever tell you it's going to? I asked Shaneel and she just laughed at me. I wonder if it always does—every time, I mean?

At first I wasn't going to do it. No way, Jose! Cassandra Scott from Catholic School? I don't think so. But then, while I was lying there feeling like that, I just thought, why not? Why not do it with him? I've got to do it with somebody sometime, and he's a grown man—been everywhere, done everything. Why not find out what it's all about?

Anyway, I made him wear a condom.

Talba handed the diary to Eddie, and asked, "How old is she, Mrs. Scott?"

"Fourteen. And you see what she says about him."

Talba said, "Statutory rape."

"Not exactly," Eddie said, "Louisiana law is tricky. Here, it's called 'carnal knowledge of a juvenile.'"

"But it's still a crime. Why not go to the police?" asked Talba. Eddie gave her a look that told her not to rush things.

"Cassandra says she doesn't know who the man was. I tried to get it out of her, and I did go to the police. They say they can't do a damn thing without a name. Then I went to find that little bitch Shaneel, and the idiot counselor wouldn't even let me talk to her. Goddammit, you see how frustrated I am? No one will *do* anything!" Talba remembered what Darryl had said about her causing a scene in the counselor's office. She hoped it wasn't going to be repeated.

Grasping at straws, she said, "There's no name anywhere in the diary?"

"Oh, yes, there's a name. Toes."

"Toes."

"My daughter had her first sexual experience with a man named Toes." She twisted the tissue till it tore, and at this moment, her anguish seemed real to Talba. She didn't care much for the name Toes herself.

Eddie said, "We need to talk to the girl."

Scott nodded. "Might as well. She doesn't talk to me, that's for sure. But I don't think it's—I don't want to be rude, but I really think she'd respond better to Ms. Wallis."

Take that, Talba thought. *Take that, Eddie Valentino. I'm the right demographic—young, female, and as dumb as the kid when it comes to guys. Scratch that. Formerly as dumb as the kid.*

She was feeling magnanimous. Instead of letting

Eddie do the dirty work, she jumped in ahead of him. "I'll be happy to talk to her, but we do work as a team. Okay if Eddie comes along?"

"I guess it can't hurt." Scott didn't seem happy about it.

Chapter Four

She was pushy, she was smart-mouthed, she was probably brilliant (or thought she was, which was just as bad). She was also cute as a button, and the whole package added up to one large pain in the ass. But after the reading, once he got home and got sober, Eddie found he didn't hate her at all. In fact, he had to admit she reminded him of someone—an awful lot, as a matter of fact. Except for the little matter of skin color, she was just about a clone of his daughter Angela.

The thing he hated was Angie and Audrey pushing her down his throat. Sometimes it seemed like he never got to make any decisions on his own. They worked on him all the way home from the damn reading. Both of them seemed to think she was Sherlock Holmes and Robert Frost rolled up in one—and in the end he ran out of excuses.

Yes, she could probably make his life easier. And yes, she was about ten times more qualified than anyone else he'd probably be able to get. No matter how hard he tried, he couldn't seem to make the mere facts that she was black, female, pushy, and had an uncanny ability to get around him outweigh the rest of it. Matter of fact, not a single one of the four facts could even be mentioned outside a poker club in Arabi.

Plus, that poem about her father had really gotten to him. He hated it when she read it because it made him so goddam sad—like maybe he was missing something. He didn't see why it was anybody's business to go and make him feel like that. But the girl really loved her father. You couldn't fake a thing like that. That had to count for something.

"Okay, okay, okay. I know when I'm licked," he had said, slamming the door of his Buick, and Angie had given him a big sloppy kiss. That part was okay, but he hated it when she followed it up with crap like, "Dad, I've been so worried about you."

Worried about him, hell. He could damn well run his business by himself.

Anyway, he thought he could until the damn *Baroness* stuck a gun to his head and walked away with everything he'd ever worked for. That was what he was going to tell Audrey, but actually, once he realized how much she was going to save him on the financial reports, he didn't mind that much—might even come out ahead.

That was an interesting thought. He had business— had plenty of business—but to his recollection, he'd never had an African-American client who wasn't referred by a lawyer. What if there was a nice little market there, and Ms. Talba Wallis could tap into it for him? Blacks did business with blacks, and now he had one on his staff. He could even give her a little commission for each new client she brought in—sweeten the pot a little, get her to put the word out.

He was most impressed with Aziza Scott as a client. Not only hadn't she balked at his considerable hourly fee, she'd turned out to be a hospital administrator. Hospitals were big businesses. They got sued; they had employees who stole; they had plenty of investigative needs. Also, from the looks of her, Ms. Scott was plenty well-fixed and likely had plenty of friends who were—and who might need a little divorce work or something.

If he could just do something about her mouth, the Baroness might work out.

One thing about it bothered him a little—the co-incidence of Scott making a scene at Talba's boy-friend's school at the very moment she was negotiating her salary. He decided to let it go. He knew it had to be a setup and a pretty transparent one—but if Scott's money was good, what the hell did he care? Let the Baroness play games all day and all night if she wanted; if she thought she was fooling him, so much the better. Being underestimated was always an advantage.

After the client left, he said, "Ya got a car, Ms. Wallis?"

She came back with, "How about if we do 'Talba' and 'Eddie'?"

Damn, she could be irritating. It was his place to say that, right? Who the fuck did she think she was? But what the hell, it was going to come to that, anyway. So he just said, "Whatever Your Grace desires. Ya got a car or not?"

"Yes sir. Nice little Camry."

"Well, get out to Delgado and sign up for the next investigators' course. But first call up the state Board of P.I. Examiners and apply for your apprentice license." He paused. "Oh, and by the way—nice of ya to include me in on the interview with the kid."

She gave him a smile he could only construe as mischievous. "I thought I had to."

"Ya damned right ya had to. Ya can't do a damn thing on this case—or any case, ya got that?—till your apprentice license comes through." He paused, his gaze boring right through her—this was something you couldn't mess around with. "Ya know why?"

"My mama always said, 'because I told you not to'—that's good enough for me."

"Well, there's three thousand better reasons— one for every dollar I'm gon' get fined if you do. Now get outta here."

While she was out, he and Eileen rearranged the copy room so she could use it for an office.

Talba was touched to find the little office they'd carved out for her—Eileen had even put some flowers in there. Still, it wasn't quite what she expected. The obvious space was the room down the hall, the one that appeared more or less empty.

"What's with that one?" she asked. "Is there another employee?"

Eileen shook her head. "Oh, no. That's the video room. It's Eddie's pride and joy."

"What do you need a video room for?"

"We do these 'Day in the Life' things, see? Like if somebody gets mangled up in a car accident and they're suing. We do a little movie showing how tough their life is when they can't even move their little finger."

Talba winced. "Omigod. I hope I never have to do that."

"No fear. Uncle Eddie loves it—he'd do nothin' but that if he could. That and divorce work— anything, so long as it doesn't involve computers."

"Did you say *Uncle* Eddie?"

"Oops, did I? 'Scuse me, I'm not supposed to do that. Anyway, it's on Aunt Audrey's side."

That was good information—there'd be no antagonizing this one. Eileen said, "Make me a list of what you need, okay? There's already a phone line in there. Oh, and I've ordered you a cell phone. Eddie thinks you should have one. You got a camera?"

"Not a very good one."

"Okay, I'll get you one."

"I'll probably need another phone line for the Internet."

"Sure. He said to get you whatever you want."

"Great. How about a nice green Jaguar?" Talba slipped into her new office and started setting things up. There were a bunch of folders in her in-box with a note on them: "Not to be touched until you have your license." They were mostly credit checks. Easy-peazy. She had them nearly all done by five-thirty, and the interview with Cassandra was at six. Eddie didn't say a word when she laid them on his desk.

"Pontchartrain Park," he said as they piled into his Buick. "Birds of a feather still flock together."

Talba racked her brain, but in the end had to give up. "Eddie," she said, finally, "what language was that?"

"It's where we're going. Where the rich black folks live."

She almost said, "I don't think so—or my brother'd be there," but that sounded snotty even to her. She settled for, "Oh. Thought that was East-over."

"Pontchartrain Park's older—must not be fashionable anymore."

"Well, I sure wouldn't know. I live in the Ninth Ward." She said "de Night Wawad," like a native, and actually got a laugh out of him.

The neighborhood was on the lake and nicely appointed with a golf course, but by nineties standards it was really pretty modest—a tasteful collection of ranch-style brick homes, nearly fifty years old by the looks of them.

Aziza Scott's was no different, being well-kept and sedate, though the Mercedes in front was one of the better cars on the street. The inside, by contrast, was mildly chaotic.

Scott had had time to change into khakis and a T-shirt, but her makeup hadn't had an update for hours. "Would you like to talk in the living room?" she asked, and Eddie shook his head, perhaps thinking the room too formal. That it was, but it needed a good dusting.

Scott said, "Cassandra's watching TV," and started toward the back of the house.

The dining-room table was piled high with papers and files—work stuff, probably the mom's or dad's, and they'd spilled over onto a buffet with a silver tea service pushed to one side.

Eddie asked "Is your husband home?" and Scott said "I'm divorced." She tried out a wry smile, but it never really took off.

Talba glanced off to the right and saw that the kitchen looked, as Miz Clara used to say, like a cyclone had struck it. A whiff of garbage that needed emptying drifted out of it.

Scott waved at it. "The cleaners come tomorrow," *Teenage girls contemplating pregnancy should be forced to visit,* Talba thought. The house was a powerful argument against single parenthood.

The family room where they ended up, by contrast looked a little better. Scott must have admonished her daughter to clear out discarded socks and leftover pizza before the visitors arrived.

The moment Talba saw the girl she had a bad feeling. Cassandra was a tall drink of water well on her way to babehood, clearly with little else on her mind. Her skin was a luscious golden color, lighter than her mother's, and her hair was curlier. She had pulled it through a rubber band somewhere near the top of her head so that it formed an exuberant pouf while exposing a graceful neck. Spidery arms protruded from a sleeveless shirt that failed to cover her navel and skinny legs from a pair of abbreviated shorts. Her bare feet revealed green-painted toenails. Sullenness enveloped her like a thick, sticky cloud.

For the first time, Talba's confidence faltered. *I don't know if I can do this,* she thought. The girl was clearly a bird with a broken wing, but not only from the rape, Talba thought. The wounds didn't seem fresh.

She and Eddie sat down while Scott turned off the television. Talba caught the way the girl looked at her mother, something nasty flashing suddenly from her eyes, and then turned away from her, toward Talba, her mouth hanging slightly open, giving her a somewhat retarded look and showing a mouthful of hardware. Perhaps the braces made it hard for her to close her mouth, Talba thought, and felt a twinge of sympathy for her. Pretty as she was, she was profoundly awkward; and so deeply unhappy you could see it from ten paces.

I know this girl, Talba thought. *I've been there. Being fourteen is like a prison sentence.*

Aziza, the mother, was trying to help her out. "Ms. Wallis is a poet, Cassandra." Darryl must have told her. "*And* a detective. How's that for a combo?"

Talba smiled at the girl. "Poetry doesn't really pay the bills. I'm a pretty good computer jockey too. You on the Internet?" She was trying to get down to it right away, find out if the girl had met her attacker on the net.

Cassandra shook her head, not deigning to speak, her mouth still hanging open and hatred coming out of her pores.

Eddie said, "Ya into music?"

The girl shrugged.

Aha, Talba thought. *An affirmative.*

"Who ya like? Lauryn Hill?"

Another shrug.

"She sings in a choir," Aziza said.

Talba tried to sound enthusiastic. "No kidding!"

The girl flared. "I don't see what you're trying to get at."

Eddie ignored her. "My little grandson's into hip-hop. Ya know what? Some of that stuff's pretty good. Ya like tigers?"

Talba could see that the girl was getting ready to shrug again, and fairly nastily, but she stopped in mid-motion, apparently taken aback by Eddie's non sequitur. "There's a group named Tigers?"

"No, I mean tigers—like at the zoo. I was askin' 'cause my grandson volunteers over at Audubon Park, and they've got this new baby tiger he was telling me about."

For the first time, the girl seemed actually interested. "Oh, wow, really?"

"He said it's just like a real big kitten—cutest little thing you ever saw."

"He gets to pet it?"

"Yeah, sure. Hold it and everything."

"Ohhhhh. Lucky!" Talba could hear the longing in her voice and thought that Cassandra was someone who seldom got what she wanted. She realized that, in spite of herself, the girl was taking to Eddie—that somehow or other he'd gotten around her. And that Aziza had been completely wrong: Talba would get nowhere with her. So far, she was anything but an asset.

For some reason, Eddie was kicking at her, gently. She had no experience with kids, no knowledge of them, and absolutely no idea what to do now. All she knew was, she was pissed off at the kid, Eddie, and herself, in that order. "Aren't we getting a little off the subject?" she said, and felt ashamed when she heard the testiness in her voice. She was being childish, and she knew it.

And yet, Eddie stopped kicking her. Even spoke kindly, sounding a little abashed that he wasn't acting properly. "Yeah, I guess we are. Listen, Cassandra, I know it's hard for you, but we've been hired to find the guy who—uh—you know—" He actually started to blush.

"The asshole," Talba said, suddenly seeing her role and warming to it: she was the bad cop.

"He is *not* an asshole," Cassandra flashed. "He's just somebody I met."

Eddie said, "My grandson's a—you know—a young male. People could say things. I know how you feel, baby."

Drunk with power, Talba said, "How'd you happen to meet him, Cassandra?"

She shrugged. "I don't know."

Aziza spoke sharply. "Cassandra!"

Cassandra telegraphed her a couple of hate-rays, and spoke to Eddie: "We were just at somebody's house and somebody knew him, so we called him to come over."

"Whose house, baby?"

Before the girl could speak, Aziza Scott said, "Shaneel's. Shaneel Johnson, the girl who goes to Fortier." Darryl's school.

"And how do you know Shaneel?"

She was quiet for a while, but Eddie waited her out. "Choir," she said at last.

"Was Shaneel the one who knew him?"

"I don't remember."

"Well, who else was there?" Talba gave her voice an edge.

"I don't *remember.*"

Eddie said, "Was he somebody's brother or boyfriend? I mean, why'd you call him?"

She looked down, obviously hating the question, but not wanting to be rude to Eddie. "He knows cool people. He said he could introduce us."

"To cool people?"

"I guess so."

"So did he bring them over?"

"No."

Aziza Scott apparently could stand it no more, the way they were tweezing information, hair by hair. "He took them over to his house."

Eddie looked at the girls from over his eye pouches. "That so, baby?"

Cassandra nodded.

"How many girls?"

She shrugged.

"And were the cool people over there?"

Slowly, she shook her head.

"You must have been together quite a while, right?" He waited for her to nod. "Ya mama says you don't know his name."

"I do know his name. His name's Toes."

Talba said, half-kidding, "Oh, no. Now Eddie's gonna think all black people have weird names."

"Toes what, baby?"

"I don't know."

Eddie considered. "Well, honey, you're a beautiful girl, you know that? Why would a beautiful girl like you . . ."

"He said he could really love me!" The words came at them like a punch in the mouth. She screamed them, eyes flashing fury at all three of them.

"But he did tell you you're beautiful, didn't he?" Eddie spoke infinitely gently. "Because you are, honey, you are. Don't ya ever sell yaself short again." He touched her gently on the shoulder, in a way that managed somehow not to be patronizing.

He got up to leave, and Talba took her cue from him, standing as well.

On the way out, he said to Aziza: "Did he hit on Shaneel? Or anyone else who was there?"

"Cassandra says not. And you saw what the diary said—about how flattered she was to be singled out."

"Ms. Scott," Talba said. "Do you have a boyfriend?"

Scott's face broke out in smiles; she all but wriggled. "Why, yes, I do. Why do you ask?"

"I think your daughter needs you worse than he does right now." She figured since she was already pegged as the bad cop, she could say anything she wanted.

They were silent for the first part of the drive home, and Talba was grateful for it. He wasn't saying a word about either her ineptitude or bad manners. Finally, deciding he wasn't going to, she got up the courage to speak. "Eccch. Can you imagine? Taking a bunch of fourteen-year-olds over to his house?"

"We got a real piece o' toe jam here. He's got the right name."

"Think she knows the real one?"

"Yep. They all do—all the kids who were there. Ya want to go with me to see Shaneel?"

"Sure." *Is the pope a bear?* she thought. She said, "Eddie, I gotta ask you something. I thought Angela was your only kid."

He shook his head. "Nope. Got a son." He stared off into space for a moment, and said, as if he wasn't used to the word, "Anthony."

"He must be a lot older than Angie."

"Younger. Why?"

" 'Cause I don't get it. How could you have a grandson old enough to volunteer at the zoo?"

"I don't."

"You *don't?*"

"Ms. Wallis, ya got a lot to learn. Lemme tell ya somethin'll be the best thing I ever taught ya: all women like babies. Even if they think they don't, they do. Ya want to get to a woman, ya talk about babies. And if she's under fifteen, ya make it baby animals—furry ones. Ya can't go wrong."

She stared at him in shock. "No grandson *and* no baby tiger?"

"Could be a baby tiger. Cats are randy as goats, ya know that?"

Feeling slightly breathless, she changed the subject on him. "Where's your son live?"

"Who knows? Haven't heard from him in ten years."

She knew she should back away from the subject, but she was in too deep to just let it hang there. She tried to sound casual. "Your choice or his?"

"Both, I guess. Neither one of us has a bit of use for the other."

Talba suddenly felt exhausted, too tired even to go out with Darryl, and that meant breaking a date. She never did that.

Chapter Five

"I t's your fault," she said when he phoned. "You got me the client."

"Whooo. Some piece of work, isn't she? I don't think I've *ever* heard that much noise coming out of that poor counselor's office."

"She strikes me as somebody who expected the kid to raise herself, and then when Cassandra got in trouble she had to point the finger somewhere else. I mean, that's the only reason I can think of for pursuing this through a detective."

"Ah. Beautiful, poetic, *and* perceptive. She's a type—every teacher's seen her a million times. The kid's grades are bad, so it's the school's fault—usually, that's what you hear them yelling about. They always want you to tell them what a good kid they've got, because if the kid's not so great, it reflects badly on them. They're embarrassed. I mean, *embarrassment's* their reaction to their kid having problems. So it's somebody else's fault—if not the school's, then the other kids'."

"Wait a minute," Talba said. "I don't know if I buy this embarrassment thing. It seems like more than that. I mean, if it's somebody else's fault, then it's not only not their fault, but they don't have to do anything about it."

"Oh, man, you wouldn't believe! I had a woman last fall at parents' night—the kid's grades were falling, he was acting up in class, the whole thing. And this woman asks, quite naturally, what she can do. So I say, 'Easy. Take away the TV, the phone, and the computer, and have the kid do his homework in a central area, somewhere near you. Like in the dining room if you're working in the kitchen, so you can answer questions if he has them.' Now tell me, Your Grace—does that sound unreasonable?"

"Sounds a hundred percent right to me."

"You know what the woman said? She said she couldn't do that, the kid would get mad at her."

"And then she'd have to deal with it."

"You got it."

"And she couldn't be bothered because she's busy getting her presentation ready for work. Or going out with her boyfriend."

"You got her down cold. Her and Aziza Scott both."

"Aziza's a type, huh?"

"Oh, yeah. A pretty far cry from Miz Clara."

Talba sighed, but Darryl continued. "And woe betide the younger generation. I swear I think it all fell apart when families stopped having dinner together."

"Well, hell. I may not think Aziza's the greatest mother in the world, but I can handle her. At least I got the job. I'll make it up to you—canceling like this."

"I don't get it. That job can't pay much. I mean, you've had *much* better ones in terms of compensation. And if you just wanted to be a detective, why didn't you go out and do it on your own? Why wait to answer an ad?" He sounded genuinely puzzled.

"There's something about this guy Eddie. I can't explain it—I feel like he might have something to teach me."

"Oh, please. Don't go mystical on me."

"I don't know. It's sweet the way he is with his family. And he came to my reading—how many potential bosses would do that?"

"You poets really live on crumbs."

"Yeah, well. I've got a day job now. Can we come interview Shaneel?"

"At school? You've got to be kidding—we got a bureaucracy going here."

"Oh." For a moment, Talba felt deflated. "Wait a minute—I've got an idea. Maybe I could get someone from child protective services to come with me."

He laughed, and it sounded like a bark. "Lots of luck with that one. But sure—*if* you could get somebody from there, it would probably work. It's a mighty big 'if,' that's all."

Later, she reported what he had said to Eddie, who made no effort to control his contempt. "Bullbleep. We don't need no stinkin' badges."

"How do we get around it?"

"You might work out real well, Ms. Wallis. Maybe I should of hired you a long time ago. Ya got the right demographics, all right. Gene Allred was right about that one."

"I'm not sure I see what you're getting at."

"Well, let me spell it out for ya. Call the counselor, say ya from Child Protection, and ya'll be right over to interview Shaneel."

Talba had a brief moment of hope, but in the end it came as no surprise to her that the lady from Child Protection had to be accompanied by her older, male colleague. Eddie trailed her like a duenna. The counselor, a Mrs. Terrell, looked a little perplexed but not enough to ask for stinkin' badges. She was a middle-aged woman, African-American, and a church lady if Talba ever saw one, but not the overbearing kind, the nice kind.

"I'm so sorry about the Scott girl. Her mother seems so . . ." She stopped, evidently remembering her manners, and left to get Shaneel.

The girl was pudgy and cute as a kitten, much darker than Cassandra, her cheeks little black apples, the light glinting off them so they sparkled like a second pair of eyes. She wasn't nearly as pretty as Cassandra, but she had a sensuality about her, and a sense of fun that probably made her a more popular kid. She was a hell of a lot friendlier. "How ya'll?" she said by way of greeting, as if she'd been properly raised, this public-school girl, as opposed to Cassandra, the zombie from Pontchartrain Park. Once again, Talba pondered Aziza Scott's mothering style.

When Eddie smiled back, Talba saw the look in his eyes a dad gets watching his kid at Little League, or maybe a recital. *I wonder how I know that?* she thought. She'd never known her own father. "Baby, we need to ax ya about a man named Toes."

"I'd tell Miz Scott if I knew. I don't know the rest of his name."

"Ya know what happened to Cassandra?"

She looked at her lap. "I know."

"Ya think that's right?"

When she raised her head, she had a great big smile pasted on the bottom part of it, plenty of teeth and no joy, little tense lines around her mouth. "I'd tell ya if I knew. You know I would."

Eddie said. "I know ya would, honey. Ya don't have to worry about that. Just tell us who else was with ya that day."

The girl wouldn't meet his eyes. "Nobody."

Talba thought, *I can't make it any worse,* and took

her shot. "Look, this man hurt your friend Cassandra. Maybe it comes down to who's the better friend, Toes or Cassandra. You really think he's worth protecting?"

Shaneel's eyes had started to glint. "He ain' my friend. I don't want nothin' to do with him."

"Then who called him, honey? Cassandra didn't know him—if it wasn't you, who was it?"

Shaneel only stared at her lap.

"You sing in a choir, don't you?" Talba wasn't much on church, but her mama was, and she knew the drill. "I know you believe in God. And in having the courage to do the right thing. Only good can come out of it if you tell us. You know that, don't you?"

The girl shook her head, not lifting her eyes, clearly torn between her conscience and something else. Whatever that was was the key.

"What could happen if you told us?"

"Cassandra my best friend. She'd never speak to me again. Pammie either, prob'ly."

There it was. The three adults looked at each other. Eddie said quietly, "Where does Pammie go to school?"

The girl raised her head, and her face, though tear-streaked, was profoundly relieved. "She go to Ben Franklin."

"And she's the one who called Toes."

"He a friend of Pammie sister. Rhonda."

"Rhonda was there too?"

"No. Rhonda wasn't there."

Mrs. Terrell cut in curtly. "Pammie who, Shaneel?"

But the girl merely sat there, tears welling and overflowing. She'd tell, Talba thought, she'd certainly tell. She just had to believe she hadn't *really* told.

"How do you girls know each other?" she asked.

"Choir. We all in choir—and all our mamas work. We all we got. We go to a different person's house every day after school. If Cassandra and Pammie cut me off, I ain' got nobody."

Eddie patted her. "Where's that choir you sing in?"

Shaneel was silent, but Mrs. Terrell said, "Gethsemane Baptist Church. That's right, isn't it, Shaneel?"

The girl nodded.

Mrs. Terrell got up. "I'll call the church. Shaneel, you can go back to class."

Eddie said, "Baby, ya did just fine. Nobody's gonna be mad at ya." To Talba's surprise, he got a smile out of her.

The Pammie in the choir was Pamela Bergeron.

O nce in the car, Talba called Ben Franklin and was told Pamela wasn't in school right then. Something seemed funny about that, she thought. Why not, "She's not in school *today*"?

She asked for the girl's address.

"I'm sorry," the receptionist purred. "We don't usually give out addresses."

"It's really very important—it *is* a police case and . . ."

To her surprise, she didn't even get to finish her sentence. "Of course. We're all terribly sorry about what happened. But it is our policy not to give out addresses over the phone."

Talba had no idea what was going on, but she wasn't above exploiting it. "Ma'am, we're really wasting time. Isn't there some way . . ."

The woman's voice softened. "Well, under the circumstances, I think there might be. Her dad owns that little card store over at The Rink—why don't you check with them?"

"Thanks." To Eddie, she said, "Got a phone book?"

"Backseat."

In five minutes, she had lied her way into the address and given it to Eddie, unable to keep the triumph off her face. "How'm I doing?"

"Ya doin' okay."

"That's all you can say?"

"Ya got a lot of mouth on ya."

Oh, well, she thought. *I should have known better.*

He wasn't done. "Ya know it's a crime to impersonate a police officer?"

"I didn't impersonate anyone. I just mentioned it was a police case."

"Which it isn't. Watch ya mouth, missy. Just watch ya mouth."

An odd thing, though. When they arrived at the girl's house, a police car was parked in front. Other cars were there as well, and people milling.

"Something's going on here," she said, but Eddie ignored her.

He hollered at a cop who was walking back to the district car. "Billeee."

The cop smiled. He was white and middle-aged. "Eddie Valentino. How you been doin'?"

"We're just here on a routine case. What's goin' on?"

The cop shook his head, and Talba thought she saw real sadness in his face. She wouldn't have expected it. "Oh, man. This is a heartbreaker. Hit-and-run. Young girl killed—just like that." He snapped his fingers, perhaps, Talba thought, thinking how easy it would be to lose his own kid.

Eddie's face went gray. "Jesus God. Rhonda or Pamela?"

"Rhonda. Ya know her? Ya know the Bergeron girls? Damn shame, Eddie. It's a damn shame."

*   *   *

They rode back to the office in silence, Talba trying all the way to get Eddie in a conversation, Eddie not, as he mentioned to her, in the fuckin' mood. The minute he said it he was sorry, too. He hated the word. He thought it showed a great lack of imagination, not to mention class, and yet, at the moment he was so completely not in the fuckin' mood it popped out of his mouth.

He rubbed his head, then realized he was doing it. Damn! One of his headaches. *No way,* he thought. *I can't get a headache now. Can't. The damn computer causes them, and now I have a computer jockey. No reason in hell I should get a headache.*

He willed it away.

This thing had him all messed up. It involved a whole lot more women than he was used to dealing with in the course of a day. Girls, really. Even Talba; for the life of him, he couldn't shake off the sense of a resemblance to Angie. She was just a kid, and she was way too big for her britches, but he had let her get away with stuff and wasn't sure how he felt about it. A little voice inside of him said it wouldn't matter, wouldn't be his responsibility once she got an apprentice license and he didn't have to witness the crap she pulled. But he also felt an uncontrollable urge to straighten her out, the way he did with Angie half the time, even though she was a grown woman.

He could have crawled under the carpet when Talba mouthed off at the client. On the other hand, the woman's idea of motherhood appeared to be letting the kid's little friends baby-sit while Aziza fucked her boyfriend. Sure the kid wanted to have sex—she probably even wanted a baby. Anything to get away from a woman who declared herself in charge, probably nagged a hundred and fifty percent of the time, and didn't enforce rule one around the house. Eddie didn't have to see it to know what Scott's mothering style was like. He could hear it now:

"Cassandra, you ready for church?"

"I'm not going."

"What's wrong, baby? Aren't you feeling well?"

"I'm not going, that's all."

"Baby, church is very important for your spiritual well-being." (Eye-rolling at this point.) *"Now go get your good clothes on."*

"Mama! You can't—there isn't time. You just can't make me do it. It's too mean."

Whereupon Aziza would look at her watch, her boyfriend would arrive in a suit and tie, and she'd dash out the door, leaving Cassandra to watch cartoons on television.

Of course, the kid felt superior to her mom—she probably won every argument with her. What the hell, Eddie wondered, ever happened to "because I said so"? The kid was a mess—even Talba, a kid herself, could see that and could see why. Eddie frankly thought Aziza should be prosecuted for neglect, but there weren't any laws to handle it, and, furthermore, she was the client. He wasn't about to mention her maternal shortcomings.

So he'd let Talba do it for him. Do it and get away with it. He wondered if he could work up the resolve to reprimand her for it.

Then there was the way she took over the interview at the school. Totally out of line. But the girl's instincts were good. When he tried to get around that one, he couldn't.

It was also sharp of her to pick up the bad-cop role at Scott's house. Or had she realized she was doing it? He had his doubts.

She was a handful. But other things were bothering him.

Cassandra was. He hated seeing a kid that miserable. He wanted to get the bastard who'd exploited her, but in truth he was as angry at the mother as he was at the rapist.

Most of all, there was this Rhonda thing. The coincidence of her death was a bit too much to buy. Eddie had been a cop for a long time, and his cop's belly told him one thing: Toes.

Maybe the kids weren't lying about his identity— maybe they really didn't know who he was. And maybe Cassandra told her friend Pamela that her mother was pulling out all the stops to find him, and Rhonda told Toes, who realized she was the only one who knew who he was, and he killed her. It was amazing how little regard some people had for human life. A guy who'd lure three fourteen-year-olds to his house and have sex with them was a monster by definition.

But taking it further—this was what bothered him the most—taking it further, maybe the others did know his identity. Maybe Rhonda was only the first.

This was why he was in no mood. He needed to figure out what the hell to do.

Okay. First call Scott and tell her to call all the other parents. That was obvious. But damn, he hated the idea of that call. Maybe Talba could make it.

Also, there was the question of telling the police the whole story. It was going to be a few hours before he could find out if anyone saw the hit-and-run. Maybe if a white woman were driving . . . nah, that was no good. No matter who was driving, Toes could be behind it. No question he had to warn Scott. Damn. He had to talk to her himself.

When they got back to the office, he said, "You

take Rhonda. I'll take the cops and Aziza," and closed the door behind him.

His head pounded. *At this rate,* he thought, *I'm not gonna make sixty-five.* His birthday was two weeks away.

Chapter Six

Talba thought, *Okay, fine, if you want to be that way,* and closed her own door. That would mean he'd have to come to her and knock—or at least send Eileen. Anyway, she had some stuff to do she didn't want him to know about.

But first the case. She hoped to hell Rhonda hadn't been married—the hardest thing about the Internet was tracing people whose last names you didn't know.

Well, there *was* a Rhonda Bergeron at the address they'd gone to to find Pamela—evidently she'd lived with her parents. She was eighteen. Damn. So far, Talba had been too puzzled and hurt by Eddie's refusal to talk to feel much for Rhonda. But eighteen! She was starting to feel plenty, including an urgent need to get going on this. Come up with something. Goddammit, *protect* her somehow, though it was too late.

No newspaper clips. Hmmm.

Talba's fingers flew like a flock of finches. Not much on the father, Lloyd Bergeron, except that he was married to a woman named Marilyn. Decent credit, good driving record. Nothing on Marilyn.

Johnson, as in Shaneel, wasn't even worth trying.

Just for good measure, she put together a dossier on Aziza Scott and printed it out for Eddie, along with the tidbits on Rhonda. No surprises there either.

She needed to talk to people, to go back to Shaneel—the most likely whistle-blower—and threaten to wring her little neck if she didn't talk. But Eddie'd wring *her* little neck if she did.

She went to lunch and lingered until she was bored. When she got back, she was faced with the same old empty in-box. She felt tense and frustrated.

And so she did what she always did to clear her head—started noodling on the net. Which reminded her—she was really going to have to set up a web site for Eddie, and soon too. Her pride wouldn't permit working in a place that didn't have one. Besides, if she was going to be a rainmaker, it was probably the best thing she could do to bring in business.

She was on Eddie's time, why not do it for him now? She needed to register a URL. Eddie-Valentino.com had a ring to it.

No, wait a minute. The name of the agency was Anthony Valentino. Anthony! He'd named the agency after his son.

She forgot about the web site and started fooling around with "Anthony Valentino." She could always do a peoplesearch, starting in Louisiana, then more or less guessing, but that was way too boring. Newspaper articles were a lot more fun. She hit a few more keys.

And there they were—news stories. About a

dozen of them, modest-sized articles in modest-sized papers all over the country. Interviews. There were schedules too, and reviews. Anthony Valentino no longer went by that name (though he mentioned it in every single interview).

Anthony Valentino, formerly of New Orleans, had metamorphosed into bluesman Tony Tino. Now *he* probably did have a web site.

Yes, indeed. There it was. Even a picture of him, looking more like Angie than either of his parents. He had on a narrow-brimmed hat like an old black man might wear, someone playing in a joint like Ernie K-Doe's Mother-In-Law Club. You couldn't see his hair, but she was betting on thick and curly. The face looked *fine*. It was an Italian face, big-nosed and bold, with a hint of the balefulness so striking in his father. In a young man, lugubriousness contrived to be sexy, and no one knew it better than Talba. It was hard to say from a head shot, but Talba's impression was of leanness, a build more like his mother's than his father's. His expression was cocky, in the manner of musicians posing for photographs, but the tiny bit of sadness and something else, something about the set of the features, suggested a vulnerability, a sensitivity, the kind of thing women went mad for. *Oh, hell, including me,* she thought. *Eddie's kid's a hunk. Wonder what he plays?*

Whoa. Harmonica. A blues harmonica player. He even had a CD out. Pretty accomplished guy.

She riffled through the interviews, which he had attached to his home page—not only that, he sounded literate and charming. Actually, not charming. Anyone could be charming. The man sounded nice.

He was . . . look at that . . . living in Austin. Practically a stone's throw. There was no mention of a wife or kids, which she supposed befitted a blues musician. A bachelor would have more time to brood.

Now why in hell didn't Eddie know where he lived? Wait a minute here—she consulted the schedules and interviews. Tony Tino had played New Orleans, but hadn't been interviewed there. Oh, well, never a prophet, she thought—or perhaps it was Tony's choice. Maybe he didn't want to fling his long-lost self in his parents' face.

Parents. Maybe it wasn't both of them. Maybe it was Eddie only.

Still, why didn't Eddie know where his only son lived? He might hate the Internet, but he was on it every day of his life. Why the hell wouldn't he type in his son's name and see what came up?

Maybe he had. Maybe he'd lied about not knowing.

Her doorknob rattled. "Ms. Wallis, what's this closed door stuff? What ya doin' in here?" She barely had time to get out of Tony's web site before the elder Valentino came crashing into her office.

"Thought you were going to call me Talba," she said, and then was sorry she hadn't been more respectful. Eddie looked like hell, his face pinched with pain. "Eddie, what's the matter?"

"Ah, it's nothin', I just got one of my headaches."

"Headaches," she said. "Have you had that checked out?"

He swatted the air in front of his face, indicating his disdain for the question. "The driver was a black male."

"Damn! Do you think we should tell Aziza?"

"Oh, yeah. Hell, yeah, I think we should tell Aziza. But she left this morning on a business trip, and her office won't say where she went."

"What about Cassandra?"

"She didn't go to school today, and nobody's answering the phone at home. For all I know she was in the car with the hit-and-run artist."

"Is there any description on him?"

"Uh-uh. Just black, average build, probably in his twenties. Two of them in one car, which was a medium-sized beige job." He paused and rubbed his head. "Cassandra might be staying with one of her little girlfriends—maybe we could get their numbers from her school. Ya want to call 'em for me?"

Talba looked at her watch. "School's already out."

Eddie shrugged, but she thought she saw a tiny tightening in the lines between his eye. "Oh, well. Maybe her mama'll call me."

"Are you going to tell the police about Cassandra?"

"I don't think yet. It's a long way from havin' sex with a teenager to killin' somebody. Think about it— you ever have sex when you were fourteen?" He looked horrified at what he'd said. "I mean, uh, excuse me, I was thinkin' out loud."

Talba had to laugh. "Sixteen. With a boy who was nineteen. My mama found out about it, and there was hell to pay. And then, what do you know, the same thing happened all over again, with another boy."

"Anybody go to jail or get killed?"

"Uh-uh. It was more like a tempest in a teapot."

"Yeah. So I think maybe we'll leave the police option up to Ms. Scott, if we ever find her. Ya get anything on Rhonda?"

"Just a DUI. I printed out the stuff on her and everybody else I could think of." She handed him the package.

He nodded briefly, letting her know he'd heard and wasn't much interested. "I need ya to do something for me." He looked like he was about to fall over.

"Sure, Eddie. Look, you think you should go home or something?"

"I'm goin'. Oh, yeah, I'm goin'. Headache like this can last two days."

"What do you want me to do?"

"I need ya to go to the funeral. And the visitation if there is one."

"Me? Without my license?"

"Ehhh, maybe it'll come tomorrow. I probably crossed the line *already* lettin' you make that appointment with Ms. Terrell. But it's the same thing again—you'd fit in, I'd stick out."

She couldn't resist interrupting him. "How on earth did you get along without me?"

He didn't dignify that with a response, not even a tilt of an eyebrow. "You won't be workin', if you catch my drift." He held out a pair of palms-up, innocent hands. "Anybody can go to a funeral."

He didn't come in the next day. A great day, she thought, to work on his web site—she'd surprise him when he came back. Not that that's all there was—Eileen popped in about ten with an armful of files. "Mostly employment checks," she said. "He said to have you work on them. Oh, and Angie called for your address—I said I'd call her back. Okay if I give it to her?"

Talba was puzzled. "Sure, but why would she need it?"

"She wants to send you an invitation to Eddie's sixty-fifth birthday party. Are you free Saturday after next? March twentieth, I think it is. Angie's throwin' it, so you *know* it's gonna be nice."

"I'm flattered. I hardly know him."

"Angie likes you. And also, uh . . . it's going to be, like, a roast. She thought you could maybe . . . um . . . I know she wouldn't come out and say it, but I *think* she's kind of thinkin', *you* know . . ."

Talba finally got it. "She wants me to write a poem? Well, now I'm really flattered."

Eileen smiled.

"Let's see, I think it's going to be about the bags under his eyes."

Eileen left, tittering politely.

She thinks I'm kidding, Talba thought to herself. *A rap, maybe. I've never done one.*

No visitation was announced for Rhonda Berge-ron, which struck Talba as strange for a girl as young as she was, as vital as she must have been. But she knew little about such things—perhaps the body had been cremated, and there'd been a private wake (or whatever Methodists called it) at Rhonda's parents' house. It occurred to her to bake a cake and take it over there. She could say she'd met Rhonda in some context they wouldn't know about. But in the end, she thought it too risky, and when she got to the funeral, she thanked her stars she hadn't done it. She was almost the only black person in the congregation.

Oops, Eddie, the joke's on you.

Evidently, Rhonda had been white, which must mean Pamela was white as well—a peculiar thing, considering this crowd, to hang with two black girls.

There was another strange thing—though there were only five or six black faces in the pews, the choir was nearly all African-American. She could pick out Cassandra and Shaneel, very solemn in their black robes, Cassandra looking drawn and miserable. Pamela, though, appeared to be sitting with her family, the little redhead with the long straight hair, Talba thought.

Rhonda, by contrast, had lustrous long black hair, clearly visible from her casket at the front of the church. Evidently, she hadn't been cremated. Talba felt her throat catch as she forced herself to look at the face, pale and thin, set off by a pale blue dress with lace; something vintage, Talba thought. It looked like silk from where she was. Her imagination roved freely, concocting, before Talba could stop it, a vision of the girl as she must have looked, alive, in that dress—tall and very thin, black hair blowing in the wind, granny boots on her feet, skin pale and delicate, body a little too wispy.

Druggie, her mind said, and her eyes overflowed. *What the hell?* she thought. *I didn't even know the girl.*

Someone from the funeral home closed the casket, and she nearly sobbed aloud.

Talba had never been to a funeral before, in fact had never set foot in a Methodist church. She and her mother were Baptists, and plenty of her friends were Catholic, but she didn't know that many people who weren't one or the other. (Except for a few Muslims, of course—there were plenty of those around. And the odd Pentecostal.) She didn't really know what to expect, but the proceedings had an antiseptic quality that surprised her.

The family came in right after the minister. They were brought in in a formal procession, after which there was a prayer and a chance—while everyone's eyes were closed—to survey the crowd more closely.

The choir was made up mostly of women, though there were a few men, most of them older than the one she was looking for, and some of them white. There was one who looked to be in his early twenties, a short round kid with a shaved head and such a cherubic expression he looked like an African-American Cupid. *Not him,* she thought. *If the rapist was Rhonda's friend, it wasn't somebody from the choir. Anyhow, that kid couldn't seduce a sheep.*

In the congregation, none of the bowed heads appeared to be Aziza's, though surely she'd come back from her business trip by now. There were a few older black couples, though. Talba guessed they were parents of choir members. She didn't see a single black male under forty.

Almost as soon as the hymn was over, the choir stood and began to sing, an uplifting hymn, the sort that church people call "joyful," but by the second bar, Talba was crying.

She was amazed at herself. What the hell was this? Not only was she crying, she was sobbing, in great big embarrassing gulps, as if she'd been Rhonda's best friend. The woman next to her reached out and put an arm around her shoulders, and the woman's touch was anathema, poison, felt like fire. Talba didn't know why. She almost screamed, but stopped herself in time, and jumped away. In the silence, she could hear sniffling from the front of the church.

When the hymn was over, the fit stopped, whatever it was.

The minister came forward to thank "the choir of Gethsemane Baptist Church, which has come to worship with us today and to help us surrender up to God the soul of Rhonda, beloved sister of Pamela Bergeron, a devout and faithful member of the Gethsemane choir."

Talba was struck by the word "devout." Somehow, neither of the girls she and Eddie had interviewed seemed all that devout, but how could you know if you didn't ask? She particularly didn't see Cassandra as a Jesus freak, but the girl *was* in a choir. Why? Talba wondered.

The minister got on with the show. He said he had known Rhonda personally, but not well, and had interviewed all her family about her and that she, too, had loved music, almost as much as she loved Jesus and her family. Oh, yes, she loved music, and she loved animals, too, and had once had a dog named Grizzy. And she had graduated from Ben Franklin High School and had gone on to pursue a lifelong interest in fashion, taking a job at Millie the Milliner's, though it took her far from home, deep into the dark heart of the French Quarter itself. And she had done well there, and she had thrived, and now this young woman had been taken from her family and her loving friends . . .

He went on like that for a while. He mentioned the way people loved her and she had made the customers feel at home, and she had been a faithful and loyal employee, but, in truth, the gist of it seemed to be that Rhonda hadn't done very much with her life except work in a hat shop.

But she had loved music and she had loved to hear her sister perform with the Gethsemane Baptist choir, and her favorite song had been "Swing Low, Sweet Chariot," which the choir would now perform and would like to dedicate to her memory and to the Bergeron family.

They hadn't even gotten to "sweet" before Talba was sobbing again. Before, it had been as if she had contracted a sudden crying disease, a bug that simply came and controlled her body, pushing out of it tears and unwanted sounds. This was different. A flood of sadness had enveloped her and invaded her and was now flailing for expression. And the flood of sadness was an old friend.

She knew it as well as she did her own skepticism, her dislike of sanctimonious ministers, be they Methodist or Baptist, black or white, and yet she could not imagine how she did.

I've been here before, she thought, and suddenly she wasn't Talba Wallis going out of control in one of the pews, but a tiny brown angel floating over the congregation, looking down at the people, staring down at Rhonda's casket, and the salt-and-pepper choir, and seeing, quite distinctly, Urethra Tabitha Sandra Talba Wallis, the Baroness de Pontalba, keening like some Third World mourner for a woman she never knew.

She must have truly been making a spectacle of herself, for once again, the woman to her right, so soundly rebuffed before, dared to touch her again, to put an arm around her. And with the touch, the vision dissolved.

Chapter Seven

Eddie had awakened Monday with yet another headache, but he damn sure wasn't going to give in to it. He downed three cups of black coffee, and pried himself into his office.

Audrey kept nagging him to see a neurologist, and if the headaches kept up, he was going to have to. He felt like shit. They always left him feeling washed-out and without enthusiasm. Depressed, Audrey would say.

This getting old most assuredly was not, as they said, for sissies. Sixty-five in a couple of weeks and he felt a hundred and five.

He had a bad feeling Audrey and Angie were up to some damn thing, mostly because they hadn't nagged him about having a party. Five or six of his old buddies from his cops-and-robber days were taking him to lunch at Galatoire's, something they never did. Therefore, Audrey had probably put them up to it to make him think that was the party.

But there had to be more. Audrey and Angie were going to try to cheer him up, he knew it.

Damn, he felt bad. He thought the reason he was so depressed was the damn machine. The way his business had changed from active pursuit—the real deal—to sitting in his office hitting a keyboard.

Well, now he had a Baroness to deal with that shit. So why did he have headaches? He couldn't figure it, unless he had a brain tumor.

"Hello, Eileen. Anything up?"

"Talba's at the funeral, like you said. Aziza Scott called. She's coming over on her lunch hour."

Charming. As if *he* didn't need a lunch hour.

He went in his office and called his doctor. What the hell. His eye bags were turning into steamer trunks.

At twelve-eighteen precisely, Scott arrived on the warpath. "Eddie Valentino, what the hell do you mean leaving messages at my office and all over my answering machine?"

Eddie leaned back in his chair and gave her his Italian-Southerner act. "The best way to reach somebody is usually to leave 'em a message. Seems like I heard that somewhere."

"It is nobody's business at my office that I've hired a private detective."

"Ms. Scott, I didn't tell 'em I'm a private detective. I needed to tell you there was a chance your daughter might be in danger."

"She was fine. She was with her grandmother."

She seemed to be calming down a bit, and Eddie patted the air to set the mood. "Well, that's fine. Yeah, you right, that's just fine." Behind her, he saw Talba walk past on the way to her office. "Ms. Wallis. Ya got a minute?"

"Sure, Eddie." She stepped in, and he noticed she was wearing a dark suit, looking fairly civilized despite her wild hair. "Hello, Ms. Scott."

Eddie said, "Sit down. Sit down. How was the funeral?"

"Sad. I saw Cassandra there."

Scott looked bewildered. "*You* went to the funeral? Why?"

Eddie spoke quickly before Talba could. "As a gesture of respect." He hoped she'd catch the subtle put-down. Damn this woman. Try to tell her her child was in danger, and she reamed you out. "Look, Ms. Scott, I don't know if you actually got the gist of the messages or not, but it's this: there could be a connection between your daughter's rape and this girl's death."

"That's ridiculous!"

"Why do you say that?"

She stood. "You people live in a world of paranoia, you know that? I'd *hate* to live like you."

Eddie patted air again. "Well, I'm sure you're right. We felt we had a duty to apprise you of the possibility, that's all."

She was tall to begin with, and she wore high heels; she looked down at Eddie as if he were a nest of vermin. "I need you to attend to the matter for which I hired you."

She left like a runway model, grand and dramatic.

Talba said, "What was that about?"

Eddie sighed. "The thing the shrinks call denial. She came over here because she's scared shitless (excuse my French), but she's not about to interrupt her big important life to do anything more than throw money at the problem." He spread his open hands. "What the hell. We tried, huh?"

Ms. Wallis had the look of a KO'ed fighter coming to, kind of dazed and disoriented. "She's batshit. Uh . . . excuse my French."

Eddie didn't want to excuse it at all—it was one thing for him, another for a young lady employee, even a black one. But under the circumstances, there was nothing to do but let it go. He rubbed his head. The fool headache was coming back. "You get anything at the funeral?"

"Well, the killer wasn't there. Unless he's really a master of disguise. I picked a few names off the guest registry." She shrugged. "I could call them about her, see if she's got any black friends they know of—there sure weren't many at her funeral. But the obvious thing's to ask Pamela."

"What ya sayin'?"

She looked at him as if he were speaking Chinese. "Ask Pamela. If anybody'd know who Toes is, she would."

"Not that—the other thing you said. Everybody in the whole case is black—whatcha mean she doesn't have black friends?"

"Oh. I forgot you didn't know. The Bergerons are white. Pamela's one of a handful of whites in that choir the girls sing in."

"She must have some voice," Eddie muttered. He was a little embarrassed, though exactly why he couldn't have said. "Give me the names from the registry. We can't talk to the poor kid the same day they buried her sister. We'll wait a coupla days on the Bergerons. Ya understand me?"

"Sure. But why don't I call the people at the funeral?" Something mischievous played in her eyes. "I mean, I'm the right demographic and everything."

He sighed, once again feeling a lack of enthusiasm. "I better do it."

"You sure?" She smiled, and waved a letter. "My license came." She looked full of beans and ready to face the world, like a kid who's just graduated. Eddie envied her.

"Well, that's a damn relief. Yeah, you do it."

"Also, she used to work in a hat shop. I'm going there first."

He put his head in his hands. "Good idea. Just be sure ya leave Eileen a list of places you're goin' to. And leave the Bergerons alone. Ya understand?"

"Eddie?" she said. "You okay?"

"Yeah, I'm fine. Get outta here, all right? Don't mess with those people. I mean it."

Hell. All he wanted to do was go home and sit in a dark room for a couple of hours. Take a few aspirin, see if it got any better.

When she saw him, Audrey's face froze in a mask of fear under its pound of makeup. "Eddie. What are you doin' home?"

"What's the matter? Got the mailman in the bedroom?" It was an automatic line, stupid and trite, but now he really looked at her. Her habitual heavy makeup wasn't quite immaculate, indeed seemed streaky and tatty. Her hair was a bit unkempt, as if she'd been lying down, but she was dressed up. "Hey. Where ya goin'?"

"I just got back." She stood tall and planted her feet. "I've been to my shrink's, Eddie."

"What are you talking about?"

"I've been seeing a therapist."

"Are you nuts or something?" He was too panicked to say anything else.

"I've been so worried about you I had to talk to somebody. I can't go through this alone; I swear to God I can't."

He covered the room between them in three steps and put his arms around her, held her tight to him, something he never did. Was everything in the world coming apart? "Go through what, baby? What'cha talkin' about? I'm here with ya. You don't have to go through anything alone."

"I have to watch you fall apart. All by myself, except for Angie. You're just letting it happen, and you won't do nothin' about it, and I *can't*. I'm going crazy, Eddie. I'm going crazy." She wasn't crying the way he'd expect her to be; just talking, sounding sad, like she was already all cried out—like some pathetic client of his, someone with problems. Not like Audrey, his wife.

"He thinks it's because of Anthony, Eddie."

He was suddenly livid. "You talk to some asshole about me? Ya talk about *me*? You can't do that—what the hell ya think ya doing?"

She shook her head, as if he were some kind of hopeless case, and got herself a drink of water. He waited for her to answer, but she just stood there drinking her water, looking at him.

Talba was starting to wonder what the hell she'd signed up for. Eddie wasn't well. She'd have to speak to Eileen about it—maybe he had a drug problem or something. But his money was good and the work was pretty fascinating.

She'd been to her first Methodist church and her first funeral, and now she was about to visit Millie the Milliner, always a treat. Millie, whose name had probably once been Thelma or Elsie, made exquisite nineteenth-century-style hats, perfect to wear with vintage clothing of the type Rhonda had been buried in. They were huge veiled bonnets piled high with flowers and fruit and foliage, each flower, each grape, each leaf lovingly handmade. They could easily have been parodies of themselves, but Millie managed by a millimeter to keep from crossing the line.

Her own work cost hundreds of dollars, but she also sold hats by lesser artists, smaller, more contemporary items more to Talba's taste, if the truth be told. But though Talba'd probably never wear one of Millie's masterpieces, she'd once spent a delicious two hours minutely examining every item in the store and finally walked away with a purple sequin fantasy that had a kind of Garden of Eden scene worked into it—entwined snakes and apples and branches—a thing entirely befitting a Baroness. The shape of the hat was African—a kind of pillbox more often worn by men than women—and the decorative work was like Haitian sequin art. She often wore it for performances.

The day she'd shopped there Millie herself had been absent, but today, she recognized the woman in charge as someone she'd seen earlier. She'd have to be blind not to have seen her.

The other woman spoke first. "I saw you at the funeral, didn't I?" She was dressed in a taffeta teal suit with a fitted jacket and calf-length full skirt, the jacket cut for maximum decolletage and trimmed with lace and black buttons. The suit was clearly contemporary, perhaps something the woman had whipped up herself, but the style was kind of a Gay Nineties variation, happily absent the bustle. With it, she wore a close-fitting hat of exquisite feathers in rusts and browns and gold, plucked from pheasants, probably.

The outfit was nothing you could miss, but on this woman, once you saw it, it was a picture you'd never forget. She had masses of tumbling flame-colored curls trailing halfway down her back, a prominent hawky nose, and about a hundred and fifty pounds over the limit. She was one of those fat women who had perfect, tint-tipped hands and moved like a wood nymph. But she wasn't pretty, and it wasn't only the nose that kept her from it. She had slightly scarred skin and a perennially wary look; her eyes moved too fast, scanned too much. Already, Talba felt like a shoplifter.

The thing to do was disarm her.

She stuck out her hand. "Millie? Talba Wallis. I'm

such a fan of yours. One day I'm gonna get my mama one of your hats. I know she'd just love one."

"Your *mama?*" The woman turned her eyebrow into an arch that could have held up a bridge.

Talba could have bitten her tongue. "Well, she's a church lady. Before today, I would have said *I* don't go anywhere good enough for them, but then I didn't know I was going to be going to a funeral, did you? That was a shocker, wasn't it? Rhonda, I mean."

Millie's wariness crystallized into action. Evidently, the thing she feared had come to pass, and it was Talba herself. She was probably about five-seven and wore three-inch heels, so that, with the hair and hat, she was a good six feet, and she drew herself to full advantage. The suit, as if not already wide enough just to go around her, was equipped with shoulder pads. She thrust her arm out to full length and brandished a needle-sharp, blood-red nail. "If you're a friend of T and T's, you can just get out of here."

Talba wasn't sure what she was hearing. "TNT? The explosive?" She was too baffled even to get out of the way.

Millie stepped forward, the point of the nail a hair from slicing Talba's nose. Her voice was low and commanding. "I said get out of here."

Talba felt her face start to lose composure. Bafflement was starting to give way to alarm. She stepped backward, stumbling in the process, and said, more or less to the floor, "I don't think I'm who you think I am. I'm an investigator looking into Rhonda's death."

"You're what?" Now she seemed as bewildered as Talba. "You're a cop?"

"Not exactly." *Not at all, actually.* "I work for a man named Eddie Valentino. To tell you the truth, I never even heard of Rhonda Bergeron until three days ago. I wouldn't know she worked here if it hadn't been for that smarmy preacher."

Unexpectedly, Millie barked out a laugh. "Oh, God. Didn't he make you feel like taking a bath?"

Talba rolled her eyes. "I suppose that's one way of saying good-bye." She looked full into Millie's face and saw that her eyes were some kind of blue-green mixture made up to match her outfit. The liner was smeared in the heat. "Who did you think I was?" she asked.

Millie's cheeks flushed. "Nobody. I just got mixed up for a minute."

Talba was starting to get the hang of this, and she liked where it was heading: Millie had evidently come to a conclusion based on color. She said, "Look. Let me be honest with you. I'm looking for a black man in his twenties who may have committed a crime. I know he knew Rhonda, but I don't know his name. Is TNT black, by any chance?"

Millie gasped. "You really don't know them, do you?"

Talba was silent, allowed her head to move only slightly.

Millie said, "What crime?"

Again, Talba was silent, though now she was buying time, trying to figure out what to say. She wasn't sure what the detectives' code was.

Again, Millie leaped to conclusions. "Murder, right? You think he killed Rhonda. The family hired you, right? Oh, shit, I knew it! I told Danielle, 'this is no accident. You don't mess with those kind of people.' "

Bingo, Talba thought. *Drugs. Isn't it always?*

The woman kept on talking. "*Goddam,* I felt guilty when that asshole was talking today, knowing all the while it happened right in my shop. She'd never have gotten mixed up with that asshole if it hadn't been for me." Her face crumpled and tears rolled.

She pulled a tissue out of her all-too-evident bosom.

Talba saw an opportunity to inject humor: "She was mixed up with the preacher?"

Millie barked her laugh again. "No, a different asshole. I'm going to tell you about it. I'm going to tell you all about it. I swear to God, I hope that asshole gets the chair."

Talba thought, *You just do that thing*, but Millie said abruptly, "You got any I.D.?"

"Sure." She brought out the letter that constituted her apprentice license, trying not to show how embarrassed she was at being not merely a novice but a newborn.

But Millie didn't seem to notice, just nodded, satisfied. "You ever heard of Baron Tujague?"

"Well . . . sure. Everybody's heard of Baron Tujague. I think he owns half the city by now."

"Yeah, and he's got about ten Grammys."

Tujague was a rapper, and that wasn't the half of it. He also had his own label, which employed a good number of people; he'd been responsible for discovering three other musicians who'd had gold records, and he had a new crop of protégés coming up. Plus, he was an extremely prominent speaker-at-schools and maker of public-service commercials.

Millie sneered. "And big in the role-model business. Tell me something—does a rapper need hats? Does he need funky, floppy hats, and fancy pimp-style hats, and little bitty pillbox hats with sequin pictures on them? Think he might need a whole wardrobe of hats? Well, where would he come?"

Talba smiled. "Pretty good customer to have."

"Oh, yeah. Great customer. I've got this designer named Danielle, who does these incredible sequin things—"

"I've got one of her hats. You mean the Baron and I have something in common?"

"He just loves Danielle. Commissions stuff from her."

"What's the deal—is Tujague TNT?"

"Half of it—T and T, I said. That's what they call themselves. The other one's a creep named Toes."

Talba almost gasped aloud.

"Look, I haven't got anything against Tujague, except maybe he's a little arrogant, but, hell, if Tom Cruise came in here, would he be arrogant? He's a *movie* star. Of course, Meryl Streep wasn't arrogant— man, does she look good in hats. But mostly, stars believe their own press." She shrugged, and it was a little like an earthquake. "It's a fact of life. For one thing, they have these *entourages.*" The last word was delivered with such contempt, you'd have thought she was a born-again with a thing against sinners.

"Ah," said Talba. "Toes."

"Oh, yeah, Toes. The motherfucker. Excuse my French."

What was it with white people and this French thing? Talba said, "Hey, it's the French Quarter."

Millie looked at her, probably actually taking in her face for the first time. "You're pretty funny. And you look . . . I don't know, like a performer. I get 'em in here, you know? Show me that license again?"

"I am a performer—this is my day job, okay?" She pulled herself tall and declaimed. "By day, a simple private eye, and by night, the Baroness de Pontalba." She bowed.

"Cool. I knew it. You a rapper too?"

"Talba's my name; poetry's my game. I don't hang in TNT circles, believe me." She handed over the license, but this time Millie didn't even look at it.

Millie sighed. "Well, the long and short of it is, poor little Rhonda didn't have any better sense than to fall for him. You really didn't know her?"

She pointed to a picture taped to the cash register, of staff members clowning. "Well, this is what she looked like, not—" she shuddered "—nothing like whatever that was in the casket."

She wasn't quite so thin in the picture; she was a beautiful, vital girl, wearing a vintage dress and a hat. "She looks like a princess."

"She was one of the prettiest girls I ever saw. And Toes—shit. Toad's more like it. Skinny, ugly little creep. Kind of a monkey face. But it was like . . . I don't know . . . I guess she thought he somehow *was* Tujague even though he's probably some penny-ante little dealer or something. I don't know what he is, and neither did Rhonda, even though she dated him off and on for three months." She paused and got dreamy. "Three months. Is that all it takes to ruin a life? Hah! Dated. Did I say *dated*? She didn't date him, she was his slave. He said rabbit, she hopped. She talked to a man, even a *customer*, he beat her up. He'd come by and get her, take her away for an hour, screw her, bring her back with her dress torn. God, she was a mess."

"Why do you think he killed her?"

Millie looked at her accusingly. "You're the one who said it. I didn't."

"I think I just said a crime. Seriously. Why do you think he killed her?"

"Come on—why do you think so?"

This is going nowhere, Talba thought. "Who is Toes, exactly? Doesn't he have a name?"

Millie shrugged. "Not that I know of."

"Do you know his address or phone number? Any way at all I can reach him?"

"No. He's a friend of Tujague's, but I hear the Baron's a little hard to get to. Being a jillionaire and all."

"Well, I know a few hundred people who can get to him. And they've all got blue uniforms."

Millie looked startled. Her smile, when it came,

started out slow and spread over her face. "I kind of like that idea."

Talba wasn't sure Eddie would, but she wasn't about to call him at home. The ethics of it seemed simple: she had information that could lead quickly to the rapist's arrest—but only if the police were involved. She could spend days running down pals of the Baron. The cops could just turn up and ask him who Toes was; if he didn't answer, they could make him miserable, at least for a few hours. She and Eddie couldn't compete with that.

She knew one cop in the whole department, and it happened to be a detective who'd worked Homicide for years. She went back to her office and put in a call to the Third District. "Skip Langdon, please."

Langdon came on the line. "Baronessa. How the hell have you been?"

"I was doing great till Miz Clara made me get a job."

Langdon was a big strong white woman with hair so thick and curly it was almost nappy. She laughed, and Talba could picture brown curls shaking all over her head. "Tough luck. You making those computers smoke?"

"I'm working for a private detective."

"Oh, God, some people never learn. Remember what happened to the last one you worked for?"

"This guy's a different animal. You know Eddie Valentino?"

"Sure. Everybody knows Eddie. Now, *he's* a good guy. But I don't see why someone with your skills . . ."

"Miz Clara's sentiments exactly. Call it the thrill of the chase. Would you know anything about that?

"Oh." The cop's voice was subdued. "That's a nasty bug to have bite you. You're going to be poor for the rest of your life."

It was Talba's turn to laugh. "I doubt it. I'm probably going to get fired for calling you. But I think at this point I might be obligated to."

"I'm all ears."

Talba ran it down for her, pausing for interruptions of "Jesus!" and "What a turd."

When she had finished, Langdon said, "Well, you did the right thing, assuming the person handling the case is a halfway-decent cop. But could I give you some unsolicited advice?"

"Sure. What?

"Keep working the case."

"Meaning?"

"Meaning don't count on anything. The Baron's got a lot of pull in this town."

"In the *department*?" Talba was shocked.

"About six months ago, a couple of baby rappers got into some trouble over a few guns and a little rock. It was kind of strange how easily they walked away from it. Guess whose label they record on?"

"Ah. I guess I shouldn't be surprised. This was still Louisiana the last time I looked."

"Let me find out whose case it is—in Child Abuse, I mean—and they can call you if that's okay."

"Sure."

"The Homicide thing's a little more delicate. I think I'll just say I got a tip that it might involve a carnal knowledge case—give the detective the name of the Juvenile officer, and let him or her run with it. That way you don't have to get involved. Okay by you?"

"Couldn't be better."

She spent the rest of the day calling people whose names she'd gotten from the funeral registry, but none would admit to knowing a Toes—or any black friend of Rhonda's.

And by the end of the day, no call had come from the Juvenile Department.

Chapter Eight

"A man named Toes. What's wrong with girls these days?" Darryl Boucree was grinning at her across the table at Bywater Bar-B-Que, which, despite its old-fashioned name, was the kind of place decorated with Barbies in birdcages.

Across from Darryl was a good place to be. That way you could look at him. He had to be the best-looking history teacher in the parish. Talba had no idea how he kept the Fortier girls at bay.

He was a little bit scholarly-looking, which befitted his day job, and a little bit devilish, which was more appropriate for his two night gigs, bartending and playing the trumpet. He was a sometime member of a band called the Boucree Brothers, which was more or less a pickup band made up of family members, not all of them brothers. Darryl was someone's nephew, Talba couldn't quite remember whose. He probably had the best smile in Louisiana.

"Do you know Shaneel? Cassandra's friend?"

"Not really. I hear she's a pretty good kid."

"Well, Cassandra's a mess. I'd like you to meet her."

"Thanks so much."

"She'd like you."

He shrugged. "Kids do. It's rare to encounter such extraordinary brilliance and wisdom in one so young and handsome. They recognize it."

Talba rolled her eyes. "And Millie said Tujague was arrogant."

"Now, him I do know. He came and did an assembly for us once."

"Hey! He did?" She saw an opportunity here. "Could you—"

"I met him is all. He wouldn't know me."

"Oh."

"I thought he was a good guy. But I bet Millie's right—there are guys who surround themselves with sycophants. Not that I know anything about the rap scene. But I guess a groupie's a groupie, no matter what their sex is."

Talba was playing with her food, her mind wandering, suddenly fixing on the pitiful image of Rhonda lying in a pretty blue dress in her nice padded casket. "Can I tell you something weird that happened to me? I cried at the funeral."

"A lot of people cry at funerals. I hear it's more or less expected."

"No, you don't get it. This had nothing to do with Rhonda."

He took her hand. "Well, stress. And that music. It always gets you."

She pulled her hand away, wanting to be taken seriously. "Darryl, I'm telling you. This was *weird*. It wasn't just crying, it was like the floodgates had broken. And I had this strange sense of déjà vu."

"Funerals are pretty much the same, I guess."

"But that's just the thing—this is the first one I've ever been to."

He made a fist and banged the table. "You know what? That's the trouble with our society. You don't get to have an experience, because you've already had it. Sure, you've been to funerals. You're been to hundreds of funerals—it's just that you were at the movies at the time; or in your own living room with the TV on."

"But I didn't *cry* then." She heard the whine in her voice, the faint childish note of desperation.

Darryl sobered instantly. "You sound like you're about to now."

She was shaking her head. "I don't know. This was just so off-the-wall."

He clasped his hands together on the table, serious at last. Apparently he'd finally gotten the picture: something weird had happened. "You know there's something we've never talked about? Whatever happened to your father?"

"My father?" She was taken aback. "Oh, I see what you're getting at. Well, he's not *dead* or anything. He just . . . left my mother."

"So you weren't at his funeral."

"No." She felt her lower lip start to quiver.

Darryl wouldn't quit. "Do you ever see him? I mean, you must have been close at one time."

They might as well have been talking about calculus, this was such bewildering territory. "Why do you say that?"

He looked a little bewildered himself. "The poem . . . 'Queen of the May.' "

"Oh, the *poem*. My mother hates that poem."

"Really? She should be glad you had such a good dad—I'd love to be a father like that."

"Well, actually, it's just about . . . oh, hell, you should never try to explain a poem. Let's just call it poetic license. I don't remember my father. I don't . . ." She stopped. She'd been about to say she didn't even know what he looked like, but that surprised her so much she didn't want to go on with it.

Darryl said, "It has to hurt."

"No, really. I didn't even *know* him."

"It has to hurt," he repeated. "It's got to. Why else would you have written the poem?"

He spoke with such emphasis that she looked him full in the face, and saw there, in the set of his jowls, in his usually laughing eyes, such sympathy, such pain on her account that she had no idea what to make of it; literally couldn't imagine where it had come from. And then, in the midst of her confusion, her throat closed; a flock of butterflies took flight in her stomach. She thought that she was frightened, that she somehow remembered these sensations, as if she were having another déjà vu— but frightened of what, she couldn't imagine. She was in a nice restaurant with nice Darryl Boucree, beloved by everyone from his students to Miz Clara. It was hard to imagine anything safer.

Her first thought was to hide what was happening to her. She drank some beer, hoping to open up her throat, and it worked, a little. But it made her feel queasy.

Darryl looked at her critically. He said, "You don't look so good."

She forced a quarter smile. "Just tired. I think I better go home." It wasn't a real date, anyhow—just a friendly supper. Darryl had a gig in a while, and she was planning an evening in cyberspace.

Once they were in the car, her throat closed again, and her eyes felt oddly tight. She didn't speak, which was unusual for her, and later she couldn't remember anything about the ride home. When he pulled up at Miz Clara's, she turned to kiss him and felt herself withdrawing instead. She went through the motions rather than give away the fact that anything was wrong, but once in the door, the flood began. She'd barely gotten to her room before the sobs rolled out along with the tears. It was exactly the same as before—like being possessed. What the hell was wrong with her?

She lay for a long time on her bed and stared up at the ceiling, not only unable to answer the question, but even to wrestle with it. When she finally stirred an hour later, she couldn't name a single thing she'd thought about. Yet she hadn't been asleep or even in some state of semiconsciousness. The whole time she'd been dimly aware of her mother puttering in the kitchen, turning off the kitchen light, turning on the television—and then the rhythmic bursts from the TV itself.

She turned on the computer and went to Baron Tujague's web site, which was considerably more elaborate than Tony Tino's. Carefully, she read every word, and not once did the word "Toes" appear. Next, she did a search on Tujague and printed out everything that had been written on him in the last year or two—about a pound and a half of material to read at her leisure. She scanned it quickly, noticing that it was all celebrity puff stuff—no reports of arrests or other nastiness.

She had drunk no more than half her beer at supper, and, frankly didn't care much for beer at the best of times. A nice glass of wine was what she wanted now—something to take the edge off the weirdness her psyche was putting her through. She rummaged in the kitchen, hollering out to the living room. "Mama, you want a glass of wine?"

"Why, I b'lieve I would," Miz Clara answered in a tone of delicious surprise, as if she just couldn't imagine anything quite so odd and yet so delightful. "It's so hot in here."

She was fanning herself when Talba brought her

the wine, though it wasn't hot in the least. But Miz Clara was a church lady; a glass of wine was at least as much a sin as chocolate cake for dessert.

"Mama, have I ever been to a funeral before?"

Her mother wore neither wig nor scarf, just a close-cropped cap of wiry hair. She had on a kind of muumuu thing with short, bell-shaped sleeves and her favorite floppy slippers. The elegant wine-glass seemed to perk up the outfit. "Why you askin' me? If you don't know, who does?"

"I mean when I was tiny, maybe. Something I might not remember."

"You ain't never been to no funeral." Miz Clara spoke huffily, as if this was a subject simply not discussed in the Wallis home. And yet she and Talba's Aunt Carrie dissected in detail every funeral they ever went to.

"Mama, why don't you ever talk about my father?"

"What? What'd you say to me?" She was way beyond huffy. She was mad. Really mad.

Talba couldn't remember it, but maybe that was a subject that really had been forbidden. She stood her ground. "I said why don't you ever talk about my father?"

Miz Clara turned back to the television, her mouth set tight, teeth clenched so no crumb of information, however tiny, could possibly escape. "Ain't worth talking about," she said.

"Would you just answer one thing for me? Is he dead or alive?"

Miz Clara whirled, nearly knocking over the wine she'd set down on the table next to her chair. "What's wrong with you, girl? You ain't *got* no father. Don't make no difference whether he dead or alive."

"But . . ."

Miz Clara interrupted, not looking at her, showing every sign of having forgotten she was there.

"Wish to God he *was* dead," she said, as if she were talking to herself.

Talba poured them both a second glass of wine and went off to her room. Once again she lay staring at the ceiling, but this time a thousand things occurred to her. She didn't even know if her parents had been married.

She thought back, back, way back to the time when a child would have wondered where her daddy was. She couldn't for the life of her remember asking; but on the other hand, she hadn't the slightest recollection of being forbidden to speak about it.

But there was something even more surprising. She had researched Tony Tino yesterday, wondering how Eddie, with a computer so close at hand, had never thought to try to locate his son. And yet she, who lived and breathed computers, had never thought to research her father.

Something was wrong with this picture.

Chapter Nine

All she wanted to do was sleep, and the flesh, aided by the splendid soporific of a nice glass of wine, was certainly willing. She slept as if drugged for five hours and woke in the middle of the night feeling ready to take on tigers.

She thrashed for an hour or two, mind racing, and about half an hour into it, it occurred to her to turn the thing to her advantage. She put her mind to the question, not of her father (anything to avoid that one for a while), but of how to find Toes, and in the morning, dug out one of the outfits comprising her "right demographics" disguise. She had a closetful of white blouses and navy skirts left over from her temp days.

She had been hired by her original mentor, Gene Allred, to plant a bug and do some other spying in an office in which most of the clerical workers would be young, black, and female. He even knew a temp agency that could get her placed.

The same thing would probably work again if she could just get past Eddie.

Eileen, a moonfaced, plainish girl under the best of circumstances, looked drawn and strained when she arrived. "Audrey just called. She says Eddie's gonna be out another day. Wants to know if you can handle what needs to be done."

"Oh sure, no problem." On the one hand, this was great news—she'd be left to her own devices. On the other, what was going on here? "Eileen, does he get these headaches a lot?"

"They just started a couple of months ago—well, I wouldn't say that. Before that, he'd have one every three or four months. Lately, he's been missing a day or two every couple of weeks. I'm getting worried. I've got to tell you, I'm really starting to worry."

"What does Audrey say?"

The girl shrugged thick, ungainly shoulders. "She doesn't say anything. And that's nothin' like Aunt Audrey." She looked as if she might cry.

Talba's stomach flip-flopped. Damn! Eddie'd gotten to her. Racist, sexist old tyrant that he was.

"What about Angie?"

Eileen made a face. "I'm not her favorite cousin."

Talba saw what the problem was. Angie was all business. She probably thought Eddie ought to hire somebody bright and attractive and competent instead of offering charity to a woman she probably considered her slow-witted cousin. Talba decided to worry about that later. She said, "I guess we'll just have to do the best we can."

"Hey, I got you something." She opened a drawer and came up with boxes and bags. "One cell phone, one camera, and one pager."

"Pager?"

"Eddie said to get you one. He thought you'd like it . . . it being modern technology and all. He said to get him one too."

Talba did like it, especially the fact that Eddie'd gotten himself one. It made her think he meant them to work as a team.

She went into her office to call CompuTemps, and asked for a man named L. J. Currie. "Hey, Mr. Currie, Talba Wallis. Remember me? From Gene Allred?"

"I remember ya." He sounded downright unhappy about it.

"Now don't be like that. You know I'm a great worker."

He sighed. "Where ya need a job?"

For the right price—or if you had something on him—Currie could get you a job almost anywhere.

"Baronial Records," she said.

"Sorry, they don't use us."

"Oh, come on. You've got connections, L. J." She wasn't sure he did.

"I could give you a referral to CompTask. Their Ms. Brown has that account, I believe."

"I need a job today."

"I'm sure Ms. Brown can expedite that, if you explain your problem right." Talba thought, *Cross her palm with silver.* "Is there a referral fee?"

"Ms. Brown will take care of that."

A kickback, then—for which Talba would no doubt be charged, plus there'd be some kind of bribe for Ms. Brown. But that was the cost of doing business. Talba could care less. It was the way the system worked, and she was going to use it.

Before she trundled over to CompTask, she checked the web for "spy equipment." Remembering the bug she'd placed for Allred, it occurred to her she'd better get hold of some tiny transmitters. Probably Eddie wasn't the bugging type, but Eddie wasn't around.

It was amazing how easy it was to find this stuff. In five minutes, she'd ordered various bugs for telephones and other locations, but passed on what she really wanted—you could now get a GPS for tracking cars. You put it in the car (hardwiring it if possible), and then you could track the vehicle at home if you liked, on your desktop computer—or if you wanted to follow it, with your laptop in your car. Now this was really her style. Unfortunately, it was way out of her price range. But she was so impressed with the concept, she phoned the seller, struck up a conversation, and eventually he mollified her with a couple of ancient "bird dogs" he knew how to get—old-style homing devices you could attach to a bumper. The problem, he warned her, was an extremely cumbersome and short-range receiver. Damn! She wanted that GPS.

But of course Eddie would probably kill her if she used any of this stuff.

Feeling cocky, she hied herself over to CompTask, where, it seemed, Ms. Brown hadn't worked for three months. Damn, she was mad! (Mostly at herself, though she thought it entirely possible L. J. Currie'd shined her just to get her out of his hair.)

Okay, there was more than one way to skin a cat. She called CompTask and said she was from Baronial Records. She had a bit more up her sleeve, but it wasn't necessary. No sooner were the words out of her mouth than the auditory red carpet rolled out. She was switched to a Ms. Lewis, in whose mouth butter wouldn't melt. *Too bad for you,* Talba thought. *Here goes.* And she did her best imitation of a bureaucrat in high dudgeon. "Excuse me, Ms. Lewis, but it's nine-thirty and my temp isn't here for the third day in a row. I've got a department to run—can you *please* tell me what in the name of God is going on?" As if the world would come to an end if the filing didn't get done.

Ms. Lewis was flustered. "I don't understand. I know Liza was there—"

"Oh, she was here—just not when I needed her. Ms. Lewis, I'm sorry to be harsh, but the girl's late for the third time—that is, if you even sent her."

"Of course we sent her. But Liza's never late—it just isn't like her."

"Are you sure she went to the right department?"

"Actually—"

"Yes? Actually?"

"Usually Ms. Regan in your personnel department disperses the girls—but since there's only one today—"

Thank you, God, Talba thought.

"—there couldn't really be a mistake. She's been there a week, and she's scheduled for another."

"Let me get this straight, Ms. Lewis. You sent her to Purchasing, is that correct? She has not arrived. Maybe you'd better send someone else."

"Purchasing? Liza's in legal. Oh my God, were there two work orders?"

Having now gotten what she wanted, Talba was feeling generous. "Millicent, what is it?" she said, as if speaking to an underling. "Oh. Very good. Ms. Lewis, I beg your pardon. Liza's here; someone sent her on an errand." She hung up quickly, hoping Ms. Lewis wouldn't catch on that there weren't actually two work orders.

The bad news was, there didn't seem to be a way to get to Baronial today. Still, tomorrow would probably do. After a decent interval, she phoned Ms. Lewis again, said she was calling for Ms. Regan in Personnel, and they wouldn't be needing Liza the rest of the week.

Still no call from the cop on Cassandra's case. Talba'd had about enough of waiting for it. She called Skip Langdon again, got the name—Officer Dinel Corn—called Corn, failed to get her, and left a message.

Hell, she thought. *That just isn't good enough.*

She called Aziza Scott at work and found her surprisingly pleasant. "Hey, Talba, how're you doing?"

"Okay, thanks. How's Cassandra doing? That's the question."

"She feels bad about Rhonda. And also Pamela—she can't get through to her. I called that family, by the way. The Bergerons."

"You did?"

"I got to thinking about what you said about Rhonda's death being coincidental. I thought they should know. They wouldn't even talk to me."

"Well, their daughter was buried yesterday."

"And they won't let Cassandra talk to Pamela. You know what I think? They're racists, pure and simple."

Talba said, "I'm sorry about Pamela," and she was. Sorry on Cassandra's account. She had her own opinion about why the Bergerons wouldn't want to talk to Aziza. "I just called to find out if you've heard from Officer Corn."

Silence came from Aziza's end. Finally, she said, "Is that someone I should know?"

"She's the cop on Cassandra's case."

"Oh. I can't remember things like that. Should I have heard from her?"

Talba itched to say, "Do you ever answer a question except with a question?" but thought better of it. Instead, she wriggled her way out of what was shaping up as an extremely unproductive conversation, and sat for a while staring into space.

She wanted to talk to Eddie.

She was starting to get a very uneasy feeling. Langdon had spooked her. Not hearing from Officer Corn was spooking her. What if she'd set something in motion that further endangered the girls?

Pamela had the information she needed. If Eddie hadn't forbidden her to talk to the Bergerons . . .

but he had. In the end, she couldn't bring herself to go against his wishes.

She paced.

There was plenty to do. She could work on setting up Eddie's web site, and she could always work on the books—she'd promised, after all. But, somehow, it didn't seem decent just to break into Eddie's accounts and start organizing them without him.

So she did work on the web site. And then, somehow or other, she wasn't quite sure how, she found herself e-mailing Tony Tino. Just one sentence— "Are you Eddie Valentino's kid?"

Within an hour, he had answered: "Who are you? Is my father all right?" and she broke out in a sweat. She had done it as a lark, hadn't really expected him to answer . . .

Who'd believe that? she thought suddenly. Why the hell *had* she done it?

She sat with her head in her hands for a while, feeling paralyzed.

And then she began looking for her father. She spent several minutes getting into a search engine and locating a peoplefinder. She was all set to type in his name when she realized she didn't know it. Stunned, she sat there holding her head, willing something to come to her. *Donald,* she thought. She had heard it once, at least. She had heard her mother and her Aunt Carrie mention her father in a conversation she wasn't part of. She'd been ten or twelve maybe. The sisters probably didn't know she was in the room. They were talking about a man they didn't like, and Talba was pretty sure it was her father. Donald or David. Something like that. She figured she'd try both and once again was all set to begin when it hit her that she didn't know his last name. Didn't even know if her mother and father were married.

How could you look for someone when you didn't know their name?

It might be on her birth certificate, she thought, almost certainly would be. Only she didn't have a copy of it.

A scrap of memory flashed uncomfortably: Needing her birth certificate to get her driver's license; her mother giving her a folded copy; unfolding it eagerly only to find herself staring, horrified, at the four words she hated most in the world.

Her name.

The unspeakably ugly words—*Urethra Tabitha Sandra Wallis*—shamed her so badly she refolded it without even looking at the intriguing tiny hand-and footprints. At that point, it ceased to be an object of interest or curiosity, and became solely a rather unpleasant device to get her license. She handed it to the clerk, and later handed it back to her mother without ever unfolding it again.

She shrugged off the memory and checked her mail, just in case. Sure enough, Tony Tino was still on her case—he'd sent another e-mail.

Okay, okay, she had to bite the bullet. "Didn't mean to alarm you," she wrote. "If Eddie's your dad, he's fine (though not nearly so tough as he thinks he is). I'm just a fool who works for him. Please forgive the intrusion—just couldn't resist."

To which he replied: "You couldn't possibly work for him if you're not a relative. And you couldn't possibly be a relative if you're in touch with me. Who *are* you?"

There was only one answer to that one: "Not to brag, but *I* am a Baroness. Check out my web site. www.Baronessa.com."

Twenty minutes later, he got back to her: "Wow. I'm impressed. But now I know you *couldn't* work for my dad. Black, female, and smart? Uh-uh. I don't think so."

Suddenly the thing was a conversation:

"Your mom and Angie made him hire me."

"How are they?" he fired back.

Why don't you know? she wondered. She wrote: "They're just great. Planning your dad's birthday party." As if she didn't suspect anything was the matter.

And if it was a gambit—she wasn't sure herself—it worked: "Wouldn't know about that. My family and I don't talk."

"Figured as much—I'm a detective in training. :) Want to talk about it?"

"I don't know if I should. I don't really know anything about you."

"What? I thought you saw my web site."

"Are poets compassionate people?"

"Ezra Pound was an asshole. And Byron was a womanizer. Sylvia Plath was crazy; Anne Sexton molested her kid . . . but me? *I* am a Baroness. Eddie's a difficult man. I like him a lot."

"It's not so easy for me."

"You're just lucky you have a dad. I'm not sure if I do or not." *Whoa,* she thought. *Where's this thing going?*

But he didn't pick up on it. "Why'd you write to me? Is my dad really okay?"

"Actually, he's home with a headache. Which, I guess, is why I wrote to you. Bored."

"Thanksalot!"

She could see it was starting to deteriorate into one of those insufferably boring e-mail exchanges, and so she made a quick exit. "Oops, phone. Nice talking to you."

"We didn't really talk," he answered, leaving her feeling oddly betrayed. Did he mean they hadn't exchanged meaningful thoughts, or simply that e-mail wasn't talk?

She worked on the "locates" and employment

checks Eileen placed in her in-box. Eventually, the day crawled by.

Now that she had her license, Eddie didn't have a real reason to get mad at her for temping at Baronial Records, but she half hoped he wouldn't be back the next day. The less he knew, the better. Still, no way around it. She scribbled him a note saying she'd be out all morning, thinking she'd call in at noon.

Instead of going home, almost without making a decision to do it, she went to visit her aunt Carrie.

Aunt Carrie lived across the river in a little brick house—a very little house—with window bars protecting a lifetime of souvenirs and mementoes. Aunt Carrie was poor, but that certainly didn't keep her from shopping. She had little of value in her house, but she made that up in volume. The place was chockablock, a jumble of junk that necessarily collected dust and grease. Talba didn't know how she could stand it.

Like her sister, Clara, Carrie had no husband, but she had had one once. Uncle Frank—a man, unlike her father, whom she could vaguely remember. She had only one cousin, La Jeanne, a girl her own age who'd had a baby in high school, but married later and had another baby. Talba was happy for her. Miz Clara had nothing but contempt—she wasn't president and she wasn't a doctor. *If you don't watch out, ya gonna end up like ya cousin La Jeanne.* Talba'd heard it a hundred times.

She rang the doorbell, knowing Aunt Carrie was there. She was home all the time when she wasn't shopping. She was on disability on account of asthma and some other things—Talba didn't really listen when she started talking about it.

She came to the door with a kid clinging to her— La Jeanne's younger boy, who was three. Carrie baby-sat him for a few extra bucks. She had other things she did too. She sewed a little, she gambled some, with mixed results. She kept thinking she'd win the Lotto.

She was wiping her hands on an old frayed apron, like some stereotype of a nice aunt. "What's wrong with Clara? Oh, Lord, what is it?" Dread sat like a spider on her round face.

"Nothing. She's fine. Why?" But Talba knew why. Belatedly, she realized she'd never showed up at her aunt's door unannounced, certainly not at this time of day.

"What you doing here, child?" She made no effort to move aside, to let her niece in.

"I'm sorry. I didn't mean to scare you. I need to talk to you."

"Come on in, then." Reluctantly, she opened the door and Talba entered. It was obvious Aunt Carrie felt the visit boded poorly.

Talba didn't know how to put her at ease, realized she didn't know her aunt well anymore, since she was nine or ten she had seen her mostly as an extension of her mother. In truth, once La Jeanne and Talba were out of the toddler stage, the sisters hadn't much use for their offspring when they were together, preferring to chatter like squirrels with each other. What they talked about, Talba hadn't really noticed, except that one time when she was sure it was about her father.

"Hey, Marcellus," Talba said, thinking it politic to talk to the kid. "How ya doing, boy?"

Marcellus took off as if chased by bears. She laughed. "Looks like he likes his grandma all to himself."

"You want a glass of tea, girl?"

"Sure." She followed her aunt into the kitchen, hoping they could sit at the small table there. For Talba's money, the kitchen was the least oppressive room in the house. In addition to being full of junk—and dusty, greasy junk at that—Aunt Carrie's house was dark, the curtains always drawn in an effort to keep the place as cool as possible, save money on air-conditioning.

But the kitchen wasn't bad. It was cluttered, two or three meals worth of dishes always piled on the counters, jars of strawberry preserves and peanut butter open with knives left in them; but at least dishes, by their nature, had to be washed now and then. Talba couldn't understand how her mother, who ran such a tight ship, and her Aunt Carrie could possibly have come from the same family. They could both cook, though; she'd say that. You couldn't tell one of them's gumbo from the other's; either could win prizes. Aunt Carrie had a pot of it on the stove now. She nodded at it. "La Jeanne coming for supper."

Without waiting to be asked, Talba sat down at the little plastic-covered table. Her aunt gave her the tea but didn't sit, letting her know she wasn't to settle in. She'd obviously made up her mind to get this over with as soon as possible. It was the worst atmosphere possible for Talba's mission.

"Well?" Aunt Carrie had her hands on her hips. "What is it, girl?"

Suddenly, Talba's feelings were mightily hurt. She felt her eyes start to water. Damn! This just wasn't like her. She swallowed a few times. "I'm your niece. I thought it would be okay to visit."

The older woman softened and sat down. "It's okay to visit." She spoke a little more kindly. "It's just fine. What ya got on ya mind?"

"I just wanted to ask you something."

Her aunt nodded. "Well, go ahead, then."

Talba couldn't think where to start. In the end, she blurted, "Why won't anyone tell me anything about my father?"

"What?" Her aunt's face clouded. She stood up,

furious. "That what you come for, girl?"

Talba nodded and opened her mouth to speak again, explain, maybe, but Aunt Carrie wasn't about to relinquish the floor.

"You come in here, no call, no nothing, scaring me out of my wits, thinking something's happened to my sister, then maybe Corey, even La Jeanne. Couldn't figure out what kind of ugly thing you bringin'." She stopped and shook her head. "Umm umm umm. And then you bring up ya *father*. That what you come here for?"

"I don't even know his name." She heard herself whining like a three-year-old.

"Girl, you be glad ya don't know his name. Last thing ya want to know's that man's name!" Marcellus, alarmed by the excitement, came in crying, and grabbed his grandma's leg. She picked him up and cooed at him. "It's all right, baby. It's all right now."

Talba thought, *Why isn't she like that with me?* and remembered that once she had been. She felt herself going utterly out of control, letting go of the last thread of adulthood, regressing to about Marcellus's age. "I don't even know if my parents were married."

"That's what's eatin' at you? Whether you a bastard or not? They was married, all right. Umm umm." She shook her head, as if she wished she could change history. "Rue the day."

"No! That's not it at all . . ."

"What is it, then?"

"It's . . . I can't put it into words. I just need to know, that's all." Suddenly she got righteous about it. "Don't I have a right? What if I wanted to have a baby? Was he bipolar or something? I'd need to know that, wouldn't I?"

Carrie grabbed her arm, hovering like a crow. "Ya pregnant, Sandra? Tell me ya ain't pregnant. Break ya poor mama's heart."

"I'm not pregnant." She felt defeated. "I just need to know."

Perhaps she sounded so desperate her aunt loosened up, Talba wasn't sure. All of a sudden Carrie stepped back and looked her in the eye. "Maybe ya do have a right. I don't know, maybe ya do." She seemed to come to a decision. "Ya daddy's name was Denman."

Talba took it in slowly. "Denman. Denman Wallis."

"Denman La Rose Wallis."

"La Rose? You telling me La Rose?" She could barely breathe. It couldn't be a joke—Aunt Carrie was hardly a student of Shakespeare. The irony of it was smothering.

Her aunt shook her head in puzzlement. "That mean somethin' to ya?"

"No kidding—that was really his name?"

"I tol' ya it was. Prob'ly shouldn't have, but I tol' ya. Ya think I'd lie about it?"

Talba thought, *Yes. At this point, I'd think anything.* She said, "I guess not. I just don't understand why everyone's so secretive about him."

" 'Cause it's over and done with, that's why. That man nearly rurned ya mama life—didn't do you and Corey no good either . . ."

"We wouldn't be here without him."

"It's a miracle you here *with* him. I done somethin' for ya, Sandra. I gave ya his name, and I done it for a reason. I want ya to promise me somethin'."

Talba knew what was coming. She felt her stomach seize up. "What's that, Aunt Carrie?"

"I want ya to promise to let it be. Ya don't know what ya do to ya mama when you bring that man up. I want ya to let her alone. Go on about ya business and leave it in the past, where it belongs."

Talba hated this. Damn if she wasn't tearing up again. Aunt Carrie, for all her gruffness, all the distance she was displaying today, had been an important figure in her early childhood, a nurturing second mother, often more tenderhearted than Miz Clara herself, who preferred Corey, anyway.

"I can't promise that, Aunt Carrie. I'm sorry, I just can't."

Carrie said, "God help ya then, girl," and there was something unexpected in her eyes and voice, something different from the anger Talba expected. It was something soft and compassionate. "God help us all."

What the hell had happened to cause that kind of reaction? Talba thought about it all the way home. *He must have molested us,* she thought. *Corey and me.*

It would certainly explain the secrecy, and the paranoia when anyone brought him up.

But Talba felt oddly distanced from the notion. She ought to be a bit more creeped out, it seemed to her, and thought it must be so thoroughly buried she'd have to dream to bring it back up.

Miz Clara had supper waiting when she got home. "Where ya been? I expected ya home an hour ago."

Now or never, thought Talba. "I went to see Aunt Carrie."

"Carrie? What ya need from Carrie?"

"Same thing I wanted to ask you."

"About what?"

Talba wondered if she was pretending—if she didn't even know how obsessed her daughter had become. "About my father," she said.

"Ya father! Honey, you ain't got no father. You an example of spontaneous combustion—or whatever they call that thang."

Miz Clara had been ready for her—that was as close as she got to kidding around. Talba knew damn well she shouldn't push it. "Mama, just tell me one thing. Only one thing, and I'll never ask anything else."

"Oh, for heaven's sake. Ya sound like ya 'bout seven years old."

"Just one thin fact; that's all I ask."

"Go ahead and ask. I ain't saying I'll answer."

"Why do you hate my dad so much?"

It was evidently the simple three-letter word that did it. Miz Clara went up like Vesuvius. "What in the name of God ya mean ya 'dad'? Sound like somebody ya know and see every day and helps ya mama raise ya, and even helps support ya. Tell me, girl, ya got one of those? I don't want to hear none of this 'dad' stuff—not now and not ever. You mention that man to me again, and I swear to God I'll boot ya right out of this house ya was raised in. Now you go to ya room, just like you was a little girl. And without ya supper too! Yeah! I mean it! And don't you ever, ever bring up that man's name to me again."

Very seldom did Miz Clara get on such a high horse.

She'd never throw her own daughter out; Talba hadn't the least fear of that. Somehow, she'd manage to stop herself on a technicality. But Talba sure wasn't ever going to bring up the man again.

She went to bed and dreamed she had a baby and it was crying. *Too trite,* she thought. *Too damn trite for words. If I had a shrink, I wouldn't even tell him.* In the morning, she picked a white blouse and blue skirt out of her closet and headed out to exercise her demographic advantage.

Baronial Records was huge, much larger than she expected, something like a campus way out in New Orleans East. She had imagined one dingy building, but this place looked like some kind of African-American Skywalker Ranch. It was a veritable anthill of activity, which excited her. Everybody looked jazzed, and almost everybody was black. She liked that a lot until she realized that almost everybody was male as well.

Wondering what her job was (but guessing it was filing), she made her way to the legal department, and announced herself as Liza's replacement, poor Liza having awakened with the stomach flu.

As it developed, she was the assistant of a Ms. Jackson, Ms. Jackson being a lawyer, apparently. Ah—she was a legal secretary. Well, she could do it. If it involved a computer, there was no question she could do it. It and lots of other things. She practically smacked her lips.

She had a plan—a plan so simple it couldn't go wrong. All she had to do was find out who Toes was, then get a picture of him, and get the kids to I.D. it. And they'd given her a computer to play with. If the word "toes" was in it anywhere, she'd find it.

She went in and prowled. Ah, yes. Toes. Toes and more Toes. Though never as a word—always as a syllable. As in tomatoes, potatoes, even pimientoes. Certainly not as a proper noun.

Well, hell. Toes had to be a friend of the Baron's, didn't he? He might even work for him. Therefore, somebody must know him. She got herself invited to go to lunch with a bunch of clerical workers and tried it out on them: "Y'all know anybody named Toes?"

Hilarity followed. Appendage jokes. Remarks about the things parents name kids. One woman had known an "Ears," and someone else a "Sweet-eyes." The one who knew a "Brown Nose" was probably joking.

The conversation was flying out of control. Talba tried to rein it back in: "No, really. He's a *good* friend of the Baron's—they call each other T and T. My sister met him at a party."

More hilarity. "Girlfriend," one of the ladies con-
fided, "every stud in the state claims to be a friend
of the Baron's, black *or* white. Which color's this
dude? Or is he that soft creamy color I could eat
with a spoon—you know, that color that's mostly
gold, with just a little red in it? Mmmmmm. Yeah."

Evidently nobody in the group knew the gentleman. But maybe the legal department wasn't the
best for picking up on who did and didn't know
the Baron. After lunch Talba took a quick tour of
the building, approaching the receptionist in each
department with "a fax for Toes." She failed to
score, but it was barely a start—there were plenty
more buildings, plenty more departments. She just
had to be patient. Had to keep working there a few
more days, asking around. Something might happen.

But they probably wouldn't keep her. She had a
pile of work when she got back to her desk, and it
wasn't computer work—she was very slow at plain
old typing, which is what it mostly was. She was behind and probably wouldn't be asked back. She had
to think of something before the gig blew up in her
face.

Somewhere near quitting time, she thought of it.
The key was the Baron. He did know Toes, had actually been seen with him. The thing was to get to
the Baron. And it could be done. All she needed
was his schedule, which was sure to be in the computer somewhere.

Excited, she thought, *I wonder if there's something
tonight?*

And then it occurred to her that if there was
something big and public, it would be on his web
site. She went there first, and wasn't disappointed.
There were three good opportunities, the first of
which indeed was that night, and it was something
she'd probably be able to get into, even this late.

But wait, she thought, I could have done this without wasting a whole day working here. So she went looking for his nonpublic schedule again, and found plenty of other opportunities. She printed it out and went back to her contracts.

Her last act before leaving that night was to call CompTask and, in the guise of Ms. Jackson, ask them to send Liza back.

Chapter Ten

"No. No way. Negative. Uh-uh. Over my dead body."

Talba stared at her e-mail and thought perhaps there was room, after all, for the Luddite opinion that not all business need be conducted on the Internet. She had simply inquired of Darryl Boucree if he would care to accompany her to a program of indigenous rap and hip-hop music featuring national artists, and even offering to supply the tickets. Surely this was too strong a reaction.

She tried the phone. "Mr. Boucree, sir, I find that usually when I ask a gentleman for a date, I get a much more polite reaction. I just don't believe you can say to my face what you said to my computer."

"Ms. Wallis, ma'am, I don't believe I heard you. Put your sweet lips a little closer to the phone."

"Perhaps we could trade. If you'd do this one little thing for me, no telling what I might do for you." She spoke in a whorehouse whisper.

"Not on your life," he answered. "Not for all the money in the world. Not even if . . ."

"I wasn't thinking about money."

"Not even for your precious smooth black skin."

"Dark brown, actually. And surely you jest." People liked her voice. Some had joked that she could make a bundle doing phone sex. She put all the sweetness she could muster into the last four words.

"You're on your own, Ms. Wallis."

She was getting exasperated. "Well, what's the big deal? Rap's an African-American art form. Why all the resistance?"

"It's also a part of kid culture that I get all too much of. You know what that asshole calls women?"

"What asshole? There are three artists on the program."

"You know what asshole. Baron Tujague."

"I thought he came to your school, and you liked him."

"All right, all right. He's civic-minded, I guess. This thing tonight, for instance. It's just that I hate that shit. It's so slick and ugly."

"Slick and *ugly* . . . mmmmm. Sounds like fun. Slick and *uuuggly*."

He laughed. "God, you're a sexy woman."

She pressed her advantage. "Listen, this thing's for the Musicians' Clinic. How in the name of your profession are you going to find a better cause? And they're each only going to do one number. Rich people are going to be there—think they want to hear rap?"

It was a promotional party for the second CD produced by the Musicians' Clinic at LSU, this one all rap, all original songs. Darryl's own band, the Boucree Brothers, had a song on the first. Tickets were two hundred bucks apiece, and Talba figured she could expense a couple.

"Why is it so important to have me with you?"

Darryl asked, and she could see she just about had him.

She thought of something to say that finally convinced him—or maybe it was the way she said it. It had nothing to do with sex and everything to do with her feelings for him.

The thing was a two-hour deal at the House of Blues, a venue of which Darryl disapproved on grounds that the acoustics of the place were wasted on rap. But there was nothing, as Talba pointed out, wrong with the drinks. She was wearing one of her Baroness outfits, flowing fuchsia harem pants with tight shiny top and the hat she'd bought from Millie the Milliner.

Because the point of the CD was to promote health, and because much of the Baron's fanship was perceived as being drug-friendly, to say the least, he'd been asked to write an antidrug song. And had. A song about dying and all your friends dying and leaving your kids behind, still little kids, "no daddy or nothin' " and your mama cryin'. "Rhymes with dyin'," Darryl noted, but even he found it hard to find fault.

"Now, listen," said Talba, when the songs had been sung and the pitch made, "you're a famous musician. Here's the deal. You go suck up to him, and while you're at it, introduce your friend who could be his sister, their names are so similar."

He smacked his forehead. "This is what it was all about."

She shrugged. "Well, the other thing and this— the thing I mentioned."

"You mean you love me so much and can't stand to be away from me, even for one evening."

"Well, yeah, sure. You know that's true. Except for the evenings I can."

"God, what I do for women." He grabbed her hand and started to blaze a trail through the crowd.

"Better lose that plural," she said automatically, but she could see he didn't really mind doing this for her, that in fact he was pleased about it, and she thought that if she had put it to him this way in the beginning, he might have been more forthcoming with the favor. But then at the time, she hadn't really been sure how she wanted it to work. She'd just known she needed Darryl; the world of rap made her nervous. To be sure, she had a poet's contempt for rhyme that wasn't poetry, or if it was, then poetry in the service of commercial interests.

Yet she did feel there was nothing wrong with making money, and in a perfect world that all poets would make money. So what, she thought, was her problem?

Commercial poetry, perhaps, that promoted violence and hatred, particularly of women. Yet not all rap did, and she knew it.

It was just baggage she carried.

When Darryl had elbowed their way within a couple of feet, the Baron himself signaled him. "Hey, man—aren't you Darryl Boucree? Been knowin' your work for years. The Boucree Brothers are an institution. Ain't that right, Thomasino?"

The man beside him, smaller and seemingly overwhelmed to be in the Presence, showed a good set of teeth, and said, "Tha's right," and followed up with a brace or two of nods.

"Hey, Kassim! Hey, Raynell—got somebody I want you to meet. Hey, Darryl, these are my buddies—and this is my brother, Thomas Toledano. Darryl Boucree, gentlemen, Darryl Boucree of the Boucree Brothers—one of the premier musicians currently residing in this town." Kassim and Raynell were wearing gangsta rap outfits—baggy pants, backward baseball caps, the whole thing, but the Toledano brothers—if that was their real name—were dressed in casual slacks and shirts, out of respect for the occasion. Talba gave them points for that.

She also observed that the Baron definitely didn't talk like a thug. He didn't speak standard English, exactly, but he came pretty close. That interested her almost more than anything else about him, because she, who always spoke correctly, didn't even say stuff like "I be ready" in jest, also wrote in dialect, and did it because, as she'd told Eddie, it was the only way she could imagine writing.

"Darryl. Darryl." The Baron spoke urgently, as if Darryl might get away from him. He seemed more wound up than he ought to be, even though he'd just performed. She knew perfectly well what that did to you. "You're gonna hear about these boys soon. Kassim and Raynell, AKA Pepper Spray. They just cut an album on our label—look out for it."

Darryl said he was pleased to meet them and Thomas as well, and he was about to get a word in edgewise when a half-drunk dude came and leaned on the Baron and tried to give him a joint, which seemed to embarrass him. "Hey, Nito, come on. Come on, this ain't no place for that shit. Come on, meet Darryl Boucree. Darryl, my buddy, Benito— Nito, you know who Darryl Boucree is?" Benito didn't seem interested. "And who," said the Baron, "is this *lovely* lady with the beautiful hat?"

He extended a hand to Talba, and seeing his chance, Darryl said, "This . . ." He paused as if waiting for a drumroll, "is the Baroness de Pontalba."

At which the Baron looked utterly nonplussed, like he knew he ought to know her, but couldn't quite place her. "You're a rapper, too," he finally said, as if he'd managed to put his finger on it.

Talba smiled, and it wasn't entirely phony. She sort of liked the guy. "A humble poet," she said. "But I *am* a Baroness."

"Well, isn't that a coincidence?" he said. "Because

I am a baron." He said it the way she did when she performed, emphasis on the *I*.

"Hey, I know you. I *know* ya." It was the brother.

Oh. shit, she thought. *He must have seen me at Baronial Records.*

"I know this chick's into that shit. She got a book with one of your poems in it. I've *seen* it, man—remembered the Baroness thing. Hey, you really are a poet—how 'bout that? Hey, Tujague, she the real thing."

"I can *see* she's the real thing." The Baron spoke with an edge of smarminess, the kind of automatic seductive note guys on the street affected without even thinking about it. "Ummm, *hmmm.*" No doubt he meant to be flattering, but this was the kind of thing that turned her off about the whole rap ethos. "Hey, maybe we could do somethin' together sometime—you know, we both rhymesmiths—some kind of thing in the schools or somethin'. Get kids interested in poetry." He turned back to his brother. "Like we been talkin' about. Hey, whatcha think, Darryl?"

Darryl smiled and settled into an easy slouch, as comfortable and natural as this man was overbearing and false. "You're welcome at Fortier any time."

"How 'bout that, Your Highness? You up for it?"

" 'Your Highness' isn't necessary. 'Your Grace' is sufficient, thank you." Talba gave a little curtsy.

He looked at her kind of quizzically, as if he'd only just really noticed her. This time, when he spoke, his voice had none of the street smarm that had crept in before: "You got a real nice voice, you know that?"

"Why thank you, Your Grace."

"No, I mean it. I'd like to work with you. You up for it?"

"Sure. I'd love to."

"*Okay,* then, we got a deal. Darryl . . ." He held up a hand for Darryl to slap. "Good to see you, my man." And he moved out among his admirers.

"Real sincere dude," Darryl said.

"You mean my new best friend that I'm going to do a gig with?"

"You mean *my* new best friend."

"Well, he did know you. He's the one called you over."

"I guess I was wrong when I said he wouldn't remember me from Fortier. But I guarantee you that's the only place he knows me from. He wouldn't know the Boucree Brothers from the Crips."

"What do you mean? You can't know who comes to your gigs."

"Well, if he had, and he really was a fan, he would have introduced himself. Now wouldn't he?"

She thought it over, imagined a shy young wannabe and how he'd behave, but she couldn't make the Baron fit the image. "I don't know. He sure knew you."

Darryl shrugged. "The principal gave him an album when he came to the school. It was kind of embarrassing at the time, but she meant well." He looked uncomfortable. "You want to get out of here?"

As they walked over to Chartres, where they'd parked Darryl's car, he said, "By the way, did you get what you went for?"

"Are you kidding? An introduction to my idol, who offered to do a gig with me? We're practically engaged."

Darryl was silent.

"What?" she said finally. It was unlike him.

"I don't know. He seemed like he was on speed—never a good sign. But not only that . . . these rappers, I just don't know—a lot of them really do seem to be gangsters. You check his rap sheet, Ms. Dick?"

She shook her head. "Even I can't get in the police computer. But you're cute, you know that? To be so concerned."

"I'm not kidding. It spooks me."

"Hey, you called it a minute ago."

"I called what?"

"When you called me Ms. Dick. Trouble is my business, know what I mean? Besides, he's got semi-good manners, except when he thinks he's being sexy. I think there's a mama in the woodpile."

"Interesting choice of words."

"Apt, I believe. If he's from a good family, he wouldn't want anyone to know it."

She thought about that. She hadn't compiled a dossier on him, in fact had read only his own press about himself. She should do that first thing in the morning.

Or maybe she should just call him up and say, "Hey, Baron, know anybody named Toes?" And he'd give her a name, and that would be the end of it.

She needed to see him again. Well, hell—she checked his schedule, and to her surprise, he was doing something in the morning—first thing in the morning. And something weird, if you considered the lyrics of his songs, which were mostly about mayhem. He was on the program at a breakfast sponsored by the archdiocese. *I wonder,* she thought, *if he's running for office.*

But it occurred to her the answer was probably much simpler. The man was currying favor. Baronial Records was big, and it was probably going to get bigger. It was going to want more land and plenty of tax breaks, and who knew what else. The archdiocese was one of the most powerful political forces in the city.

She didn't see crashing the breakfast after meeting the Baron the night before—he'd probably have her arrested for stalking.

Or wait. Maybe that wasn't a bad idea. She could pretend to be a groupie—hang out, get to know some of the female hangers-on, and chat them up. She'd have Toes's name within a week. Come to think of it, the man had practically invited it—that stuff about her voice and how he'd love to work with her. Sure. He'd just love it. He'd probably love a few other things as well, and that was the dicey part. How long could she hang out without having to put out?

One thing, she thought ironically, she did have groupie credentials; she'd been with a musician the night before. For all the Baron knew, she went out with a different one every night of the week.

The strategy was dangerous, but it might be the shortest distance between two points. Before she went to bed, she left a message on Eddie's phone telling Eileen she'd be late, she had an errand to do.

She woke up to a downpour.

Chapter Eleven

Miz Clara banged on her door. "Sandra, you gettin' up? Who you think you is? Queen of the May?"

That was what the title of the poem was about. When she was a little girl, her mother used to do that, and she'd think, *If my daddy were here, he wouldn't treat me like that. He'd treat me like I really was Queen of the May.*

She rolled over and laughed at herself. Queen of the May indeed! Where in hell had Miz Clara even gotten the phrase?

She thought: *What shall I wear to a prayer breakfast? Ah, I have it. How about a nice white shirt and a blue skirt?*

Uh-uh. Not if I'm playing a groupie. That calls for Baroness clothes.

But if Eddie comes to work, he'll fire me.

She ended up in flowing bronze with a change of clothes in her car. But as it turned out, she just

could not make herself get out of her car and walk
blocks in the pouring rain, ruining her Japanese silk
kimono and her cute sandals that went with it. Absolutely couldn't. Anyway, was a sodden groupie
sexy?

How about if I surveil him? she thought, and wondered if she'd just invented a word.

The idea appealed to her. She parked half a block
away from the Ramada Inn, where the breakfast was
being held, and about fifteen minutes later the
Baron walked out, along with one of the men she'd
met last night, and got in a warm, dry limousine.

Right decision for once, she thought, and took off
after the limo, trying to remember the name of the
man with the Baron. Kassim, she thought. These
people all ran together.

The limo turned around and threaded its way
back down St. Charles to the interstate. Evidently it
was going to New Orleans East, where Baronial Records was. She followed on I-10. The car took an East
exit, all right, but it didn't go to Baronial Records.
Instead, it stopped at the Shoney's near Home De-
pot.

She did a double take. Shoney's? All the money
in the world, and these guys were having fast food.
She figured they'd send the driver in for supplies,
but instead, four men tumbled out of the limo and
went in, as if one of them wasn't one of the hottest
stars in the country. She parked in the lot, thinking
the groupie routine wouldn't fly in this all-male
atmosphere. These dudes were definitely not going
to be in the mood for chicks.

The rain had let up, and she could actually see
pretty well through the window. The four guys met
two others, and they all sat down to have breakfast.
Real breakfast, unaccompanied by prayers.

The record company was pretty close—maybe this

was a hangout, someplace where the Baron knew he could go and be left alone.

Surely you wouldn't take a business acquaintance to Shoney's. And she recognized three of the men—Kassim, Raynell, and the Baron's brother, Thomas. These were probably the rapper's best pals, and the brother fit the description Millie had given: he was pretty much a toad and had a name starting with "T."

She decided to take a chance—if it paid off, she was the hottest shot in Louisiana. If it didn't, she didn't think she'd lost anything.

She got out her camera and her cell phone, got the number from information, crossed her fingers, and dialed Shoney's. Someone answered on the fifteenth ring.

She said, "This is Cassie from Baronial Records. Is Toes in there with the Baron? I've got a little emergency here."

The employee who answered put the phone down on the counter and went over to the table. She could see just fine, but she couldn't hear. What did the woman say? Did she say "Is one of you Toes?" or did she say, "Emergency at the office"?

Oh, who cares? she thought, *I'll just photograph them all when they come out.*

But her heart speeded up when the Baron's brother got up to take the call.

Could it be this easy? She moved her car, so she'd be in a better position to photograph them when they came out, but even so, she only managed to get two, the brother and one of the ones she didn't know.

She dropped the film off at a one-hour-processing joint and hurried back to the office. Too late, she remembered she'd forgotten to change clothes. If Eddie was there, it was going to be embarrassing.

Eileen Fisher's bland features showed something,

but Talba wasn't sure what. Excitement, maybe.

"Is he here?"

Fisher nodded. "He wants to see ya."

Glancing into his office, Talba couldn't bring herself to enter. Eddie was like a dragon in there, breathing so much fire she was afraid of getting scorched from the doorway. What in hell had she done?

Well, plenty, but what that he could know about? Where to start? She decided on, "Eddie, I'm sorry I'm late . . ."

He said, "Where in the *hell* do you get off?"

I'm fired, she thought. *Damn. I was liking it, too. Crazy little job, but never boring.*

"Listen. Eddie. I think I've got the guy."

He stood up and shouted her name. Shouted it. "*Talba!* Talba, sit down."

She was quite honestly afraid to. She hovered at the door, not sure whether to flee or what.

"Goddammit, get *in* here." He sat down and spoke a little more softly.

Okay, he'd backed off a little. She took a tentative step into the room, but she wasn't about to sit.

"Sit down, goddammit." The bags under his eyes were black. Nothing like her own skin, which was brown and smooth. These were darker, a mottled gray-black that she hadn't associated with human skin. It crossed her mind that he was really very ill, that the headaches were either a cover story or a symptom of something much more dire than she'd imagined.

She more or less slunk into a chair. "Are you all right?" she said, unable to focus on anything else.

"Whaddaya mean am I all right? Do I look all right?"

She opened her mouth to speak, but he said, "Or do I look like I'm about to kick your ass all the way to Canada?"

She closed her mouth, thinking that this was no way at all she'd expect him to speak to a woman. Whatever she'd done, it was worse than she thought. Her mind leapt to the worst. Had she endangered Cassandra? It must be that. There must be some eventuality she hadn't foreseen. Her skin was suddenly clammy. "Has something happened to Cassandra?"

"Cassandra?" Eddie stared at her, absolutely blank. What the hell kind of monkey wrench was this? Who the fuck was Cassandra?

The call had come half an hour before. He had simply picked up and the voice, a voice he didn't recognize, had said, "Dad, it's Anthony," and there was a collision in his brain.

It was the last goddam thing in the world he wanted to hear. And yet, all the turbulence, all the spiked, barbed, jagged, nasty, hateful projectiles flying around in his head had suddenly stopped their yammering and all was quiet in there, as if their motors had turned off and they were gliding now, gliding peacefully, simply sailing around between his ears in harmonious silence. He had listened to the silence for a while, not a thought in his head. *Shock,* he thought later. *It must have been shock.*

"Dad, are you there?"

And that's when the collision came. The motors that had turned off flicked on at triple speed, so that everything flying around in there, everything in that momentarily peaceful cavity, everything ugly and barbed and jagged, crashed into everything else, and threatened to blast his skull open. It sounded like a thousand ringing phones, a dozen roaring beasts, a season of hurricane wind. "I can't talk to you," he said to his son, and it was literally true.

"I got an e-mail from someone who works for you.

She said you were out sick. I thought I'd call and see how you are."

Eddie couldn't stand the noise, couldn't take the roaring and the ringing, the cacophony, the stroke it was giving him, the apoplexy. He was going to be dead in a minute. His heart was going to stop from the strain of this.

"I can't talk to you," he said again, and his voice was raspy, something like the sound a bear might make after a winter of hibernation—aggressive but none too alert.

He hung up the phone, and when it rang again, he let Eileen Fisher take it and when she came into his office bearing a pink message memo, he said, "Where the hell is Talba Wallis?"

He had sat there staring at the wall until his assistant came in, letting the debris inside his skull grind itself into particles, letting it grind his soul along with it, letting it grind up what was left of his life, and when she appeared in the door of his office, dressed for Mardi Gras or something, he had to restrain himself from grabbing her by the shoulders and shaking her till her teeth rattled.

Cassandra.

Cassandra was the fucking client, that's who Cassandra was. What was *wrong* with this girl?

"How the hell should I know how Cassandra is? What the fuck's that got to do with anything?" He didn't even bother to excuse his French.

To his utter frustration, she said, "What have I done?"

He truly couldn't believe it. "Idiot! Goddamn little idiot!"

"Did they fine you the three thousand dollars?" She was almost whispering, she was so scared.

"The what?" he said, and suddenly got it. She was a retard. He couldn't believe what he was hearing.

"Fuck the fuckin' three thousand dollars. Where in hell do you get off talking to my kid?"

But there was no contrition on her face, only bewilderment. "Angie? I haven't talked to Angie today."

"Anthony!" he bellowed.

"Anthony? Oh, Tony. I didn't talk to him, I e-mailed . . ."

"For God's sake. That *chair* is smarter than you."

And finally, she caught on. He could see the light dawn on her face. She talked fast, shaking her head. "Eddie, I'm sorry. I'm really sorry. I didn't mean to intrude on your privacy."

"I got family problems, all right? Ya think that's ya business? Who the *fuck* ya think ya are?"

She shrugged in that helpless way people do when they've exhausted their reservoir of apology. "I never thought he'd call you. I thought we were just talking."

"What *right* did ya have?"

"I didn't have any right. I don't know. I just . . ." She squirmed, trying to think up some excuse. "I just think he's lucky to have a dad," she blurted, and looked as if she could die of embarrassment. What an unspeakably stupid thing to say, he thought. She rambled on. "I mean, I don't even know if I've got one."

"And so you thought you'd fix us up. My son and me."

"No, it wasn't that."

"What are you saying, then?"

"I don't know. I just wanted to talk to him. I was being playful, I guess."

Without realizing he was doing it, Eddie rose up out of his chair and stood over her, his face close to hers. "Playful? You were *playing* with other people's lives?"

Her chair scraped on the floor as she pushed it

back, alarm spreading like a stain over her features. For some reason, that made him even madder. "Get outta my sight! Just get fuckin' out of here!"

She was already at the door. "Okay, Eddie," she said, evidently feeling safer. "Sure I'll excuse your French."

He knew what was going to happen, and it was unacceptable. He needed her gone. Completely gone; off the premises.

He stomped out into the hall. "All the way out! Eileen, you too!"

Neither of them needed to be told twice. He was speaking to their backs.

Only when the door had snicked shut did he allow himself to acknowledge that he was choking to death, that his throat had closed. He gasped; and a howl came out of him, a baying, as if he were an animal. He half expected the women to come running back in alarm, but nothing happened. He locked the door with shaking, sweaty hands, still roaring, bellowing, and when his throat was raw, he sat down on the sofa in the anteroom and let the tears go.

The funny thing was, he didn't even know what he was crying about.

Chapter Twelve

For Talba, the hardest part, almost, was going down in the elevator with Eileen Fisher. They both understood that something more embarrassing than scary had happened, but Talba had other baggage as well. She thought, *Eileen's going to say, "he's not himself," and I'm gonna puke.*

But when Eileen said it, she didn't puke, instead cracked, "No, he's the Antichrist," which set the girl to giggling, and allowed her to stare at the elevator walls in peace.

When she was safely in her car, she bent over the steering wheel, trying to get her breath, heart pounding, hands shaking. She was sweating too. She blasted the AC up to Arctic and sat there, contemplating the enormity of her sin.

He had asked her why she did it, and she had had an answer, had been on the verge of saying, "It didn't involve you. It wasn't about you." But that sounded so stupid and lame and phony she couldn't

get it out. Now, seeing what had happened, she
didn't even believe it.

She had meddled, whether she had the sense to
realize she was doing it or not. Without meaning to,
she had wounded this great male beast, had hurt
him so bad he might never forgive her.

And in turn that hurt her, made her realize how
fond of him she was. Sure, he'd been abusive. Sure,
he'd cursed her out, called her an idiot—a *chair*, for
Christ's sake. But he was out of control in a way she
couldn't have predicted. She'd gone someplace forbidden, opened some sort of secret door, and it had
unhinged him. Actually unhinged him.

For a while there, on the short walk to her car,
she'd considered calling Audrey or Angie. But she
recognized instantly how wrong that would be. Even
if Eddie committed suicide, he had to be left to do
it in dignity. Not that that was going to happen. She
didn't know what the future held, hadn't a clue
whether she still had a job, but there was no doubt
in her mind Eddie would weather this. At least if
there was anything to the ancient maxim that you
shouldn't hold things in. The sounds that came out
of him after she and Eileen left were a lot like an
explosion. If they didn't rip him apart, nothing was
going to.

She looked at her watch. Not quite lunchtime, but
getting there. She might as well work as not. The
film she'd dropped off would be ready by the time
she got there; if it turned out, she'd have an excuse
to go shopping on Eddie's nickel. But first, she
needed comfort food.

For Talba, that meant a shrimp po' boy, something in which she indulged about once a year. Today, she decided, was going to be the day, and she
was going to drink a Barq's with it.

She had to go to the French Quarter anyway—
she'd get one there. In her opinion, this was na-

ture's most nearly perfect food. Talba liked hers dressed—nativespeak for "decked out, baby-child," as she'd written in a poem once. Slathered with mayonnaise, topped with crisp tomato slices, then blanketed with lettuce, cut in strips and tucked in like confetti. The shrimp, of course, would be fresh and flash-fried; the bread sweet, French, and so fresh it would still be fragrant. The Barq's would be cold and sweet as running creek water, but a good deal more caloric. Maybe she'd write another poem about this particular lunch—"ain' nobody po' that's got a shrimp po' boy"—well, no, but she'd work on it.

Actually, she kind of liked it. The sentiment, not the line—that was far too cornball. Ah, she had it— she could put it in Miz Clara's mouth. That would work just fine. In fact, she wasn't altogether sure her mother hadn't said it at some point. She'd been forever making points about what did and didn't make you poor in some kind of spiritual sense that wasn't Christian (though Miz Clara was). Some kind of thing that went beyond Christian.

Talba stopped to eat at a place on Conti Street, a place where they charged about three times what she'd have had to pay in her own neighborhood, at least a few years ago. There had been a little store around the corner where she and her brother Corey went when her mama gave them money.

He was a butt now, but Corey had been a great brother to have at the time. He had warded off the bullies and taken care of her when Miz Clara couldn't. Hey! She could write him a poem. That would do a lot to heal the chasm that had opened between them when she drifted into a life that wasn't about money, and he married Miss La-di-da with skin more like cream than coffee.

That's some silly shit, Talba thought. She shook her head at her own absurdity, able, with a bite of nectar and honey in her mouth, to be generous toward her sister-in-law. This was far from the best shrimp po' boy she'd ever had—couldn't even touch the ones she and Corey used to go get—but it was still nectar and honey. It was greasy and the bread was old— the shrimp fried too slow, the tomato limp and lame, the lettuce going brown—carelessly, lovelessly made. But it was still a shrimp po' boy and a shrimp po' boy was still finer than nightingales' tongues.

The poem was coming. She took out a pen and started scribbling.

> *My brother used to say, "Little Bird . . ."*
> *(he call me Little Bird)*
> *He say, ". . . Little Bird, I'm gon' get you a wriggle*
>   *o'worms*
> *You ain' goin' hungry with Big Bird around . . .*
> *You ain' goin' hungry with worms in your tummy,*
> *You ain' goin' hungry this fine day in June . . .*
> *Dry those tears and flap those wings . . .*
> *Open that beak and . . .*

And what? Talba stared at the paper, wondering where on earth this stuff came from.

Little Bird? She had no recollection of Corey ever calling her that. And yet it came out so naturally. She focused on her chewing, staring out the window, trying to clear her head.

A picture came gradually into her mind—of herself, watching television. *Sesame Street* was on. And she was crying. Corey came into the room and left again, perhaps saying something to her.

Then he came back, wearing some sort of yellow outfit—pajamas? His? Miz Clara's?—and he'd used something to simulate feathers. Maybe it was the kind of grass that came in Easter baskets . . . something like that, anyway. And he pretended to be Big Bird, and she laughed.

And maybe then he took her out to get a po' boy. That wasn't part of the memory, if this *was* one, and she had a feeling it was. It was too vivid simply to have popped from whatever mysterious place poems come from.

How strange, she thought, *to forget a thing like that.* And then:

He was the only father I had.

Her eyes started to water, taking her by surprise. It wouldn't have occurred to her in a million years to go all gooey over her yuppie brother.

With the aid of the Barq's, she swallowed the last of the sandwich—a good thing, since she felt her throat swelling. She was getting into father territory again, and she hated it. But it was more than that—it was a sense of wonder that so much of her childhood seemed lost—specifically, that whatever tenderness there had been between her and her brother had been allowed to die.

By me, she thought. *By me. Corey didn't do it.*

But in some ways he had, and she understood that, even as she romanticized him. He chose to go snobbish and materialistic and judgmental when he became a doctor. She didn't do that to him. In spite of it, though, Miz Clara still loved him. Why couldn't Talba?

Maybe I do, she thought. *I guess I still do. I wonder what he knows about our father?*

The last thought, the thought about her father, came tacked on to the rest of it, clear out of left field, and, as with so many things lately, she wondered why she hadn't thought of it before.

Probably because they walked on eggshells around each other. She never voluntarily asked him for anything. If Miz Clara needed something other than medical care—where Talba happily bowed to her brother's expertise—she'd customarily get it herself even if it meant taking some job she hated.

Like the one at United Oil, which had replaced the rotting stoop and painted the house. The cottage looked like new now, put the others on the block to shame, and Corey had chided her for it—said he didn't see why she hadn't asked him for the money.

She hadn't said what was on her mind: *You could see what she needed as well as I could.*

And she wondered why she hadn't.

She picked up the photos from Shoney's and found herself pleasantly surprised—not bad at all, though she only had two of the men. Still, she had hopes.

She strolled into Millie the Milliner's, happily full of her favorite food, confidently carrying a possible break in the case, happy to be there. She'd put the morning behind her—the rain, the near faux pas of barging in on the prayer breakfast, Eddie's wrath, and most of all, her shame. She had done a truly bad thing, and she knew it, but she hadn't thought of it for half an hour. She was looking forward to a little browse through Millie's, and also to a chat with Millie herself.

Millie was helping a customer. She was dressed today in purple—flowing purple pants worthy of Talba herself, gorgeous purple top in tie-dyed silk, knee-length lavender jacket. Her *chapeau du jour* was something D'Artagnan would have been proud of, royal purple felt with a luxuriant black feather. Her nails were blood-red.

Talba caught her eye and gave a little wave and a smile, but evidently Millie didn't see her. Either that or she ignored her, and Talba couldn't see that. Still, she seemed to be taking a lot of time with her client.

Another came in, and Millie went right to her,

leaving Talba feeling snubbed. *Oh, well,* she thought, *I'm not a paying customer.* She amused herself trying on hats.

And finally, when the second customer had gone, and they were alone in the shop, Millie disappeared into the back. Something was up.

Talba followed her, but with care. She had no idea who else was back there. But no one was there except Millie, organizing bits of trim as if it were the most pressing job in the world.

"Hey, girlfriend. What's going on?"

"This part of the store's my private space."

Talba shivered. "Wooo. Have you got a thermometer? It got real chilly all of a sudden."

Millie smoothed out a piece of bronze velvet. "I'm afraid I can't help you today."

"Today? Why not today?"

"Look, Miss, I've spoken to my lawyer, and I really can't help you." She was keeping her eyes on her workbench, not meeting Talba's.

"Oho. You seem to have forgotten whom you're dealing with. Not 'miss.' 'Baroness.'"

"Baroness." The way she kept her eyes down made Talba distinctly uncomfortable.

Talba opened her purse and brought out the folder of newly printed photos. "I've got some pictures to show you."

At last, Millie raised her eyes, and they were formidable. "I need you to leave my shop, please."

"Hey, I thought we were friends."

"I'm ordering you to leave."

"I thought you were Rhonda's friend. I thought you wanted to get the creep who killed her."

For answer, Millie picked up the phone, dialed information, and said, "The number for the Eighth District, please."

Probably just for effect, Talba thought. Nobody

wanted police in their shop. But she was making her point, loud and clear.

"Okay, I'm out of here. Call me if you need me." She scribbled Eddie's office number on a piece of Millie's gift wrap, and made a mental note to ask Eileen to get her some business cards.

She breathed deeply as she walked back to her car, trying to regain her composure. She was more shaken than she wanted to admit. *Toes got to Millie,* she thought, and the thought wasn't pretty.

Whether he did it with money or threats, he'd realized it had to be done, and done it fast. He was covering his tracks well. Talba was afraid for Shaneel and Cassandra. Close to panicked, in fact.

Fingers shaking, she dialed Aziza on her cell phone. "I need to talk to Cassandra right away. Can you call the school and fix it?"

"For heaven's sake, Ms. Wallis. What on earth is it?" She was irritated, a woman accustomed to full reports, not cryptic requests.

"I may have an I.D. on the perp."

"What? Who is he?"

"I don't have a name yet. Just a picture."

Aziza sighed. "Okay, show her. Where are you?"

"Just leaving the French Quarter."

"I don't think you have time to get to her school. Today's choir practice. She takes the bus to the church—why don't you head there?"

"Okay." She took down directions so precise it was like talking to a cartographer.

By the time she got there, choir practice had started. Her mission was certainly urgent enough to interrupt, but Talba didn't, at first, preferring to listen for a few minutes to the voices, male and female, young and old, blended in the pure joy of singing. Shaneel was there too, openly having the time of her life, and Cassandra, while not exactly abeam with delight, seemed at peace. Maybe she wasn't enjoying herself, maybe she wasn't even able to, but Talba could see she was finding something in herself most people didn't have. Whatever it was, it was getting her through, and God knew she needed it. *Or Goddess knew,* Talba thought. *The girl needs a mother.*

Listening to the choir, watching the girls, she was catching on to why they did it when they didn't seem even slightly religious. They had a beautiful gift, something special, something outside the mundane. She was happy for them. It was the thing she told kids to look for in themselves when she went to high schools to talk about poetry. Not many of them had a clue what the hell she was talking about.

Where's Pam? she wondered, scanning the choir for the little redhead. Since almost everyone was black, she'd have stuck out like a snowball. She wasn't there; still in mourning, perhaps.

Talba listened for twenty minutes, absolutely unable to bring herself to interrupt, and did so only when the choir stopped for a breather. She spoke with the leader, who called the girls down from the choir loft to mundane ground.

They were avoiding her eyes, sneaking glances at each other. "Hello, women," she said.

Shaneel couldn't help a smile; Cassandra couldn't manage one for the life of her.

"I've got some pictures for you." She gave them each a picture of the baron's brother, and one of the other man, the man she didn't know.

Cassandra said, "So?"

"Have you ever seen either of these guys?"

Cassandra shrugged, not even deigning to answer.

Slowly, as if she really hated to, Shaneel shook her head. "No'm," she said, finally. "No'm, I don't b'lieve so."

"I think one of them might be Toes."

Cassandra shrugged again, managing to pack so

much contempt into a simple shoulder gesture that Talba wondered if she might have a future in the theater.

This time Shaneel shook her head vehemently, apple cheeks shining in indignation. "No'm," she said. "Absolutely not." Talba looked at her quizzically, struck by a false note somewhere or other. "He don't look a thing like him. Neither one of 'em."

She was lying, and very poorly too. "Which one of them doesn't look like him?"

Cassandra said, "Neither one of them does," each word a dagger. The girl was so full of hostility Talba thought she might burst into flame.

"Girls. The man's dangerous. What's the deal here?"

"Thought we was women." Shaneel sounded disappointed.

"I think you're about to get demoted. If you're afraid of this guy, let's get him behind bars."

Cassandra was wearing overalls and a pink T-shirt. For once, she looked no older than her age. The little puffball atop her head gave her the look of a baby animal—fuzzy and vulnerable. She gave another of her mighty shrugs. "Who's afraid of him? He was just somebody to fuck."

"Young lady, you might shock your mother, but you can't shock me. At your age, I'd done more rebelling than you ever thought about doing."

"I'm supposed to care?" Cassandra could have been made out of caramel-colored stone. Shaneel looked panicked, as if she'd somehow been betrayed—whether by Cassandra or Talba herself, Talba couldn't tell.

"Shaneel, could you excuse us a minute, please?"

Tears started to glisten in the girl's eyes, but she turned back to rejoin the choir. Talba stopped her. "Can you wait a minute? Sit over there, will you?" She was embarrassed at having "young lady'd" the girls; it was the sort of thing she told herself she'd never say. She turned to Cassandra. "You remind me of somebody, you know that?"

Not even a shrug this time. Just a blank stare.

"It's me, honey. I used to hurt as bad as you do. I used to hate the world as much as you."

Nothing.

"It'll get better, I promise you."

The girl turned faintly interested eyes on her.

"Do you believe me? Fourteen's the worst age in the world, unless you count twelve. I swear to God it'll get better."

"No, it won't." There was still no expression on Cassandra's face. She might as well have been a doll. But her voice had a slight catch.

"I promise you."

The shrug was back, the contempt.

"You're smart to sing, you know that? It's the way to get through. Here's my phone number." Talba ripped out a deposit slip, imprinted with her home phone, something she hadn't been willing to do for Millie. "Call me if you need me. I mean that; I'm there for you." It was a lot like talking to one of the pews.

She called Shaneel over again. "Honey, you're not a very good liar."

"What you mean?"

"You know one of those men is Toes."

"You ain't no welfare lady—you Miz Scott's detective, ain't you?"

"Yes, and I'm pretty good, don't you think? I got past your principal."

She was amused. "Yeah. Yes'm. Guess you are."

"So which one is it?"

"Ma'am?"

"Which one's Toes?"

"I ain' know."

"Yes, you do."

"I was asleep that day—when Toes come by the house."

"You went to his house with him. You already told me that."

"I ain' remember."

This was going nowhere. Talba gave her a deposit slip, her "card" and left feeling like a failure. There was no doubt in her mind that Eddie would have opened up the girl like a calzone—gotten secrets flowing out of her like cheese-and-mushroom filling. She missed the man.

Maybe I should send him some flowers, she thought. *By way of apology.* But she dismissed the gesture as too theatrical.

If she got to thinking about Eddie, she was going to go into a funk. The thing to do was to keep moving, to do something constructive. She headed for the Bergeron house. Eddie hadn't lifted his embargo on the dead woman's family, but she felt a decent amount of time had gone by. And getting to Pamela was absolutely crucial.

The woman who came to the door was thin and drawn, no one Talba remembered from the funeral. Her hair and lipstick were too dark for her skin, making her look older than she probably was. She had on neat polyester slacks in a charcoal color, and a tailored print blouse. She was dressed for doing errands, perhaps, or receiving visitors. Talba remembered that Shaneel had said the three girls hung together partly because their mothers worked. This woman must still be on bereavement leave, still trying to accept the finality of her daughter's death.

She had deep lines between her eyes, a perfect eleven, and the forehead above them was furrowed as well, contorted so heavily Talba was reminded of a shar-pei. Her eyes were frightened, darting behind and around her visitor. It made Talba uneasy.

"Mrs. Bergeron?"

"Yes?" The woman wasn't openly hostile, but she was on the verge.

"I'm a friend of Aziza Scott. Cassandra's mother."

"Cassandra?" Her brow curled further in on itself; her eyes became wilder still.

"Pamela's friend from choir practice."

"Pammie never mentioned a Cassandra."

Talba was at a loss. Aziza had said she phoned and talked to the Bergerons; Talba was sure of it. And that Cassandra had phoned, but couldn't get through to Pamela. *I couldn't have dreamed it,* she thought.

But it was clear that being Aziza's friend wasn't going to cut any ice. "Look. I'm a detective . . ."

Mrs. Bergeron didn't wait to hear any more. "Lloyd! Lloyd come here!"

Almost instantly, a man appeared, his arm encircling his wife's waist as he stepped up behind her. He was quite a bit taller than she was, and he carried a pillow of fat at his center. He wore a short-sleeved white shirt that fit him in such a way that it emphasized both his spare tire and his sloping shoulders. It was an odd shape for a man of his size; perhaps he had never done manual work or exercised.

He was almost bald, but still had a few strands of light brown hair between the two side tufts, worn too long, so they were limp and lifeless. He wore a pair of thickish glasses with thin-rimmed frames, and his face had a vague, confused look.

"Lloyd, this woman says she's a detective."

The man held out his hand, as if entreating a child to give back the butcher knife. "Lemme see ya badge."

"I'm not a police officer. I'm a private detective, and I'm extremely concerned about your daughter. Let me show you some I.D." She started to reach into her purse, but the man grabbed her forearm. She raised her chin, alarmed. Behind the glasses, Bergeron's eyes flamed.

What the hell was going on here? She was starting to panic.

She spoke softly. "Okay, now. Okay. Everything's all right."

She started to step back, but Bergeron pulled her into the house, slammed the door, and slung her across the foyer. She crashed into a wall and tried to come back to her height with dignity, suddenly remembering the sensation of playing statues as a kid. The door was closed, and Bergeron had his back to it, blocking her from leaving. His wife stood at his side, forehead still furrowed. Talba's heart thundered. *What the hell* is *this?* She hoped she hadn't spoken aloud.

Bergeron spoke in a controlled, menacing voice. "Now you get on the phone and you get her back over here." His arms were folded over his chest and his feet were about a foot apart. He sounded like a poor man's Clint Eastwood.

How in hell to defuse this? Talba found she wanted nothing so much as to curl up and have a nap. She knew the impulse well. Miz Clara had been sick once when she was a child—confined to the hospital—and Talba and Corey had gone to stay with Aunt Carrie. Talba had spent the whole time under her cousin's bed sucking her thumb. When she came back to herself, the grown-ups talked about her "coming out of her shell." It happened to her again the first time a boyfriend broke up with her, yet again the time she saw someone struck by a car. By that time, she had a name for it—the turtle response, she called it. It was her invariable reaction to stress, and she was never more aware that it could hardly be less appropriate.

Struggling to lift the veil of lethargy that was settling over her, she ran her mouth, blurting just to keep herself animate. "You mean Pamela?" she said. "Get Pamela over here?"

"You heard me. Do it. Marilyn, bring her the phone."

Mrs. Bergeron left, and Talba kept talking. "Mr. Bergeron, I'm really sorry about what happened to Rhonda. I'd like to help you, but I need you to . . ."

He spit on her. "Don't you mention my daughter's name."

Talba was still trying to assimilate the fact that she was standing there with saliva on her face when Bergeron spoke again. "Nigger."

Talba jumped back and hit the wall again, revolted beyond anything she'd ever experienced, though whether at Bergeron or his saliva she couldn't have said. It was pretty much a toss-up.

Her anger was starting to come up, which, in this circumstance, might be more dangerous than the turtle response. The man was a racist who'd probably see anything she said as an excuse to hit her. She had to keep calm. "Mr. Bergeron, let me leave, please."

"You ain't goin' nowhere."

Even in her fear, Talba almost laughed. The man had seen too many movies. She said, "I need to go now, please."

Marilyn Bergeron returned with a cordless phone. He took it. "Force your way in here, like that . . . I'm gon' call the police on ya."

Talba could feel her shoulders lower an inch or two. *Call them! Tell them I'm the reincarnation of Bonnie Barrow. Say I shot down Amelia Earhart and killed Jimmy Hoffa. Just call them, please.* Eddie would kill her, but it was better than being killed by Lloyd Bergeron.

"Give me that phone, Marilyn." He grabbed it out of her hand and turned back to Talba. "I'm callin' the police."

His wife said, "Lloyd, for God's sake."

But he focused on Talba. "What you think if I called the police?" Talba was quiet. "Huh, nigger? What you think?" He kicked her, barking her shin, but once more she didn't respond. "Answer me!"

"Do what you have to do, Mr. Bergeron."

It was the wrong answer. He threw the phone across the room and looked straight at her, yelling so loud she thought the windows would break. "That was my daughter in her coffin the other day!"

Something had happened to him, something Talba had never seen before. Before her eyes, he'd grown a good three feet, and his eyes had somehow assumed the size of personal pizzas, red and flaming behind the glasses, which only served to magnify them. His breath was a dragon's and his voice a hammer, pounding at her. "That was my daughter! That was *my daughter!*"

He took a step toward her. "What the fuck do you mean comin' in my house like this?"

Talba turned and ran, flat-out pounded through the house hoping to hell she'd get to a door. There was a long hall, and then, blessedly, a kitchen, and—yes!—a back door.

Bergeron was following. She shrieked, "You're scaring the shit out of me!" and it was true, but she realized later he wasn't exactly trying to catch her. In fact, if he had a purpose at all, it was probably scaring the shit out of her, but more likely he'd just lost it. And no telling where it was going to lead, once started.

The door had a button lock on it, which slowed her down not at all. She was out in a trice, and down the three steps to the side of the house. Outside, she felt secure enough to slow down a bit—she could be heard if she yelled for help, though actually, she'd prefer a quiet to a noisy exit.

However, no such luck. Bergeron stood on the stoop and hollered after her, continuing till she was out of earshot and for all she knew, long after. "This is *my* house. *My* fuckin' daughter! Who do you think you are?"

She was in her car with the door locked before

she understood just how unnerved she was. She was clammy all over, heart racing, limbs weak. Her hands were shaking badly.

Adrenaline, she thought. *It's the fight-or-flight response. Guess I'm a flyer.*

She felt badly disoriented—figured it must be part of the same thing.

She breathed from her belly until she felt calm enough to turn on the ignition, and, as she drove back, worked on what she was going to tell Eddie. That wasn't too hard: everything, probably. She'd just have to hope he wouldn't be too sarcastic.

That is, if she was still working for him, and if he ever spoke to her again. In either case, she still had to tell him she'd called on the Bergerons, because she'd learned one important fact—Pamela was missing.

She called the office but got no answer. Eileen must not have gotten brave enough to reenter. Talba didn't see why she should be the first.

What do I need? she thought. *What do I need to get back to normal?*

Coffee and water, came the answer. *One to drink, the other to look at.*

She was starting to feel drowsy, maybe the crash from her adrenaline high; the coffee ought to help with that. She stopped and got some at a place on Veteran's Highway and made her way out to the lake, where she parked and got out to drink it. She tried to clear her mind of the case, of her fear, of her shame at her fear, of the memory of being spat upon and bullied. She tried just to breathe and drink and look at the lake. She didn't succeed, or even come close to it. But by the time she got to the bottom of the cup, she knew she'd gotten far enough away to address it again.

Chapter Thirteen

She had a little spying to do.

She drove over to Aziza's and knocked boldly on the door. No answer.

She knocked again, making it as scary a police knock as her small knuckles would allow.

Still no answer, so she did it again.

Maybe nobody was in there, but she was working off a lot of her aggressions. Just when she was about to go sneaking around peeping in windows, she heard steps coming toward her, small uncertain ones. Only then did she realize she'd probably terrified the very kid she was trying to help.

"Cassandra? You in there, baby? It's Talba Wallis."

The girl flung open the door. She looked pale, her face drawn as if she was about to cry. "I didn't know who you were." Her voice was panicked. Poor kid was home alone. She should have considered that possibility.

"Listen, I'm really sorry. I didn't mean to scare

you. I just thought you couldn't hear me knocking."

A voice called out from somewhere in the house: "Cassandra? Who is it, baby?"

Aziza. She *was* home.

The girl turned and shouted, "That detective." She made it sound like "that whoremongering child-beater."

"I'll be there in a minute."

Hell with that, Talba thought. "Can I come in?" she said.

Cassandra shrugged as if she couldn't waste words on so pathetic a being as Talba. But she stepped resentfully aside.

The girl led her through the same chaos Aziza had a few days before, to the same snug back room. Talba could hear the low drone of Aziza's voice on the telephone.

"Cassandra, listen," she said. "If I asked you something, would you tell me the truth?"

The girl laughed. It came out a short, nervous bray, perhaps meant to convey contempt.

"I get it," Talba said. "Depends on the question, right? Okay, how about this one—can I have a drink of water?"

Cassandra was openly contemptuous now. That and puzzled. "Can you have a drink of water? That's what you want to ask me?"

"Well, the first thing."

The girl heaved her shoulders yet again, shrugging being a mode of expression she obviously preferred to speaking in the affirmative. She padded off to get the water.

Quickly, Talba looked for a place for one of her bugs, but Aziza buzzed in before she had a chance to plant it.

Damn! The tiny things were so useful!

The mother was as cheerful as the daughter was sullen.

"Hi, Talba. How'd you enjoy choir practice? They're good, aren't they?"

The question took Talba aback. Choir practice seemed weeks instead of hours ago.

"Yes . . . they're quite good." She was trying to collect her wits, having lived several lifetimes, or so it seemed, since then.

"I just got home." Aziza had changed clothes, though—she was wearing shorts. And she'd had an extended phone conversation. "Cassandra said you didn't have anything."

"I showed the girls two pictures. They said they didn't know the guys."

Aziza sat down opposite Talba, kicking off a sandal. She curled her legs under her. "I didn't get the details. The phone rang."

Cassandra returned with the water and gave it to Talba. Talba passed the pictures on to Aziza. "These are the photos."

"Oh, my God. It couldn't have been one of these guys. Could it?" She looked at her daughter.

Cassandra gave the teenager's "no," the one that comes out like a whiny screech.

"You're sure?" She gave the girl a level look, not even halfway stern. The woman wasn't scary enough to frighten a moth—Miz Clara could give her Mom lessons. Even Talba could.

"Oh, Mom!" Another screech.

Aziza lifted a what-can-you-do eyebrow, and said, "She says she's sure."

"One of them's a friend of someone who's extremely powerful in this town. The other's his brother."

"Can I go, please? I've got homework." Everything the girl said had a whiny edge to it. Maybe she was always that way, but Talba thought she was under a lot of pressure. She spoke before Aziza could. "I'd like you to stay a minute."

Cassandra sat down hard on a sofa, a little black cloud that plopped rather than floated.

"What man?" Aziza said. "What powerful man? These guys look like gangsters."

"Baron Tujague."

Aziza said, "Who?"

Cassandra said nothing. Talba watched her face. Absolutely inscrutable.

Okay. That proves it. "You know who he is, don't you, Cassandra?"

"Of course."

"You don't seem surprised that these guys are close to him."

Aziza said, "Will someone please tell me who Baron Tujague is? A drug dealer or something? I know very few African-American barons."

Cassandra's silence was so deafening she almost had to hold her ears. Finally, Talba answered herself. "He's a rapper."

The girl said, "Can I go now?" and Aziza nodded, not even looking at her.

"I think I know who you mean," she said. "The guy who owns the record company?"

"The same. I think his brother's called Toes."

"But Cassandra says no."

"Aziza, tell me something. What teenage girl wouldn't react if you showed her pictures of anyone—not even someone she'd had sex with, anyone at all—and said he was the brother of a big-deal rapper? None. Not one—unless she was hiding something."

Aziza considered it. "I don't know. Rap's not Cassandra's thing."

"Oh? What kind of music does she like?"

"She likes . . . well, she . . ." Aziza stopped cold, clearly at a loss. "She sings in a choir, for Christ's sake!"

"Does she have a Walkman?"

"Of course she has a Walkman. She's a kid. What does that have to do with it?" She was getting testy.

"She may be playing music you aren't aware of." Talba felt stupid, stating the obvious so wimpily, but this woman had a lot of hard truth to wake up to. She had a set of nasty blows to deliver—she might as well start out with a love tap.

As casually as she could, she said, "Did you know Pamela Bergeron's missing?"

"Cassandra didn't mention that."

"She may not know."

"How do *you* know?"

"I went to show Pam the pictures. Her parents told me." (That was close enough to the truth.)

"Look, if Cassandra and Shaneel say you don't have the guy, you probably don't."

Here was a woman, Talba thought, who'd go through near-boggling mental acrobatics to avoid looking at the truth.

She felt utterly out of her depth, feeling as she did that Cassandra was in grave danger, yet not wanting to drive Aziza farther into her shell of denial.

This was a job for Eddie. She realized it suddenly and certainly. There was no way in hell she was going to get through to this woman, but Eddie might be able to.

She said, "Back to Pam a second. Is she here, by any chance?"

"Here?"

"Staying with you."

"No, of course not. Don't you think I'd have told you?"

"Could Cassandra be concealing her?"

"Are you kidding? The way she keeps her room you couldn't get a kitten in there, much less another kid." She raised her voice. "Cassandra! Come out here a minute, please."

The girl appeared with her Walkman still in place. With a show of huge inconvenience, she removed the headset. "What?"

"Cassandra, is anyone visiting?"

"What? You *know* no one's visiting."

"Tell me the truth. Is Pamela Bergeron here?"

Wonderment appeared on Cassandra's face, so far her only expression besides clamped shut and angry. "Pam? Are you kidding? She wasn't even at choir practice."

"Okay, you can go."

The girl hesitated. "Why? Why do you want to know?"

Talba said, "Her parents are worried about her."

Disdain appeared briefly on the teenage features, and then Cassandra showed them her cute little backside switching down the hall. If it involved parents, it had all her contempt.

"Ms. Scott," Talba said, "I think you've got a bigger problem than you think you have. I'm going to have Eddie call you."

"What are you talking about?"

"You may have a dangerous situation here."

Anger flickered on Aziza's face. It was quickly replaced by suspicion, and then a certain wiliness, the sort that could outsmart itself. "Oh, I get it. Oh, yes, it's all coming clear. Don't tell me: you and Eddie probably want to recommend a bodyguard. And your firm just happens to supply them. That's it, isn't it? We came to you in good faith, and you're trying to scam us."

There was no doubt in Talba's mind she really did believe it.

Oh my God, I've blown this so completely. I'm not cut out for this shit. If that kid gets killed, it's my fault.

She felt so miserable she wasn't even angry at the insult. She said what she always said when things were so badly out of control she felt she was about to hit a tree at high speed: "I think we'd better talk about it later."

And for the second time that day, she got yelled at: "What kind of fool do you think I am?" Aziza just took the one shot and left it at that. Considering the kind of day Talba'd had, it seemed the mildest of attacks.

When she was in the car, she thought, *That's three times if you count Eddie. I wonder what my horoscope for today is.*

The unaccustomed experience of tears left Eddie feeling punchy and bewildered. What in all hell had that been about?

Anthony. It was about Anthony.

I miss him, he thought. *Well what the hell, he's my son. Sure I miss him—but why would I cry about that?*

Because of the way he is and what he did.

He was getting up a little outrage, and that felt better. He was stronger, surer, the minute the grudge started to gather. This was familiar territory, the place he needed to be.

Goddammit, the kid never . . . Anthony always . . . His mind was blank. It was huge what Anthony had done. Unforgivable. He'd left home without Eddie's permission, refused to finish school, sashayed off . . . and then he'd . . . Eddie didn't want to think about it.

The phone rang. He ignored it.

Goddam that Talba. Where in hell did she get off? How *dare* she? He found it absolutely incomprehensible that one human being could invade another's privacy like that.

Would I do that to her? he thought. *How the hell could she?*

Dad, for Christ's sake, you're a private eye. It was Angela's voice, implanted somehow in his brain. *You do shittier stuff on a daily basis.*

He really wished his daughter would clean up her language. Also, get out of his head.

He picked up the phone and listened to his voice mail—Angie again. In his head and out of it. "Dad, I got the weirdest phone call. Where's Eileen? What's going on over there?"

He went to find some aspirin. He had some kind of tired, naggy headache, but nothing like one of those big babies that kept him out of work. Surprising, he thought. His eyes hurt from the tears, that was about all.

He choked down the aspirin, washed his face, looked in the mirror, and thought, *I want to see him. I really want to see him.*

It was a big fat mistake. A horrible sound came out of him, and then more tears. Damn. He hoped nobody came in before he could get this thing under control. But what in hell to do about it? Every time he turned around, it ambushed him.

Lots of things ambushed him. Things Anthony had said to him wouldn't let up, kept cycling round and round his brain, leading nowhere.

Dad, I've been thinking about you a lot. I mean, with your birthday coming up and all.

This was the son who had defied him, left home at sixteen, quit school. Quit school when Eddie himself had had to work two jobs just to finish high school, and never had gone to college. Mr. Big Shot Spoiled Brat Anthony just thought he could up and do anything he wanted.

"I just wanted to pursue happiness in my own way," he'd said. *"I don't understand why the people I love most want me out of their lives."*

"Because you're a bum, Anthony," was what Eddie wanted to say. "Because you don't care about us. Why the hell should we care about you?" But something prevented him, something in his son's voice, some remembered note, a remnant from the boy's childhood that brought back his feelings for his son before it all went sour.

He had loved that kid. Loved him more than Angie, and that was the truth. He saw bits of himself in Anthony, little inklings of an innocence he couldn't remember having, but must have had—a purity of heart that might once have been his, that maybe he could recapture. Intelligence as well. Lots of it. More than he had ever had, he was damned sure of that. Of course Angie had it too, but Angie was a girl; she intimidated him. She was foreign. Anthony was familiar. Like Eddie himself, only better.

Could have been better. Should have been better.

What the hell was he thinking? He had no idea what Anthony was. For all he knew, his son was now the junior senator from Idaho.

What was "better," anyhow? Some part of his brain was asking a question: Does it mean *doing* better? Or something else?

I don't understand how all these years have gone by and now you're almost sixty-five. I got this e-mail today from a girl who works for you and I thought I might not see you again, or Mom or Angie either.

When Eddie heard those words, something exploded within him. He felt it start in his stomach and shoot up to his skull. It was pear-shaped and purple and when it popped open it was spiky inside, like the inside of a fig. It was fury.

He honestly believed he would have killed Talba Wallis if she'd been near enough at the time. He wanted to smack her across the room and stomp her.

It wasn't an urge he'd ever had before. It scared the hell out of him.

Goddam you, he had shouted, and hung up the phone.

Now these tears.

And the headaches, Audrey had said. The headaches were about Anthony.

Oh, Audrey. Audrey, what have I done to you?

The shame of it, of her going to a shrink, going on his account, because of what he was putting her through—that was more than he could take. It sat on him like a boulder.

He closed his eyes. He was lying on the sofa in the reception room with all the lights out, and now he just wanted to rest.

His brain kept cycling, round and round and round, endlessly, endlessly, and then it stopped.

He slept.

He dreamed he was in a courtroom, and Talba Wallis was the judge. She stood before him like a crow in her black skin and black robe, and then he was led to the guillotine. He wanted to tip the executioner, having read that it was the done thing, but the man turned away from him, muttering.

No words were spoken in the dream, but in the clarity of the dreamscape he understood his crime.

It was doing the unforgivable.

He awakened moaning, trying to call for help, to be heard, and tried to remember what it was that he had done in the dream. *What* was unforgivable?

He knew.

It was something so contemptible, so petty and mean, so wrong and immoral, so childish and stupid and arrogant and utterly vile he couldn't even think about it. It couldn't have been he who had done it, it was impossible. The best thing was just to bury it, never to name it in his mind again, never to put words to it, never to let it into his consciousness.

But now there was this thing with Audrey and the shrink. That was right in his face, and it was his doing. That he had to own up to. And if he did that . . .

If he did that, the whole house of cards came down.

Let it, he thought. *Goddammit, let it.*

His son had left a phone number on his voice mail—he didn't know if he had the balls to dial it.

Chapter Fourteen

Ms. Wallis came creeping in like an old cat in a yard full of new smells, unsure what might leap out of the dark.

"Eddie? You in here?"

"Waiting for you. Audrey called." She had called the house thinking he'd be there—as he would have any other time. But tonight he wasn't ready yet. What had happened to him was far too intimate to talk to Audrey about.

"Come on in, Ms. Wallis. I'm not gonna bite you. Hell froze over."

"Eddie, let me just say . . ."

He stopped her with a slap at the air. "Ya know what we guineas say? Fuggeddaboutit." He took a sip of the scotch and water on his desk. "I learned that in a mob movie. What's ya pleasure, Ms. Wallis?"

"Nothing, thanks."

"Ya better have one, or we won't communicate. I'm way ahead a ya."

She seemed to relax a little. "You have any white wine?"

"Are you kidding? Detectives don't drink white wine. It ain't macho." When he was drinking, he couldn't be bothered watching his grammar.

"This one does."

"Oh, all right. I'll get ya some." There was a little refrigerator in the copy room that now served as her office.

"I'll get it."

While she was gone, he had a little more of his own drink. He had a real nice buzz, and he wanted to keep it going. She came back with the glass in one hand, the bottle in the other. "I ran into some problems, Eddie. It's nice you've forgiven me, but . . ."

"I didn't say I forgive ya."

"Well, anyway, we're talking. We might not be after I tell you what's going on."

"Damn, Ms. Wallis. Can't it wait? I talked to my son tonight for the first time in ten years."

She forced a smile. "I'm happy for you, Eddie."

He could see that she was, or rather he somehow felt that she was, because of a certain softness that had crept into her voice and the set of her shoulders. But she was so tense she could barely bring herself even to utter the social niceties.

He went into his tough-guy routine. "Yeah, so, we'll get to that. What's on ya mind? You were gon' talk to the hat-shop lady, weren't ya?"

"Omigod. Is that where we left off? That was about three lifetimes ago."

He found himself getting irritated. "You been doin' stuff I told ya not to?"

She was gulping her wine. "Yeah. Oh, yeah. I think I really blew it too."

"Oh, shit, is anybody hurt? Excuse my French."

"Maybe. But that part isn't my fault. What *might* happen is."

He held up his glass and saluted her. "Good thing I'm drinking this stuff."

She tapped his glass with hers. "Me too." She giggled.

"That's it. Ya gotta keep smiling."

"The good news is, I'm pretty sure I know who the guy is who had sex with Cassandra. The bad news is, I'm afraid she's in danger."

He snorted. "Danger's a way of life with that kid. Mama like that, she'll be lucky to get through high school."

"Shall I start at the beginning?" She looked as if she were trying to get her breath.

Eddie nodded. "Take ya time."

"Millie the Milliner told me Rhonda used to date a black guy. And guess what his name was?"

"I don't know. How'm I s'posed to know?"

"Toes."

"Well, great. Toes who? Mystery solved. Older sister's beau seduces kid sister's kid friend. Toe jam, like I said."

"Toes Who is the question, all right. I found out he's a friend of Baron Tujague."

It took Eddie a second to place the name. "The rapper?"

"Uh-huh."

"Damn." That struck him as not a good thing—too much power and ruthlessness on the loose.

"So I did a little investigating . . ."

"Wait a minute. Not so fast. What exactly did ya do?"

"I went to work as a temp for Tujague."

"You what?" He really couldn't help laughing. She had more balls than Spalding. "Little lady, you got *cojones*."

"I'm not little, and I'm not a lady."

"You right about that—if that trash mouth of yours is any indication."

To his surprise she let that one go by, even though it was practically an invitation for a "fuck you." "To make a long story short, I met him, I met his brother and some of his friends, I followed them, and I figured out Toes is probably the brother."

Eddie was starting to grasp the seriousness of the thing. "Whew. Heavy-duty."

"Yeah."

A light sweat had broken out on his upper lip, an instinctive sign he sometimes got about trouble.

"So I took some pictures and showed them to the girls—Cassandra and Shaneel."

He leaned back in his chair and rocked. "Good," he said. "Good." She was brash, but she knew how to get the goods. Actually, he was kind of proud of her.

"They denied knowing either of the guys I showed them. So I thought, okay, I know someone who knows the guy for sure—Millie the Milliner."

Eddie approved. He actually approved. It must be the scotch.

"Well, that's when the fun began. She tossed me out of the shop."

He might have known. "What'd ya do to her?"

"Nothing. I swear to God I didn't even say anything."

"Come on, Ms. Wallis. What'd ya do?"

"Just walked in. And she said she'd talked to her lawyer."

"Lawyer? Well, what'd ya do the first time?"

"Eddie, you've got to trust me. I probably did make some wrong moves, but not with Millie. What I think is, somebody got to her."

"Paid her off, ya mean?"

"Or threatened her. Could have been that."

He thought about it. "Yeah, you right. Could have been that."

She hunched up her shoulders, as if to ward off an attack. "So I had no choice but to try Pamela. I know you told me not to, but—"

"No. At that point ya had to." Only, he should have done it himself, Eddie thought. But he'd been out of commission, covering up a ten-year-old sin.

Talba put her hand on her chest and exhaled. "I thought you were going to kill me."

"Give me time. I might still."

"Well, her parents were abusive from the start. They're obvious racists—"

"I don't want to hear that. I will not tolerate calling people names as a result of your failure to get along with them."

"Eddie, you hired me. Would you just try to trust me? They're the ones calling names. The father called me the 'n' word."

Eddie realized she was right. She was brash, but she was showing pretty good judgment on most things. He really should try to trust her. He was embarrassed, both by the conclusions he'd been drawing and by Bergeron's use of the epithet. Unfairness always embarrassed him. "You right, Ms. Wallis. You right. I ought to trust ya. And I'm real sorry ya had to go through that. But would ya mind telling me what set it off?"

"I reached for my license and he grabbed my arm and pulled me in the door—I think he thought I had a gun."

"Why would he think that? Ya think he's just paranoid?"

"He might be; he sure acted crazy. And one thing I'm sure of—he's really distraught about his daughter dying. It might just be that. But I think he's got a reason."

Eddie said, "Now why would that be?"

"When he had me inside, he said—wait a minute . . ." She set down her wineglass and prowled around in her purse until she found a tiny notebook. "I wrote this down later; I thought it might be important. He said, 'now you get on the phone and you get her back over here.' "

Eddie's sweat-alarm had spread from his lip to his pits. "They've got Pamela."

"Yeah. And I guess he thought I'm one of them. Because I'm black."

He saw she was right. They would think that because they wanted to; their imaginations, in their panic and disorientation, would tell them that any black person must be at fault for the disappearance of one daughter and the death of another; and therefore that any black person could deliver Pamela back to them.

They must be out of their minds with fear. Eddie thought briefly about Angela, his own daughter dead or missing, but let it go quickly; you didn't think about the unthinkable.

"Bergeron kicked me, by the way."

"Ya want to press charges? Ya could, ya know."

"Nah. Goes with the job."

He could tell she was trying to impress him. *Well, hell,* he thought. *She's succeeding.*

"It did occur to me Pamela was hiding out at Cassandra's, so I went out to her house to check, and she wasn't. But I did lay it out pretty thoroughly for Aziza—Rhonda dead, Pamela missing, people who might think they're God in it up to their eyeballs."

"How'd she react?"

"Like always. Utter and complete denial. She says if Cassandra says Toes isn't one of the guys in the pictures I showed her, then he isn't." She shrugged. "And he might not be. I honestly don't know if Toes is the brother, or a friend I wasn't able to photograph."

Eddie reached for the telephone. "Well, hell, Ms. Wallis, it's time to get the police in on this. They can just walk up to Tujague and ask him. If he don't want to answer, they can sweat him."

"I thought of that."

"Ya thought of that? Well, did ya call 'em? What's the point of thinking about it if ya didn't call 'em?"

"I called them several times."

He was getting pissed off—she thought of every damn thing. "And?"

"And they didn't call me back."

"Oh. Well. Ya have to call somebody ya know."

"I did. I called Skip Langdon. By the way, she says she knows you."

"Skip Langdon didn't call ya back?" He had a hard time believing that one.

"She did, but the Juvenile officer didn't. The one on Cassandra's case."

"What's his name?"

"Her name's Detective Corn." She emphasized the "her" ever so slightly, and perhaps a bit triumphantly. Eddie recognized it as the sort of thing that usually irritated him, but he was getting used to Ms. Wallis. And he was pretty mellow from the scotch. And beyond either of those things, he wanted his assistant to have dinner with him. He wasn't ready to go home yet, and he wanted to practice talking about his son, try out saying his name a few times, before he did.

"Well, I'll call her," he said. He did, and he also called a buddy of his, exactly as Talba had, and left messages for both of them.

He was about to ask her to come grab a bite when he noticed she was staring intently at him. "Eddie?" she said. "How bad did I screw up?"

He thought about it. "I don't know that you screwed up at all. Sounds like you might have done a pretty good job, all things considered."

He was deeply ashamed that it had fallen to her to work the case by herself. "Come on. Let me treat you to dinner. Ya like the Bon Ton?"

"I just keep thinking about Cassandra. Eddie, tell me something. Did you ever lose a client?"

Talba was way too tired and discouraged to eat, but if ever there was a business dinner, this was it. She couldn't imagine what Eddie was going to tell her—everything he knew, she hoped ("Secrets of a Hard-Boiled Dick—Revealed At Last")—but if he was going to impart knowledge, she was going to be there to receive it.

Of course, maybe it wasn't that. Maybe he was just trying to cheer her up for screwing up so badly.

She'd never actually been to the Bon Ton, though the minute she saw it, she knew it was Eddie all over. These days downtown was full of fancy new places— the Metro Bistro would have been more Talba's style—but the Bon Ton was the exception. It was all checked tablecloths and crawfish bisque—an old-line Creole joint famous for its bread pudding with bourbon sauce.

It was a comfort food kind of place, a restaurant for rainy winter days, not a see-and-be-seen, crawfish-eggroll-with-caviar kind of place. She and Eddie both ordered the shrimp étouffée. "I think I've had enough scotch" he said, and ordered a bottle of wine to share, though Talba didn't think she'd drink much, especially if there were things to be learned, wisdom bytes to be stored.

It was a good bottle, too. Eddie tasted with relish. He might talk like something out of an old movie, but he'd been around, and not just on the mean streets. She said, "You know a lot about wine."

He gave her a raised eyebrow. "How do you know? I just ordered one bottle."

Her cheeks heated up in embarrassment. She raised her glass. "Well, so far, so good."

"Ya stereotyped me, didn't ya? Ya think just because I'm a wop, I gotta be ignorant."

"I didn't. I . . ."

"Client cultivation, Ms. Wallis."

"I beg your pardon?"

"That's why I learned about wine. Had this old guy, rich as Croesus, used to hire me every couple of months to follow his wife. She never was up to anything, but he was." Holding a wineglass, he really looked quite sophisticated. "See, he used to come over from Houston to see this lady, but she worked as a secretary or something, so he had nothing to do in the daytime. He liked to go to this one place for lunch, so I'd go with him. Usually turned into an all-day thing, and over the course of it, my favorite waiter'd teach me a little and then a little more about what wines to order."

"An all-day thing sounds like Galatoire's."

"Ahhh. That was the punch line. I was savin' it. This guy—the client—called it Galatorey's; always, no matter how many times he heard it right."

"You kidding? *Galatorey's?*"

"Swear to God."

And all of a sudden, they were laughing, the two of them; belly laughing, carrying on far out of proportion to a simple mispronunciation. It was a great tension release.

Something was wrong with the story, though. "I don't get it," Talba said. "The guy was from Houston? You had to go there to spy on his wife?"

"Noooo. No way. She lived Uptown. They'd been separated for years."

"Worse and worse. Let me try again—they were separated, but he came here to see his mistress and while he was here, he used the time productively to get the goods on his wife."

Eddie shrugged. "Guess he was tired of supporting her. She later turned up dead—accidental overdose."

"Woo. You believe that?

"Could have been. She liked her booze and pills."

"But did you do anything about it?"

"Sure. Told the cops. What else could I do—solve the case myself? Ya think I'm Sherlock Holmes or somethin'?"

She had to smile. "More like Mike Hammer."

"Who's that?"

"He's not real, either."

Their étouffeé came, and Eddie tore into his with a gusto she was glad to see. Though he didn't show the least sign of being drunk—except, perhaps, for an unaccustomed affability—she definitely didn't want to end up driving him home.

And yet, when she really thought about it, it wasn't that. She just didn't want to see him drunk.

"Lady, ya want to know who I am? Want to know who I really am?"

"I'm not sure. I mean . . . I looked you up on the Internet. I know enough."

"No, ya don't. Ya really don't."

"Okay, who are you then?" Actually, she was curious.

"I'm a guy who always wanted to be a cop."

"Well? That makes sense. You were one."

"I never was. I was a deputy sheriff."

"I didn't know there was that big a difference."

"To me there was—real cops wear blue. And I was too short to be one. You got any idea how that affected my work? You're an amateur psychologist, aren't ya? Everybody is these days."

"You don't have to be too much of one to figure that one out. Especially since I've read a bunch of news stories on you. You overcompensated, I gather?"

He laughed again, though this laughter lacked the purity, the unadorned enjoyment of their mutual belly laugh. It was a bittersweet laugh, a laugh contaminated by regret. "You bet I did, Ms. Wallis. I'm 'on tell ya. I was the best damn Deputy Dog this state ever had."

"So I gathered from the clips."

"Give me a case, and I'd work it till it was raw. Somebody ended up behind bars or dead, always. Every damn time."

Talba hated this kind of talk. It was the kind of macho posturing that gave rednecks a bad name.

"Quit wincin', Ms. Wallis. Only one of 'em ended up dead. Thirteen years on the job, and I only drew my gun once."

"What happened?"

He held up his glass as if about to give a toast. "Ah, that's for another day. Tell me about, you, Ms. Wallis. Tell me about you."

"Me?" She could hardly have been more taken aback. "Well, I haven't lived very long, so there's not a whole lot to talk about."

"In that case, where you get off writin' poetry?"

"Well, I . . . I don't know. I think about things a lot." She was deeply embarrassed, hadn't dreamed he'd get personal with her.

"Tell me about ya dad."

"My dad?" This was going from awkward to nightmarish.

"Yeah, ya dad, remember? The one that took ya to the park and let ya ride the flyin' horses. You know, the guy whose lap felt safer than a real horse—is that part real, by the way—about the horse? Come on, where would ya keep a horse in New Orleans?"

It was a lifeline; something to grab on to. She conjured up a smile. "Poetic license. They fine you three thousand dollars without one."

"So ya didn't have a horse?"

"Pony ride at a fair once—does that count?"

"Well, ya dad musta been a pretty nice guy—sounds like ya loved him a lot. How'd you lose touch with him?"

Talba was feeling a little sick.

"I mean, ya said ya weren't sure ya even have a dad. I'm a detective, ya know. In case ya'd like me to find him."

She nodded, not meeting his eyes, unable to speak.

Evidently, he caught on that this wasn't her favorite subject. "Sorry to intrude, Ms. Wallis. I'm 'on tell ya somethin'—can I tell ya somethin'?"

Talba was trying hard to swallow. She'd taken a bite to distract herself and now discovered that her throat was closed.

She nodded and pointed at her cheek, as if she had way too much in her mouth, and had to chew for a while.

"I been thinkin' about Anthony ever since I heard ya poem."

He must have seen her jump.

He patted the air. "No, now. I have. I gotta say I'm sorry for getting so mad at ya. I talked to my son today for the first time in ten years, it's like a milestone or somethin'. But all I did was, I just called up and said was he all right and I was doin' good and Angie graduated law school and his mama's fine, ya know? And then I didn't know what else to say so I got off the phone. I been drinkin' ever since—that and trying to figure things out."

What things, Talba wanted to ask, but she had enough sense to respect his privacy.

"So I was wonderin'—what do you know about him?"

"Me? What do *I* know about him?"

"Well, I mean—you found him. How'd ya do that?"

"Oh, I see. I did what I always do." She spread her plams in the what-else gesture. "Went on-line. He's got a web site. He's a musician, you know—or didn't you?"

Something happened on Eddie's face, something complex and regretful. It took a long time; he didn't bother hiding his emotions while he thought it through, but it wasn't something you could follow like a play. All Talba could really tell was that this had resonance for Eddie. When he finally let something win on his features, it was a pleased smile, but he could have been acting. "Is he now?" he said.

"He plays harmonica, and seems to do quite well for himself. Oh, and he's known professionally as Tony Tino."

"Catchy." Eddie put his wineglass down and poured himself some more. He'd quit drinking all through the étouffée, but as soon as the talk turned to his son, he started in again.

She kept talking—it seemed to be what he wanted. "He lives in Austin—did you know that?"

"Austin." He looked genuinely surprised. "That's close."

"Good place for blues—that's what he plays. The web site doesn't say if he's married or has kids."

Eddie looked away from her. "He's too young for that."

"How old is he?"

"Let me think about it. He must be . . . I guess he's twenty-six or seven."

"Well, it's not impossible."

But the next thing that happened was, Eddie's eyes misted over, a sight she'd never in a million years expected to see.

It was so pronounced, he actually dabbed at them. " 'Scuse me, Ms. Wallis—it's the wop in me."

"What is?"

"I was imagining what it might be like to have a grandbaby."

Grandbaby. That was the way her mama and her Aunt Carrie talked. Old people talked that way. Black people. Talba found something infinitely touching in the way it came out of Eddie's mouth.

He was recovered now, though having himself another little sip. "Does he—you know—tour? Is that what they call it?"

"It is, and he does. I know the jargon 'cause my boyfriend's a musician."

All of a sudden, he busted out in smiles. Old, sad, pathetic Eddie, who even seemed miserable about talking with his son, beamed out big-time. "Ya got a boyfriend, Ms. Wallis? Good for you."

She wished she hadn't turned the spotlight back on herself. She said, "Your son had a lot of really great reviews."

"Tell me somethin', Ms. Wallis—did he ever play New Orleans?"

She had known he would ask that question. "I'm not sure," she said. "I kind of don't think so."

But he would go to the web site himself, and know that she lied. Maybe he wouldn't mind. "You're really going to be proud of him, I think. Oh, by the way, did I mention he's a hunk?"

"Oh, yeah? Ya mean his picture's on there? I can't get used to this stuff."

"He looks a lot like Angie."

"Yeah. He always did." He stared off into space for a while, as if there were a very interesting fly on the wall of the restaurant, and once again, something sad came over him. Something about Angie. Talba wished she had the nerve to ask what it was. "Bread pudding and coffee?" he asked.

She looked at her watch. "No, I really should be—"

"Come on. Help an old man sober up."

In fact, she'd already thought of that. He needed a break from the alcohol before he got in his car. "Okay. Let's split the bread pudding, though."

He put in the order, and when he turned back to her, he had a new alertness about him. "Let's talk about the case a little more. You satisfied you've identified Toes?"

"No. I'm really not. But I don't think Cassandra's going to confirm any I.D., and everyone else who could is clammed up. I do think the kid needs protecting. Probably Shaneel too."

"Maybe that's who we need to lean on. She a nice kid?"

"A lot nicer than Cassandra."

"Mmm. Mmmm. Child with problems. I'm gon' try Shaneel myself. Who are her parents?"

"I, uh, haven't gotten that far—her last name's Johnson. But the church could probably help."

He leaned back and nodded. "Guess that's the way to go." Talba could hardly believe this was Eddie Valentino. She didn't know what to make of this new, mellow version.

Booze, she thought. *He'll be the usual old crank in the morning.*

She said, "What about Cassandra?"

"She'll be all right in school. Needs watchin', though. This thing's out of hand."

"I mentioned that to Aziza, and she accused me of trying to sell her bodyguard services."

"I better have a little talk with Ms. Scott. Meanwhile, you ever heard of a little thing called client reports?"

Well, hell, she thought. How dare he pull that on her after what she'd been through? "Eddie, that's not fair. I haven't had a second, and you know it."

"Relax, Ms. Wallis, relax. Don't go touchy on me

just when we're gettin' along so well. I'll do the damn report. Just need your notes, that's all."

"Okay. I'll give them to you first thing in the morning."

"Mmm. I don't think so. I want ya to stay home tomorrow morning. Did ya taste this bread pudding? Nectar of the gods."

She felt as if he'd hit her. "What are you talking about?"

"It's a late night, and you've had a hell of a day. Besides, you're kind of green around the gills—have been ever since I mentioned your father."

"Oh, come on, Eddie, I'm just tired."

"My point, Ms. Wallis, my point. Take the morning off and organize your notes. You can e-mail 'em and come in after lunch."

That was better. At least she wasn't fired. And a morning off would suit her fine. She might still be able to see Darryl tonight—in which case she'd be up late. "Okay, Eddie, sure. But, as you would say, can I ask you somethin'?"

"Ask me anything. I might not answer, is all."

"Are you ever going to call me Talba, or not?"

He didn't even hesitate. "Well, Ms. Wallis, I expect I will every now and then. If I'm real mad at you."

"That certainly bodes well."

"I'm 'on tell ya somethin'—I'm probably gon' say ya name pretty often."

Chapter Fifteen

His wife, having heard the car, was standing in the door when he came in, wearing a robe that zipped up the front, not meant to be sexy at all. But it couldn't hide who she was. She was skinny, always had been, but she had a good chest on her, and that beautiful heart-shaped face. She'd been a platinum blonde the whole time he'd known her, though they had two dark-haired children. She had hair that pouffed and bounced, hair that got a lot of attention. Even now, it looked as if she'd spent a while puffing it up nice.

"He called here, Eddie. I know what ya did."

"Anthony? Anthony called here?"

"I know what ya did, Eddie." She was like a sentry waiting for the countersign.

He didn't know what it was. He didn't think there was anything in the world he could say to entitle himself to admittance. "I was a fool, Audrey. I could kill myself."

"Ya shouldn't have put us through it, Eddie." She moved aside and he entered, but her voice was like a metal blade left out in the cold.

"Audrey, I been drinkin' . . ."

"Yeah. You been drinkin'. Ya couldn't face it. Ya couldn't face it now and ya couldn't face it then and ya body nearly couldn't take it, all that stress ya put on yaself. I was wrong about those headaches, wasn't I? It wasn't the reason I thought—it wasn't because ya missed Anthony. It was because ya told all those lies."

He didn't know about the headaches, but it occurred to him his heart was going to be the next to go, and pretty soon, if this kept up. He felt as if he were splitting apart.

He could have argued with her. He could have ignored her. He could have walked past her to bed and dropped into unconsciousness.

Instead, he held out his arms and said the thing on his mind: "Audrey. Ya think ya can ever forgive me?"

To his surprise, she moved a step back, something she'd never done in the history of their marriage. She said, "I can forgive ya. I just don't know how long it's gonna take." Her voice chilled him.

"Audrey, I love ya." Again, it was all that came to mind.

"Ya better sleep in the guest room." She turned and left him there, staring after her like an idiot.

What he had done was so monstrous that he had every idea she was right—it probably was what was giving him the headaches. Probably it was some feeble attempt of his brain to purge itself of the information it held—to explode and destroy it forever.

Sometimes in dreams, Eddie could hear his own smarmy voice saying the things he had said, and he would wake up clammy, unbelieving. He had to believe he hadn't said them. Because if he had said them, there was no hope for him as a husband and a father and a human being. Therefore, he couldn't have said them.

He'd almost convinced himself of it. Could a thing like that give you headaches? he wondered.

"Your mother doesn't ever want to see you again as long as she lives. After ya left, she cried for a week and couldn't eat, and then she was sick in the hospital. She's so ashamed of ya she won't even let me say ya name. You ever call here again and I'll track ya down and get ya knees broken for ya."

It was worse, what he told Audrey—that he'd fought with his son because he found him with a young cousin—"hurting" her, Eddie said, refusing to say more so she'd draw her own conclusions.

For Angie he had only had to make up a fight in which Anthony had said hurtful things about every member of the family, especially her. He cringed now at the phrase, *"my fat-assed ugly sister,"* coupled with Anthony's supposed abuse of his parents. Angie was a beautiful girl, but she thought she wasn't; she was thin, but she worried about her weight; and she couldn't tolerate injustice. He knew all that about her, and he used it against her.

And for what? Why? How in God's name could he have gotten angry enough to sink so low?

In his heart of hearts, he knew how—out of stupid pride. He wanted to control his son's future, and if he couldn't, he wanted to destroy it. But only for a moment! Only for a millisecond, it seemed now, looking back. Yet by the time he came to himself the damage was done—Eddie was something less than a man, and he'd been living with it ever since.

He heard Audrey sobbing into the night, and after a long time getting his nerve up, he went to comfort her. She jammed a chair under the doorknob.

*   *   *

Talba had drunk enough wine to cloud her judgment and enough coffee to keep her awake. Her mind was hopping around like a kid with a sugar high. There was Eddie, there were the Bergerons, there was Cassandra. And there was her father.

Eddie, with his off-the-wall question, with his improbable tale of reconciliation (precipitated by her—she couldn't forget that) had stirred it all up again.

No question it was a riveting subject, but there was so much else. Just now, it wasn't appropriate to obsess over it. But she had been warned off, and that had to mean something. That was the part that had started to gnaw at her.

She couldn't work on the case. In all probability, she'd already done too much. Eddie had told her to go home and rest.

Fat chance, she thought. *Wired like this, I'd pace all night and keep Miz Clara up.*

She wanted to see Darryl. Badly.

Mentally thanking Eddie for her cell phone, she called, but got his voice mail. Maybe he was home, but in the shower. She could try back in a few minutes.

She looked at her watch. It seemed like midnight, but it was only nine-thirty. *I could go see Corey,* she realized. *Even he doesn't go to bed at this hour.*

She thought about it. Corey and Michelle were overscheduled and didn't enjoy Talba's company a whole lot, anyway. If she tried to set something up, they'd just put her off.

Because of the wine, perhaps, or because it was time (she thought that later), she took the unprecedented step of driving out to Eastover to see her brother.

Eastover was not the kind of place you went unannounced. Aaron Neville lived there. Several Saints lived there—the football kind, not the martyred kind—and a few well-known politicians. It was said to be nearly equally divided among wealthy blacks, whites, and Asians, but Talba had been there only once, and most people she saw were African-American. It was a gated community in New Orleans East, an area not otherwise known for its affluence.

The guard asked if Dr. Wallis was expecting her. For a wild, panicky moment, she thought simply of turning around and pretending it never happened, but she said no, tell him his sister was there. Admission approval came so fast she realized why—it was going to be an instant replay of the scene with Aunt Carrie. Quickly, as she picked her way to her brother's house, she called on the cell phone: "Nobody's sick. Everything's fine. I just need to see you."

"Sandra! It's the middle of the night."

"Omigod. Are you in bed? I didn't think it was *that* late." She thought, *This is the dumbest thing I've ever done.* "Listen, this can wait. Really. I'll call you later in the week."

Corey said, "You're here. You might as well come on," and she could hear the tiredness in his voice.

He was wearing shorts and a T-shirt, hastily thrown on perhaps. He wasn't even wearing his glasses. Michelle, standing in a half-dark kitchen in silhouette, wore a satin robe that showed Talba something she hadn't known. She was so taken aback she gasped instead of making her manners.

Corey was trying to calm an overexcited dog. He looked up, alarmed. "What is it?"

Michelle took a step forward into the light, and the curve Talba had seen straightened a bit. She was smiling. "I think she thinks I've put on weight."

"Oh, that." Corey smiled back at her, a caressing, intimate smile that made Talba feel as if she were peeking in their bedroom. He strode forward and took her hand, his shaved head shining. "Well, you have."

"And there's a lot more to come."

They turned away from each other and toward Talba, as brides and grooms do when the ceremony is over. They were grinning like hyenas. "Congratulations," she said. "This is a little bemusing."

Michelle frowned. "How's that?"

"I just wondered when you were planning to tell us. When the kid goes to first grade?" She sounded so petty she hated herself, but she spoke on her mother's account.

They weren't even slightly daunted. "Matter of fact," Michelle said, "we called Miz Clara tonight, but there was no answer. We wanted to have you all over this weekend."

Corey said, "Don't tell her till we do, okay?"

"Of course not."

Michelle said, "Well, why don't we all sit down?"

"Actually, if you don't mind . . ."

"Oh, you need to see Corey alone? Sure. I'm dead tired anyhow." Michelle was so damned cooperative, even *that* was irritating. Talba never had liked her, and she didn't want to start now.

She didn't like her because Michelle was so patently a trophy—the perfect figure, the show-stopping face, the near-white skin (this part embarrassed Talba); most of all, the fact that Michelle didn't work, did nothing all day but arrange flowers, it seemed to Talba. And now this Stepford-wife routine.

She'd have liked for Corey to marry someone with a little more edge, some bite, maybe. A brain or two. Someone more like the women in her own family. And now there was going to be a mini-Michelle. She wasn't exactly jumping up and down.

Talba said no, thanks, she didn't need anything,

and when Michelle was out of earshot, Corey said, "You been drinking?"

"Wine with dinner. Why?"

"You smell like you bathed in it."

He was making her mad. It was obvious this whole damn thing was a mistake. Here she was in her brother's "great room" with its cathedral ceilings and its sleek Italian furniture, and that alone made her uncomfortable. Then he had to come at her like that. She stood up. "Maybe I better just go."

The dog wagged its tail, as if *it* liked her, anyhow.

Corey looked at her a different way, a gentler way, like he was beginning to see her distress. He said, "What's wrong, little bird?" and that did her in.

She sat back down as if struck. "You did call me that."

"Well, yeah. I did. That supposed to mean something?"

"I don't mean now. You did when we were kids, didn't you?"

He looked a little hurt. "You don't remember?"

"I just did. You dressed up like Big Bird, didn't you?"

"Best performance of my life. You mean you don't treasure it every day of your life?"

She laughed, suddenly delighted with him, seeing a side of him she'd almost forgotten about. Maybe the baby had softened him up. "I remembered today."

"And you just had to come over and shout a belated 'bravo.' Well, now, I appreciate that."

"Corey, something strange is happening to me. I think I've forgotten a lot of stuff."

"What's strange about that? You're getting old is all. We're all losing brain cells."

It wasn't like him to kid around like that and yet . . . it used to be. He really was more like his old self than he'd been in years.

"Listen, I want to know something. Do you remember . . ." She stopped, unable to get the word out.

"Do I remember what?"

"Our father." It came out in a dull monotone, barely audible.

He sank back on the white leather. "Woo. What are you thinking about? Why would you bring up something like that?"

Suddenly she was angry. "Corey, you should hear yourself. Since when is a person's father 'something like that'? Since you're about to be a father yourself, seems like you'd have a little more understanding."

His forehead was rumpled up like a bed. "I hear you." He seemed to be trying to stave something off, keep it out of his own mind. "I shouldn't have said it that way. But I can remember things you can't . . . and you should count your blessings."

"But, Corey, I want to *know*." *Whiny*, she thought. *Ever the whiny little sister.*

"You were two when he left. For practical purposes, he wasn't your father at all. You've got no reason to do this."

"He did something really bad, didn't he?"

Her brother stretched, putting his feet on a glass coffee table. He looked exhausted. "I don't know. I don't know that he did. He drank and helled, I guess. He led Miz Clara a merry chase. Maybe there wasn't much more to it than that."

"Then why doesn't anyone talk about him? You just said you could remember things. What things, Corey? I need to know. Do you realize I didn't even know his name before yesterday? Isn't that a little weird? Having a father so bad you don't even mention his name in the family?"

"If you didn't know his name, it's your own fault. It's on your birth certificate." He was back to his old supercilious self, the Corey she knew so well.

"Corey, if you mention him, Miz Clara goes through the roof."

"Well? She was married to him—what do you expect?"

"Aunt Carrie too."

"Look, all I can remember is being miserable. All of us being miserable. I can't really remember details." He shrugged and looked very sincere. She knew he was lying. "I can't help you, Sandra."

"Corey, please. Please." She hadn't dreamed she was going to beg. "I really need you to try."

"Why?" he said. "Why all of a sudden?"

"Oh. Well, that's a good question. Something really strange happened to me. I went to a funeral. Now, I've never been to a funeral in my life and yet, it felt like I had. I could remember things about a funeral. Like I knew I'd been to one. And there was something else—I mean, something *really* weird."

He was sitting up straight now, had lost his wary look. Something she'd said had piqued his interest.

"Well. I started crying. I mean crying and crying and crying, like it was my own funeral, the minute they started playing the first hymn."

He started laughing.

"What?"

He was roaring, out of control.

"Corey, what the hell is wrong with you?"

"I'm sorry." He was coming around, starting to pull himself together. "I'm sorry, really. It's just that . . . that music. It's happened to me a million times."

She was offended. "Well, I hope for your sake, you haven't been to a million funerals."

"Only four or five. But I cried at every one of them."

"Cried how much, Corey?"

"What kind of question is that?"

"I mean, a little bit or a lot?"

"Oh, you know. Teared up."

"Listen, Big Brother, I'm talking buckets. The Mississippi River."

"Oh, please."

"Okay, the Atchafalaya."

To her surprise, he actually cracked a smile. He almost never laughed at her jokes. In fact, it always seemed to her he disapproved of them, considered them somehow a sign of her frivolous nature. "Look, you must have been under pressure."

"Okay, don't take me seriously. Nobody else has. But I'm telling you something. Something happened to me at that funeral. I had some kind of flashback. I'm not a baby anymore. I have a right to know what happened."

He crossed his arms and stared straight ahead, lips together as if honoring a long-ago promise to keep them that way.

I'll wait him out, she thought. *I'm not going to blink first.*

And finally, still not looking at her, he spoke to the wall. "I guess you do," he said. "I guess you do." He spoke so gently he hardly sounded like her brother.

Fully five minutes had passed by then, so much time she couldn't remember what he was responding to. "I do what?"

"You've got a right to know."

Her stomach did a somersault. A bullfrog or something leapt into her throat and clogged up her breathing. "Tell me," she said, and was surprised to hear no sound at all. She knew she had moved her lips.

"I've got to get a drink." He rose, went into the kitchen, and started rattling ice cubes. "You want one, too?"

"No, thanks." She felt icily calm. Detached. She just sat there while he made himself a tall cold one, not thinking anything, not seeing anything, not moving, suspended in space.

He was drinking scotch, she thought; anyway, something tawny. He took a sip, and she could have sworn he made a face, as if he didn't really enjoy it. She realized he wasn't much of a drinker, that she must be putting him through a version of hell if he felt he had to do something he didn't like in order even to talk. But she rationalized that it had to be done—she couldn't continue to live like this.

When he could look at her, he said, "Look, he's dead."

"Dead?" It was what she was looking for, but it seemed anticlimactic. Was this all there was? "What's the big deal if he's dead?"

He gave her a smile that was just on the edge of goofy—the scotch was doing its work. "I guess we still think you're the baby girl."

"So you're trying to protect me?"

He gave her one of those tiny neck shrugs that are meant to be self-deprecating, but, to Talba's mind, often signal a guilty conscience. "Kind of silly, isn't it?"

"Corey, it just doesn't fly. I never even knew the man. How's it going to hurt me to know he's dead?"

Corey gulped down a big swallow. "Miz Clara's proud; she didn't want you to know."

"To know what? The way he died?"

He was silent.

"What happened? Jealous husband shoot him? Something like that?"

He couldn't meet her eyes. "Something like that."

"Well, what, Corey? Tell me the story. You can't just leave me with one little shred of it. Listen, you want to know something really, really weird? I have this feeling. I've got this feeling I know a whole lot about it—I've just forgotten it."

"Oh, Sandra, hell! He died of an overdose, okay?

Yeah, you've got memories—but you just remember the funeral, that's all. That's why you cried when you went in that church—it's that simple. But know one thing, girl, and know it well—if Mama finds out I told you any of this, she's going to kill me. I wasn't even old enough to know what I was saying, and she made me promise I'd never talk about it with you. You know how hard it is to go back on a promise to Mama?"

She thought that once, a long time ago, she might have seen him wear a look of anguish like the one he had on at the moment, but she couldn't place the time. She could only place the feeling, and it was desolation. She touched him, something she seldom did. "Oh, Corey, I'm sorry. I had to know."

He nodded, once again looking at the wall. "I know you did."

"Mama's some lady, isn't she? Trying to keep something like that a secret. Half the daddies in our neighborhood probably died of overdoses."

"A bit of an exaggeration."

"It's not exactly stigmatizing. That's what I'm getting at."

"Mama's old-fashioned."

"Yeah, but something's wrong here. Mama doesn't lie. Now, let me think about this." Miz Clara had some kind of pact with herself—with Jesus, she might have said. She might dance around the truth, but she'd never tell an outright lie.

"She tell you he wasn't dead?"

"Let me think. No, not exactly. She said something like, 'wish to God he was.' "

He snorted. "See? That's Miz Clara."

"I don't know. This sure seems like a stupid thing to keep secret."

For once, he did look at her. "I agree. I agree with you. But do me a favor—please save my behind and don't tell Miz Clara we talked about any of it. Promise?"

"I don't know." She was dead against it.

Corey looked at his watch. "It's getting late, you know that? Michelle's going to kill me. Hey, listen, there's something I've been meaning to ask you." His mood had lightened—he seemed almost happy, almost normal, as opposed to the Type-A Corey she was so used to.

"Okay. Sure."

"I was kind of wondering—how come Michelle and I have never met your beau?"

"My beau?" She was taken aback.

"Darryl."

"Oh, yeah, I know who you mean. I just thought—"

He chuckled. "Quaint usage, huh?"

"I'd say so." She couldn't help laughing as well—Corey was actually making fun of himself, an unprecedented occurrence.

"How come you haven't introduced us?"

"That's funny—I really don't know. I guess the time hasn't been right." In truth, it had never occurred to her to introduce Darryl to Corey and Michelle. She preferred to tell him amusing stories about her stuck-up, pompous ass of a brother and his BAP of a wife.

"How about we make a date?"

"Oh. Okay. Sure."

"You don't seem that enthusiastic."

"No, really. Let's do it. How about Saturday?"

He frowned. "Umm. No go—already booked. Tomorrow's good, though. How about tomorrow?

"If Darryl's free, you've got a deal. How about something simple? Sid-Marr's, maybe."

"Oh, no. Hell, no. We don't go out that often. We'll take you to Brigtsen's."

"Who could say no to that?" And yet, she kind of

wished she could; kind of, but not really. She also kind of liked the idea.

But, driving home, she felt disoriented—the dad thing, the Darryl thing, the baby thing. You name it, it was wearing her out. She felt as if she'd eaten a meal of chocolate bars—unsatisfied and under-nourished, with a strange, sticky taste in her mouth.

Chapter Sixteen

She was wired, and it wasn't late—only twenty of eleven. She pulled out her cell phone and called Darryl from her car. "You'll never guess what. Brace yourself—it's not all good."

"I've got it: Oprah wants you—but only if you clean up your language."

She laughed at the ludicrousness of either possibility. "This is only slightly less likely. My brother wants to meet you."

"Hey. What's so weird about that? I'm an okay dude; halfway famous, even."

"No, it's weird for him to be interested in me. He wants to take us to Brigtsen's. Tomorrow."

"Oh, hell, I'm playing the governor's mansion."

"Oh."

"What do you mean 'oh'? Tomorrow's good. Count me in."

Talba was quiet. She'd half hoped he'd refuse.

"What's wrong," he said. "You don't want to do it?"

"No, I just . . . I'm going to be with you tomorrow, and it's late, and everything . . ."

"So?"

"Well, okay. I was kind of hoping to see you tonight. But I guess that would be superfluous. I mean, I know it's a school night and everything."

"Talba, what's wrong?" If he'd sounded tired, he didn't now. His voice was all concern and alertness.

"Nothing. I just wanted to see you."

"Should I put the coffeepot on, or chill the wine?"

"Wine. Definitely wine."

Darryl had recently moved to Algiers Point, and a more peaceful place would be hard to imagine. It was part of Orleans Parish—therefore part of the city—but it was on the west bank of the river. Though the houses were strictly old New Orleans— neat little shotguns and larger Victorians—it had the sleepy feel of a small town. Each well-kept home was set back from the street on a nice-sized yard, and the residents took pride in their gardens.

Young families could afford to live there—and did—but because of the neighborhood's age and a sprinkle of gay couples, it escaped the sterility of a suburb. Darryl said he'd picked it because the price was right and on the weekends, it was like being on vacation. Talba, who frequently went out for the weekend, had to agree—yet if you wanted dinner, you got on the ferry and six minutes later got off in the French Quarter.

She went by ferry tonight, thinking how odd it was to be going there this late, and in the middle of the week. *I should call Miz Clara*, she thought, and yet it was really too late. Maybe that was good. If she stayed over, she could go home after Miz Clara left for work. She didn't much want to see her mother right now.

Darryl met her with a glass of wine in each hand. "For you, Your Grace."

"Woo. Do I need it. I've had one hell of a day."

"Sit down and tell me." Darryl had guy furniture—big and comfortable. He liked to sit in an old, beat-up leather chair he'd gotten at a garage sale, with his feet on an ottoman. Talba, in turn, would lounge on the deep, soft sofa upholstered in brick red corduroy.

They assumed the positions, Talba setting her drink on a massive wooden coffee table. She looked around her, getting her bearings. "I love this room."

"Come on. Talk."

"I'm feeling better. Really. Just being here."

"Talk, girl."

"Okay, here's the short version. The day started out with a prayer breakfast, moved on to almost getting fired, getting frozen out by one person, yelled at and chased by another, and finding out my father's dead."

Without missing a beat, he picked up on the relevant part. "Your father's dead?"

"If Corey isn't lying. Which he might be. Everyone seems to be trying to keep me from finding out anything about my father."

"Oh, God. This is tied in with that funeral thing, isn't it?"

Talba, lying down on a fat cushion, stared up at the ceiling. "Well, now, my mother says I've never been to a funeral, and if I ever mention my father's name, she'll throw me out of the house. However, two days ago I *couldn't* mention my father's name because I didn't know it. My aunt, who practically threw me out of *her* house, finally deigned to tell me it was Denman La Rose."

"Your mother wasn't married?"

"Oh, yes. It was Denman La Rose Wallis. But that's all I know. No matter what else I ask, a hundred roadblocks go up. Nobody wants to talk about him, but most of all, nobody wants me asking about him.

Finally, I went to Corey, and you know how desperate I had to be to do that."

"More wine?" He poured them both a glass. She was beginning to feel better. The wine was helping, but mostly, being with Darryl was, in his peaceful, comfortable little house.

"Darryl. This really means a lot to me."

He held out his glass. "I know. But don't worry—they have AA chapters everywhere."

"You know what I mean."

He smiled at her. "Glad to be of service, ma'am." They locked eyes for a moment. Darryl broke first. "So what'd Corey say?"

"He told me our father is dead—even though Miz Clara told me he wasn't. You know Miz Clara's lying thing? How she never will lie, but if she can wiggle around the truth, she doesn't think it's the same thing?"

He laughed. "No, but it sounds right for a church lady."

"Well, she wiggled *and* she lied. Or else Corey did. I realized it on the way over here. She says I've never been to a funeral; he says I was at my father's, and that must be why I had that weird experience at Rhonda's. She also says he's not dead—but that's the wiggle part. What she really said was 'wish he was,' or something like that."

Darryl considered. "Hmm," he said finally. "Are we overanalyzing?"

"About Miz Clara, maybe. Who knows what she's up to? But, still, it remains clear no one wants to talk about the man."

"Talba, has it occurred to you that something really bad happened. Like maybe he . . ."

"Molested me?" Her stomach gave a little shudder. "Yeah, I've thought if it. Maybe she found out and threw him out. Kind of depressing, isn't it?"

"How old were you?"

"Two."

"Jesus."

"Yeah." Once again, she inspected the ceiling. "But I just thought of something. It's perfectly in character for Mama and Aunt Carrie to behave like this. But what about Corey? He's a doctor. He must be aware that you're supposed to talk about these things. Like—you know—how can you have a healthy relationship with a man if . . ."

"Hey! Maybe that's why he wants to meet me."

"What?"

"You know. To vet me. Make sure I'm not a pervert. See if we really do seem healthy."

Talba sat up, suddenly amused. "Oh, man. What an opportunity. You got a dog collar I could wear? Something with spikes, maybe. And I could get a nice latex dress . . ."

"See? You're better. All you needed was a drink with Uncle Darryl."

"That's not *all*, Uncle Darryl."

"Well, it's all you're getting. School night, remember?"

"Never stopped you before."

"Okay, Your Grace. Anything you like."

She shook her head. "No, I'm kidding. To tell the truth, tonight a good long cuddle's more to the point."

"That's what I thought."

"Listen, I want to ask you something. You know that poem, 'Queen of the May'? You said you'd like to be a father like that."

"Uh-huh. I would."

"Well, I was wondering—what kind of father are you?" She paused, but he didn't answer. "I mean— how come you never talk about your kid?"

"Oh, man. Let's don't get into that."

She looked at him hard. "More secrets?"

"Raisa's a great kid. I wish I could see more of

her." He stared at the old-fashioned ottoman with his Nike-clad feet on it. When he looked up at her, he was clearly so miserable she wished she could withdraw the question. "What made you ask?" he said.

"Nothing. I didn't realize it was such a sensitive subject."

"It's not. Really." He gave her a smile so forced it looked squeezed out of a toothpaste tube. "What brought it up?"

"I just thought . . . with Corey suddenly asking to meet you . . . I was wondering why I've never met Raisa."

"Oh." He sat back in his chair and blew out his breath. "Good question."

"Maybe for another occasion?"

"Almost certainly for another occasion. Are you staying here tonight?"

"If I may."

"I insist."

She couldn't imagine Darryl having a secret. And yet, he hardly ever talked about his daughter. Never, in fact, except to mention her in passing.

Hours later, she blinked awake, terrified, Darryl touching her face. "Talba. What is it?"

"Whooo. Nightmare."

"You're soaking wet. You were moaning."

"There was all this blood . . . a horrible noise, and then people split open, and blood poured out of them. Rivers, I mean. Like a cartoon or something. It was like rain—it just kept getting deeper and deeper and deeper."

"What kind of noise?"

"I don't know. Like a crash. A boom or something."

"A gunshot, maybe."

"Too loud, I think." She shuddered. "Can I have some water?"

He got her some, as if she were a child, and once again, she fell asleep in his arms. She felt as if she might cry when he got up and dressed and left for school.

It was raining out, and she fell easily back to sleep. Eddie was right. She needed to decompress.

She slept as long as she could and went in to make herself some toast. Darryl had made coffee for her. *Maybe*, she thought, *I should marry him.*

But you could hardly marry a man who didn't know your brother. And who had a kid he never talked about. *I wonder*, she thought, *if we really do have such a healthy relationship. God knows I'm no judge.*

One thing she did know—Darryl made her happy where many men had made her cry. *Good enough*, she thought. *Good enough. And Miz Clara likes him.*

On the other hand, Miz Clara might not be infallible in these matters—by all reports she'd chosen poorly herself.

The rain made her want to stay put, but there was little point without Darryl there. Her own house— Miz Clara's house—seemed lonely without her mother, who had left a tart note asking please to call her at work and say whether she was dead or alive. It brought a small lump to her throat, made her realize how accustomed Miz Clara had become to their arrangement.

Originally, her mother had permitted her to move back in for a reason—she had some poems to write, and a project to do, involving her given name and the intern who'd stuck her with it. When she'd gone back to her day job—which she roughly thought of as "computer genius"—she had never moved out. Neither she nor her mother had ever mentioned it. She'd just started working for United

Oil, paying rent, and putting money into the house when it needed something.

Of course, she'd met Darryl in the original move-back period. If she had had a different boyfriend—somebody like Lamar, the last one, Miz Clara would have thrown her out on her ear. But she was probably more smitten with Darryl than Talba was; she was happy to put up with her daughter to have him around.

Talba dressed for work, but it was only midmorning. She was so depressed, so disoriented as a result of yesterday's events, that she thought of going in early.

Instead, she did a search on the name Denman La Rose Wallis. As expected, she came up with nothing. It was an odd name.

Well, hell, she thought. *If I want to see it written down, I know where to go.*

After a maddening phone search to find where the records she wanted were kept, she drove to the State Building, went to the Office of Vital Records, and applied for three documents: First, a copy of the marriage certificate for Clara Suzanna Guidry and Denman La Rose Wallis. It cost her, but she asked also for the birth certificate of Urethra Tabitha Sandra Wallis, grateful she had to write the name so she wouldn't have to say it.

The cruelty of the name—to Miz Clara: she didn't care about herself—at one time had made her so angry it ran her life. But now her mother's innocence moved her more. That, and her genuine wish to give her daughter a pretty name. Her second name, indeed, was not TABitha, but TaBEETHa, to rhyme with Urethra.

Third, she requested a copy of the death certificate for Denman La Rose Wallis.

And then she settled down to wait. After an hour, she left, cursing bureaucracy and uncooperative civil servants. She tried to walk off some of her nervous energy, returning flushed, sweaty, and just as antsy as before. She still had to wait another twenty minutes.

Finally, having sweated a quart of blood, she had the documents—at a collective cost of $27, the marriage license being the cheapest. She folded them carefully into her purse and found a place to have coffee before she looked at them. Urethra Tabitha Sandra Wallis, (later to become the Baroness de Pontalba) had been born to Clara Suzanna Wallis and Denman La Rose Wallis in 1977. Seven years later, her father had died. That was wrong, she thought. Corey had said she was only two when he died. Had he made a mistake or lied? She looked at the cause of death: *Gunshot wound to the chest.* Not an overdose. He had lied, and about more than one thing. She was seven at the time, not two.

No one, it seemed, could be trusted on the subject of her father. She closed her eyes in frustration, and immediately felt sick, felt something the size of a porpoise leap out of her stomach and into her throat, something slimy and thrashing. Something she recognized.

It was fear.

The world in front of her, the backs of her eyelids, turned red. She snapped them open, but it didn't help. She felt as if her body was swaying, as if she might fall. She closed them again, against the disorientation, and she was a child, almost a baby. Someone was lying on the floor on an old rag rug, bleeding from the chest, and there was an ancient red upholstered chair in the room. The loudest noise she'd ever heard echoed in her ears.

The memory—if it was that—flitted so quickly away she had only the vaguest impression of the person on the floor, but the room was vivid. And the fear was monstrous.

The leaping porpoise had grown quickly to the size of a whale, and it was no longer in her throat, but had liquefied and seeped into her cells, contaminating them and making it impossible to focus, even to . . .

She felt a steadying hand on her back. "Are you all right, Miss?"

She turned to look at the good Samaritan, a white man. "I think so. I . . ."

The look on the man's face stopped her cold. "Put your head down," he said. "Head on your knees." He helped her lower it. She wondered if she was going to throw up.

But in fact she felt better in a moment, and the man, holding the back of her neck, let her up. "Are you ill?" he asked.

She faked a smile. "I'm fine, I think." She held up her cup. "Too much sugar in my coffee. Thanks for your help. I'm okay. Really."

He said she was welcome, and walked away frowning, as if he didn't feel his work with her was done.

And truth be told, she still felt shaky. *I was there,* she thought. *I saw him die. And I wasn't any two, either. I had to be seven. Why'd Corey tell me two?*

Why, in fact, had anyone told her anything, even that she should keep her nose out if it? They were trying to protect her, she knew that, but from what? Not just the memory of her father bleeding, though that was plenty.

More than that.

Talba thought about it hard, and tried to come to terms with the notion that her mother might be a murderer. She wondered how to research it. First the newspaper, she thought, but there must be something else. Police records? Could she ask Skip Langdon?

No, she could not. No way in hell. And she was

suddenly aware that she wasn't going to look it up in any newspaper files, either. She was going to forget about it. She hated to admit it, but they'd been right, the whole damn batch of them. She was wrong to pry into this thing, and she was going to drop it.

If Miz Clara had shot her husband, she must have had a damn good reason.

Was it about me? she thought, remembering her worry that he'd molested her, that that was what the silence was all about.

If it was, she didn't want to know.

Chapter Seventeen

Eddie was in the office early, even before Eileen, having slept barely at all. Listening to Audrey cry like that, knowing he couldn't go to her, was probably the hardest thing he ever had to do. It made him think of something else almost as bad—the time the maid had called him at work and told him to meet Audrey at the emergency room.

When he got there, he could hear his son screaming behind walls and curtains, stranded somewhere in a labyrinth of treatment rooms he couldn't have navigated even if he'd managed to penetrate the shield of bureaucracy that was the first hurdle.

The boy had been five, stricken with acute appendicitis, but at the time Eddie didn't know that, knew only that his son was in agony somewhere that Eddie couldn't go. It was the first time he realized how much he loved his son, how crazy he'd go if anything happened to him.

It was the night he'd taken the vow, too. *The vow. The pledge.* He'd completely forgotten.

And that was what this whole ten-year thing was all about.

He thought about that. He'd forgotten the thing this was all about, the thing that was so important it had kept him from speaking to his son for a decade.

He could get mystical about that, if he let himself, his taking the vow, never being able to break it, then forgetting it, and now Anthony back and Audrey reminding him of it with her crying. There were people who'd say things about it being meant to be and everything happening for a reason, but Eddie didn't have two seconds for people like that.

So far as he was concerned, there was nothing beautiful or symmetrical about this, it only made him feel like a piece of crap, which was what Audrey thought, anyway. Angie would, too. Maybe he should try to get to her first, before Audrey or Anthony.

But what would I say? he thought. *"I can explain?"* He couldn't, not even to himself.

The vow was this: *I'm going to send my son to college no matter what.*

How was he supposed to explain that it had become the most important thing in his life and that Anthony had made it impossible for him to keep it? The damn vow had become more important than the kid.

He brushed at his face, as if he could make it go away. *It just got out of hand,* was the best he could do.

That was so lame it made him want to puke. He couldn't say something like that to Angie. He couldn't say anything. Hell, let her think he was a piece of crap; he thought so himself.

His mind wouldn't stop. It kept going on like that, never giving him a minute's peace. Finally, he'd just gotten up and dressed in yesterday's clothes. He thought he'd go to the office, at least try to make peace with his business—do *something* right. Audrey had come into the kitchen while he was puttering around. She'd walked up to him and taken his hand and squeezed it and looked into his eyes, her own overflowing.

He didn't know what to do. His tongue seemed to be nailed to the roof of his mouth. Finally, she said, "Eddie, ya did what ya thought was right," and released his hand. She poured herself a cup of the coffee he had made, all the while keeping her back to him, and finally, she said, "Ya look terrible. At least go put on some clean clothes." And that was how he knew he was once again welcome in the bedroom.

So here he was with a bad taste in his mouth from too much coffee too early, and a head spinning from the barrage of memories, the fusillade of guilt that had besieged him in the night. He was staring balefully at the pile of papers on his desk, trying to think of a way to avoid it, when he was startled by the phone.

He looked at his watch. Eight-thirty. Way too early for anyone to call. Still, it beat unloading his in-box. He picked up and was once again startled by a little female gasp; of horror, it sounded like. "I was going to leave a message. I didn't think anyone would be there."

He was surprised that he recognized her voice. "Good mornin', Ms. Scott. Lovely mornin', don't you think?"

She'd apparently gotten over her initial panic, and moved on to haughtiness. "Mr. Valentino. I'm in a terrific hurry. I called to leave you a message. I won't be needing your services any longer."

He pulled out his drawl for her. It was slow and sounded halfway stupid; with arrogant people, it tended to put him at an advantage. "Well, I reckon not. Ms. Wallis tells me she's about got to the bottom of things."

"Ms. Wallis! Ms. Wallis is who I want to talk to you about."

"I thought you didn't want to talk to anybody. Idn't that why you called so early?"

"I don't have *time* to talk to anybody. But it would seem that we're talking. So let me be brief and to the point. I am extremely sorry to report that Ms. Wallis has behaved unprofessionally. She came highly recommended and indeed I chose your firm because of her reputation. But I do not feel she is an asset to you, and I feel you should know. She has been very disappointing, and that is why I am turning the case over to another private investigator."

Eddie reflected how strange it is that people stop using contractions when they get up on their high horse. He made his voice even slower and sleepier than before. "Well, now. Just what did Ms. Wallis do to get ya so upset?"

"It wasn't what she did to me. It was what she did to my daughter."

"And what was that, ma'am?"

"She badgered her. She visited her at choir practice and then again at our private home, trying to get her to identify a man Cassandra has never met. As a matter of fact, she behaved as if Cassandra were the suspect rather than the victim. She made her cry, Mr. Valentino. She made my fourteen-year-old daughter cry!" Her voice rose with every sentence. Eddie made sure his dropped.

"Well, now, I'm real sorry to hear that." He spoke so softly he even annoyed himself. "Ms. Wallis is one of my best investigators." The words came out about one every three seconds.

"I was under the impression she is your only investigator."

He allowed himself a chuckle. "Well now, I guess you've got me there, ma'am. Tell me, what exactly did Ms. Wallis say that Cassandra found so offensive?"

He heard her draw in a breath. He could almost hear what she was thinking: *If I'd been able to leave a message, this conversation wouldn't be happening.*

"It wasn't what she said, it was her manner."

"And what was that, ma'am? Was she belligerent?"

"I'm not sure I'd . . ."

He didn't let her finish. "Was she threatening?"

"She just wouldn't let up."

"Ah. She was persistent."

"You can call it what you like, Mr. Valentino. My daughter's been in tears ever since her visit."

That he could believe. "I want to thank you for tellin' me about this. I'm gon' make a note to give Ms. Wallis a talkin' to."

"You do that, Mr. Valentino."

"I enjoyed meetin' your lovely daughter. I wonder if I could could tell her so myself?"

"I think she's been upset quite enough."

"Well, I enjoyed meetin' you too, Ms. Scott. Let me know if I can do anything else for ya."

"I think that, under the circumstances, you ought to return the retainer."

He'd known that one was coming. People like Aziza Scott didn't cut you an inch of slack. "I don't know, Ms. Scott. We put in a lot of work on this. Maybe we could negotiate something in between."

"If a check for the entire amount is not on my desk before the end of the week, you will be hearing from my lawyer."

Once again, she'd lost her contractions.

"Well, like I said, it's been real nice workin' for ya." He figured even she would see through the sarcasm, but he didn't have it in him to excise it.

*   *   *

Eileen was at lunch when Talba arrived, but the minute her foot crossed the threshold, Eddie's voice boomed out, "Ms. Wallis, get in here."

She almost wished she'd stayed out the whole day. She was in no mood for Eddie's blustering. Something about her face must have made that clear. She'd gotten only as far as his door when he said, "Good God, what is it? I give ya the morning off, and ya come in looking like ya haven't slept."

"Not to be rude, but that's a perfect description of you."

"Touché, Ms. Wallis. Touché." He shook his head and his eye bags jiggled. They looked to be developing cellulite. "Sit down, why don't ya? Now tell me what's wrong."

"It's nothing. I mean, it's nothing to do with the case. I just . . . you know, a female thing."

It was all she could do to suppress a giggle when, on cue, Eddie's color deepened. She didn't know all that much about white men, but one thing she knew well—any mention of menstruation, no matter how oblique, and they were on the next train out of town. She truly treasured this about them; it afforded her the one foolproof form of manipulation she had. She wished she could remember to use it more often.

She shrugged, as if in apology. "Sorry. You asked."

"Hey, I got a wife and daughter. Hell, Eileen too. Misses three days every month. You gonna do that?"

She even loved the way they got defensive about it. "Uh-uh. I'm going to give you worse things to worry about."

"I got a little taste of that first thing this morning. Client called and fired us."

Nice segue, she thought. *Just when we were playing so nicely.* "I'm not surprised," she said. "I got the feeling she's rethought the whole situation."

"How so?"

"I don't think she really wants to find the guy. I think she's thrown money at it and assuaged her conscience. End of story."

"That sounds a little self-servin', don't ya think?"

Alarm bells went off. "I don't understand."

"She complained about ya, Ms. Wallis. Said you're unprofessional, and she's hiring another detective."

"I see. And what was the nature of her complaint?"

"I think you know."

Frantically, Talba flipped back through her encounters with the Scotts. Nothing came up. "I'm not getting anything. I wonder if it had something to do with what happened at the Bergerons'."

"Said ya made the kid cry."

"Oh. She didn't cry while I was there. She was damn surly, though."

"Did ya reprimand her?"

"That's not my place."

"Did ya cuss her?'

She was outraged. "No! Did Aziza Scott say I did?"

He chuckled. "Take it easy, Ms. Wallis. I'm teasin' ya."

Talba closed her eyes in frustration, sorry she'd taken the bait. "Well. Sorry she wasn't pleased. Does this mean we don't get paid?"

Eddie drummed his fingers as if the question wasn't worth his time. "Ah, hell. It ain't no big deal."

"Well, what was that we just went through, then? What was, 'Ms. Wallis, get in here.' "

"That was me bringing out the rubber hoses. If you were guilty, ya woulda confessed."

"Oh, come on. Pretty gentle for an interrogation."

"If you were guilty, it wouldn't have been. But you weren't. I can read people."

Oh, right, she thought.

"I put a pile of stuff on ya desk. See if ya get through it today. If you're done by four o'clock, I'll start showing ya the books—so you can take 'em over."

Her chair scraped on the wood floor as she got up. "I was hoping you forgot."

She turned on her computer and checked her e-mail. Tony Tino had written her. Had thanked her and invited her to write him again. She didn't know if she dared.

There were various other missives from various friends—mostly fellow nerds—and there was something so unexpected she wondered if it were real:

Talba—I'm writing on a cokmputer at school. I enjoyed meting you. Im really really relaly worried about paemla. dont tell anyone i wrote you. cassandra

She printed it out and took it in to Eddie. "What do you make of this?"

He read it and looked up at her, keeping his chin down, so that his eyes looked like two brown moons over the purple ponds of his eye bags. "The kid's scared to death."

"If I'm the only one she can talk to, she really is in trouble. Before this, I'd have said she hates my guts."

"You think this thing's authentic?"

"All I know is, it really did come from her school. Xavier Prep, if you recall. I don't think any of the other players would have access to it. Shaneel goes to Fortier."

Eddie drummed his desk. Talba noticed that he did that a lot. "We're out of it," he said.

"What about Pamela?"

"We've got to assume if she was missing, her parents would report her missing."

She was disappointed. She realized she'd been expecting more; hoping for more.

I'm losing it, she thought. *I'm getting a dad thing for him.* For times like this, she kept a diary file in her computer.

She went back to her office and started messing around in it: *Repeat after me, please: Eddie Valentino is no knight in shining armor. He's just a guy in business. If nobody pays for it, it isn't his job, okay? You got that?*

Yes ma'am, Miz Talba, yes ma'am. You sure are one good mama—darn near as good as Miz Clara herself.

Good. Now go do your job. Think you can manage that?

I don't know. What if I went to Skip Langdon and told her everything?

You've already done that, idiot. She knows about Toes.

Yes, but Pamela.

You can't report a missing person if you don't know she's missing. What are you thinking of? Just do your job.

Okay. Pep talk over.

It was as good a way as any to warm up for work. For a while, she hacked away at the pile of employee checks Eddie had put on her desk. Fortunately for their potential bosses, they were all upstanding citizens. Unfortunately for her, however—it was turning out to be one of the most boring afternoons she could remember. And to top it off, she was about to have dinner with Corey and Michelle. That didn't sound a whole lot livelier.

About four, Eddie popped his head in. "How ya comin'?"

"Drowning in paper."

"Now ya know what this job's all about. Forget about the mean streets. Ninety-nine percent of it's as routine as filing ya nails. Listen, let's do the books another day—I've got to go see Angie about something."

"Sure. I've got plenty to do."

"By the way, **Pamela's okay.** Her parents sent her out of town for a while."

A sunburst of relief fanned out in Talba's chest—

and it had nothing to do with Pamela. "How do you know that?"

"I'm a private dick—you hadn't heard?"

But something was funny about it. "Why would they send her away in the middle of the school year?"

"Distraught about her sister—near nervous breakdown." He put on his sport coat. "It happens. Have a nice weekend."

Talba stared after him, feeling like a dog newly rescued from the pound—falling in love with the hand that feeds it. Love was about right. The moment she realized he'd checked up on Pamela, she had an unreasonable surge of affection for him. The trouble was, she knew what it was; she knew exactly what it was.

And that old white man is most assuredly not my father! she told herself. *He's not even a good father. Ask Tony Tino.*

In the end, she did. After a premarital investigation (or sweetie snoop, as she'd quickly dubbed it) that had proved to be lots of fun—*Impostor Caught Red-handed by Brilliant Computer Jockey*—she e-mailed Tony, and caught him on-line.

He wrote back, "Shall we have a drink? Meet me in my favorite cyber-bar."

A few directions later, they were ensconced in a private chat room.

"Got your martini?" he asked.

"I'm having tea. You?"

"Beer—this is Texas. Listen, I have a lot to thank you for. You know how long it's been since my dad's spoken to me?"

"Ten years, I gather. He's born again, Tony—a completely new person. He even took me out to dinner last night."

"Your treat, I'm sure."

"I'm not kidding. I think he wasn't quite ready to

tell your mother he'd talked to you. Also, he wanted to tell me about you."

"All bad, of course."

"He's really missed you."

"Actually, I called my mother and told her. And I found out something really bad."

Talba's mouth went dry. "He's not sick, is he?"

"Nothing like that. I'm not ready to talk about it yet—and probably shouldn't, to one of my dad's employees. Still, unloading to a stranger is what chat rooms are all about. Families are a pain—you know that? Didn't you say your dad passed away? I'm sorry about that."

"No, because I didn't know it when I wrote you before. I think I just said, 'You're lucky to have a dad.' Since then, I found out he is dead. But it's not like I ever knew him."

"D-i-v-o-r-c-e?"

"Yes. But there's some big mystery going on— nobody in the family ever mentions his name—and I mean that literally. I didn't even know it till this week—I mean I didn't know it for sure. Get this— his middle name's La Rose!"

"La Rose by any other name . . ."

"As far as I can tell, nothing about him smelled sweet. I've started to have flashbacks."

"Of memories? Do you think your family's protecting you from something?"

"They even say they are. You know what I think? I think I was there when he died—and I know he died of a gunshot wound. That's a matter of record."

"Who shot him?"

"That's the question. My mother hated him enough—that's for sure."

"What's your memory?"

"Just the shot. The body on the floor; some furniture. Funny thing, though—my brother said it happened when I was two, but going by the date on the death certificate, I was seven. He also said my father died of an overdose."

"Weird. Was there anyone else in the room?"

"Arrrgh. I don't know if I want to go there."

"Uh-oh. I don't blame you. Know what—I'm getting the feeling this isn't fun for you. I don't want to make things worse—especially after what you did for me."

"I'm fine, really. I'm pretty detached from it."

They said their electronic good-byes, and Talba closed down her computer with a big fat exhale. The truth was, she couldn't believe she'd done what she'd done—talked to a perfect stranger about something so intensely personal. For her, computers had always been a tool to work with—not a social or therapeutic avenue. She felt embarrassed and drained. And not at all like having dinner with Corey and Michelle.

Chapter Eighteen

Because she'd had plenty of time to get to work, she hadn't brought her car, instead had ridden in on the 82 Desire, the bus that replaced the streetcar when progress progressed. Talba gloried in it not only for the literary reference, but also for the thing that had captured Tennessee Williams's imagination in the first place—the innate poetry of it. Except she had a layer the playwright hadn't had— this was a much faster, uglier, fouler-smelling vehicle than the one he'd had to work with. She never rode it without thinking about that.

She'd once had an ambition to call a collection of poems *82 Desire*, just because she liked the name. But she'd since refined the idea. Now she had a plan to write a cycle of poems about her fellow riders— not their real lives, about which she couldn't know, but their imagined lives. It had come about because that was what she did when she was on the bus— make up stories about the people, try to put herself in their houses, in their marriages, feel what it must be like to be them. She had a notebook full of thoughts and observations and three or four drafts of poems, but since she'd gotten the car, she'd sort of forgotten about the project. She thought about it on her way home and felt ashamed.

And yet this was no night to write. Her mind was in such a swivet she could barely focus long enough to find the fare, much less to think literary thoughts. She should never have gotten into that discussion with Tony Tino—and not just because it was stupid and embarrassing. Because she couldn't get the damned movie out of her head.

Another thing she shouldn't have done—referred to it as a movie. It was running over and over, an endless loop, and everything was different. She knew perfectly well what repressed memory syndrome was, and also knew some people said it didn't exist. She could see the problem.

There was no doubt in her mind that what she was seeing was real, it was someplace she'd been, something she'd seen, but yet she also knew that it was both embellished and diminished. It was clear to her that her imagination was filling in blanks, adding details, and also that her mind was withholding data. For instance, in the first flashback, the shot, the unbearable loud noise, had come *after* she saw the body. Therefore, she concluded, her brain had simply provided it because it ought to be there.

Sometimes now, when the movie ran, it came before, but that, she figured, was because she knew it ought to go there. *Perhaps there were two shots,* she thought. Whichever it was, this wasn't a detail added by an overwrought imagination. She had most assuredly heard that shot. She knew by the way she felt about it. By the terror; by the bafflement; most of all, by the sorrow—the inconsolable sense of regret.

So either there were two shots, or she'd remembered the sequence incorrectly. In that case, what else was wrong? Not that it mattered much—there weren't really enough details to piece together a story. She couldn't tell one thing about the body except that it was bleeding. Maybe it had on jeans. Had her father worn jeans? She wasn't even sure of that. And she couldn't say why except that the memory-movie was like a dream, in which you *know* you're with a particular person, yet he looks entirely different from the way he actually looks; in which things sometimes appear three-dimensional and perfectly normal, except that when you try to remember later, all you recall is an impression. This was like that. An impression.

Why the hell, she thought, *did Corey say it happened when I was two—and the death certificate says five years later?*

She kept playing the movie. Sure enough, she had the definite sense of being very young, almost infinitesimal. Was it something to do with height, with how far above the floor she seemed? That was crazy.

She closed her eyes and tried to think of something else.

And when the movie came again, she saw something different. Looking down at the floor, she could see a shoe tossed carelessly near the chair, as if the owner were a child who had simply left it there. It was her own shoe—one she remembered perfectly. A pink sandal, half of a pair she'd had the summer before first grade. Now that made *no* sense—she hadn't had the shoes at either age, two *or* seven.

She had no idea if it had been there all the time, or if her overactive brain, abhorring a vacuum, had thoughtfully filled it in.

She went in and stood in the shower a long time, hoping to get her balance back.

She chose her clothes carefully. She had the distinct feeling her brother's wife hated the way she dressed, but she could hardly change her personality just for the evening—Darryl would never speak to her again.

She chose an ankle-length dress in deep green, the most conservative thing she owned, accessorized it with a full-length flowing jacket in an African print, six-inch-wide orange-beaded belt, and three or four silver necklaces. Looking in the mirror, she thought, *Oh, well* and quoted herself aloud:

> *I* am the Baroness de Pontalba and *Michelle*
> Can kiss my aristocratic black ass.

For good measure, she turned around and mooned her own reflection.

Darryl was in the kitchen with Miz Clara, sitting at the old black-painted table that Talba suddenly realized she really ought to replace.

Miz Clara said, "Well, ain't you the Queen of the May."

"Indeed not. *I* am a baroness."

Darryl said, "You're a queen to me, baby," thus earning one of Miz Clara's rare ear-to-ears. Darryl was a person of whom she thoroughly approved, which was the only thing that made Talba suspicious of him.

Corey and Michelle were waiting for them, Michelle in a little pearl gray suit with pink-pearl blouse fastened with white-pearl buttons. Her only jewelry was a pair of pearl stud earrings. Her hair was caught back in one of those little George Washington ponytails that men wore. Talba honestly couldn't recall ever seeing a black woman with that hairstyle.

Michelle's mouth flew open at the sight of her sister-in-law.

Talba beat her to the punch. "Like my outfit?"

Michelle blushed.

Talba wagged a finger at her. "See, your face gives you away. It's okay; really—everybody's different. *I* don't go in for bivalve by-products."

Michelle's giveaway face announced that she was struggling to get the reference. Corey got there first. "Pearls. Pretty good, little bird."

Michelle said, *"Little bird?"* in a tone of pure horror, as if Corey had used a pet name for a mistress.

Darryl simply stared at Talba, evidently feeling a new and unpleasant facet of her personality had just been revealed.

As it has, she thought. *As it has—even I didn't know I was that bad. We've got ourselves an inauspicious beginning here.*

Corey ignored his wife and held out his hand to Darryl. "I've heard a lot about you."

Darryl said, "I've heard about both of you. I think congratulations are in order."

Michelle looked down at her stomach. "Oh. I didn't think . . ."

Darryl chuckled. "No, Talba told me. Nobody could guess."

Corey said, "Hey, I'm a doctor, and I couldn't tell if I didn't know."

Oh, right. Of course he had to announce that in the first five minutes. They hadn't even gotten inside the restaurant and Talba was embarrassed three times over—though as much at herself as her relatives.

Evidently, Corey and Michelle came to the restaurant a lot. The maître d' fussed over them and the waitress called them by name. They ordered drinks, and when Corey asked for "the usual," Talba could have puked.

But she couldn't have said why.

She was in a rotten mood, that was why. Something like a headache was lurking just behind her eyes. Maybe a drink would help. She slurped down a couple of glasses of wine in short order, and found her instinct exactly right. It helped a lot.

She listened with detachment as Michelle turned her well-bred charm on Darryl. "I hear you're a man of many talents," she said.

Michelle was from a famous old New Orleans family, a member of the class of people known in the city as Creoles. In other places, the word may mean as little as "mixed race." In New Orleans, it connotes an entire culture, dating back to the Free People of Color of the previous century.

Before the Civil War, they formed their own tight-knit, often profitable community in the French Quarter and the Treme. They were artisans, dress-makers, professionals, and most important, property owners—even the women, who were frequently participants in a genteel body-exchange called placage. Under this system, girls as young as fourteen were taken by their mothers to the Quadroon Balls, where, if they were lucky, they might catch the eye of a wealthy white man and end up under his "protection."

But a would-be protector would first have to strike a deal with the girl's mother, preferably for ownership of a house and a proper education for the children of the union. Then, having bought himself a mistress, he'd move her into her new house and spend as much time there as his life with his white wife permitted. Because of the racial makeup of the arrangement—the lightest girls were considered the prettiest—the offspring of the placées became whiter and whiter over the years, frequently becoming *passants blancs*.

Many who retained color, however, became wealthier and wealthier, more and more respected and influential, until eventually they became the city's power elite—and not the city's *black* power elite. They were its political center, period.

This was what Michelle Tircuit came out of. In her own hometown, she was as much a blueblood as any *Mayflower* descendant in the country.

The Tircuits originally owned stables, eventually, as cars came in, moving on to become manufacturers and merchants. They now owned a locally famous foundry, which made high-end hardware and accessories for old houses—doorknobs, shutter hinges, heavy-duty latches, faucets, and cabinet handles. Tircuit's was the place to go if you were restoring a house, or even building a new one—and with all the yuppie developments cropping up, they'd now branched out to contemporary goods.

Michelle's brothers, sisters, and cousins were doctors, lawyers, fund-raisers, accountants—not a blue-collar worker among them. Miz Clara was deeply impressed.

And, truth to tell, so might Talba have been if Michelle had not, with a Howard University education, taken a job as a receptionist, apparently to mark time till she was married. And then, having caught Corey, quit her job to devote her life to shopping and grooming.

The woman had never shown the slightest interest in anything else—and to think, with all that time and money, the best she could come up with was a little gray suit and pearl earrings. The lack of imagination made Talba almost as mad as the lack of ambition.

Darryl was telling her and Corey about his three jobs—schoolteacher, bartender, and musician. (Actually, he was laying it on a bit—he hardly ever tended bar any more except as a substitute.)

Corey was trying to steal the floor—getting up a good whine about how hard he'd had to work during his residency.

The weenie-waggling began in earnest just as the

entrees arrived—at least Talba imagined that was what it was. She wasn't privy to it because Michelle was bending her ear.

"God, I wish I could have a drink. Do you *know* how careful you have to be when you're pregnant? My older sister developed placenta previa, and couldn't get up for the last four months—can you imagine?"

"Not really." *But I bet* you *could. I bet you'd love it.*

"Talba, that is the most *amazing* outfit—where *do* you find these things? I could shop and shop and never even come across anything like it."

"I've got a feeling we go to different stores."

Michelle laughed, filling the air with malice. Her Ms. Niceguy act of the night before had withered after Talba's bivalve crack. "Well, there's no doubt about that."

Change the subject, Talba thought, and drank the last of her fourth glass of wine. *Get out of this file before you lose it. But what the hell to talk about?*

Kids were always good. "Tell me—are you hoping for a boy or a girl?"

"Oh, a girl. Of course."

"Why 'of course'?"

"Well, every mother wants a girl. So she can dress her up and teach her things."

Oh, God, Talba. Don't say 'Things like, what color pink to put on her nails?' Just don't say it. Instead, she said, "Things like Faulkner and Shakespeare?"

She knew she was starting to lose it.

"Why . . . no." Michelle looked uncertain, not really wanting to believe she'd been insulted. "Things about life."

Things about life. What the hell does the Black Barbie know about life? Her fury was getting out of hand. She nodded to take up the slack while she broke off a piece of bread, buttered it, and stuffed it in her mouth to avoid saying the wrong thing. Which would be just about anything, considering her mood. She tried to analyze it.

She was nice to me last night. She got all dressed up and came out just to honor me and my boyfriend. Why am I so hostile toward her?

The answer came so fast it shocked her: *It's the baby. I don't want her having a Wallis baby.*

Wallises were achievers; Michelle was a parasite.

The humor of it eluded her—the likelihood that Michelle's family would feel the same way about a Wallis baby, for entirely different reasons. She turned furious eyes on Michelle, who seemed oblivious. She had used the time to think of a way to change the subject. "Sandra, I've been thinking."

"Talba."

"I beg your pardon?"

"Talba. My name's Talba. Why can't my own family even call me by my name?"

"Oh." Michelle seemed genuinely startled. "I thought that was just your professional name."

"No, it's my everyday name. The name everyone calls me."

Michelle took a bite of lettuce. Talba was sure nothing fat, sweet, salty, or chocolate ever entered her mouth.

"Corey says you've really had it tough with that name of yours. And there were other things too. I want you to know that we understand how badly damaged you are, . . . ah, how deeply it affected you, and we just . . ." Her hands flew and her perfect red talons were arrowheads. ". . . that is, we want to accept you for who you are and we're trying to . . ."

Talba set down her wineglass so hard it spilled. "How badly *damaged* I am?"

She realized she must have spoken loudly. Both Corey and Darryl were staring at her. A pool of silence had fallen at the surrounding tables.

Corey said, "What's going on here?"

"I didn't mean that. It came out wrong."

But Talba knew she was quoting her brother, and the knowledge was balling up in her stomach, as hard as a baseball and about that size.

Michelle's face flashed a distress call. "All I meant to say . . . I know you've had a really hard time . . . even *you* don't know . . ."

"You're goddam right I don't know. And why the fuck don't I?" The little pool of silence had overflowed into every corner of the restaurant. Even the wait staff had frozen. Darryl put a hand on her thigh, but she ignored it. "It makes you feel so damned important to have a secret, doesn't it? You're so pitiful. Just *so* insecure with your little half-baked psychological homilies—as you damned well ought to be. Anybody as inadequate as you *should* feel inadequate—and if your pathetic little secret knowledge makes you feel like a real person for once in your pathetic little life . . ."

The maître d' appeared, running. "Everything all right here?"

Talba would have expected Corey to grovel and snivel. To her surprise, he barked at the man. "Everything's fine. We won't be needing your help." He turned to Michelle. "Leave. Quickly."

"*Me?* But Sandra's the one . . ."

"Michelle. Leave. Wait in the car." She stared at her husband in astonishment, biting her lip, then pushed back her chair and swept out.

This turn of events was so unexpected that Talba's anger began to abate, and the restaurant came back into focus. It was as if she'd passed out for a moment. Darryl had risen and put an arm around her, but it was Corey's face she was staring at. He said, "You okay, little bird?"

She couldn't speak to him, only stood and let Darryl steer her out. Corey followed, having apparently made some deal to settle up later with the restaurant. Talba could only imagine what sort of apologies he'd given—"under a strain," "medication," something like that.

She was intensely moved by the way he'd rescued her; and constitutionally unable to face him. Saying nothing, she let Darryl lead her to the car, and bundle her into it. He tried to hold her, but she couldn't stand being touched, couldn't even stand to look at him. He started the car.

"You taking me to the emergency room?" she said.

"Would you like me to?"

She shook her head. "No. I want to go home." Her voice was a watery trickle.

She didn't speak again till they'd arrived at Miz Clara's, and neither did Darryl.

Her mother met them at the door. "Ohhhh, baby. Oh, my baby. Come on in this minute."

Corey had phoned and told the whole sorry story. Talba felt a sudden automatic jet of fury, but humiliation smothered it. She covered her face with her hands. Darryl said, "I think she needs to be alone," and what happened next was at least as amazing as Corey's ordering Michelle from the restaurant.

Miz Clara said, "You take her to her room—will you? In case she needs any help."

Even in her stupor, Talba knew that her mother had just given Darryl permission to enter her daughter's bedroom, indeed to stay with her all night if need be. She was too far into her turtle shell to contemplate the meaning of it.

She lay down on the bed without even thinking, but Darryl lifted her shoulders, took her by the arms, and pulled her to a sitting position. "You can't sleep in that."

And she had let him take off the African-print jacket, the three silver necklaces, the beaded belt, and, finally, her green dress and bra. He had let her keep her panties, but she wriggled out of them. "I'm cold."

He found her a T-shirt to sleep in, and asked her if she wanted him to stay. She shook her head, once again unable to speak. He kissed her forehead and left.

She heard him talking to Miz Clara, but she was past caring.

Chapter Nineteen

Her mother woke her as usual: "Who you think you is, Queen of the May?"

But it was Saturday, and Talba was damned if she was getting up. Miz Clara was gone by the time she got around to it—she worked every other Saturday for a lady in the French Quarter. A note on the kitchen table noted tersely that: *Darryl Boucree is as fine a Christian as I have ever seen.*

Not just any old thing could amuse Talba that morning, but that did. She'd never asked Darryl if he was a Christian; she herself was not, though she'd never mentioned that fact to Miz Clara.

She made herself coffee, and as she waited for it, considered a drink instead. She wasn't really going to have one, she knew that in advance. But the idea was certainly appealing—anything to avoid the shame of the previous evening. The shame and the ramifications:

Corey would never be able to go back to his favorite restaurant.

Michelle would divorce him, and he'd never see his child.

Miz Clara would choose between her children, and she'd pick Corey.

Darryl would never call her again—no one would date a crazy person.

Did she dare call him?

She didn't think so.

She found his note when she went to make her bed, pinned to the pillow like a good-bye in a country song. She picked it up with dread. But all it said was, "Your Grace: Call me, why don't you? Your faithful servant"

What to make of that one? "Faithful" was good, maybe all wasn't lost. Then again, maybe it was. If the news was bad, she wasn't ready for it.

On the other hand, the note poked her out of her shell. She was ready for something—but what? She went back into the kitchen, poured herself a second coffee, and sat down to think.

Uh-uh, that didn't work. Too painful.

She wasn't actually conscious of any transition, was simply aware that she was back in her room, sitting at the computer, having utterly renounced her vow of the day before, to forget about her father. This thing wouldn't wait.

The only thing was, she couldn't get what she wanted on-line. She'd give anything to be able to hack into the *Times-Picayune* library. Frustrated, she wondered if the public library was open on Saturday, and then had a better idea. She had a friend at the paper, a reporter who'd once done a story on her—maybe Jane Storey would look up what she wanted. She gave her a call.

Unfortunately it meant telling a lot of her personal business, but that was what it took to get a reporter intrigued. Even so, it looked like it wasn't going to work until finally Talba blurted, "Dammit,

Jane, I'm a baroness! You have to do what I say." A good laugh, it seemed, was almost as good as information. "All right, all right." Storey giggled. "Anything you say, Your Grace," and went off to check the old files.

It was a thumb-twiddling thirty minutes before the phone rang. "Hey, Baroness, I think I've got it. Listen to this: 'Body Found in Apartment.' But I warn you, it's not pretty."

"I can handle it."

"Okay, here goes. It's mercifully short."

It was only about two paragraphs, and all it said was that Denman Wallis had been found in his own living room, dead of a gunshot wound. Or that was almost all—it said he'd been found after neighbors reported a foul smell. The body was in an advanced state of decomposition.

When she had thanked Jane and hung up, Talba closed her eyes to see if she could still run the movie. It was there like before, only now she saw only the blood, a flowing, fearsome lake of it. For the first time she heard a voice—"Sandra! Oh, baby, baby, baby! Oh, baby!" Miserable. Keening. "Come here, baby. You all right. Everything's okay." And then arms around her. Being picked up and held by someone.

Not Miz Clara. A man.

Her eyes were open now, staring at the screen, but she was still watching the movie. Only now it was more like a video game, with characters interchangeable at her whim. She played it as it must have happened.

If mother-as-murderess was what they were keeping from her, then who had picked her up? Could it have been Corey?

No. If she was seven, he'd have been fourteen, and even now he wasn't a big man—as far as she remembered, he'd been a runty teenager. This was definitely an adult. She couldn't think of anyone close enough to the family to be there at a time like that. There must have been an argument—nobody would argue in front of guests.

Unless the argument was *about* the guest.

Did Miz Clara have a lover? The idea was so preposterous, Talba almost laughed. If she and Corey hadn't existed, she'd have thought her mother had never had sex in her life—never had the slightest interest in it.

Maybe Miz Clara had learned the hard way.

Talba's overloaded brain was screaming with the effort of it. *Come on, folks, is this worth driving me crazy for? Give me a fucking break!*

She realized she was furious.

"Goddam it to hell!" She yelled loud enough to be heard on the north shore and threw a shoe across the room. Unsatisfied, she threw the other shoe. "Motherfucking motherfucker!" No doubt Mrs. Glapion down the block had heard her, but she was well beyond excusing her French.

She sat down hard on the bed and lay back, staring at the ceiling. *This is what made me so mad last night. The goddam conspiracy.*

They are not getting away with it. There's got to be something.

There were several things. There was an old cedar chest in which her mother kept—what? She didn't know.

There was a hall closet that hadn't been cleaned since her childhood, that she knew of.

And there was an attic.

It was Saturday, and she had all day.

Every instinct told her to go for the cedar chest, that that was where it would be, if it existed. She'd never even known Miz Clara to open it.

But she couldn't do that quite yet. She was angry at her mother, but such an invasion of privacy was going to require an act of will she wasn't yet up to.

She figured the heat in the attic would be unbearable, but she was still willing to go there first. To get to it, you had to pull down a door in the ceiling and climb a folding ladder. Armed with a flashlight, she ascended gingerly, on fastidious alert for crawly things.

But it was remarkably clean up there. This was where her mother kept her winter clothes in summer, and her summer clothes in winter. There were garment bags there, and some black-plastic leaf bags closed with a twist of wire.

Talba worried them open. Clothes were inside—clothes of her mother's that she could remember Miz Clara wearing fairly recently. Certainly nothing from another era. They were probably things waiting to go to the Goodwill, or maybe a rummage sale at church.

She was drenched when she descended and folded up the ladder. Okay, it was done. Some iced tea and then back to work.

Was she ready for the cedar chest?

Now or never, she thought. *Let's do it.*

She popped briefly by the closet, just to reassure herself, and found it so packed with things she couldn't identify, she found she actually preferred the chest.

Ms. Clara used the top for a catchall. It was stacked with old church bulletins and boxes of pledge envelopes. There was a little shell-encrusted figure of Jesus on a cross that Talba had brought her from Florida once when she was a child. It made Talba wince, as it had even at age nine, but she'd known her mother loved Jesus, and there wasn't that much of which Miz Clara did approve.

There was a cardboard stationery box of cards her mother had saved, birthday and Mother's Day cards from Talba and Corey, which made Talba tear up.

Things like that were private; they shouldn't be seen by anyone but the collector—especially not by the collected. There were some pills, too, and some old magazines, mostly copies of the *Watchtower* left by Jehovah's Witnesses. She had heard Miz Clara promise the Witnesses she'd read them, and Talba was sure she still meant to, though some were seven years old and had never been touched.

Talba took careful note of where everything was and then laid it all out in the same pattern on her mother's carefully made bed.

She opened the chest. The smell of cedar filled the room. Startled, she jumped as if an animal had leapt out.

Fitted onto an inch-wide wooden shelf that ran round the perimeter of the chest was a sort of shallow drawer that lifted out, divided into two small compartments and one large. Lying there right on top, in the middle of the large one, was something that took her breath away. Her parents' wedding picture, framed in silver.

She picked it up, taking in every detail. Miz Clara thirty-odd years younger and wearing a white dress! She couldn't get over it. Absolutely could not imagine such a thing.

It was a long, beautiful, lacy white dress, with veil to match. Absolutely the whole nine yards. Ten minutes earlier, Talba would have bet money that Miz Clara had worn a church dress down to City Hall to get married.

But her mother had been a real bride, as radiant as the cliché held. Talba kept staring, inspecting the picture for signs of her mother's cynicism, her brittleness, even her stoicism, and all she could see was happiness. And hope. And real hair, she was pretty sure—Miz Clara had been buzz-cutting her hair and wearing wigs for dress-up ever since Talba could remember.

She thought: *Why don't I know about this? What little girl doesn't know about her parents' wedding?*

A memory came blasting back—Talba playing with her dolls, humming the "Wedding March," Miz Clara yelling at her. "Girl, you stop that foolishness. You want to end up pregnant at fo'teen? Ya want to finish school or not?"

She had been nine at the most.

Talk of marriage was as *verboten* in the Wallis household as talk of Daddy. Miz Clara had always said, "Don't you ever depend on some man to take care of you. You got one person you can depend on, and her name's Sandra Wallis. That's all you got in this world."

Hurt, she had asked, "What about you, Mama? I thought I had you."

And her mother had laughed. "Baby, you got to take care of *me*."

She looked at her father's picture. He was handsome. So handsome she was instantly drawn to him, though perhaps that was because she knew she was looking at her father. He was a nice medium brown color, like she was, and he had an Afro (though her mother's hair was straightened). He also wore a lush moustache, a masculine attribute for which she'd always had a weakness. He was dressed in black tie, proper as you please, standing politely behind his bride. You'd never have guessed he'd become a druggie and die of a gunshot wound.

Talba felt herself tearing up again. *What a waste!*

She was disgusted with herself: *Get a grip, girl. The guy was worthless. Everyody says so.*

Still. You only get one father.

There were other pictures in the drawerlike compartment, though this was the only framed one. The others were loose, as if carelessly tossed, though there was nothing careless about Miz Clara. They must be things she couldn't bear to part with, no matter how much she professed to despise her husband's memory. The first one Talba saw was a two-by-three-inch photo of herself, snaggletoothed and pigtailed; a school picture, probably from second grade. Again, she felt like an intruder. She didn't want to know that her mother had saved a picture like this of her, and she knew her mother wouldn't want her to know. It was far too sentimental a gesture for Miz Clara to acknowledge.

There were more pictures of her, and some of Corey, and some of Aunt Carrie. One that really got to her was of all of them, six-year-old Corey all dressed up in a suit like his dad's, their father wearing a tie, Carrie and Clara in dresses and hats, each holding a baby daughter, each daughter decked out in white lace. On the back, someone had written, "Easter, 1974." Talba wondered who had taken it.

It was hard, looking at those pictures. She wanted to stare at each one forever, and yet the most cursory glance made her feel so guilty her stomach hurt. The phone rang, and she nearly threw herself under the bed.

Darryl, she thought, and let it go. Pausing now wasn't going to make it any easier.

She did stare at them for a while, even laid some on the floor and looked at them in the aggregate. There was so much so see . . . so much it took her nearly an hour to find the flat, green-leather album at the bottom of the pile. It was trimmed with gold and looked bought at a stationery store, an extravagant purchase for someone like Miz Clara. It was no one's idea of a wedding album, yet that was what it was—and indeed it had a dignity that one of those white shiny ones wouldn't have had.

For the first time, she saw a picture of her grandmother. Her grandfather had died when Carrie and Clara were in high school, and her grandmother, when Talba was a baby. Talba thought it odd that there were no photos of her anywhere in the house—but then, there were no photos at all. They were all, it seemed, in the cedar chest.

If her father had parents, they hadn't come to the wedding—perhaps he had come from too far away for poor folks to travel. Aunt Carrie had been maid of honor, and there was a best man—someone named William Green whom Talba didn't recognize. He'd be difficult to trace with a name like that, but she could try. There were no bridesmaids and no groomsmen.

The photographer evidently hadn't shot pictures of the guests as well as the wedding party, in the casual manner of the late nineties. But there was a face she knew. There was a great shot of the bride and groom saying their vows, the preacher's solemn brown face peering out above their clasped hands. And he was someone she knew. He was a man she remembered from her childhood, when her mother had made her go to church every Sunday—the Reverend Clarence Scruggs, as nasty an old devil as she'd ever met in her life.

Old. The thought chilled her. Maybe he was dead. Still, though—she remembered the Easter finery— her parents had gone to church. She looked closely at the pictures, and there could be no doubt—it was the same church her mama went to to this day. Surely someone there would remember her father. Someone. Surely.

There were no papers, no other clues in the shallow compartment. What on earth was in the chest proper? She tugged the container off its narrow shelf, no easy job, since the chest was probably two and a half by five feet.

It was only about a third full, and what was in it was underwear. A satin robe and nightgown; some lacy slips and panties. She knew instantly what it was—her mother's trousseau.

Talba had been a fairly decent history student—she was perfectly aware of the turmoil of the sixties. She knew all about Black Power and Black Panthers and Black Is Beautiful. (And personally, she thought of herself as black—"African-American" was too cumbersome and sounded like a euphemism. She'd run across the old rallying cry, "I'm black and I'm proud" and wondered whatever had become of it.) When all that was going on, her parents were getting married. Her mama was shopping for a trousseau, dreaming a dream.

It was enough to make you cry.

She felt around in the bottom of the chest, just in case, and, in fact, felt something hard, something in a little plastic envelope. Fishing it out, she beheld her mother's diaphragm, which she dropped like it was radioactive. Quickly, she pushed it to the bottom and fluffed some underwear around it, so maybe Miz Clara would never know her daughter had done this. Talba was numb with remorse.

She had the whole thing back together, church bulletins, seashell Jesus, and all in ten minutes. She would die, would absolutely, no question, croak if Miz Clara ever knew she'd touched her diaphragm and eyeballed her undies.

She went in her own room and flopped again on the bed, feeling the turtle response setting in.

Uh-oh, she thought. Gotta fight it. She breathed some, counting the breaths, a technique she'd learned from a boyfriend who was into martial arts. In fact, she promptly went to sleep, which was full-tilt turtle, she knew from experience, but she slept only a few minutes, waking refreshed and hungry.

She took a shower, fixed herself some lunch, and made up a story to tell when she called the church. She checked her voice mail, but if Darryl had called, he wasn't owning up. Maybe it was Corey, she thought, and realized for the first time she was going to have to apologize to Michelle.

Oh, God. Maybe I could find a fairy godmother to turn me into a real turtle. Permanently.

A machine answered when she called the church. The days of full-time church secretaries were apparently over—but then it was Saturday. Still, things would be going on there. Maybe some ladies cooking for a needy family, something like that—maybe someone's house had burned down, and they needed a casserole.

Aha! She had an idea. The latest church bulletin was on the cedar chest, and she was in luck—it listed a White Elephant Sale for the Wednesday Night Prayer Group. That meant plenty of ladies, some of them old. Most of them, probably. She thought about taking the plastic bags from the attic, but the minute she did, Miz Clara would declare the missing garments her favorites—there was a law about that.

So she packed up some stuff of her own and drove on over, surprised she could still find the place after her long absence.

She made her manners and her donation and started asking around, getting all the wrong answers: "Why, no, I don't b'lieve I do recall a Clarence Scruggs."

"Brother Scruggs? Why, he's been gone a long time. Must be ten, twelve years."

"I haven't thought about that old man in a month of Sundays—I wonder whatever did become of him?"

"You might ask Lura Blanchard. She said she'd pass by later on."

Anybody might pass by later on—maybe even Clarence Scruggs himself. But Talba was a woman on a mission; if she lost her momentum, she'd go back in her shell. She started wandering.

It was amazing how things came back to her. She

knew exactly where to find the downstairs powder room, the social hall, the Sunday school rooms, and that indispensable repository of records—the church office. Mailing lists and tithes were probably computerized now, but they hadn't always been. Talba was hoping for some old-fashioned file cabinets. Unfortunately, the office door was locked.

Could she unlock it with a credit card? Getting caught would be ugly, but what the hell.

She gave it a shot, but couldn't make it work.

There was always the window. She could heave a rock through it.

She heard footsteps. Quickly, she knocked, to give the appearance of innocence. An old woman came into view, a woman who looked at least ninety. She was wispy, thin like old people get, and the kind of short that has once been tall. Her skin was light and her wiry white hair was cut in an ear-length bob and parted on the side. She walked with a cane, but that didn't stop her from wearing two-inch heels. She looked elegant in her white hair, navy dress, and spiffy shoes. She was the sort of old lady who'd probably bury all her friends and die with her funeral perfectly planned, right down to the hymns.

"Hello, Sandra Wallis," she said. "I heard you were looking for me."

Talba was speechless. She'd never seen the woman before in her life. Maybe she was the church ghost.

"I know ya," the apparition said. "Been knowin' ya all ya life." She waved an encompassing arm. "All those sisters out there—they know ya. This a Christian church, girl. Once you in it, ya in it forever."

That wasn't Talba's understanding of the way the thing worked, but she understood that that was a technicality—Miz Clara had raised her in this church, and no matter what kind of heathen she'd since become, they were always ready to take her back—even if she didn't remember them.

She gave her new pal a great big granddaughterly smile. "I know your face—I just can't recall the name."

"Lura Blanchard, dollin'. You axed for me, didn't ya?"

Talba put out her hand to shake, but to her surprise, the woman gathered her up in a hug. "Welcome back, child."

"Why thank you, Miz Blanchard. I was just wondering if anybody's in the office."

"Well, I used to be—every day of my life." ·

The same face, much plumper and smoother, appeared on Talba's mental screen. "You were the church secretary."

"Tha's right, dollin'. For thirty-odd years. See, ya do remember."

Talba was starting to worry about the old lady. She looked around wildly, hoping for a couple of armchairs. "Is there anyplace we can go to sit down?"

"Sho' honey. Got my key right here." Lura Blanchard reached in her elegant dress and pulled a key from her bosom. "Never gave this up for just that reason. Every now and then, I like a quiet place to sit down."

Without an apparent second thought, she broke into the church office. Talba must have been showing her amazement. Lura Blanchard said, "It's all right, dollin'. What belongs to the church belongs to all of us."

Sure enough, there were a pair of good chairs in there. Each of them took one. "I understand you looking for Reverend Scruggs."

"Yes, ma'am. I wonder if you know where I can find him?" Talba hoped she didn't sound too phony. The effort of behaving genteelly was getting to her.

"*You* want him or ya mama?"

It was a tough one. Talba didn't know which was the preferred answer. She decided she'd better not lie. The whole thing was going to get back to Miz Clara, if it hadn't already. She had no idea these people kept such close tabs on one another. "It's for me," she said. "I need to ask him about a bit of church history."

"Is that right, now? Well, I might be able to help. I been here longer than anybody but God."

"Miz Blanchard, are you a close friend of my mama's?"

"Clara Wallis? As fine a Christian woman as I've ever met in my life." That didn't actually answer the question, but it was rhetorical anyway.

"I'm asking because I thought she might have told you about my job. I'm doing some confidential investigating for a security company. I'm afraid it involves something I'm permitted to talk about only with those who're directly involved." She babbled on, to cover the awkward moment. "I'm awfully sorry—for *me*, I mean—'cause I'll bet anything you do know."

Lura Blanchard gave her a wry smile that didn't tell Talba whether she'd bought the lie or not. She said, "Well, let me see what I can do for ya." And proceeded to rifle the church files.

She knew exactly what she was looking for and where to find it. In less than a minute, she had an official-looking card in her hand. "Uh-huh. Here's an update on his address. We don't see much of Reverend Scruggs anymore." Her small, proper mouth assumed another wry little twist. " 'Course, some folks think tha's a *good* thing."

Talba matched her smile for smile. "He was kind of an old terror, wasn't he?"

"Wasn't much joy in him—all hellfire and damnation. I don't believe tha's God's message, but that was Reverend Scruggs's path, so who am I to criticize?"

"Surely the church paid him. I'd have thought you'd have some say-so."

"Well, we must have needed him—he was what God sent us. And I certainly wouldn't argue with His plan for us. Would you?"

Talba sidestepped that one. "Guess you right," she said, in her one habitual lapse of standard English—she found it smoothed over a multitude of sticky situations. "Shall I copy down Reverend Scruggs's address and phone number?"

"Help yaself, child. Help yaself." The old woman sighed in what might have been resignation. Talba wondered again how good a friend of her mother's she was. On impulse she said, "Did you know my father?"

"Ya father? Why no, I didn't. I don't b'lieve he was a member here."

And yet he had worn that Easter suit.

Talba helped the old lady back downstairs and thanked her as curtly as she politely could—a process she managed to pare down to twenty minutes or so. She was itching to get to the Reverend Scruggs before her mother found out she'd been trespassing on her turf.

Chapter Twenty

The good reverend had evidently fallen on hard times, or perhaps Baptists simply didn't pay their ministers much. These days he was living in public housing for seniors.

She dreaded going to see him. She could remember his flashing, angry eyes, the way he pounded and paced when he really got going. One sermon she particularly remembered, delivered when there had been a lot of gang activity: "The Lord will not *tolerate* such as this. He will destroy these young people as he destroyed the Canaanites, as he destroyed the Philistines, as he destroyed all the enemies of Israel. Destruction shall rain down upon them and peace shall be restored."

So far as she knew, peace hadn't ever been restored, but within three months, seven or eight young men in the gangs had been destroyed. Talba was young enough to be impressed. When she thought about it, that particular sermon had done more than anything else to make her lose interest in the church.

Considering the neighborhood she was going into, she wished she had a steering-wheel lock. The kids in the streets looked pretty much like the ones upon whom the Reverend Mr. Scruggs had called down destruction all those years ago. He must have lost his touch.

Now don't you worry, she told herself. *Crime is down all over the city.*

Still, a woman alone didn't go places she shouldn't, and Talba really shouldn't be here. She wondered if she should get a gun, and almost laughed: *I'd probably shoot myself.*

The man who came to the door looked about as old as Lura Blanchard, but he'd fattened up where she'd thinned out. He had quite a watermelon on him, showed off by a wife-beater T-shirt. Chest hair that peeked out of it was as white as the hair on his head. He was barefoot and struggling to get a pair of specs on his face. "Are you the lady from the home health? We weren't expecting you today."

"Reverend Scruggs?"

He smiled at that—he must not hear it much anymore. "Brother Scruggs is fine."

"Lura Blanchard told me where to find you."

"Why I'll be darned—Lura Blanchard! Come in, come in." And he opened the door. "Will you 'scuse me a moment?" He looked hugely uncomfortable.

A female voice called from another room: "Clarence? Who's that?"

" 'Scuse me, will you?" The Reverend Mr. Scruggs hitched up his pants as he departed.

His hair had been black when Talba knew him, and his manner so fierce even some of the congregation's adults found him scary. More than his belly seemed to have softened up.

Talba checked out the room while she waited.

It was short on furniture and long on mementoes. In fact, there was really nothing large in it but a couple of bookshelves, a television, a table against a wall, and two chairs with a small table between them. Bookshelves, tables, and walls were loaded, however—with pictures, diplomas, newspaper clippings, scrapbooks, awards, certificates of appreciation, everything he could scare up to remind him of the life he used to have. Talba wondered which was better—the remembered or the current one. This one looked meager and hard, but the man seemed more at ease with it.

He returned wearing a fresh white shirt and a clean pair of trousers. Talba could see that he'd also splashed water on his face and guessed he'd brushed his teeth as well. He extended his hand. "Well, now. Well, now. Whom do I have the honor of addressing?"

"Talba Wallis, sir. I used to be called Sandra. My mother's Clara Wallis. Perhaps you remember us from First Bethlehem Baptist."

"Wallis? I remember your mama. Yes."

The voice called to him again. "Clarence? Who is that with you, Clarence?"

"Excuse me a moment, will you?" he said, and this time she heard him speaking softly to someone. When he came back, he closed a door somewhere behind him. "My wife," he said. "She is an invalid, I'm afraid. She had a stroke several years ago, and has never fully recovered. Her memory is very poor."

Talba was intrigued. The notion of being what amounted to this man's prisoner would have horrified her at one time, but he had spoken to his wife as gently as any nurse. She asked if he was her principal caregiver.

"I am, yes. It pretty well keeps me occupied."

"It must be hard on you."

"On the contrary. Had it not been for my wife, I

might have lost my way entirely. She is my dearest love, and I find it a privilege to care for her." The words would have been difficult for most people to say—far too intimate to fit into the twenty-first century—and yet he had spoken them simply and sincerely, without the pastoral bombast of previous years.

"You seem different from the way I remember you."

He nodded. "Yes, ma'am, I am different. And I am proud of it too."

"What did your wife say to you? I mean, how did she . . ." Talba felt she'd gone too far, but didn't know how to extricate herself. "I'm sorry," she said. "It's none of my business."

"No, it is not, and yet I am quite happy to tell you. It was not what she said, but who she was. We had a child who was stricken with a rare and painful disease. I felt as though the Lord had turned against me. I was devastated and I was angry—after all, I was the fiercest soldier in His army. And then I gradually came to see that the God I had been looking for, the holy spirit itself, dwelt in this woman who took such loving, uncomplaining care of our stricken child, and I vowed to remake myself in her image."

Talba wasn't quite sure what she was hearing. "Are you saying that . . . uh . . ."

"Not that I worshiped my wife. Certainly not. I worshiped her only in the sense that any man worships the woman he loves. I mean only that the holy spirit dwells in all of us and that in her I was able to see it shining through and to understand its shape and its texture, its beauty and its glory, to see for the first time that which had eluded me for so many years. And I felt that I was home."

"Well." Talba hardly knew what to say—the simplicity of his belief, his lack of bombast, was really quite moving. "You still preach a beautiful sermon."

"I meant that as no sermon, young woman. Simply as a statement of fact."

She smiled at him, beginning to get over her embarrassment. "And I thank you for it, sir." She was starting to talk like him.

"What can I do for you, Miss Wallis?"

"Ah. Me." She had actually forgotten about herself for a while. This felt a lot more like being in church than sitting in First Bethlehem ever had— maybe the Lord really did move in mysterious ways. "I don't know where to start."

"Why don't you start at the beginning?" Kindly old uncle eyes looked out at her from behind the specs. She might as well have been talking to Santa Claus. It occurred to her she could unload on this man—he was a perfect stranger, and he used to be a preacher.

"Have you got a while?" She asked, "I might need a little pastoral counseling."

"Certainly I have. Let me just go see to Ella."

While he was gone, she halfway considered bolting, but coming back would be too hard. At the very worst, maybe he'd tell her if she needed a shrink.

"Would you like some coffee?" he said. "Mine is not very good, but it may pump you up for the ordeal to come."

"What ordeal?"

"You are not looking forward to talking about it, are you?"

"Listen, let me just dive in while you're making that coffee."

He motioned her to come to the kitchen, and began to move clumsily about it.

"I made a scene in a restaurant last night. My brother's probably never going to speak to me again. My boyfriend's probably given up on me."

"If you have come to me, this is not the beginning of your problem."

"Everybody's keeping a secret from me. A big, big deal of a secret."

"I see." He nodded, and held out a cup of coffee. Indeed he looked like a shrink. Maybe it wasn't going to be too bad.

Seated at his old kitchen table (which was every bit as disreputable as Miz Clara's), she poured out the story in little clumps of remembrance—some from childhood, most from the last few days, and some the gray-mist ones of the movie in her head—ending with the scene from the night before, the compulsion that had come over her this morning, even the White Elephant Sale and Lura Blanchard, whom she ratted out for breaking and entering, thinking she and the reverend might have a big old laugh about it. And indeed, they were such pals by that time, that it came, as he might have said, to pass.

He filled her cup again and looked at her over the top of his glasses. "What are you afraid of, child?"

She wondered why he hadn't read as much between the lines as she did. "I think my mother killed him. I think . . . maybe . . . there might have been another woman, and it might have even have been . . ." She had a thought way the hell in the back of her mind. Was it too stupid to say it? *Spit it out, girl. Come out of your shell.* "My aunt Carrie," she said at last. "That man? You know, that man I remember? It could have been my uncle. That's the only person it really could be—he killed my daddy because, you know, he caught him with his wife . . ."

"Slow down. Slow down now. I can't tell whether you think your uncle killed him or your mama."

"I'm *afraid* it's my mama. I guess I was just hoping maybe it was the man—because nobody loved me like that that I can remember. My uncle would have been the only one, you see? The man picked me up and hugged me and tried to comfort me . . ."

"Well, your mind can play tricks on you."

"I guess it can." She was deeply disappointed—she wasn't getting much in the way of wisdom out of Reverend Born-Again.

"But I want you to rest easy, now. Your mama didn't kill your daddy."

She looked at him curiously, unsure if he was speaking from knowledge or opinion.

"I remember a lot about the story. No ma'am. Your mama didn't kill him and your Aunt Carrie didn't carry on with him. I don't care what her name is." He laughed at his own small pun. "That I can promise you. Yes ma'am, I can promise you that. But there *was* another woman—you're right about that. And that's what broke your parents' marriage up. Your daddy left home when you were just a baby."

"Oh. I thought they lied about when he left—I guess I took 'left' to mean disappeared or dead or something. I didn't catch on that he moved out."

"Oh, yes, I remember it well. He and your mama were separated. Not divorced, though; don't believe they ever divorced."

"Did he move to another city or what?"

"He didn't move to another city—that I remember. Wait a minute, why do I think that?" He closed his eyes for a minute and bent over the old table. He could have been praying, for all Talba knew. "Yes. Yes, I do remember. I saw him in church after that, with you and your brother."

Talba couldn't feature that one, considering the way Miz Clara felt about him to this day. The wound would have been much fresher then, more tender and sore. "You mean, he sat with mama and us?"

"I don't think so. I can't seem to recollect seeing your mama with the three of you."

"Well, I appreciate what you're saying, but I'm still

not getting why you're so sure Miz Clara didn't kill him."

"I know what I know, girl." A touch of the old fierceness had crept into his voice. "I can't divulge your mama's secrets, but I know what I know."

There it was—the same old thing again. "What *is* this thing with secrets?"

"Now, hush, Sandra. You just hush now." He spoke just above a whisper; Talba could imagine him speaking that way to his demented wife. "By the time your daddy died, your mama had moved on. She had other things on her mind. Yes, ma'am. Yes, she did."

"You sound as if you remember when he died."

For the first time, he seemed confused. "Well, now, I can't say I do exactly. The service must have been somewhere else—maybe his woman's church, or his parents'. But one thing I can say for sure. Miz Clara wasn't studying on that man anymore. She had moved on from that."

Suddenly the light started to dawn, so clearly she didn't see how she could have been so stupid. "Are you saying my mama had a boyfriend?"

"Child, you know I can't talk about something like that. You know I can't. If Miz Clara won't talk about her own life, far be it from me." He stood up. "Let me just check on Ella."

When he came back, Talba had readied herself to leave, a process that took only a little longer than leaving Lura Blanchard had. After many thank-yous and be-goods and take-care-of-yourselfs and promises not to be a stranger, they finally severed the connection.

Talba was a little disoriented, but otherwise okay. Feeling turtlelike, that was all. And utterly unprepared to see Darryl's car in front of her house when she arrived. Darryl was coming down the walk, just leaving.

"How's Your Grace this fine afternoon?" He was trying to be his old easy self, but there was something stiff about him.

"Embarrassed," Talba said. "Humiliated beyond all imagining. Abject. Do you think you could possibly ever forgive me?"

He relaxed a bit. "Consider it done. But we do have to talk—I'm not kidding. I got worried when I couldn't get you on the phone."

"I was too embarrassed to call."

"Can we talk?"

She shrugged, wondering what fresh hell this was. "If we go somewhere else. I'm not in the mood for Miz Clara right now."

"Nor am I. Let's take a walk, why don't we? City Park, maybe. Or maybe not. Too many flying horses. Maybe out by the lake."

Talba thought that ideal—the man was better than a doctor. She got in the car with him and started up again. "I don't know what got into me—I swear to God I don't."

"If I had to guess, I'd say it was frustration. You're right. They're all lying to you. They even kind of know they're wrong, but they can't *not* do it."

She whirled toward him. "You know something I don't."

He laughed. "Uh-uh. Not till we get there. Think about something else till we get there."

He thought that was funny. He didn't have a clue how blank she could make her mind, how easy it was for her to settle back in her shell—the more stress, the easier. And this was stress. Smugly, she idled her mind, and not until they were walking did he speak.

"You're not going to blink first?"

"You challenged me. But enough's enough. Out with it."

He picked up a stone and skipped it across the silvery surface. "Unfortunately, there is no it. Nobody told me what it is—just *that* it is. Goddam, Baroness. Something's funny in your family."

"Come on—everything! Now."

"Well, first Corey. Frankly, my dear, you were a tiny bit out of line . . ."

"Don't remind me."

"But did he get upset? No, he got protective."

"Yeah, I noticed it too."

"And there was Miz Clara, waiting up for us with hot milk . . . he'd called her, of course. But you'd have thought she'd be panicked. I mean, what it looked like, speaking from the outside, was that the very distinguished Baroness de Pontalba had just flipped her famous lid."

"Oh, God, it's going to get around town."

He dismissed that one. "You're a poet. You can get away with it. But Miz Clara almost seemed to be expecting it. And she did talk to me."

"You've been holding out on me."

"Uh-uh. I didn't learn a thing, except that *they're* holding out on you. She said I had to be especially nice to you, that you'd been a real nervous child, and the family was always 'scared something would happen.' "

"Scared what would happen?"

"You got me. I asked her specifically. All she'd do is put her lips together and shake her head. So I got tired of it, finally. I said, 'Look. Did something happen to Talba when she was little?' "

"Ha. What'd she say to that?"

"She narrowed her eyes and gave me the mother look—you know that look? All kids know that look. And she said, 'Chew mean, boy?' I know that ploy. I do it with my students all the time. And so, plung-

ing boldly into the abyss, I said, 'Did Talba see someone shoot her father?' "

Talba heard blood pounding in her ears. Whiz-
zing through her temples. *Zing. Zing!* An artery was
probably going to burst. "Oh, my God. I've got to
sit down." Instead, remembering the man who'd
kept her from fainting, she leaned over and touched
the grass, as if stretching her back. That was no
good—what she needed was less blood to the head.

She did sit down, and Darryl with her, rubbing
her back, sharing his warmth. Gradually, her run-
away heart began to subside. "What did she say?"

"She said, '*Oh,* no. Didn't see *no* such thing. Sandra didn't see *no* one shoot her daddy—you crazy
as she is, boy.' "

He did such a perfect Miz Clara that Talba, in the
midst of a near heart attack, burst out laughing.
"You shouldn't make fun of my mama."

He was laughing too. "I know. I hate myself when
I do it. But you think maybe she's protesting too
much?"

"Sounds like it, doesn't it? But I'm halfway relieved you actually asked her. See, Mama doesn't
lie."

"She was lying. Maybe you had to be there—I was
as sure of it as I am of . . . of . . ."

"Of what?"

"Oh, you know. Sky's blue, water's wet—that sort
of thing."

"Your baby loves you?"

"Does she?"

"Does he?" She was feeling better, but after the
night before, looking for a little reassurance.

"Can't. Sorry."

The blood started to *zing* again.

"A common man is not permitted to love a Baroness."

She relaxed. "How about if commanded?"

"Maybe if commanded."

"I so command."

He laughed. "Pushy, aren't we? Listen, I need to talk to you about something."

"Oh, God. I definitely need to lie down. Can I lie down for this?"

"No. Sit up, damn it. This is serious. I had kind of a revelation last night."

"Oh, shit." She put her hands over her ears. "I don't need to hear this. Not *today*, Darryl."

But when she looked at him, he was laughing. "Don't be silly. I'm not trying to break up with you— is that what you think?"

She executed five or six whole-body nods.

"Well . . . no. Not that I didn't consider it for a while—there in the restaurant. You know how sometimes you can think you know a person and yet . . ." He didn't have to finish. She was doing nods again. It was exactly what she thought he'd be thinking.

"And then, one look at Corey's face, and I knew something was badly wrong—and not with you. Your brother loves you very much, Talba."

"He does not. If he did, he wouldn't have married that . . . that marshmallow fluff."

"Oh, come on. Michelle isn't so bad."

"She is. You know she is."

"Just because she doesn't dress like a baroness . . ."

"Okay, okay." She wanted to get to the meat of this, whatever it was.

Darryl stood up. "Come on, let's walk some more. I want to walk."

She sensed that he wanted her beside him, so that they weren't looking into each other's eyes. "Fine with me." She dusted off her butt.

They were quiet for a few minutes. Talba was afraid to speak, but the suspense was so severe she had to take giant breaths to keep from hyperventilating.

It was getting late now, low sun glinting on the lake. The world was still, except for a faint lapping, and the occasional pelican's dive. She tried to absorb the calm.

When the words came, they glided to her out of nowhere, seeming not to be in Darryl's voice at all. "I wanted to protect you. I wanted you home with me."

The sentiment was so unexpected she blurted "What?" in a loud, outraged-sounding whine.

He put his arm around her waist. "It's okay. I'm not pushing you. I'm not asking you for anything. But I was thinking . . . maybe I will someday."

Talba's throat started to close. A turtle attack was coming, and she wasn't sure why. She loved Darryl. Why should she be afraid of this? This was what women wanted.

Darryl said, "Hello?"

"I, uh . . . sorry. My software's slow or something. I'm still downloading."

She could feel him withdrawing from her, knew it was a response to her own aloofness. "Look, there's a reason I'm saying all this." He was nervous. She heard it in his voice, and it amazed her. By day, Darryl Boucree taught high-school kids and by night, he played music all over the city. It took a lot to make him nervous. "All this talk about secrets is starting to get to me."

"Fine. I won't talk about it. Forget I ever said anything."

"Hold it; you're not getting it. I want you to talk about what's bothering you. Like I said . . ." He seemed to be having trouble getting it out.

"Yes?"

"I want to protect you. I want to help you. But I've started to feel like I'm not all there for you."

Was it reassurance he wanted? "Darryl, no one

could have been more kind and understanding . . ."

He stopped walking, turned toward the water.

He was standing with his hands in the pockets of his jacket, braced against the breeze. He looked like a god. She had an image suddenly of a man standing just like this, hands in pockets, the wind blowing as it was now, only he was a white man and so his hair moved when the wind blew, and he was smoking a cigarette and the wind blew the smoke as well. It was a kind of déjà vu, perhaps something she'd seen in a movie, and it was inexpressibly sad, the man remembering something he'd lost.

She knew in that moment that this was not the kind of sadness she saw in the eyes of men who could never be cheered up, that at least some of his sadness had been caused by her, and that she was capable of causing it again, and that any person who could cause this man to feel this way was not worthy of him.

"Darryl, I swear to God I'll never be such an asshole again."

"Get off that, will you? What I'm trying to say is that you were onto something the other night—there's a reason you've never met my daughter." He frowned. "How to say this? She's kind of a handful."

"You mean a brat?"

He looked hurt, and she remembered how she'd just seen him and what she'd realized. She could have kicked herself.

"It could be more than that—she's being tested. For now, let me just say she's difficult."

Talba knew what she should say—even wanted to say—but now, under pressure, it was a fight to get the words out. "Could I meet her?"

He nodded, slowly, solemnly, then he grinned.

That gave her courage. "Do I have to?" she said.

He swatted her on the backside. "Yep. You do." He was smiling like his old self.

Chapter Twenty-one

Eddie had it out with Angie over the weekend. She was tougher than Audrey, tougher than Tony. Hell, face it, she was tougher than Eddie.

But, knowing it was coming, he developed a strategy—he'd just say, yeah, yeah, she was right, and he didn't know what got into him, and it must have been temporary insanity, and then when she ranted on, he could act hurt and say why was she so mean to him?

It worked, too, up to a point. At least it freed him for thinking up anything to say to defend himself. Because it wasn't a strategy at all—it was really a decision just to lie down and take it. That was how it was with Angie. She wasn't a lawyer for nothing. She had things to say, she was going to say them— usually two or three times. Listening was no picnic— but on the other hand, it was the only alternative to fleeing the country.

So that was how his Saturday went. Sunday, he

went to Mass with Audrey, and, afterward, they took a drive. This was something they never did together. But he found himself suggesting it, and then there they were, off to the Gulf Coast to have lunch. Audrey was like a girl, she was so happy—happy that the last ten years had been wiped out and things she'd thought were true weren't and never had been. Happy that her baby boy was back. Even happy with Eddie. She had forgiven him big-time.

They ended up gambling in one of the casinos and-what-the-hell, spending the night there and, most amazing of all, having a nightcap and making love. Really doing it, not just Eddie getting off, which was what it usually felt like anymore—as if Audrey weren't there at all. Like she was just a prop.

All of which is to say, that was how he missed the eleven o'clock news, which it was his religion to watch. He picked up the paper Monday morning with a twinge of guilt, but it was nothing to what he felt when he actually saw what he saw—a picture of Aziza Scott, missing person. She hadn't come home from work Friday night; her ex-husband had reported her missing after his daughter called him, terrified. There was a picture of Cassandra on an inside page.

Eddie had dropped the ball.

He had let the case go when she fired him. Hadn't followed up with Shaneel. Goddammit, what was wrong with him?

"Audrey, we're going." She was still asleep, still in the afterglow of the night before.

Eddie was in another world by then. Because he took confidentiality seriously, he couldn't even tell her what was wrong with him, why his mood had suddenly turned demonic.

He had a very bad feeling about this. So bad he felt a tight metal band close on his midsection. He'd had this before; he knew all about it. It could be an

ulcer symptom, but in his case it probably wasn't—
it was stress. And he lived his life under stress. It
took an awful lot to cause something like this.

He dropped Audrey off without so much as going
in to change his socks and underwear. It was nearly
nine o'clock. He drove straight to the Scott house.
A man answered the door, colored fellow, seemed
nice, but a little sad. The kid's father, in from Baton
Rouge. Eddie explained who he was and said he had
to see Cassandra.

She hadn't gone to school that day. She was still
in bed, probably crying. She got up and dressed to
talk to Eddie.

He said, "How ya holding up?" and all the oblig-
atory stuff, and then he got down on one knee to
talk to her, just the way he had with his own kids
when he had something really important to tell
them. "I'm 'on tell ya something. I'm gonna find
your mama for ya—you believe that?"

She shook her head. Her father said they couldn't
afford Eddie's services.

He ignored the dad and spoke directly to Cassandra. "Listen, honey, ya mama fired me. I'm not
working for her or anybody else now. Just you. And
I work for you for free, ya got that?"

The dad said, "We really don't need your services," but Cassandra said, *"Daddy!"* in that teenage
way, and he shut up. The kid was scared spitless.

"Now I need ya to promise me some stuff."

She was nervous, kept glancing at her dad. Finally
she said, "Daddy, can I talk to Mr. Valentino alone?"

He said, "Certainly not. I'm your father. Anything
you say to him can be said in front of me."

He didn't know about Toes. Eddie realized suddenly that Aziza hadn't even told him—was probably afraid the whole incident would reflect badly on
her. He said quickly, "It's okay. Just stay with ya
dad—will ya promise me that?"

"I have to go to school."

"Just today, okay? Promise."

She nodded, utterly miserable. The phone rang, giving Eddie, after all, a minute alone with her. He said, "You know Toes has her, don't you?"

She screamed, "No!" so loud he saw he wasn't going to get anywhere.

He left her and drove to the office, where he kept a few clean clothes he could change into. He'd just done that, and was coming back from the men's room, when Talba came in fit to be tied.

"He's got Aziza."

"Yes, Ms. Wallis. I b'lieve you're right."

"Well, what if he goes after Cassandra next? Or Shaneel?"

"Now calm down, Ms. Wallis. Just try to be calm. Cassandra's father is with her. And Toes can't get Shaneel during school hours."

"How about after school?"

"We'll just have to get there first, won't we?" He hoped he sounded calm; if he did, it was a front.

Her eyes were wild things, operating with a mind of their own; her voice vibrated with panic. "Shouldn't we call the police. I mean, this is two murders that we know of . . ."

He sat down, moving slowly to calm her. He patted air, slowly. "Ms. Wallis, Ms. Wallis. For all we know, Ms. Scott took off with her boyfriend. We don't even know she's dead, much less that this is a murder. We had information about Rhonda Bergeron, and they weren't even interested. Now, we could call the police again. We could. But what would we say?"

"How about if we just call the tip line and say check out Baron Tujague's brother in the Scott case?"

"Now what's that gon' do?"

"I don't know, but it's something."

"Go do it then. Ya got my blessing. Whatever works. And whatever doesn't work, I don't care." He waved her away and called the church to see if he could get Shaneel's home phone number.

They said they didn't have one. Hell.

And Talba, with all her machines and magic, couldn't find out where the parents worked. Their only chance to see her was after school, and there was a small problem with that. Eddie shrugged it off—a *very* small one. He stopped in his assistant's office on the way out. "Ms. Wallis, I got a lunch date I can't break."

When she turned from her screen, her eyes were scooched up again, and flame shot out of them. He wondered if she had any idea what a presence she was—how easily she made herself known without ever saying a word. He said, "I see you think I should break it," and Eileen Fisher's voice sang out from the anteroom, "You're going, Uncle Eddie. Forget about it. You're going."

"Yeah, yeah, I'm going. Look, there's nothing I can do until after school, anyway—I'll meet ya at Fortier, okay?"

She tried to smile, but it didn't come off. Well, hell. He gave her points for trying.

Talba had been trying so frantically to come up with something—anything—that she hadn't even checked her e-mail. She had brought herself a tuna sandwich from home. She could eat that at her desk and catch up—she was way too hyper to try to relax.

But she did go out for a second—to a deli to get a Diet Coke, and, during her errand, she let her mind wander in Darryl's direction. Their relationship had unquestionably changed, whether for the better she didn't know. It was both more intimate and more distant, both states caused by his revelation. They were wary of one another now, each circling till there were further developments, yet both knew the meaning of what he had said, the longterm point of it. It was an incredibly brave thing to do. Talba deeply admired him for it. Loved him for it. And wished he hadn't done it quite yet.

Talba wasn't much on kids. Did she really need Darryl's difficult daughter in her life?

She scolded herself: *Stupid! Shallow! Hateful! That man is so good to you, it's like eating love-colored ice cream. After the way you acted Friday night too! Women would kill to have a man like Darryl Boucree. What the hell's the matter with you?*

You are going to love this man. I don't care how mean and small-minded you are—you are going to get over it!

She was genuinely ashamed of herself. But she'd turned a corner—she'd had a talk with herself and gotten through to what was real. And what was real was Darryl's simple, honest love for her; his decency; his choice to be honest with her. A rolling tsunami of love threatened to overwhelm her. She felt tears coming and blinked them back.

Nonetheless, Eileen greeted her with, "What's the matter?"

"Oh, nothing." She switched the Coke can from one hand to another—she had refused a bag, and the thing was giving her frostbite. "Just worried about the kids, that's all—Shaneel and Cassandra."

"You know, today's Eddie's birthday lunch."

She'd forgotten all about the damn birthday. "I thought there was a party. I'm supposed to be writing a poem, right?"

"Oh, the party's still on. This is just some old pals of his taking him to lunch. Aunt Audrey put them up to it, so he won't suspect anything."

Well, that explained why he had to go. She couldn't fault him for it.

She went in her office and attacked her tuna fish and e-mail. Ah. Tony Tino had dropped her a line:

Guess what? I'm coming to town! Mom invited me to Dad's birthday party. This is a big deal—I'm bringing my fiancée. Did I mention I'm getting married? Also, I'm the entertainment—or part of it, anyhow. I hear you are too. Looking forward to meeting you.

And there was a p.s. that was the real heart of it:

About this getting married—we've been meaning to do it for a long time, and now Cara's pregnant. So it's sooner rather than later. When I got your e-mail, I'd been in a funk for days, thinking about my family, and how my kid would never know its grandparents. See, what happened— Dad told Mom and Angie some lies about me and he told me some lies about them. That was how he kept us apart. So I couldn't just call—or anyway, I didn't think I could. Your e-mail was what it took to push me over the edge. I was so ripe for plucking I was starting to ferment. I owe you a lot, Baroness.

Quickly, she composed an answer:

Wow. For once, the Baroness is humbled.

And she was, more or less. What she had done she did on impulse, and it nearly went the other way. *I ought to be more careful,* she thought.

She got to Fortier half an hour early, wondering how she was going to spot Shaneel in the swarm of kids leaving the building. She didn't even know what the girl was wearing. With two of them, though, they'd have a good chance—and they'd almost certainly be able to see it if Baron Tujague's brother approached her.

When the bell rang, Eddie still hadn't shown. Talba thought, *Must have got sloshed.*

Shaneel was a big girl and fortunately, she'd picked today to wear a sweater of bright orange— the color hunters wear so they can see each other.

Talba's eye was drawn to it. *A break,* she thought. *Maybe this'll go right.*

"Shaneel! Hey, Shaneel—can I talk to you?"

The girl waved, even, under the circumstances, seemed happy to see her. "Hello, James Bond. 'Zat who you are? Or ya Jessica Fletcher?"

"Neither one, exactly." Talba thought what a shame it was, there wasn't a female analogy in popular culture. She forbore to mention Nancy Drew. "Got a minute?"

Shaneel waved good-bye to the kids she was walking with. "Sure. I got a minute."

"You know about Cassandra's mother?"

"Oh, yeah. She didn't come home from her date or something."

"Her date?"

"I don't know. She's always out on a date."

"Shaneel. She still hasn't come home."

Alarm flooded the girl's plump, carefree features. "She gone the whole weekend?"

"You haven't talked to Cassandra about this?"

She shook her head vigorously. "No. Haven't talked to Cassandra." And then she got a sort of stupefied look, as something came back to her. "Didn't talk to her *today.* I talked to her; sure I talked to her."

"Talk to *me,* Shaneel."

When the girl turned her face up to Talba's, it was like a lovely dark moon, wide and innocent, not overbuilt with suburbs and subdivisions; a small place in the universe that hadn't yet been wrecked. "Whassup?" she said. "You look kind of funny."

"I think Toes got her. Kidnapped her." She said it for shock value, didn't really expect it to have any resonance, but to her surprise, Shaneel's eyes grew into cookies, a dark raisin punctuating the center of each.

"Why you say that?" she asked.

"Shaneel, you know something. Tell me. We don't have any time to waste."

The girl took a step back, horror smeared like mud on her face. "Her mama called him. Her mama talked to him."

"Aziza called Toes?"

"Yes'm. She called Toes."

"Come on, honey. Keep talking."

"She told Cassandra they could get money from him—she said he owed it to her for what he did to her."

"So he was one of the men in the photos."

"Yes'm. But Pammie said he was a friend of Baron Tujague. You come in, sayin' he's the Baron's brother, well, Cassandra's mama smells money. She called the Baron's office and made a stink—Cassandra heard her do it, right on the telephone. Finally, she got Toes and made an even bigger stink, and Toes said she was right, he did owe her money behind it. He was gon' pay her the next day."

Talba suddenly felt steely and hard inside, for once calm and capable. She found that, often, with her worst fears confirmed, a great calm descended, and she was feeling that now.

"See, Cassandra . . ."

But Talba interrupted her. There was something she wanted to make completely clear. "That was the day she disappeared, Shaneel."

The girl wouldn't stop. "See, Cassandra wasn't like—like you think. Cassandra loves to sing more than anything in the whole world—me and Cassandra both; Pammie too. Well, Pammie's sister Rhonda knew this dude who knew the Baron and Pammie said maybe he could help us get started. You know, the Baron's got his own recording studio."

"Ah. The light dawns." Shaneel looked at her like she was speaking French, but she couldn't really help the outburst. She realized she'd just gotten a piece of the puzzle that had been eluding her—exactly what flavor of toe jam she was dealing with. "Go on, honey."

"We thought maybe we could make a CD—the three of us, you know? Maybe we'd get high with this guy and he'd listen to us sing. Only, Cassandra . . . I don't know . . . he said he had something special to talk to her about."

"Okay, Shaneel. This is not a nice man we're talking about."

"You got that right."

"A man who would have sex with a young girl isn't nice. But Rhonda's dead and Aziza's disappeared. This is way beyond 'not nice.' "

Shaneel wouldn't meet Talba's eyes. "Pammie's gone too."

"Her parents sent her away."

"No'm, I don't think so—they call my house last night to see was she there."

Damn! They'd lied to Eddie.

The girl looked miserable. "After Rhonda got run over, Pammie say maybe Toes done it. She say . . ."

"Rhonda knew about Toes and Cassandra?"

"I don't know. Why?"

Because she had to—otherwise Pammie wouldn't have put it together. And, sure enough, just like we thought, that's what started it all. Talba could see the whole thing: Rhonda gets outraged, partly on behalf of her own baby sister, pitches a fit, and threatens to go to the cops.

It had to be that—if it were blackmail, he probably would have just paid her. But by the time Aziza got around to blackmail, the stakes were a lot higher. Now he couldn't just pay—he'd already killed one Bergeron sister and maybe two.

And thanks to me, Aziza knew.

"Never mind, baby," she said. "A lot of bad stuff's

been going on. It's time to go to the police about this."

The girl took a step backward, dread inching over her face. "No po-lice. *Uh-uh.* No po-lice!"

Talba tried to think how to talk about this without scaring her—if she hadn't already figured out she and Cassandra were in danger, she was plenty scared about something. Adding to it was only going to make it worse. "Why not?" she asked. "What are you afraid of?"

Shaneel took off running. Talba started to chase her, but a boy, a football player from the size of him, bumped her out of the way. She tried again, but everywhere she turned, someone else blocked her. Apparently, the kids at Fortier stuck together. Shaneel was gone by the time she threaded her way to the sidewalk. Gone, and she didn't know where the girl lived.

But there was always choir practice. She called the church and learned it wasn't being held today.

Okay, she thought. *Back to Uncle Eddie. Also the drawing board.*

Chapter Twenty-two

It was possible to walk to Galatoire's from the office, but Eddie's limp posed a problem. He could make it fine, but his leg would ache tonight. And right now he was feeling good. Anthony was back in the family, he and Audrey were lovers again, and he hadn't had a headache in almost a week. No point messing it up with an aching leg—there was a perfectly good parking lot at Dauphine and Bienville.

He was meeting three guys from the old days—Calvin, a deputy along with him; Sal, a prosecutor; and Philip, a judge. Of the four, only Philip still had his old job. And why not? It was a good gig. The other two reeked.

Sal and Calvin had long since gone into business for themselves, much as Eddie had. But one had a video store and the other worked for a shipping company—as far as Eddie was concerned, he was the only one still in the trenches. A couple of days ago, he'd have said that was a bad thing. Today he was feeling smug.

The others, in keeping with New Orleans tradition, had come early to save a table. Eddie sailed past the jealous folk still waiting for one, greeted the maître d', shook hands with his favorite waiter, and nearly teared up at the sight of his old buddies. He wanted to hug them, but Galatoire's was more a handshake kind of place, more French than Italian. A lot of masculine back-clapping was a pretty good substitute.

Sal started the bidding. "Eddie, ya lookin' good for an old coot."

Philip said, "Eye bags are the latest thing in Paris."

"That's what I tell my wife," said Calvin. "She still wants a face-lift. Audrey still gorgeous?"

They could go on like that for hours, and did insult piled upon courtesy, thrust following parry, joke chasing joke, crab salad disappearing, trout meuniere appearing, crumbs from the crispest, sweetest bread blanketing the table.

There was wine too—not too much for Eddie, because of the kid he had to see after school—but enough to make everybody sentimental. Eddie rose and proposed a toast: "To my three oldest friends. And to friendship. And to living so goddam long we've known each other forever—excuse my French." They'd barely gotten their glasses to their lips, much less thought of a countertoast when he said, "I got good news. Anthony's back in the family."

And then of course he had to tell the story, which produced such an orgy of storytelling, they might have closed the place down if such a feat could be accomplished—on Fridays, men who go for lunch just call their wives to come join them when they check their watches and find it's dinnertime.

Eddie took quite a bit of ribbing about his new assistant being black, female, smart, computer literate, and a poet—all stuff of which he vigorously disapproved. But, hell, it was worth it—she'd gotten the kid back, glued the family back together. This week he was running a one-time-only special—she was in his good graces if she didn't get anyone killed. He was in one hell of a mood.

By the time the coffee came, they were all young and fearless again, back at their old jobs and kings of the hill. Sal was punching Eddie on the arm. "Goddam! Remember those illegal wiretaps?"

Philip said, "I didn't hear that."

"Aw, Phil, we did boocoos of 'em—everybody did it."

The judge pretended to hold his ears. "Not for my shell-pinks."

They ignored him. Sal said, "Oh, yeah, you guys were famous—how the hell did you get those telephone-company trucks?"

"Trade secret. But it worked like crazy. We'd get enough for a warrant and say—"

Philip abandoned all pretense. "—ya got it from a 'confidential informant.' Oh, yeah. You guys single-handedly gave snitches a rotten name. Confidential informant, my ass. You guys were the original fruits of the poison tree."

"Watch who ya callin' fruit, big boy. We got past you a time or two."

More than a time or two. They all knew it and acknowledged it with big sloppy laughs.

Calvin said, "It's just too bad Eddie had to get shot for it."

And Sal said, "What's that?"

Philip wrinkled his brow.

Calvin said, "Uh-oh. Did I speak out of school?"

Eddie'd been shot by the widow of a serial rapist who hung himself in jail. Guilty as sin—two women mutilated for life, three destroyed every other kind of way.

Entrapped by Eddie.

The guy knew it too—figured it out, and told his wife before he died. She believed hubby, tried to kill Eddie. He deflected the gun and took the hit in the thigh. Nearly bled to death.

Almost no one knew the story. It made Eddie cringe.

He said, "What the hell, Calvin. What the hell— we're all friends here. Nothin's gonna mess this day up. I've done some things I'm not proud of, and maybe that's one of 'em." Another was the thing with Anthony—lying to him, lying to Audrey and Angie. Jesus! Yeah, that was another. It was behind him now. Everything was fresh and beautiful.

"Hey, let's have some cognac. I got time." School wasn't out for forty-five minutes. "Did I tell ya Anthony's comin' home? I don't know when yet; we're working it out. He's gettin' married—I gotta meet the bride, don't I?"

When the brandy came, he had another toast: "Here's to all the stupid stuff ya do before you're old enough to know better."

Philip said, "Hear, hear."

Eddie tossed down the rest of his drink. "Okay, old farts—whose birthday's next?"

Calvin said, "Mine," and they agreed to do it again, if they all made it that far.

Eddie left them to settle up the bill while he went to intercept Shaneel as she came out of school. For two hours, he'd been able to leave the case completely alone. He had a twinge of fear on the way to the parking lot. But he was in way too good a mood to indulge it.

He was crossing Dauphine, wondering with some interest what it might be like to be a grandfather, when he saw the white car barreling out of nowhere.

*   *   *

Talba figured Shaneel's sudden departure was a good enough reason to interrupt Eddie's birthday lunch. Nonetheless, she was slightly relieved when he didn't answer his cell phone. She paged him and left the number of her own cell phone, then called the office. "Eileen, is he there?"

"Still at lunch. You know how it is when these old guys get together."

"I'm on my way in—if he calls or comes in, tell him it's urgent that he call me."

She didn't expect to hear from him. Consequently, when her cell phone sang out from the seat beside her, she nearly crashed into the car in front of her. She picked it up. "Eddie?"

"Talba, it's Angie."

"What? Angie, what is it?" Whatever it was, it was bad. She could tell by Angie's voice.

"I'm at Charity Hospital. Dad's been . . ." Here she broke off, unable to form words. All Talba could hear was a kind of gasping.

And then Eileen's thin, frightened voice came over the line. "He's been hit by a car. I just got here."

"How bad is it?"

"I don't know. Audrey's with him. We're waiting."

The emergency waiting room at Charity is grim and depressed; most people there are in pain of one kind or another. Those who aren't work there and live with pain on a minute-to-minute basis. They know far more than people should about life and death, and it's made them slightly brittle. What is worse, though, is that the room itself seems alive, the air writhing with the spirits of people in pain or dying or grieving or half-worried to death. It sounds frightening in the telling, and could be, but in the end, it is oppressive instead. Entering,

Talba felt as if someone had dropped a cement apron over her.

There was no sign of any member of the Valentino family. Panicked, she approached one of the guards outside the accident room, noticing that another was in a near-comical encounter with a man holding a handkerchief over his bleeding hand, jerking his head periodically, swearing under his breath, and trying to explain that what he had was Tourette's, not a rotten attitude.

"I'm looking for Eddie Valentino. Accident victim, came in about half an hour ago?"

"You're a family member?"

She shook her head. "Employee."

"Let me see what I can find out."

Figuring she was in for the usual interminable wait, she settled down to chew her nails, only to be interrupted almost immediately by a smart-looking woman in a burgundy smock announcing on the left chest that she was an "Emergency Department Patient Liaison." Once again, Talba explained who she wanted and was left to her own devices. And once again, she got action almost immediately.

"He's in surgery," reported the patient liaison. "May I escort you to the family waiting room?"

Dazed at the contrast in what she expected— good service versus bureaucratic attitude and sloth— she followed the woman to the elevator.

She found Eileen and Angie and Audrey sitting in a triangle of grief and worry, Angie looking like a mourner in her usual black. Audrey had on a gray sweat suit, something Talba felt sure she'd never be seen in, given the choice. She looked at Talba with dull, shocked eyes.

Talba said, "How is he?"

Audrey merely shrugged. Angie said, "If they know, they won't tell us. They're operating. That's all we know."

"Does anybody know what happened?"

This time, Audrey answered. Her elaborate coiffeur was flat in the back, wild in the front. She must have been napping when she got the news. "Some bastard ran him down. One of those idiots who barrel through the Quarter, think they own the town."

Talba wouldn't have believed she even knew the word "bastard," half expected her to excuse her French. Audrey's shocked eyes were suddenly snapping.

"Some Texan."

Talba realized she'd been holding her breath. "A Texan. So they got the guy. It wasn't a hit-and-run."

"It was a hit-and-run. People saw it—ran him down like a dog. Left him to die in the street." She was shaking with anger.

Talba said, "They got his plate number?"

Angie came to the rescue. "Mom, we don't really know it was a Texan." She turned to Talba. "We don't know anything."

"But we do know Eddie was on foot and somebody mowed him down?"

Angie nodded. "Bastards," said Audrey. Talba noticed how thin she was, and that she looked old, her skin gray and cracked.

"They didn't give you any idea what his injuries are?"

"His face looked terrible. They broke his nose." She turned to Angie and started crying. "They broke ya poor father's nose."

That was probably all she knew right then. Talba sat down to wait for news, her mind working. "What about the car? Did the witnesses say what it looked like?"

Angela shook her head. Audrey was already back in her own world. Eileen sat like a stone, withdrawn and miserable.

Toes could have followed him from the office. He could

have watched him park and waited for him to come out of
the restaurant. If he already knew where he'd parked, he
didn't have to follow him from the restaurant. All he had
to do was lurk near the parking lot.

She fidgeted for a while and then she could stand
it no longer. "Angie, can I talk to you a minute?"

"Sure. Let's go get some coffee." She seemed glad
of the chance to flee her mother's fear.

Talba hadn't the patience to go for coffee and
then drink it. As soon as she had Angie in the hall,
she said, "Has he talked to you at all about the case
we're working on?"

Angie looked shocked. "He never talks about
cases."

"Well, I'm talking about it. I think there's a very
dangerous person involved. And there's been another hit-and-run."

"Oh. So much for the Texas theory." The words
were brittle, but Angie's voice wasn't. It was tired,
and her face was drained. Her usual slash of red
lipstick was long gone.

"Did the cops say anything at all about the car?"

"There weren't any cops here when I got here."

"The paramedics then."

"All that was over by the time they called us. He
was already in some cubicle being felt up for frac-
tures."

"Listen, I'm going to the police. Eddie and I
should probably have already done it. I guess I'm
kind of in the way here, anyway."

Shyly, Angela put a hand on her arm. "No.
Thanks. Thanks for being here."

Talba only nodded, a little embarrassed.

"Could you do us a really, really big favor? I mean
really big. If you don't want to, you can say no."

"Sure."

"Anthony's coming in in a couple of hours. I can't
leave Mom. Could you possibly . . ."

To save her embarrassment, Talba interrupted.

"Could I meet him at the airport? It would be a pleasure. It would sure beat sitting around the hospital."

She was looking for a pay phone when she remembered she had a phone in her purse. Unselfconsciously she pulled it out and dialed, walking down the corridor with it pressed to her ear. If it had been anyone else, she would have thought them terribly self-important.

Skip Langdon, her friend at the Third District, was just about to leave. Talba begged; she had to talk this out. "Listen, just stay till I get there. Please."

"You're not confessing to anything, are you?"

"Are you kidding? This is informational. That's it. Except that I'm worried to death about my new boss."

"Eddie? You don't have to worry about him—he's honest as the day is long."

"Skip, it's not what you think. Eddie's in surgery at Charity—hit-and-run."

"Oh. That kind of worried." She sighed. "How is he?"

"Nobody knows yet."

"Come on over."

Langdon was a tall white woman, and Talba was no giant, but there was something about the cop that reminded her of herself. Or maybe that was wishful thinking—Talba admired Langdon for her quickness, her authority. *Maybe when I'm seasoned,* she thought. That was what it was—Langdon was seasoned. She'd seen enough strange things that they were familiar to her. She knew what was coming next most of the time. It was a stage of life Talba'd be happy to reach.

She said, "You're looking good, Baroness."

"I'm a wreck, but thanks. Look, you know that stuff I told you about Baron Tujague? It's escalated. Remember that other hit-and-run—Rhonda Bergeron? Well, now Eddie."

"Could be coincidence."

"Skip, I know I'm supposed to observe confidentiality, but I'm too green to handle it. The client's Aziza Scott—the woman who disappeared over the weekend."

"Whoa. Mind if I tape this? That way I can just ship the tape out to the relevant officers."

"No, of course not." Talba filled her in a little more. When she'd stopped talking, Langdon turned off the tape and thought a moment. Finally, she said, "There's something I don't get. How'd Toes know Eddie was working for Aziza?"

Talba mulled it over, rocking slightly in her chair. She was a good deal more taken aback than she wanted to let on. "I don't know. Maybe somebody saw something." But she knew as soon as she spoke that it wasn't Eddie they'd have seen.

Skip said, "Or somebody ratted."

"Maybe Aziza."

"Could have been. Certainly could have been. But you do realize, don't you, that if Toes knows about Eddie, he knows about you?"

"Yeah. I think I do." The possibility hadn't occurred to her until thirty seconds ago, a circumstance that amazed her.

"You watch your back, Baroness."

"Yeah, thanks."

"And call me in the morning—if you're still alive."

Cop humor, Talba thought as she left. She didn't find it funny. Her hands slid on the wheel, slick with sweat.

Chapter Twenty-three

S he called Darryl from the car. "Bad, bad, bad news. Somebody tried to kill Eddie—he's in surgery now."

Silence filled the line.

"Darryl? You there?"

"Yeah. Bad news thing threw me—I thought it was Miz Clara."

"Listen, I don't think I can see you tonight. I have to go get Tony at the airport."

"You wouldn't want company, would you?"

"Oh, I would. I really truly would. But I wouldn't put you through all this—after I get him, I have to take him to the hospital."

"Talba. You know what we talked about yesterday? Did you think I meant it or not?"

She sidestepped that one. "Nah, it wouldn't make sense to come get you. I'm already out by Bayou St. John."

"When does his plane get in?"

"In forty-five minutes."

"I'll meet you there."

It was crazily quixotic—then they'd have two cars at the airport. But she didn't care; she gave him the particulars.

She had no wish to be alone tonight, even alone with Tony. She wanted someone with her whose hand she could squeeze if they got bad news. And she wanted all the company she could get. Toes wouldn't try anything in front of witnesses.

She thought of the lonely walk from the airport parking lot and phoned Darryl again. "Hey, listen. I'm going to stop at Barnes & Noble and get some coffee at their café. Can you meet me there? We'll leave my car and take yours to the airport."

"Sure, but why?"

"Toes got Eddie—he might know about me too." She wasn't happy to sound like a wimpy female, but Darryl had a right to know what he was getting into.

All he said was, "Pick me up a latte, will you?"

When he'd arrived, gathered her up, and collected his latte, he said, "So. This guy's a one-man crime wave. Don't you think it's time you went to the police?"

"Skip, you mean." She'd always suspected he had a crush on the cop. They'd met through her, in a sort of a way. No, actually, now that she thought of it, that wasn't it, exactly. Skip and Darryl had both been part of a group that came to hear her read. The woman he was with that night was the police psychologist.

"I saw Skip an hour ago; she said to watch my back."

He was having trouble driving and drinking his latte. Talba reached out to take the cup from him.

His fingers feathered her thigh, barely touching. "How's Eddie? I've been afraid to ask."

"Nobody knows. Maybe Audrey does, but she's

not talking. Everybody's pretty glum, though."

"I'm sorry."

Speaking of Eddie had caused a curtain of pain to descend, a reminder of death and of fate, and they dealt with it silently, each in his or her way. When Darryl had parked, they reached automatically for one another and walked to the gate hand in hand, Talba's fingers squeezing Darryl's. They waited nearly half an hour, barely speaking at all. But she was glad to have him there.

Tony looked tousled and tired when he stepped off the plane. He was alone, and Talba was glad. The Valentinos had all they could handle right now, without a pregnant fiancée.

Talba stepped forward. "Tony. Talba Wallis."

"Ah. The Baroness." He managed a bow, but no smile. She introduced Darryl, and then spoke before Tony could. "Your father was still in surgery when I left. I'm sorry; I don't have any more news than that."

He nodded that he understood, and she noticed that his cheek was working, as if he were biting it. He seemed jumpy and irritable, like someone who'd just quit smoking.

They stopped at Barnes & Noble, where she and Tony transferred to her car. Being in it with him was like being locked up with a lion. She wished she had a cigarette to offer him.

When she got him to the waiting room, Angie and Audrey melted onto him. They were all three crying and kissing when she left, unnoticed.

She asked about Eddie at the desk. He was still in surgery.

She followed Darryl home after that, tears streaming at last. Being caged with Tony's grim self-containment was the thing that had finally gotten to her.

* * *

It was an odd night for Talba and Darryl. They ordered out for a pizza, and drank some wine, but neither one could seem to relax. Neither did they want to make love. The tension tugged at them, the strange dance of the last two days embarrassed them. They needed a break from each other, and yet they didn't want to be apart.

Talba didn't want to present a target for Toes, and she sensed that Darryl wanted to watch her. One thing: they hadn't been followed to Algiers Point. The neighborhood was too quiet, the streets too narrow for concealment.

She phoned Miz Clara. "I'm at Darryl's. You all right?"

" 'Course, I am. Why wouldn't I be?" Her mama's intuition at work.

"I don't know. I guess I'm paranoid—Eddie got run over today."

Miz Clara tried for composure, but Talba heard her gasp. "He all right?"

"I hope so, Mama. They're operating."

"You say Darryl's with you?"

She was exhausted all of a sudden. "St. Darryl's right here."

"What's that, girl?"

"I'm kind of tired, Mama."

"You watch yourself, Sandra." Everybody seemed to be telling her that.

Sometime in the night, she found peace. She woke up in full sunlight, tucked into Darryl's armpit, leg flung over him. He was trying to extricate himself.

"No," she said. This was way too good to give up.

"Got to go to school. You sleep some more."

She slept two more hours and woke up with the

strength of ten women. *Eddie!* she thought, and called the hospital.

He was in "guarded" condition. She didn't like the sound of it but it beat "deceased." She ordered him some flowers and made some oatmeal.

When she had eaten it, she called Skip Langdon. "Hey, Skip. Talba. How's it going? You got anything for me?"

"I'm going to turn you over to Sergeant Aucoin on that." The cop spoke in a clipped, distant voice. No, "hey, Baroness," no "Your Grace," no nothin'. Talba might as well be speaking to a stranger.

"What's wrong?"

"Sergeant Aucoin is coordinating that case. Would you like his phone number?"

"Uh, yeah. Sure. Certainly." She was so disoriented, trying so hard to recover her equilibrium she wasn't sure she was getting the words right. Finally, she managed to break through it. "Can't you tell me anything?" She knew she was whining.

Skip's voice was low, hardly more than a whisper. "Your man has alibis for every minute since the second he was born."

"I'm starting to get it. Alibis and connections."

Skip said, "Glad I could help," as if someone was listening.

"Wait. Listen. Hold it."

"I've got another call."

"What about the girls? Can't you protect them?"

"It's not in the cards, Baroness. I'm as sorry as I can be." Talba could almost see her swiping curls off her forehead, cupping her head in frustration. Something was going on here.

She called Sergerant Aucoin, who made a big show out of using Ebonics and calling her "sister." She had a mental picture of him: forty-fiveish, portly, and possibly bald; as dark as she was, conservative dresser; the kind of man who went to church, but tried too hard and sweated too much. *Smarmy,* she thought.

"Sergeant Aucoin, I gave Officer Langdon some information."

"Yes ma'am. How can I help ya, Ms. Wallis?"

"I'd like to come in and talk about it, maybe fill in some details for you."

"Sister, I don't think that's gon' be necessary. We got everything under control. You don't need to worry about nothin'. We the po-lice here."

She thought, *Try scaring me with that po-lice shit.*

"I have reason to believe two teenage girls are in danger."

"From Mr. Toledano?" He came right out with it.

"I think they could be."

"Well, you ain' got nothin' to fear from that quarter. Now, don't you worry about a thing. We 'bout to get this thing handled. Mighty nice of you to call, though."

"Anything new on Aziza Scott?"

"Lots of things. We developin' a case. But we can't discuss it with the public, ya unnerstand? We got it under control, Ms. Wallis. We got it under control."

She asked him if he knew Eddie, tried a few more ploys to try to get through, but every time came up against a blank wall. *Or a closed door,* she thought. *Something is very wrong here.*

She could see what the thing was, too. She saw its reverse all the time. She saw rich white people get away with things. She saw them exercise power and get smug behind it. This was a city where black people could do it, if they were rich enough and powerful enough.

And dishonest enough.

Toes was all three, it would seem. Or his brother the Baron was. Power was happening here. Male, monied power. It was making her mad.

But it was scaring her too. Someone had to look out for the girls.

She closed her eyes and felt tears of anger squeeze out of them. *Eddie, I swear to God I won't let anything happen to those girls. And I will get that bastard. Single-handedly. I promise you I will.*

She was so mad there was no question in her mind she was going to make good on the promise or die in the attempt. She had half a mind to take Aucoin down too, mostly because he'd called her "sister." She was no sister to pond scum, she didn't care what color he was.

The question was, how was she going to protect two girls at two different schools, single-handedly? She couldn't, obviously. She needed help. Darryl was out of the question for many reasons, one being that he not only wouldn't do it, he'd try and stop her as well. Another being that she was damned if she was going to run to her boyfriend every time the going got tough. A third being that she needed someone in the business, someone cued in to the case. Eileen Fisher was the only person she could think of, and she was an even more absurd idea than Darryl.

Angela, though—now there was a thought. A little on the hysterical side, but game, very game.

Suddenly the solution occurred to her. Not Angela. Tony. He was an Italian male whose dad had been shot—and who had plenty of guilt about said dad. She figured he'd already have hit the streets if he'd known where to look.

She reached him at the hospital. "Tony, Talba. How's your dad?"

"Hanging in there." He sighed. "He's still in a coma. That's the scary part. *Goddam,* this is frustrating."

"What is?" she asked innocently.

"I just wish there were something I could do."

"Tony, I think I know who did this."

"Who *did* it? You mean it wasn't an accident?"

"I don't think so; I really don't. You want to get together and talk about it?"

They got together over some truly terrible hospital coffee, and Talba told him everything. She started with Cassandra, then graduated to Toes-as-the-Baron's-brother, the death of Rhonda, the disappearance of Aziza, the disinterest of the cops, and ended, finally, with the hit-and-run attack on Eddie. He listened with a great deal more attention than she'd have thought an Italian male had in him, not once interrupting her, until that last, crucial chapter.

"Wait a minute. Hold it. Why just Eddie? Why not you?"

She nodded. "Yeah. Good question. Maybe not *yet* me. But I've been watching. So far, no tails."

He shook his head and made a sound like someone with a mouthful of food. "Mmmmf. Not yet's right. If there's anything to your theory, you're an endangered species, baby."

She didn't mind that he called her "baby." She liked it. She'd long since realized that in a city as affectionate as this one, feminist objections applied only if there was malice involved. She said, "It's not me I'm worried about. It's those two girls."

He stood up, slapping his own face. "Oh, shit. This guy's not a crime wave, he's a tsunami. He'll go for 'em. Sure he'll go for 'em."

"Yeah." She was letting it sink in.

"Maybe we can hide them somewhere."

"I thought of that. Cassandra's scared, I can tell you that. I could try to convince her. If it worked, maybe she could help us with Shaneel. The problem is, their parents."

"Why don't we just whisk them away?"

"And face kidnapping charges? Besides, where would we take them?"

"Yeah, yeah. Yeah, you right. I used to say that all the time."

"I still say it."

"Well, what's the alternative?"

"Just be there. Keep an eye on them—be ready in case he tries anything." She flung her arms wide, feeling helpless.

He pulled at his lip, maybe to stimulate thought. She had an image of him as a child, a fifth-grader maybe, doing the same thing and getting scolded for it. On the adult, it looked cute as anything.

She kept talking. "The only problem is, they go to different schools."

"Well? There are two of us."

It was what she was hoping he'd say, but she was suddenly overcome with doubt. "I don't know, it could be dangerous. And you're about to get married—and with the baby and all . . ." What had she been thinking? But it was too late now.

"Oh, for Christ's sake. I'm a man."

You sure are, she thought. *That's how they think.*

They went back and forth a time or two, and then they were both in it, both determined, both unstoppable. And when it got to that point, they were partners.

Talba volunteered to take Shaneel because this way, once and for all, she could follow her home and at last confront the parents, maybe talk them into sending Shaneel away for a while. It made sense for another reason—Tony could recognize Cassandra by the picture of her that had run in the paper when her mother disappeared; he'd never find Shaneel in the crush at Fortier.

Talba gave him directions to Xavier Prep School and left, the better part of the day still ahead of her; school wasn't out till after three. She decided to go to the office, just in case—there could be voice mail or e-mail, or even snail mail that needed attending to.

On the short drive over, she thought about what Tony had said about her being an endangered species, and what Skip had said about watching her back, and about the role she'd played in this case. If Toes wasn't after her—and careful observation told her he wasn't, at least so far—it could only be because he didn't know about her. He certainly knew her as the Baroness; but if Cassandra hadn't ratted her out, he'd have no reason to connect her with Eddie. Which still left a mystery—how the hell did he know about Eddie?

Maybe Eddie'd called him. It was the sort of thing he'd do without telling her. Maybe it was something like that. And if so . . . well, then, she was free to approach Toes in her other persona. If she could think of a point to it.

Was there one? She needed data.

And if anyone knew how to get it, it was Talba Tabitha Sandra Wallis, AKA the Baroness.

She was surprised to find Eileen in the office, trying to keep things together and keep the hysteria out of her voice. But despite a human presence, the place had a forlorn, ghostly feel. Talba shivered and turned on her computer, as if it could warm her. Whatever voice and snail mail there was, Eileen had already taken care of. Talba briefly perused the e-mail and answered what couldn't wait.

Funny, there was one thing she hadn't done. Depending on Cassandra to solve the Toes mystery with a photo I.D., she hadn't bothered going online to research the Baron's brother. She did it now—went to Yahoo and typed his name in: *Thomas Toledano*. To her amazement, he had his own web site.

Well, why not? He'd probably behave as his famous brother behaved—be much more savvy about self-promotion than most people—and a lot more arrogant about needing it.

She clicked on the web site and there he was, looking ugly as ever, sole proprietor of Big Easy Sound, whatever that was. Closer inspection revealed it to be a music promotion company, whose clients included Baron Tujague and various lesser rappers, all, Talba'd bet the ranch, Baronial artists. In other words, as far as she could see, Big Easy Sound—hence T. Toledano—was simply the promotion arm of Baronial. Probably, to give his brother a little dignity and something he could call his own, the Baron had spun it off as a separate company. For all she knew, it wasn't even real—it stood to reason the Baron had actual professionals out there working for him. Maybe this was just a shell to make the brother feel good. *Well, I'll make him feel good,* she thought. *If only for a minute.*

A minute was all she needed, and a plan took shape in her head in another minute. The address on the website was in New Orleans East, probably on the Baronial campus, she figured. And she was almost right. It was about two blocks away, on its own little spit of property, though in truth it was a pretty primitive structure that might have been an abandoned garage. Several cars were parked on the premises. She checked them all out, even going so far as to record their plate numbers. If Toledano was Toes, at least one of them was probably his— she was betting on the Lincoln Navigator.

She got out of the car and swept into the building, hoping she was being observed. Despite her hurry to get here, she'd taken a quick detour home to get into Baroness mode. Royal purple was appropriate, she thought, and, fortunately, she had a lot of it— caftans, harem pants, flowing pants, even dresses. For this occasion, she dressed for freedom of movement, in a silk outfit she'd had made for her in the style of Indian pajamas—long, loose top over tight-fitting pants. She wore boots with it because she could run in them if she had to, and for warmth and dash, she threw over it a red-velvet cape. Finally, because it was intimidating, and also because it might jog his memory, she added the purple sequinned hat she'd worn the night she met him.

This was a performance like any other. She intended to pass herself off as a representative of a distinguished organization—as well as royalty.

Chapter Twenty-four

The Toledano version of Eileen Fisher was quite a bit more glamorous, though not half so well dressed—she wore baggy bell-bottoms and a T-shirt meant for a smaller girl. Talba took a second look at her. She wasn't half as old as Eileen, either. In fact, she looked a lot like Cassandra—same light skin, snaky little body, attitude to burn. She was chewing on a hunk of bubble gum as big as an egg.

Somewhere not far away, a card game was in progress. The riffle of cardboard and dollars, the clink of change, the rat-a-tat fuck-fuck-fucks of young, black world-by-the-tails was so loud you couldn't have heard the phone ring. Testosterone hung in the air like jasmine in spring.

Bad time, Talba thought, and considered leaving. These dudes might be drinking, though, come to think of it, there was more in the air than hormones. Smoking made people mellow—at least she devoutly hoped it had in this case.

The receptionist mouthed something, which might have been "May I help you?", and Talba mouthed back that she was there to see Mr. Toledano, and then the receptionist put her hand behind her ear, engaging in what Talba could have told her was a losing game. She motioned for something to write on, and when the girl ducked to find it, saw Toledano himself, walking down the little hall behind the front counter, checking his zipper. Today, he was dressed in a deep red custom-made suit and walking like a pimp. Whether the walk itself was a pimp or whether the man thought he was fine, Talba couldn't have guessed.

He spoke before she could. "Well, hello, you fine thing. Be right with ya. Lemme just exterminate some vermin." The phrase chilled her.

He went into the room with the card players. "Listen up, y'all. We got royalty out here. Y'all get ya sorry asses out my office and do it now. Come on, yeah! Go 'head and do it." Like he owned the world.

And in a moment, the men came out, baggy-jeaned and sullen, sneaking glances at the woman he had called royalty. When they had gone, he spoke to his young helper, "Mika, we got a Baroness here. Don't she look *fine?*"

Talba almost regretted the getup, but not really. She understood that it was what had moved him to action. This was a man who was into appearances, a man so unsure of himself the mere fact that she was in his office was an event.

"I didn't mean to break up your game," she said.

"Wasn't no game of mine—motherfuckers come in every day, try takin' over my office. Can't get no business done, that racket goin' on."

"I won't take much of your time. I wonder if we could talk for a moment?" She'd decided, in view of his evident insecurity, to play it haughty. She remembered how he'd been the other night—

overshadowed, seemingly overwhelmed by his brother; excited as a kid to report that he'd actually heard of her.

"We can sure do that. You come right on in." He led her into an office so littered with papers, CDs, cigarette butts, every kind of thing you could think of that she found it hard to believe he did any business here at all. *He probably doesn't*, she thought. *His brother probably just gave him this to keep him out of trouble.*

There was a round table in the room, piled high, with several chairs around it, and a desk with a chair for the owner and two facing it, for supplicants. He sat her in one of the supplicants' chairs and assumed the owner's position. Exactly what she'd expected.

The desk had a nice lip on it, she noticed. Perfect for her purposes. How the hell to get him out of here so she could go to work? She could ask for coffee, but he'd probably just send the receptionist.

"What I owe the honor to? Little bit unusual," he said, "Baroness comes to call."

"I've got a proposition for you, Mr. T." He opened his mouth, but she held up a forestalling hand. She wasn't about to let him get going with that one. "Are you familiar with NOAAP?"

"NOAAP?" She could see he hadn't a clue; therefore, he was going to ridicule it. "What the fuck's a NOAAP?"

She chose that moment to start coughing. She screwed up her face and held her throat. "Allergic," she managed to gasp. "Dust." Hack, hack.

He shouted, "Mika. Get your ass in here. We need some water. Now!"

Talba was practically throwing a fit, bugging her eyes out, letting the tears roll down, twisting her whole body into scary spasms. "Mika!" He was out of there—just couldn't stand to look. She dipped a hand into her bosom and pulled out a tiny transmitter wrapped in a tissue. There was banging around outside. She took her time fixing the bug to the underside of the desk lip and then coughed some more into the tissue. Standing now, as if she could somehow calm her troubled body. On the desk she saw something that froze her—the burgundy binder Eddie used for client reports, with his name embossed on it.

It was Aziza's; had to be. Which left little doubt about what had happened to her.

She understood that she could go to Skip Langdon with this, that this was evidence Sergeant Aucoin couldn't brush off. She needed a picture of it, though, and footsteps were coming down the hall. She hacked a little harder.

Toledano handed her a glass of water; Mika followed him into the room, carrying a pitcher. She drank long and convincingly, she hoped. "Thanks. It happens sometimes. If there's—uh—dust." She paused, as if suddenly remembering her manners. "Or mold, of course. Do you have allergies, Mr. Toledano?"

The question was meant to throw him off-balance, and did. "Shit, no, I ain't got no allergies," he said, sounding half furious, half-embarrassed. Perhaps he found it an affront to his masculinity.

But maybe he had something else to be angry about. She was undoubtedly named in the client report. Would this ape connect the poet with the baby detective? Probably not, she thought, if he'd even read the thing—Mika'd probably given him an executive summary.

"Say, what you think of Mika?" He was admiring the rear view of her as she returned to her post.

Talba was so taken aback she almost started coughing for real. "She my girl," he said proudly. "My oldest."

"Your daughter?" Now, there was a wrinkle. "She's beautiful. Smart too, I bet."

He nodded. "Yep. We got her fillin' out applications for college. She gon' be the intellectual in the family."

That won't take a lot, Talba thought, *unless the mother has it quite a bit over this piece of garbage.* God, she *hoped* the girl hadn't seen the client report. "Well, anyway, about NOAAP," she said, eager to stop thinking about this man as someone with a family, people who loved him, and just as eager to leave behind the recognition of Mika's similarity to Cassandra.

He nodded. "Yeah. Ya proposition." He was almost smiling normally, hardly leering at all.

"It stands for New Orleans Association of African-American Poets."

He nodded again, looking almost alert.

"We had this idea. We'd like to put together a book of rap lyrics."

"And you'd like to use some of the Baron's."

"We sure would. And some by those artists I met the other night—Pepper Spray, wasn't that it?—and some by other indigenous groups. The idea's to use only New Orleans artists . . ."

She half expected him to ridicule the word "indigenous," since she figured he hadn't a clue what it meant, but instead, he said, "Now what'd we want to do that for?"

"You're the Baron's promotional manager, aren't you?"

"Ya got the right department. I'm just askin', what's in it for us?"

"Money, you mean?" She perfected her posture, looking elegantly down her nose; she could do haughty pretty well. "I wasn't under the impression the Baron really needed any."

"Get real, lady. Ain' nobody work for nothin'."

"They certainly do, Mr. Toledano. It's called *pro bono.*"

"Pro boner?"

She ignored his stupid shit-eating grin. "The collection will benefit children with birth defects caused by drugs—" She was making this up as she went along. "—I recall that the war against drugs is an important cause of the Baron's."

"Lady, you got to be kiddin'."

"But . . ." She made herself the very picture of confusion. "Wasn't that how we met? He wrote that song . . . we thought it could be the centerpiece of the collection . . . the title could come from it, perhaps . . ."

"Shee-it." He was laughing now. "The Baron don't care 'bout that shit. That was just P.R. Ya know what I mean? Just P.R."

She smiled, ever so knowingly. "And so would this be, Mr. Toledano. So would this. We thought you could get quite a lot of good press out of it—and so could we. It wouldn't cost anybody anything—the songs have already been written. And the kids would get a little money, too. Which is really the important thing."

The light dawned on his slow features like the first rays of the day. "Uh, yeah. Yeah, tha's the important thing. I don't mind tellin' ya, I thought ya was hustlin' me when ya first come in wi' that. But I see you really got somethin' to say. Ya really got a idea there."

"I thought you'd think so."

"I'm gon' run that by the Baron. I think it's somethin' he might like to do."

"Great." She stood and held out her hand. "That's all I can ask."

"You got a card?"

"The best way to get me's on my cell phone. Let

me give you the number." For good measure, she threw in her pager number as well.

She mentally congratulated herself—it really was a good idea. She'd damn near convinced herself. Her only regret was that she hadn't had a minute to photograph the client report. Still, maybe there was a way to get back in; she looked at her watch. Not now. She just had time to grab a quick bite and get to Fortier before Shaneel got out of school.

But on the way out, there was one little thing she could do. She noticed most of the cars had been driven away by the card players. When she was near enough to the Navigator, she surreptitiously opened her purse and upended it. With a little squeal, she squatted to pick up the mess, taking a moment first (very carefully, so as not to set off the alarm) to place one of her magnetized homing devices on the underside of the car—it might not be his, but she'd bet a hundred dollars it was.

She was in her own car, thinking about the Shoney's where she'd seen the Baron's gang, when her phone rang. Her stomach shimmied—with Eddie in the hospital, any call could be bad news. "Hello?"

"Your Grace, it's the Baron."

"Why, Your Grace. Wha's up?"

"I hear ya been to see my brother."

"News travels fast."

"I got my feelings hurt. Why didn't you come see me?"

"You're kind of an important man. I didn't think I could get an audience."

"Pretty lady can *always* get an audience. You got one now. How soon can you get here?"

She thought about it; this was going to make things tricky, but the opportunity to bug the big man's office was too good to pass up. She could do it if she forgot about food. "Where are you? I've got a three o'clock."

"Come on. Give me five minutes. You got to be in the 'hood—you just saw Toes."

Toes. There it was, crouching on the line like a spider made out of words. "I saw *who*?"

He laughed. "Tha's what we call my brother. T-h-o-s, Toes. It's from Thomas."

"Oh. Gotcha." She made him give her directions, though due to her recent foray, she really didn't need them. Seven minutes later she was standing in his office.

Today he was dressed in the universal baggy rap uniform. She gave a little bow. "Your Grace."

He nodded, not standing to receive her. "Welcome." He leaned back. "I know you're in a hurry, so listen up. That's a dynamite idea you got."

"It wasn't mine—it's the organizations."

He waved at her. "Yeah, yeah."

Seeing her chance, she said, "I got the impression your brother didn't think much of the idea."

"Oh, yeah? That's not what he told me. He sounded real excited."

"Oh. Well. I guess I got the wrong idea. I got the feeling he thinks you don't like to do *pro bono* work." The Baron made no attempt to conceal his annoyance. "And that he thinks my project's kind of small-time."

"Goddammit, if I've told him once, I've told the sucker . . . !" He caught himself and let the sentence trail off.

Talba was drunk with power. "I mean, I didn't really appreciate it when he called the kids freaks."

"What kids?"

"You know—the ones we'd like to benefit, the kids with birth defects. He called them 'deaf-and-dumb freaks with flippers'—it's . . . you know . . . kind of an expression that sticks in your mind."

"*Goddammit!* I'm gonna . . ."

"Oh, no, no. I didn't mean to get him in trouble.

It's okay—he did tell you about the project and I think, after we'd talked a little bit, he was genuinely convinced of its value—at least from what you tell me. Funny, though, when I left the office I still thought he was hostile to it."

"Well, I don't know what to tell you, Your Grace." He rose and started pacing, eventually turning to look out the window in the direction of his brother's office. Hardly believing her good luck, she slipped a transmitter under the lip of his desk.

This was working out a lot better than she thought. The idea of turning brother against brother had strictly been an impulse. She was astonished by her own strength, and trying hard not to get too carried away, pull back before he caught on. But for the moment he seemed lost in his own private anger. "He's gon' be the death of me, you know that? You got relatives, Your Grace?"

"I'm an only child—but I've got a mama, and watch out for *her*."

"Whooo, I know what you mean." He turned to face her again, and it occurred to Talba that the whole thing might have been a performance for her, a ploy to show off his famous rear. But surely he wasn't so vain he thought it looked attractive in baggy jeans—it must have been real, especially given what she knew about Toes. He was going to be a big embarrassment, and soon. The Baron had to suspect that.

She glanced at her watch. "Well, look, let me describe the project . . ."

"No need. No need at all. You just go ahead and count me in. That's all I wanted to tell you." He took out a checkbook. "And I wanted to give you a little something toward publication . . ."

"Oh, no, really." She was horrified. But what the hell, she could just tear it up.

"Yes, ma'am," he said. "Yes, indeed." He seemed

determined to undo whatever damage his brother had done.

"Well, we're grateful. Could you make it to NOAPP?"

"Oh, that takes too long—tell you what, you just endorse it to them, why don't you?" And he made it to her, for five thousand dollars.

When she saw the size of it, she wondered if it was intended as a bribe. Walking back to her car, she felt her legs go rubbery. All that self-congratulation must have been premature. It looked like the Toledanos were onto her.

She walked fast. Surely the Baron would call his brother after her visit. The whole damn thing could be over by the time she got to her car.

Fumbling, she tuned the radio to the frequency she'd set up for the Baron, and was immediately reassured. Her luck was even better than she'd hoped—the Baron was on the speakerphone. Quickly, she retrieved a tape recorder from the glove compartment and let it roll.

She'd just tuned in to the Baron in high dudgeon, an event not nearly so aristocratic as the Baron granting an audience. The "motherfuckers" were flying thick and fast. Talba was having a ball, taking it all in and laughing to herself till she got to this part:

"Goddammit, motherfucker, *goddammit!* Every time I turn around you're fuckin' up again. And after I sent Bingo and Pig to take care of that goddam woman for you. Did I do that for ya? Huh? Didn't I do that? I'm goddam sick and *tired* of doing your goddam dirty work, cleanin' up your motherfuckin' messes. I swear to God I'm cuttin' you loose if you don't start gettin' somethin' right for a change."

Talba heard Toes answer, "I'm sorry, man, I'm sorry. Look, I've got to hang up; I'm almost at the school."

Chapter Twenty-five

She'd cut it way too close. Kids were swarming out the door by the time she got to Fortier. Heart thumping, she stopped in the middle of Freret, willing someone to pull out of a parking place. She swiveled her head, panicked, looking for anything at all to focus on, and there it was—Shaneel, talking to two adult men. Horns blatted behind her; the men looked up. They were two of the no-accounts she'd seen earlier that day, hanging out at Toes's office. Whether or not they saw her, they were evidently moved by the horns. They melted into the crowd, crossed Joseph street, disappeared. Shaneel fell in with a group of girls, walking toward Talba—and then past her.

Talba was moving now, having no choice unless she wanted to be the latest victim of road rage. She circled the block and saw no sign of Shaneel's group. Finally, she thought she recognized a purple top on one of the kids. She gave that kid's group a pass. Yes! There was Shaneel. She needed to park and follow on foot. Damn! Toes had said he was on the way to the school. She could kick herself for her detour. And yet, she might have gotten some evidence. To her, the tape sounded like a confession of murder, though she figured a defense attorney would make mincemeat of it. Still, it might be enough to get someone's attention—if not that of the cops, maybe the media's. She loved that idea. *The media.* By all means. If she could just keep the kid alive in the meantime.

The hell with the car. She parked in someone's driveway, praying they weren't home and wouldn't be till she could got back.

Ah, that was better—like getting rid of a couple of tons of excess weight. This way she could slither unobserved. A car shadowing at five miles an hour was about as unobtrusive as a spaceship.

There was no sign either of Toes or his two thugs. She was doing fine until the group split in half, some kids continuing their happy, giggling journey, the others settling at a bus stop. Shaneel was among the latter.

Talba cursed. The kid would see her if she got on the bus, and she wasn't ready for that. She'd have to get the car. She took off running, hoping Shaneel wouldn't glance in her direction.

She arrived back at the bus stop, once more behind the wheel, just as a bus was closing its doors. It peeled out, and Talba didn't see Shaneel in either direction; she could only hope the girl was on it. She followed its stop-start progress, inspiring hatred in her fellow drivers as she halted at each stop, inspecting the exiting passengers. Just as she was about to decide she'd been tricked, that Shaneel wasn't on the bus at all, the kid alighted. And once more the trick was to follow her home.

She lived in the Magnolia Project, or at least she

was going there. The idea of entering alone made
Talba shiver. Miz Clara'd kill her if she knew. And
yet, this kid apparently did it every day—unless she
wasn't going home, but was paying a visit to one of
the thugs Talba'd seen at the school. Her blood ran
cold. Goddess help her if that was the case.

Shaneel pulled something from around her neck
and inserted it in the lock—latchkey kid, true to
stereotype. Talba hollered, "Shaneel!"

The girl turned and, to her surprise, broke out in
a grin. "James Bond."

Sometime she really did have to enlighten this kid
about the difference between a spy and a detective—
if they both lived long enough. Right now she said,
"How're you doing?"

"What you doin' in the projects?"

"I came to talk to you. This where you live?"

Shaneel nodded, once, hand still on her key, still
half-turned toward the door, half toward Talba. A
perfect metaphor for ambivalence.

"I've been worried about you. Who were those two
guys you were talking to?"

Talba almost answered with her: "What two guys?"

She said, "I saw you with them at school. Adults.
Looked like gangsters—I don't know what your
mama would say."

"Oh, you mean Bingo and Pork? They're real nice
guys."

Talba's gut jigged. "Pork? Is he ever called Pig?"

"I don't know. I don't even know 'em. They were
waiting for me when I got out of school, said they
were friends of Baron Tujague's and they had to talk
to me. Man, you should have seen my friends when
they said that. I was a hero. You 'magine that?"

"What did they want?"

Evidently whatever it was was important enough
to distract her attention. She released her grip on
the key, turned toward Talba, and reached in her

pocket. She pulled out a handful of cardboard strips. "They gave me free concert tickets. A whole *lot* of 'em—for me and all my friends."

"Did they ask you to do something in return?" *Like keep your mouth shut about half a dozen serious crimes?*

She looked bewildered. "Do something? No. Why would they do that?"

Either she was so slow on the uptake the bribe hadn't worked, or it worked so seamlessly she'd forgotten what she knew. Talba wasn't sure which, but at any rate it beat the hell out of kidnapping. If Shaneel had been followed home—that is, by anyone else—Talba was reasonably sure she'd have spotted him. She decided to find Tony now and catch Shaneel's parents later that night. "This where you live?" she repeated.

"I told you I did. Why you care?" The girl was almost pouting, an unusual attitude for this kid.

"Maybe I want to bring you a present too." Perhaps some candy—she'd have to remember to pick something up. "When do your parents get home?"

Shaneel shrugged. "It's just me and my mama." She barely spoke above a whisper.

"Well, when does your mama get home?"

"I don't know." She turned the key and disappeared.

Talba fast-walked to her car and dialed Tony. She'd snagged Eddie's cell phone for him, and they'd agreed to leave both phones on, but for some reason he didn't answer. *Take it easy,* she told herself. *If Shaneel's okay, Cassandra's okay—it follows, right?*

But it didn't. Cassandra was the one who'd had sex with Toes; the one with the missing mother. *Damn! Why the hell didn't I think of that? Why didn't I take Cassandra? Toes must have been going to* her *school.*

She could think of a million reasons why Tony wouldn't asnwer his phone, why everything was probably just fine and dandy, but that did nothing to keep her heart at a normal pace. Should she check out Cassandra's school? She looked at her watch. Pointless. School had been out for an hour. Tony should have reported in.

She turned toward Pontchartrain Park. Maybe he was out of his car. But, no, that wasn't their deal—they'd agreed to keep their phones with them.

Traffic was nasty. It took a century to get to the lake.

But she breathed deeply when she saw Tony's car in front of the Scott house. Okay. Everything was fine.

Half-smiling, she went to the door, rang the bell, and waited. She'd been there a long time when she remembered how far it was to the front of the house, how long she'd waited before. She rang the bell again, went through the whole thing one more time, and in frustration finally tried the door. It opened.

Shocked, she poked her head in, trying to decide whether to call out or creep around. Oh, hell. If they were there, they already knew she was too. It hardly made a damn.

She found that was a good thing because she was suddenly aware of her panic. Creeping was no longer an option. Her mouth opened and her feet stomped. "Tony? Tony, you here?" The answering silence was more frightening than a scream. "Cassandra?" She was racing, raging against that deathly quiet, willing it broken. She kept yelling as she ran through the house, so loud she started to get hoarse. "Tony, where the hell are you? How the hell could you do this?" Exactly what he had done she couldn't have said, other than fail to answer. "Cassandra, come *out* of there!" No one answered.

And when she reached the dining room, she knew no one would. Two chairs had been overturned on their sides, a pile of books knocked off the table, as if someone had come in, gotten this far, and met with resistance.

Even after that, she couldn't stop screaming their names, though she knew perfectly well that if they were there, she was about to find them dead.

She found nothing. No sign they'd ever been here. They must have been taken out the front door and forced into a car.

She righted one of the dining-room chairs and sat down, shaking, sweating, trying to get her thoughts together. But there was no choice. There was one thing to do and one thing only. She had to call the cops. And yet . . . and yet, there was something wrong with that plan, something that niggled at her. She did deep breathing and tried to get at it.

Ah, there it was: They'd ask her her name and make her wait there.

Still. It had to be done. She called Langdon.

Not in, and she had no voice mail.

Not having her pager number, Talba left a message with some anonymous detective: "Tell her to call the Baroness right away. It's extremely important—can you page her?" The detective snorted. Too late, she realized the word "Baroness" had probably identified her as a nutcase. He might or might not page Langdon.

And then she remembered something—the bird-dog homing device she'd attached to the car parked in front of Toledano's office. She just might be able to pick up a signal. If she could, and it was Toes's car, she could find him.

But the thing had a very short range. No time to wait for the cops. She had to get going. And there was one other thing. She was unarmed. What the hell was she thinking of?

Without a second thought, she ransacked Aziza's house, turning up what appeared to be an automatic handgun on a shelf of the woman's closet, along with several clips of ammunition. She'd never shot a gun in her life, but how hard could it be? She knew damn well she was smarter than the humanoids who had Cassandra. If they could do it, she could.

She rushed to her car, did a makeshift hookup on the receiver and . . . against all odds, started to get something.

The beep was coming from the east. On the road, she used her cell phone to dial 911, and ran the whole thing down to a dispatcher who kept interrupting with pleas for her name. Finally, she exploded, "Jesus, lady, I'll be in touch!"

The signal was getting strong.

It took her to the river, and then she lost it. What had he done, driven into the river? The closest thing to doing that was driving onto a ferry, and she ought to know. She did it often enough. She did it now. And sure enough, picked up the beep on the other side. The car was headed north.

Algiers Point wasn't only delightful, colorful streets. Uh-uh. There were woods and swampland to the north, with mosquitoes the size of bats. It was a favorite place for dumping bodies and dealing drugs.

It was where Aziza probably was.

Maybe Cassandra and Tony were dead already; maybe Toes was taking them out there to dump them.

But surely not. There'd been no blood in the house. Where would he have killed them, and how? She was feeling desperate. She tried calling Langdon again. No go.

Who else to call? There was one person, but it might not be a good idea. A person who disapproved of Toes's activities and felt threatened by them. Yet also a person who had a big fat stake in keeping them quiet. But she couldn't call the Baron. Could she?

She damned well had to. She had to do anything she could.

The cops again? Sure. Anything. And she had the license plate. She tried a different tack this time—terrified motorist.

"Nine-one-one? I just saw a man with a gun pointed at a little girl—a teenager. Omigod, I'm losing the car—*yeah,* he's in a car. Yes. Yes, I *have* got the plate number." Pretty suspicious given the rest of the message, but what did she care? "Algiers Point. Near those woods—you know? Omigod, I just heard shots. Hurry, Officer. Hurry! It's a black Lincoln Navigator."

It probably sounded phony as hell, like some angry wife with a grudge, but she knew they couldn't ignore it.

She couldn't stop her fingers, they moved on their own, dialing up Baronial Records, and then her mouth got out of control. "The Baron, please. Tell him it's the Baroness de Pontalba and if he wants to save his brother's sorry fucking life, he better get on the phone now."

Excuse my French, Eddie.

The Baron came on the line. "Baroness, what the hell's going on?"

"Your crazy-assed brother just kidnapped a teenage girl and my partner's son. I'm in a car right behind them." (That was close enough.) "We're in Algiers Point."

"You on drugs, Your Grace?"

"You killed the mama, didn't you? Listen, I know the whole story. How Rhonda Bergeron made stink and ended up dead. Then so did Cassandra's mama. The detective she hired's in a coma. If he dies, that's three."

"You are the craziest chick I ever met in my life."

So why didn't he hang up? "He's got two more in his car, and I'm on their tail. If he takes us all out, that'll make six. It's not going to fly, Baron. You can't save your brother. I'm giving you an opportunity to save yourself. Take it."

She could see the Lincoln SUV now; it was parked by the side of the road. She was sweating. The Baron said, "What do you want?"

"Call him. Call him now. Page him. You must have some kind of emergency code." She could hear the panic in her own voice.

"Why should I?"

"What?" She was struggling to see if they were still in the car.

"Why should I call him?"

"Because I have a recording of you admitting you sent Bingo and Pig to take out the mother."

"Sheeit! Ya got no such thing."

"Walk around to the front of your desk and feel under the lip. Go ahead, do it. Remember when you turned toward the window and gave me a look at your fine black ass? Know what I put there? Go see. Feel it?"

She thought she heard him swear under his breath. "That's a little transmitter I put there. I put one in your brother's office as well. I've got a recording of the conversation you had when I left your office. You stop him, I give it to you. He touches that kid, and the rest of your life you're doing the midnight show at Angola."

"Give me your number."

She rattled it off. "Baron, there's one more thing. I'm armed. I'd as soon kill your brother as swat a fly. In fact, I'd love to. You don't want to make me mad."

He laughed, and for a moment she thought she'd overdone it. Probably she sounded like some fifties

TV detective. But he said, "That'd be the best thing for everybody, now wouldn't it?"

He hung up, leaving her shaking her head to clear it. It had to be a pose. He'd hired killers to protect the man, he wasn't about to throw him to the lions—or rather, the lioness. She liked the sound of that.

She dialed 911 again, and with appropriate histrionics, gave the dispatcher her location.

Her cell phone rang as soon as she hung up. The Baron said, "I can't get him. Where are you?"

"Why?"

"I'm coming. I'm in the car."

He could of course send a fleet of thugs to whack her. Better come clean, she thought. "Baron. The cops are on the way."

"The fuck! My brother's crazy, you understand? I'm coming."

The fuck! she thought. He had a point. She told him her location.

And then she put a clip in the automatic and another in her pocket. She got out of the car, and started toward the SUV, wishing for a bulletproof vest, a motorcycle helmet, suit of armor, anything at all. "Toes?" she hollered. "Toes, I've got a message from your brother."

There was no answer. She had a bad feeling no one was in the car, and it proved out.

That meant Toes was in the nasty, swampy woods with Cassandra and Tony. She'd have to be crazy to go in there. Nevertheless, she was going to. She took off her hat and her red cape and started walking, glad she had on boots.

She moved timidly, taking very small steps in the hope they'd be quieter. She had no idea which direction to choose, and she paused frequently to listen. Finally, she thought she heard a male voice. And another noise, some kind of repetitive thumping. She headed toward it, ever so slowly and quietly.

She saw them before she could figure out what was going on—all three of them, alive. One of the men was sitting on the ground, and so was Cassandra. The other was bending over and straightening up, the same action over and over again. At this distance, she couldn't see color, and if the three had been strangers, sex might have been questionable.

Moving closer, it was a nightmare tableau. The man on the ground was Toes, the action was digging—he was forcing Tony, probably at gunpoint, to dig his own grave.

Yes, the gun was there. Talba felt for her own. She had no idea what its range was, but decided not to go any closer. If the situation changed, she could at least fire warning shots.

The boots that were even now saving her from snake and mosquito bites were too noisy to try any kind of surprise attack. The only thing she could think to do was wait, and there was nothing she hated more.

The change, when it came, surprised her as much as Toes. It was a shout, impossibly loud, right in her ear (or so it seemed). "Toes Toledano!"

Goddammit, don't! she thought. *Shut the fuck up. He's going to go crazy and shoot them both.*

Instead, he rose and broke into a big silly grin, ready to high-five the newcomer. "Hey, T!" he hollered, and Talba whirled to see the Baron behind her, megaphone in hand.

He said, "Give it up, brother. It's over."

"Whatchu talkin' 'bout? What's that shit you talkin'?"

"It ain't no good, Toes. Give it up. The bitch called the cops."

"I didn't do nothin'. I was just gon' give the bitch some tickets." (Presumably not the same bitch who called the cops.) "Asshole comes along, says he's a cop—what I'm s'posed to do? Huh? Answer me that?"

"Hey, brother. The bitch called the cops. The Baroness."

"The poetry bitch?" There were probably plenty of bitches in Toes's life. "Where she now?"

"Her car's here."

And Talba suddenly realized neither one of them had seen her. She heard sirens.

It was over. It was as *good* as over.

And yet . . . and yet . . . as long as they couldn't see her . . .

It occurred to her she could walk in a circle and come up behind Toes. It would be tricky—her purple outfit wasn't exactly invisible. And it would be dangerous—if the cops started shooting, she'd be right in their line of fire. On the other hand, wasn't this what backup was? Being there just in case?

It was a terrible idea. A perfectly awful idea. But curiously, she didn't feel the fear. She felt calm and detached. This was probably the other adrenaline response, the one that didn't result in a turtle imitation. *It may never happen again,* she thought. *I may as well enjoy it.* She started moving.

She was so intent on her own stealth, she didn't notice that the place was overrun almost before she had a chance to notice. Stealthily, cops fanned out in a semicircle around Toes. And there weren't only cops. Television crews were right behind them—dangerously close, she thought, cameras like great, metal pets on their shoulders. How the hell had they gotten into it?

Talba stopped and watched. The cops were apparently in the act of trying to arrest the Baron, or at least get him the hell out of there, and Toes was going crazy. "You let him go! Let my brother go! Swear to God if you don't let him go, gon' kill this motherfucker!" He jumped Tony, pulled him into a death hug, and stuck the gun in his ear. Cassandra whimpered. Talba was close enough to see that the girl's hands were tied behind her. She couldn't see her feet.

She continued moving. What if she came up behind Toes and shot him in the back? She didn't rule it out.

At this point, she certainly didn't.

Some cop told Toes to take it easy, and backed away from the Baron, who talked quietly with him a few minutes. After some amount of palaver, they both nodded and the Baron again picked up his megaphone. "Let him go, bro'. S'pose you kill him— what happens then? Then they kill *you*. And our mama never stop cryin'."

"You don't own me, T. I'm my own man, goddammit! You don't *own* me!" He sounded like Pamela's father yelling about *his* daughter. What was it the sound of? What did it mean?

Furious.

Well, sure.

Powerless and desperate.

What could she do with that? Desperate for what?

Pamela's father needed his daughter back; Toes needed what he said he had—to be his own man. To feel free of his brother.

She was somewhat to his left now, still a long way from his rear flank. But this was her shot. She saw the one thing she could do.

She rolled down the sleeves on her Indian-style top and measured. Both covered her hands, and the right one almost covered the gun. An inch or two stuck out, but maybe he wouldn't notice. She stepped into the clearing where he could see her; she was close, no more than fifty feet from him. She held her hands at her sides.

A roar went up from the cops. "What the fuck! Get that woman out of there! *Goddammit!*"

As if they could do anything about her.

She said, "I didn't call the cops. He did." She jerked her head toward the Baron. "I tried to talk him out of it."

"Fuck you, T!" He shoved Tony to the ground and pointed the gun at his brother.

Talba fired.

Chapter Twenty-six

S he had no idea the shot would be so loud. She stood there in shock, half-deaf, and men were pointing guns, shouting. "Drop the gun!"

"Drop it!"

"Put your hands on top of your head!"

It didn't occur to her they were talking to her until she heard Tony calling her name. "Talba! Drop it, or they'll shoot you!"

She'd forgotten she was holding a gun. It was like part of her now aching arm, but she felt her fingers release it, saw it fall to the ground. "Cassandra?" she said, and the girl answered. For a second, a second fragment, really, a blink, she had that sick feeling again, that about-to-faint feeling, and once again, she heard her name: "Talba!"

When she opened her eyes, a cop was standing over her, taking her pulse, putting something under her feet. The noise was unbearable—people shouting, sirens blaring, newscasters mouthing their spiels. Nasty harsh lights shone in her eyes, from the televison cameras. She closed them again.

It was big-time turtle-time. She stayed like that, in a near coma, for nearly the whole time it took the ambulance to get there and whiz back to Charity, coming out of it only once. When they got her on a stretcher and put her in it, when she caught on that that was what they were really doing, she said, "Am I shot?"

And someone answered, "No, you're okay. You'll be fine."

She wanted Tony with her in the ambulance, but she couldn't poke her head far enough out of her shell to mention it.

They had an awful time with her in the emergency room, couldn't seem to bring her around. She knew because she was partly awake; what she was doing was perhaps a form of playing possum, she wasn't sure, honestly didn't know if she could come fully back if she wanted to. What she did know was she didn't want to.

She had learned things in that sorry swamp. It wasn't even a swamp, just a wet piece of woods, a pathetic, ugly place, and she'd learned pathetic, ugly things there. She had seen her whole life pass before her in the moment she shot Toes. Or enough of it to know the rest was a sham.

When she felt the kick from the gun, she knew. She knew she'd felt it before. When Toes fell, when she saw the blood, the unstoppable scarlet fluid flowing out of him, flowing toward her in a thick, sticky ribbon, she knew she'd seen it before. She understood why the flashbacks were so terrifying. If the stream of blood touched her, she would die. She'd felt it today in Algiers, and she felt it that other time, God knew where it was, just *that* it was. She'd felt the same inconceivable terror when she shot her father.

*   *   *

Eddie's dream was too loud, too chaotic; he'd as soon be awake for all the rest he was getting. His son Anthony was in it, looking handsome, heavier, more grown-up—more manly, truth be told—than he had a decade ago. Audrey and Angela were there as well, Angie wearing that eternal black of hers, looking pinched and pale. Something about her was way off. Her confidence was gone. Fear was coming out of her pores like sweat. She seemed small and dried-up and not herself at all.

The other person there was his new assistant, Talba Wallis, and she was worse off than Angie. Her rich brown skin seemed to have turned gray. She looked like an animal someone had beaten. She was telling some crazy story about a police shootout, except that, in the weird way dreams twist things, she was telling it as if she'd been there, had actually done the shooting.

Anthony was trying to calm her. "Far be it from me to tell a lady she didn't save a gentleman's ass, but you probably missed him by a mile. The cops shot too, you know—it stands to reason a trained marksman's the one who actually hit the mark."

She seemed meek and subdued, like she was halfway somewhere else. Like she'd just lost a relative. Except that the person they were talking about wasn't a relative. Whoever it was had apparently been holding Anthony prisoner and Ms. Wallis was claiming to have rescued him, only she didn't seem real proud of it.

"How'd you get there?" she said. "What in hell happened?" She sounded agitated and furious, more or less her usual state. He wondered if Ms. Wallis was ever going to settle down.

"The thing was," he said, "I saw the car before I ever saw the kid. That big old Lincoln Navigator you told me about. It just stood to reason and sure enough, a black dude was driving, looked kind of like a toad.

"*Looked* like a toad, but he was acting more like a hawk. Just lurking there in that big old black car. Then the kid comes out. I knew her right away from her picture. She'd be cute if she ever smiled, you know that? And she gets in the car with someone else—with some other kids, I mean. I guess it was the car-pool person. And he follows. The Lincoln follows. Man, my heart was thumping!"

Ms. Wallis said, "You should have called me on the cell phone."

"Yeah, well, I tried."

"Mine was on," she said. "Did you have the wrong number or something?"

"It was my dad's phone, remember? I guess he forgot to charge it up. I tried to plug it in but—I don't know—it was hard enough trying to follow all those cars . . . I couldn't seem to do two things at once. And then things started happening so fast I had to keep moving.

"The car-pool mom took her home, and she got out and ran in. Then Toes pulls up in the driveway, and rings the doorbell. By the time I could get the car parked and get out, he was banging on the door and saying he had to talk to her. I came up behind him and he turned around and . . ."

He seemed to be groping for words, but Ms. Wallis wouldn't cut him any slack. "Well? And what?" Pushy as ever.

"I did something kind of stupid. I said I was a cop. And the guy tried to kill me!" Anthony was outraged. Eddie didn't really know his son these days, but if he had to guess, he wouldn't expect him to be too worldly-wise. Sounded like he'd have been right.

It seemed the guy had jumped him or something,

and then the person inside, a kid, panicked and opened the door. And that was it—the Toad had a lot more experience and a lot more meanness in him than either Anthony or the kid. He pulled a gun on 'em, bundled 'em into his car, and made Anthony drive somewhere else. And that would have been all they wrote if it hadn't been for Ms. Wallis—or so *her* story went.

Goddam! What a bunch of crazy fools he had in his life. It wasn't a good dream to begin with, but it suddenly got out of control.

Angie shrieked, "What the hell was that?"

Audrey sounded like some hysteric at a funeral: "Eddie! Oh, my Eddie, my Eddie. My *Eddie*!"

Anthony just said, "Dad!" in wonderment.

Jesus! Crazy fools was right. They were calling doctors and nurses. Now that he thought of it, this place was a hospital. He knew by the smell.

The medical personnel were acting hysterical. They were doing things with instruments and firing staccato questions at the rest of them. "You sure he spoke?"

"Well, some of us heard it."

Ms. Wallis said, "I didn't." Right. Way too busy listening to the sound of her own voice.

"What did he say?"

"It sounded like 'racy bush.' "

"No, boost."

"Foos. Like water racing. Racy foos."

"Foolish, maybe."

"Racy foolish?"

He hadn't said a *damn* thing. This was ridiculous, and not only that the crazy fools were talking too loud. He took the pillow and put it over his head. And still they wouldn't shut up.

"Hey, look. He's trying to move his hands. Like a dog dreaming about running—look at his wrists."

* * *

Talba called her mother as soon as she came back to herself, but it was too late. Miz Clara had already been besieged with calls from reporters and, hysterical, had called the police and been referred to Detective Skip Langdon. She'd just put down the phone when Talba herself called. By that time she not only knew her daughter was fine but had also realized that she was enjoying her fifteen minutes of fame. Further, that this was something she could piggyback onto. In the midst of their conversation, Miz Clara had to excuse herself because the evening news shows were coming on. Talba would have laughed if she'd felt up to it.

She didn't want to see anyone except Tony, to tell him how sorry she was that she'd sucked him into this, and to touch him, to reassure herself that he really was all right. But he was in his father's room, and that meant braving Audrey and Angie and the gray, shrunken, pathetic Eddie, for whom she really wasn't ready at this point. But she had to see him.

Tony caught her in a bear hug that said it all. To her surprise, Audrey and Angie hugged her too, apparently hadn't caught on that it was she who'd nearly gotten him killed.

She stayed a few minutes to hear Tony's story, and she was glad, because Eddie mumbled something, and that had to be a good sign.

And then the cops took her away. They were there the whole time, hovering, awaiting their chance. She had had to insist, to threaten a scene, even to get the few minutes with Tony, because she knew it was going to be a long haul.

When they finally let her go, Darryl was there for her. She hadn't called him, but she knew he'd be there. She should have been happy about it. She was miserable.

She didn't want to be with anybody for a while. But home meant Miz Clara and a hundred reporters. She gratefully accepted his offer to stay at his house.

She was surprised that she couldn't talk to him. He wanted her to tell him everything, to fill him in, but she couldn't. All she could do was lie on the bed and stare at the ceiling. He was dying to watch the footage of the scene, but she couldn't bear it. She couldn't even let him hold her.

When he went to work the next morning, she found some bourbon and drank enough of that to put her out again, and she slept until he came home from school. He let her sleep until early evening, when he made her some spaghetti with red gravy—a known comfort food—and forced her to eat it.

They talked small talk until he said, "Listen, you've really been through some shit."

It didn't seem worth the effort to answer.

"You want to talk about it?"

"I can't think about it."

It was a mistake to say that. He gave her a lot of guff about what was healthy and what wasn't and how victims have to tell their stories, and that kind of crap.

"No, you don't get it. I *can't* think about it."

"Listen, I think I should call Cindy Lou."

Cindy Lou. The damn police psychologist. The one who was with him the night they met. She was going to have to kill him.

"Talba, you're hurting yourself, just lying around like this. Your mother's worried about you, your brother's worried about you . . ."

"You've been talking to them!"

"Hey, don't be mad. Be grateful. I've kept them away so far. You know *that* wasn't easy."

"I've got to work this through on my own terms."

"All right. Okay." He didn't sounded surprised.

"You've got to do what you've got to do. Look, would you like to be alone tonight? I could go stay with a friend."

"Let me think about it." But even then she knew she was going to break through it. It was probably the simple act of his backing away that did it. She wasn't ready yet to say, *No, stay with me!* but she was pretty sure she was about to be.

She thought about it for half an hour or so, and then she asked him to stay and she told him why she couldn't even think about the shootout at Algiers Point. "It's because every time I try, something weird in my mind takes over, and I'm back in that room again, with my father."

He started making "it's-only-natural" noises, but she had to stop him. "No. The gun brought it all back—shooting Toes." She choked over the words. "Darryl, I didn't see someone shoot my father. *I* shot him."

"Oh, my God." He spoke in a matter-of-fact tone, as if he'd suspected all along, but his handsome face was tragic. "Oh, my *God.*" He was barely whispering. "That's what they were trying to protect you from."

She nodded. "Yeah. It all makes a crazy kind of sense when you know. If I saw it, then they just seem like a crazy, overprotective family, but if I *did* it, they've got a reason not to tell me. I almost agree with them."

"You do?"

That was when the first tears came. "Darryl, I *do!* You don't know how awful this is—to realize something like this!" She cried a long time, and then she told him all that she remembered and all that she didn't. When they had hashed it over a thousand times, they went to bed, and when she awakened he was gone.

Again, she got drunk and went back to bed. Sometime that afternoon, one or two o'clock, maybe, she was awakened by the smell of coffee brewing, and bacon cooking. It had to be Darryl, but how had he gotten off from school? She didn't try to figure it out, just closed her eyes and went back to sleep. The person who shook her awake was Miz Clara.

"Who you think you is? Queen of the May?"

"Go away, Mama."

"Come on, girl. You got to eat."

"I'm not hungry."

"And brush your teeth. You smell like a brewery."

Talba closed her eyes. Miz Clara pulled the sheet off. And Talba got up and brushed her teeth.

She went into the kitchen and drank coffee and ate eggs, bacon, and toast while her mother bustled around the kitchen swiping at surfaces, removing ancient fingerprints, doing what she did all day at white ladies' houses and then again at home. Miz Clara talked too, all about Talba's star turn on the news and about how good she looked and how proud she was of her.

Very atypical talk for Miz Clara.

Talba didn't trust it, but her mother was in an unusual mood—she might answer a straight question if Talba asked it. "Did they show me . . . pulling the trigger?"

"No, girl, they ain' show that. They show *him* aimin' at the camera."

"At his brother. He'd have killed his own brother." And then she realized what she'd just said, how close to home it was, and her throat closed.

Miz Clara sat down at the table. "Now listen up, girl. You didn't kill your daddy."

She had said the "D" word. Even now, now that Talba *knew,* her mother'd do anything to keep her from knowing. *How goddam misguided,* she thought, overwhelmed by the wrongheadedness of it. But at the same time, she was touched by it. She laid her hand on her mother's. "Mama, you don't have to lie anymore. I remember it."

"You don't remember nothin,' Sandra. Not nothin.' *You didn't kill your daddy.*"

Talba didn't even answer, just closed her eyes and bowed her head in frustration.

"You kill his woman."

Her head jerked up. "What?"

Her mother spoke as softly as she ever had in Talba's memory. "We didn't want you to know, baby."

"Mama, tell me. Tell me now!"

Her mother stroked Talba's arm. "You just shush and listen. That's what I'm here for." She had on a bandanna, and Talba realized she'd taken off from work to come; she was losing half a day's pay.

Miz Clara took a breath. "He was a bad, bad man, your daddy. Denman La Rose Wallis. Umm ummm ummm. Rue the day I take *that* man's name. Bad? Girl! He done it all—alcohol, drugs, women. The other thing, too."

Talba would have thought "the other thing" meant sex. But Miz Clara had just mentioned sex. "What other thing?" she said.

Miz Clara bowed her head, something she only did in church so far as Talba knew. She raised it abruptly. "He hit us."

"Both of us?"

Her mother nodded. "Corey too. But one thing— the man *only* good quality—he love his chirren. He did love his chirren. I wouldn't try to stop him from seein' y'all, no matter how much I want to."

I love this, Talba thought. *She sent us over there to be beaten.* But that was unfair, and she knew it. Her mother had done what she thought best. That was all that could be said about it.

"Women? Wooo, he had women. But one in partic'lar. One he live with." She looked down again. "One he have a baby with."

"A baby? You mean I've got a sister?"

" 'Nother brother, maybe. I don't remember."

"A *baby*?"

Miz Clara moved right away from that one. "We had some real hard times with yo' daddy gone." She looked so sad Talba patted her.

"I know, Mama."

"And maybe I say some things I shouldn't." Her eyes filled up. "Baby, you was always such a *good* little girl."

"What? What, Mama?"

"Nothin', honey. Nothin' atall. You was a good little girl. Yo' daddy was a bad man. Tha's the whole story in a nutshell. He hang out with the criminal element and he carry a gun sometime. I know. I find it once or twice. Baby, precious . . ." Tears were spilling out of her eyes. ". . . you find it too."

"I found it?"

"You weren't but five, darlin'. You weren't but five. What kinda man leave a gun lyin' aroun' where a five-year-old could find it? You answer me that? What kind of man do that?"

Until now, Talba hadn't entirely trusted the story, had thought Miz Clara was still trying to soften the blow. But the movie was playing again. The man who picked her up, the one who tried to comfort her, was the man in the photo she'd found. Was unquestionably her father.

Unless my memory's playing tricks again.

"Was my father there when it happened?"

"Ohhhhh, yes. Yes, ma'am, he certainly was. He'd left the gun on the coffee table. On the *coffee table*! Can you feature a thing like that?" Her voice was shrill with outrage. "He left his gun on the coffee table!"

"Well, what happened?"

"You was playin' with the gun and it went off. Tha's what happened. The woman died, your life rurned. Or could have been. Could have been rurned.

"Honey, we tried *so* hard to protect you. All in the world we was doing was tryin' to keep you from knowin' somethin' ugly like that."

She was crying in earnest now, and Talba felt her own tears ball up in a big clot at the back of her throat—they weren't going to melt out of her for a while. She knew how it worked—she was going to have to feel lower than a worm until the crying worked its way to the surface, and there was nothing she could do to hasten the process. Nothing but lie down and stare at the ceiling.

"I know, Mama," she said. "I know."

She wondered if she should try to embrace her mother, but she thought not. This was a private grief.

"But why would I shoot the woman?" she said.

Her mother looked at her squarely. "I ain't know, precious. The good Lord the only one know the answer to that. The good Lord the only one."

Later, during the three subsequent days she stared at the ceiling, another movie took shape in her head: Corey spilling milk on the kitchen floor, Miz Clara screaming in frustration and despair. "Look what you done now! We ain' got no money to buy more! Ain't got enough for a quart of milk. And your daddy don't even care. Livin' with that woman, neglectin' his own two chirren—oh, *Lord,* I wish that woman was dead!"

Talba asked her mama if she'd ever had a kind of paisley overblouse, a sort of blue-and-gold print, that she wore over jeans, and Miz Clara said, "Girl, how come you remember a thing like that?"

Talba said, "I remember Corey spilling some milk and you were wearing it."

Miz Clara's face closed down as if Saran-wrapped. "I don't remember no such thing."

There was another memory she tried to tease out. So far she hadn't succeeded, and there was comfort in that. In her worst moments, she had the sick, scary feeling that she'd said something like: "I thought you wanted me to, Mama. I thought you wanted her to die." But if she had, it was staying buried, at least for now, and she could only pray it would forever.

She hoped to God Miz Clara hadn't had to live with that.

Chapter Twenty-seven

Once during her lying-in period, someone other than Darryl and family had tried to come see her—but she wouldn't get up even for the Reverend Clarence Scruggs, which deeply embarrassed her and scandalized her mother. But she couldn't do it. Truly couldn't.

The thing that finally got her up was the discovery of Aziza Scott's body in the woods at Algiers Point, buried in a shallow grave. Or more properly, Miz Clara was the thing that got her up. She brought in the *Times-Picayune* and thumped it. "Bless that poor little child's heart, her mama dead! Bad enough, ya won't even get up and go see ya own boss in the hospital. Ya can't be bothered visitin' a little girl whose mama died a horrible and violent death, the good Lord forgive ya."

Miz Clara was right about this one. Even if she had to take Prozac, she had to visit Cassandra.

She made it without benefit of chemicals, and she

was touched by the girl's reception. As soon as she walked into the crowded living room, Cassandra ran to her, threw her arms around her neck, and held on. Cassandra's dad thanked her for saving his daughter. Shaneel was there, too, with her mama, a nice woman who seemed to consider her an old friend.

And so was Pamela. "Girl!" Talba blurted. "You don't know how worried I was about you."

The little redhead looked bewildered.

Remembering they'd never actually met, Talba introduced herself.

The girl's face glowed. "Oh! The woman who saved Cassandra. Let me shake your hand." While Talba complied, Pammie kept talking, nervously. "I'm a little embarrassed that I disappeared, but you have to understand how freaked out I was. See, Toes called and threatened to kill me if I ratted him out. I didn't even think—all I wanted was out." She laughed a sad little laugh. "I wish I was more proud of myself. I found out later I wasn't the only one— he called Shaneel and Cassandra too."

"You did the right thing, little pumpkin head."

"I don't know—I was scared, that's all. I didn't even tell my parents—just took the bus to Millie's. She's like my aunt, kind of." The girl said the last part shyly, as if confessing a secret crush. "You know—Millie the Milliner? She felt bad about freezing you out—she thought she had to do it to protect me."

"Well, that clears that up. I thought she had a sudden attack of racism."

Pamela was clearly mortified. "Oh, no! She'd die if she thought—"

"I was just kidding. But one thing puzzles me— your parents said they sent you out of town."

The girl looked at the carpet. "I guess they were

embarrassed they didn't know where I was. I did call to say I was okay."

Cassandra had stood by during the conversation, listening mutely, wearing a slightly dazed expression but conveying as well an aura of urgency, as if she had something on her mind. Talba bided her time till she could get the girl aside. When it was finally accomplished, Cassandra said, "I thought about you a lot—about what you did, how you saved me and Tony."

Talba was embarrassed, but Cassandra was even more so. She kept talking, fast. "I wanted to . . . well, I wanted to . . . I can't say it. I thought you were really great, and so I did something really weird. I wrote a poem."

Talba was so bowled over by this revelation that she could only repeat the words: "You wrote a poem?"

The girl nodded. "Uh-huh. About my mom. About what she meant to me. Maybe when . . . when this is all over or something, you could take a look at it."

Talba said, "Sure. I'd be glad to. I think that's wonderful, baby."

The girl had something else to say. "Is Eddie okay? How's he doin'?"

"He's better." That was the rumor, anyway.

"Listen, I . . ." She was squirming with embarrassment. "Could you tell him it's okay? I know he did all he could. Could you tell him I know he tried?"

"Well . . . sure. But I don't understand, exactly."

The girl closed her eyes and water squeezed out the bottom of each. She could only whisper. "He told me he'd find my mama for me. I know he feels real bad."

Talba felt as if someone had sprayed her face with rosewater. She couldn't believe what the kid had done—how she was handling this thing. The girl seemed to have grown up overnight.

Talba thought, *She's doing better than I am,* and felt ashamed. She went home and wrote a poem about the kid who wrote a poem about her mother.

After that, she didn't go back to bed except during normal sleeping hours. Somehow or other, she and Eileen Fisher had to keep the agency going. Also, she had a bit of unfinished business. She had to figure out how her father happened to get a fatal gunshot wound.

Eddie had broken his nose, left scapula, two ribs, and his right tibia. Once he came out of the coma, his most serious injury was the leg break. That took a while to heal, and it made him cross.

But he was coming in to the office after about a month, tearing apart everything Talba and Eileen had put together. They'd gladly have sent him back, but Angie and Audrey were being very Catholic about the thing. Or maybe just Italian. Talba wasn't sure where it came from, but it went like this: they felt guilty about Eddie's injuries, largely because, as Talba understood it, he'd missed his own sixty-fifth birthday party, which it was their duty to throw for him. Thus, the only way to expunge their guilt was to throw it anyway. Only the hotel ballroom they'd booked for the occasion was now booked until July with conventions, graduations, and weddings.

So the second week of JazzFest, they took advantage of the gorgeous weather to throw a crawfish party at their own gorgeous house out by the lake. Eddie agreed to it for one reason and one reason only—it was also a party to announce the engagement of his son Tony Tino, the well-known blues musician, and Tony's very pregnant bride-to-be. This scandalized Audrey—which was probably what

Eddie liked about it—and amused Angie no end.

Eddie was feeling so expansive, he said to her, "Ya got a boyfriend? Always room for one more."

To which Angie replied, "I thought you thought I was a dyke."

Damned if Eddie didn't blush. "Goddammit. Bring yours then, Ms. Wallis."

"Audrey already asked him. Along with his daughter, my mother, Cassandra, her father and *his* girlfriend, Shaneel, and her mama. Is that too many black folks for you?"

He looked at her seriously. "No. No, Ms. Wallis. That's about the right amount—just so long as Miz Clara doesn't bring a boyfriend."

Miz Clara had brought him greens and chicken twice a week during his recovery, and he claimed to have fallen in love with her.

Talba, meanwhile, had met Darryl's daughter, Raisa, twice, and found her as difficult as advertised. Yet it was Darryl's weekend to have her, and it wasn't a good time to mess with her schedule. So Raisa was coming.

The air was thick with citronella when Talba got there. Tables were all over the backyard, covered with newspaper, and two great cauldrons of crawfish, potatoes, and corn bubbled away. There were also tubs packed with beer and soft drinks for the children, of whom, Talba was relieved to see, there were quite a few. *What did I expect?* she thought. *These people are Italian.*

To her immense relief, Shaneel and Cassandra took a shine to Raisa, who, even Talba agreed, was an exquisite child.

Though her mother was black, some ancestor hadn't been. The girl had taupe-colored skin and shiny hair that billowed behind her in a golden cloud. Talba had never seen anything like it on any child, black or white, and it was probably going to turn dark in a year or two; but right now, it was ethereal.

Because she looked so much like an angel, you could almost forget that at any given moment she might throw a tantrum.

With luck, she'd grow out of it. And with more luck, she'd remain angelic at least another few minutes.

Talba had a poem to perform—the one she'd promised Eileen Fisher so long before. Between the consumption of crustaceans and the playing of blues, she took the floor.

"For all y'all who don't know me, I am the Baroness de Pontalba, also known as Eddie Valentino's humble assistant. While I do write and perform poetry on a regular basis, I've never exactly written a poem in this form before. But because of the kind of person we all know Eddie is, I put in a lot of special effort to come up with something ethnically appropriate. Y'all ready?"

Tony, who'd been carefully coached, led the cheering.

"It's kind of a new thing for me, now. Okay, here goes."

Tony, who'd borrowed a drum to accompany her, tapped out a rap.

Mistah Eddie Valentino he a one of a kind
He a crime-fightin' private eye that ev'rybody know
He talk like a thug, but he ain't your average Joe
He look like a thug, but he really know his wine—
He'd act like a thug if his family weren't so fine.
Got some moves when he clash with Mistah
  Dangerous Foe
Gettin' old, but got his ducks pretty much in a row

You a thug, you a gangsta, make you cry and
     make you whine
But ain't none of that stuff what makes the dude
     unique—
Got backpacks hangin' down the front of his mug
Now you could carry the mail in them pouches on
     his face,
'Cause the baldface truth is the man is a freak,
He got sleepin' bags for squirrels, they big enough to
     hug
'Cause the baldface truth is the detective's a case!

When she was finished, and had received her share of foot-stompin' appreciation, she bowed in her usual regal fashion: "The Baroness myself thanks you."

She was leaving the stage in triumph, when Tony, next on the program, took the mike and fed her the straight lines she'd requested: "Not so fast, Baroness. Come on back up here."

When she had obeyed, he said, "I don't quite understand your logic here. I know you wanted to honor my father and all, but just how exactly is a rap ethnically appropriate to a man whose last name ends with a vowel?"

"Baby, that wasn't no rap."

"Come on, Baroness. If it walks like a duck, and it quacks like a duck . . ."

"Well, then, it's a wop poem."

"If that's a wop poem, you and I were listening to some different quacking."

"No, we heard the same quacking. My interpretation threw you off a little, that's all."

"What do you mean, your interpretation? I think I know a rap when I hear one."

"Well, Tony, honey, I just said your daddy a fourteen-line poem in iambic pentameter with one octet and one sestet, and a rhyme scheme of ABBA

in the octet and CDE in the sestet." She turned full
face to the audience. "You know what you call that,
Mr. Eddie Valentino? *That* is a very ethnically appropriate Petrarchan sonnet. Known familiarly as an
Italian sonnet." She bowed again, but before the expected applause could get started, Eddie slipped in
and got the last word:

"Good night, Gracie," he said. Which got the last
laugh.

Chapter One

U nder normal circumstances, getting a Louisiana PI license is so routine as to be boring—
you take a course, you pass a test, and you pay your
money. Usually, there's only one slight catch—you
can't be issued a license unless you're already hired.
But Talba Wallis seemed to have found another one.

She *was* already hired, and she'd made ninty-
seven on the test. For nearly five months, she'd
worked as an apprentice for Mr. Eddie Valentino of
E. V. Anthony Investigations.

And still, she almost didn't get her license.

You have to submit a few little things with your
application—a copy of your driver's license, five-by-
seven-inch photo, and fingerprints. For the last, the
State Board of Private Investigator Examiners pro-
vides official FBI cards. All you have to do is take
them to any law enforcement agency that offers a
fingerprinting service and plunk down a few small
bucks.

"Piece o' cake," Eddie said. "Take ya ten minutes, max." So one gorgeous September day on her lunch hour, Talba drove out to 715 South Broad Street, headquarters of the New Orleans Police Department.

A good thing it's close, she thought. She had a client coming in at one, and at three, she had to resume her surveillance of a suspected errant wife. The woman was a college professor whose last class was over then, and Talba was in a hurry to wrap up the case. Eddie's jokes about "extracurricular activities" were getting tedious.

Nonetheless, she was in a great mood. She sailed in feeling buoyant and powerful. Finally, finally, she was getting the damned license. She liked the job a lot. A whole lot. And a funny thing, it was a great way to make friends. It wasn't something anyone ever thought about on career day at school, but once you said the words *private investigator*, it was amazing how many people blurted, "I'd love to do that!"

They wouldn't, of course. For one thing, there was the tedium—of records searches, surveillance, online research, court appearances, intake interviews, half a dozen other things. For another, most people thought divorce cases were sleazy, and these were a good chunk of the work. Actually, Talba liked them—she liked catching scumbags (of either sex) and, though originally hired for her computer skills, she'd turned out to be good at it.

It wasn't a job for everybody, but, despite the fact that she was such a computer wiz she impressed even herself, a sensitive and talented poet (in her opinion), and a baroness (she'd decided), it suited her.

So she was in an excellent mood as she entered the building. A female functionary sporting two-inch purple nails with a tiny picture on each of them pointed to a door on the right. No stairs, no elevator. Couldn't be more convenient.

Talba stepped through to a nearly dark, closet-sized anteroom opening onto a large, light, comfortable-looking room, which was populated by two people—an enormous, seated woman in a black dress and a smallish, standing, wiry-looking man in uniform. Both were African-American, as was Talba herself. The well-padded woman had a motherly look to her. Pencil in hand, she was poring over something in which she seemed to have a deep and abiding interest.

She may or not have heard Talba enter, but either way, she didn't look up. The man was talking on the phone. Talba stood politely for a few minutes, curious as to what was so important the woman couldn't take time out to serve a customer. And finally, she got tired of it. "Excuse me," she said.

The woman looked at her over nondescript glasses that couldn't hide a pair of bulging eyes. *A thyroid thing*, Talba thought, figuring it was causing the weight problem.

"I'm here to get fingerprinted."

"Whatcha need prints for?"

"I'm applying for my PI license."

"That'll cost ya thirty dollars. You can get it done for fifteen dollars at the Jefferson Parish Sheriff's Office."

"Here's fine. I don't mind the charge."

The woman raised an eyebrow, as if she disapproved of spendthrifts. "Ya filled out ya cards?"

"No, do I need to?"

"Use black ink and be sure ya print."

In the anteroom, there was an end table she could probably write on, but not enough light to see. "May I come in to fill them out?" There were at least five empty desks.

"This room's part of the police department." The

woman went back to her paperwork, leaving Talba rummaging for a pen and hoping if she found one, it would be black.

She ended up going outside to fill out the card.

When she returned, the large woman seemed almost cordial. "Come on in," she said, with a near-smile, and Talba opened the dutch door separating the spaces.

The other woman came forward to sit at the front desk. "Let me have the cards and ya driver's license." The instructions on the application had been explicit—the fingerprinter must see the applicant's license. The woman studied the documents for almost five minutes before she finally raised her head, face outraged, suddenly a different person.

"You got different names on these things!"

It was true.

Talba's birth name was an embarrassment to all concerned—to herself, to Miz Clara, and to the human race in general. A white obstetrics resident who thought he was funny had named her. However, the state required the same name on your driver's license that appeared on your birth certificate.

"Talba" was her own name, the name she'd given herself and always used except when performing her poems, at which times she used its ceremonial form, "the Baroness de Pontalba."

She pointed out where she'd written her official name on the FBI card, in the space asking for aliases and AKAs. "I'd prefer to use 'Talba' on my license," she said.

"You can't do that. Ya name's Urethra." It took all Talba's strength not to wince.

Damn! Something was severely off here. The license was issued by a state board—what right did a city functionary have even to express an opinion on the subject?

But the fat lady wasn't the sort you argued with.

Talba said, "The board might agree, I don't know. Can't know till I apply."

The woman wasn't listening. She'd begun paging through a copy of the Yellow Pages, holding Talba's license and FBI cards tightly in the hand that also held the book. "There's no Eddie Valentino in here."

The card had asked for her employer's name and address. "I work for E. V. Anthony Investigations. Eddie's the 'E. V.' part." She pointed out the agency ad.

"I'm gon' call the state board." The woman got up and waddled to a glass cubicle in the back of the room. Talba heard her dial and say, "This is Sergeant Rouselle."

This woman was a cop? That was a shocker. She wasn't in uniform and she wore no badge. Besides that, she seemed not to have either the personality or the build for it. *Minor bureaucrat* was the way Talba'd pegged her. The sort who got off on ruining people's days.

Cop or no, she suddenly realized, she was about to become snarled in a bureaucratic snafu that was going to make her miss her one o'clock.

She walked back to the cubicle and held out her hand. "Sgt. Rouselle, I think I'll go over to Jefferson Parish, after all. May I have my license, please?"

The sergeant turned on her, shouting, bulging eyes blazing behind dirty lenses. "You're going to jail if you snatch this out my hand!"

Talba backed away, "I wasn't going to—"

The other officer got off the phone quick and strode over to the cubicle, patting air as if to calm a child. "Now, ma'am, just calm down. Just take it easy now."

"But I didn't . . . look, all I want to do is go. I'm on my lunch hour."

"I get the feeling you're worried you're going to

get your boss in trouble. This is nothing to do with you and nothing to do with him."

What language was he speaking?

Who cared?

"Look, Officer, I'm on a schedule."

"Just take it easy and nobody's going to get in any trouble."

It suddenly got through to Talba exactly what the situation was: He was telling her the sergeant really could throw her in jail if she wanted to. All she'd have to do was *say* Talba assaulted her to get her license; or had pot breath; or anything she wanted to. In a word, she was trapped.

She sat and steamed. After about twenty minutes, Officer Rouselle waddled on out. "All right. You want to get fingerprinted?"

Talba looked at her watch, considering. There was still time to make her one o'clock—barely—if the show could just get on the road. "Can we do it now?"

"*Now?*" the sergeant shouted. "Can we do it *now?* You don't respect my title or my position, do you? I need a little more respect out of you, missy. Hear me: you must use the same name on these cards as is on your driver's license. . . ."

Talba was desperate to scream at the woman: *It's not up to you, Fat Stuff! It's up to the state board.* But that was definitely going to get her arrested.

It developed the sergeant could read her mind. She just stared, heaving a huge sigh. And then, still clutching Talba's license, she picked up the phone.

"Captain Regilio, please. Well, then, the lieutenant." Talba's heart thumped in a way it hadn't since she'd gotten in a shootout the previous spring. *It's the adrenaline,* she realized. *Damn! This petty bureaucrat has me scared to death.*

That pissed her off almost more than the rest of it.

Then there was the problem of how the hell she was going to explain to Eddie (or her mother or even her boyfriend) that she was innocent—whatever the charge. The fact was, she did have a mouth on her. The irony was, for once she was keeping it shut.

Eventually, two uniformed male officers and one white woman in shorts arrived to receive another ten minutes of Sgt. Rouselle's rants. "I called y'all in because this woman's trying to provoke me."

Take it, Talba told herself. *Keep your mouth shut or you're going to jail.*

Her teeth hurt from gritting them. Finally one of the other officers gently pried the license from Sgt. Rouselle's grasp and handed it back to Talba, who once again held out her hand. "May I have my fingerprint cards?"

"I'm gon' confiscate those. They're not your property, they're the FBI's."

Oh, yeah? So now you're the FBI?

She looked beseechingly at the others, but they only stared back poker-faced.

Well, who cared? At least she was legal to drive back to the office. She never had to breathe a word. She'd just go tomorrow to Jefferson Parish and no one would be the wiser.

She arrived back at the office at five after one. Her client was sitting in the reception room, and Eileen Fisher, Eddie's office manager, looked way too nervous for comfort.

"That Ms. Wallis?" Eddie hollered. "Ms. Wallis, could you come in here a minute? I just had a phone call from the state board. What's this about you gettin' arrested?"

It was a hell of a way to begin a career.

But Eddie had been gentle with her. "I'm gon' let you off this time, Ms. Wallis. So long as ya learned somethin' from this experience."

"If you mean I'm supposed to suck up to some power-hungry harpie out of Kafka's worst nightmares . . ."

"I don't mean that a'tall, Ms. Wallis. I mean I hope ya learned to never, ever, for any reason do anything in any New Orleans city office you can do somewhere else. I mean that, now. Save us both a lot of time, lot of headache."

She was about to say, Yes sir, she sure wouldn't, and leave clicking her heels together, when he held up a finger. "And one more thing if you don't mind—could ya make some kinda effort not to be more trouble than ya worth?"

That was a month ago. She had her license now—in the name of Talba Wallis, thank you very much. But the whole gig looked to be falling apart again.

S he could barely hear the words through the fuzz in her brain: "*Miss, are you all right?*" The speaker was the other driver, a white man in his forties.

Hell, no, she wasn't all right. Four days of surveillance and she finally had the pond scum in the Cadillac with the paramour, feet away from her camera lens. Inches from delicious triumph.

But now nothing. Nothing but a hurting back, a totaled car, maybe a missed paycheck. Maybe even the ax—after that little episode with Sgt. Rouselle, Eddie's patience was pretty thin.

And her mama, Miz Clara, did so love having her baby daughter employed. Even as a PI. Time was when Miz Clara thought there were only three suitable jobs for a Wallis child—doctor of medicine, speaker of the house, and first African-American president. But that was before she caught onto the stage-mom potential of having a flamboyant daughter who happened to be not only a poet, performance artist, and computer genius but also a detective.

And now a little thing like a missed stop sign was about to ruin it all. One minute Talba was barreling toward truth and justice; the next, a force from hell struck with a sound like a gunshot, leaving her humiliated and hurting. For a moment she thought maybe it *was* a gunshot. She wouldn't put it past the lying, low-down sack of manure she was following.

But, no, it was a Ford Explorer—a car about twice the size of Talba's Camry—which had been lawfully moving through the intersection. She hadn't seen the car or the stop sign. A crowd was beginning to gather. A siren wailed in the distance. And Talba's back was killing her.

In her current state she really couldn't go back to the office and deal with Eddie about this thing. He could be slightly more of a pain in the patootie than Miz Clara herself.

There was only one good thing about this—that it wasn't Eddie's car that got wrecked. And not just because his was really his wife Audrey's Cadillac. It was handsomely appointed with the Global Positioning System that Talba had bought half-price from some fly-by-night spy shop having a fire sale. She had a weakness for shopping at spy shops; her idea was, with the GPS Eddie could track her if she got in a tight spot. But after spending a week's salary on it, she realized he didn't even have a laptop for the tracking system. So, under great protest, she'd made him let her install it in his own car.

Under *very* great protest. Eddie claimed the twenty-first-century PI needed only six pieces of equipment, one of which was a child's toy and only two of which were electronic—cell phone, tape recorder, video camera, conventional camera, binoculars, and Tee-ball bat. The last was the closest thing to a weapon he ever carried. "It's well-balanced, with a good grip, and heavy enough to do some damage. *And* it's absolutely legal," he told Talba when he presented her with hers.

Groaning, she retrieved it now, along with her maps and the other five items. She put the entire PI kit in a Guatemalan bag she had in the trunk, thinking that where it really belonged was in a new car. But she sure couldn't shop for one bent over like she was.

So she called Babalu Maya for an appointment and got the tow truck to drop her at Whole Foods on its way to Camry heaven. Babalu, bodyworker extraordinaire (whose real name was probably Barbara), lived within spitting distance of the only store in New Orleans where you could buy a head of lettuce for the cost of a new Camry. Talba could walk the block and a half if she didn't collapse first; she could hobble it, anyhow. Or so she thought. She found the effort made her nauseous.

"Girl!" Babalu's face said Talba's pain was her pain. "I swear to God you're pale."

Babalu was white; she said things like that. Talba was not merely African-American but black. *Good* and black, thank you very much. She knew she was nowhere near pale, but she couldn't be looking her best.

"Give me that bag and sit down. Just sit down, now." Talba still had stairs to climb. Babalu exerted pressure on her shoulders; Talba yielded. And before she knew it, Babalu had done something, she hadn't a clue what, that made it possible to straighten up.

"Can you make it upstairs?"

Talba nodded gratefully and hobbled up ahead of Babalu, who evidently thought she might have to catch her if things didn't go well. Talba knew the drill so well she didn't even pause, just went into the first room off the hallway, removed her shoes and earrings, and slid gingerly onto the massage table.

Babalu said, "Tell me about it."

"Well, I didn't see the stop sign. This tank or something hit me on the shotgun side—caved in my whole front end."

"You are one lucky female." Babalu's pretty face screwed itself up. She had short blond hair that she wore in a careless, shaggy bob, clear, satiny skin, and some kind of chain tattoo crawling up her arm— Celtic knots, she said, but it gave Talba the creeps. Like some kind of metaphorical half-handcuffs. Babalu had smiled the time she mentioned it—and not a nice smile, either; as if the effect was deliberate.

Talba said, "Lucky. How come I can't quite see it that way? I'm pretty sure my car's a total."

"Oh, I'm so sorry. Wish I had one to lend you." That was the way she was, Talba thought. A nurturer; a healer. She knew Talba only as a client, and yet she behaved like a friend.

Talba groaned again and changed the subject, hoping for distraction from the intermittent pain. "Okay, enough about me. What's new with you?" She arched her back against Babalu's fingers.

"You haven't been here in too long, or you'd know. Feel that? These muscles think they're bone. A little stress, I'd say."

Talba ignored the last part. "Or I'd know what?"

Babalu waved her left hand provocatively; its fourth finger glinted. "I'm getting married."

Talba tried to sit up, just to take in the news. Babalu leaned over her chest and pushed her down. Tough. But her cheeks were flushed and she was smiling. Talba gave up. "Hey, that's fantastic!"

"Yeah. I'm pretty happy." The blush deepened.

"Well, tell me everything." This was good. There was nothing so distracting as a little romance.

"He's . . . cute."

"Yes? And?"

"Well, he's from Mississippi, and his name is Jason. He's about six feet tall with dark, gorgeous hair. . . ."

"Umm hmm. Blue eyes, I bet."

"Yeah. How'd you know?"

"You like that. I remember." A bodyworker, she reflected, was like a hairdresser or an exercise partner. There you were for an hour, just the two of you—of course you were going to talk about who you were dating. "He's probably an actor."

Babalu nodded. "Pretty good, too."

"I knew it. You're such a stage-door Jenny."

"I like people with talent—the way I grew up was just so . . . I don't know . . ."

"Stuffy?"

"What makes you think that?"

"You've got that deb look. Except for the tattoo, of course. And the zany hair."

Babalu laughed. "Carefully cultivated. We were trailer-trash, actually."

"Back to the guy. Does he have a day gig?"

"He's . . . ummm . . . a stock trader."

"A *trader*? With the market in the toilet?"

Babalu shrugged. "He seems to do okay at it."

"That's a fair-sized rock he gave you, anyhow." She realized Babalu hadn't said one really personal thing about the man. "What about him really, though? What's your favorite thing about him?"

"My favorite thing?" The question seemed to catch her off guard, but she recovered quickly. "You think I'm going to talk about *that*?"

"Don't. Ow. It hurts to laugh. Also, you're mashing a tender spot."

Instantly, Babalu's fingers lightened up. Talba sought once more to distract herself. "Okay, what do you like least about him?"

"Least?"

"Yeah, least. I know you're crazy in love and all that, but search your conscience—there's got to be something."

Talba could have sworn Babalu's hands tightened on her back—even pinched a bit. She heard a sound like a sniff. Damn! She sure didn't want to get a cold.

But it wasn't that. The sniff was followed by a sound like *snurf*, a smothered sound, but there was no mistaking it; Babalu was crying.

"What is it?" Once again, she tried to rise, thinking to hug the healer, but Babalu held her down.

"No. Let's finish the session."

Talba didn't move, but she wasn't about to keep quiet. "Girlfriend, what is it?"

"I think he's cheating on me."

Oh, boy. Talba had heard plenty of this kind of thing lately. Louisiana might have no-fault divorce, but there was still the issue of spousal support, which was why she was surveilling a low-down scumbag cheater when the Explorer slammed her. Proof of catting around could pay off handsomely, but that was irrelevant in Babalu's case. What was relevant was, the marriage was off to a rocky start and it hadn't even happened yet.

"You can't marry an asshole who's cheating on you. Babalu, hear me—you do not deserve this. Give the man his ring back."

"You're scrunching up again."

"You're getting me upset."

"Well, I just said he may be. He's probably not. Maybe he's . . . I don't know—maybe it's something else."

"Talk to me. Tell me about it."

"I can't. You're scrunching up. You want to walk out of here or not?"

Talba tried to relax.

"You know what I need? I need a detective."

"No, you don't. You need out."

"Could you relax, please? Look, can I come to your office tomorrow? Talk to you about it?"

She sounded so pitiful Talba said okay, maybe they could trade services. But she never thought Babalu'd show up.